The Critic

"A MAGNIFICENTLY ENGAGING NOVEL...
Makes us murmur, 'Yes, this is what it's like;
I've felt it — this is true.'"
Chicago Tribune Book World

"I HATED TO PUT IT DOWN."
Newsday

Meet JANE...thirty-four, single, an American journalist living in a colorful London loft with a cat, a vibrant sense of humor, and three carefully scheduled lovers: Anthony, a charming, snobby British lord; Franklin, black tennis-playing law student; and Tom, who falls into Jane's life through her skylight (he was just casing the joint).

One carefree young woman...three devoted lovers (none of whom knows about the others)...and everyone content — until Jane becomes pregnant. And "Whose?" and "What color?" are only the first questions Jane must wrestle with!

150,000 HARDCOVERS SOLD
SELECTED BY THE LITERARY GUILD
SOON A MAJOR MOTION PICTURE
FROM COLUMBIA PICTURES

The Critics Adore

Jane

"JANE is an immensely entertaining and engrossing first novel...The story is told with a great deal of warmth and humor. Ms. Wells has a talent for reproducing effervescent, witty dialogue which captivates the reader from the very first page."
San Francisco Chronicle

"Highly readable...bright, brittle, witty."
Cleveland Press

"What from another author might have been banal is witty and perceptive from the pen of Dee Wells. Her dialogue is dazzling, her characters precisely drawn. Mixed with the comedy are insights on contemporary society..."
Milwaukee Journal

"If Jane is a woman who did what 'good' girls don't, Wells is a writer who did what 'good' writers don't—she wrote a very good novel about women."
The Washington Post

The Critics Acclaim

Jane

"Dee Wells pours out her satire naturally and engagingly...combining reportorial accuracy with an outsized sense of the ridiculous."
Minneapolis Tribune

"It's brilliant and on the mark...you're with Jane all the way, and your own feelings of tristesse are exactly what this marvelous first novel aims for and touches...You're going to love Jane."
Providence Sunday Journal

"Jane is the quintessential modern female ...Dee Wells has created one of the finest and most sympathetic characters since Yossarian won the war..."
Chicago Daily News

"Engages your sympathies and succeeds in being both amusing and affectionate...

The Critics Praise

Jane

The novel is clever with scenes set, issues raised, and characters noticed with just the right touches..."

Kirkus Reviews

"It's funny and deftly satirical, it's bittersweet if ever the word had a meaning, and as they say, a 'very good read.'"

Greensboro Daily News

"Jane's wrestles with gestation and fate make a novel of laughter, valor, suspense and poignance, and give us a heroine who takes a permanent place in our affections."

Sacramento Call Enterprise

"Some of the wittiest dialogue I've read recently...lightness, taste, and more than a dash of human insight."

Buffalo Evening News

Jane

A Novel by Dee Wells

AVON
PUBLISHERS OF BARD, CAMELOT, DISCUS, EQUINOX AND FLARE BOOKS

To the memory of V. R. Lang
poet and playwright
who died in July 1956

AVON BOOKS
A division of
The Hearst Corporation
959 Eighth Avenue
New York, New York 10019

Copyright © 1973 by Dee Wells.
Published by arrangement with The Viking Press, Inc.
Library of Congress Catalog Card Number: 73-7087.

ISBN: 0-380-00222-1

First Avon Printing, January, 1975.

AVON TRADEMARK REG. U.S. PAT. OFF. AND
FOREIGN COUNTRIES, REGISTERED TRADEMARK—
MARCA REGISTRADA, HECHO EN CHICAGO, U.S.A.

Printed in Canada

1

At the first ring her head turned automatically on the pillow away from the phone. By the second ring a more cunning defense reflex transformed the ergh-ergh of a London phone into the old double buzz of Paris for busy. It was so real that she almost believed it.

She was in a booth in the Gare de l'Est. She was calling Odeon 78-51. She could smell the stale Métro smell of Gauloises and out of the corner of her eye she could see anxious-looking people hurrying by outside. She read the ads on the wall. "*Les femmes qui savent vivre, s'habillent aux . . .*"

She read the directions again. "*Décrochez le recepteur. Mettez un jeton . . . composez le numéro d'appel . . .*" Ergh-ergh.

She pushed a button and her *jeton* came rattling back. She could feel the second, harder tug it took to get the phone-booth door open. But the double buzz didn't stop. She gave in to reality, woke up, undid Anthony's arm from around her, and reached for the phone.

"Hello."

9

"Eyeh hevacall from Ington Dacey for Miss Jayun Cornell-uh. Is Miss Jayun Cornell-uh available?"

"Call from whom?"

"Eyeh hevacall from Wash-ing-ton Dee-uh Cee-uh for Miss Jayun Cornell-uh. Is . . ."

"Yes, all right. This is Jane Cornell. Speaking."

Silence.

"Hello? Operator?"

"Hold the lion, please. I am trying to connect you."

Enough dirty pinky-beige early morning was coming through the skylight over the bed to show the time on her drugstore alarm clock as five past five. Not an attractive time. Not even aesthetically satisfying, like the twenty past eight of clocks in ads. Probably not even true.

Wedging the phone between her chin and her collarbone, she lit a match and squinted at the numberless lapis-lazuli dial on Anthony's watch. Quarter to five. Well, that's Liggett's for you, she thought. But everything cuts two ways, and you can't get a tuna on white with extra mayo to travel at Cartier's, can you?

Then, irritatingly chirpy, Angela's voice.

"Hello, darling. Happy Lent."

"Angela, for the chrissake. It's five o'clock in the morning."

"Don't be silly, it couldn't be. It's not yet midnight here, and the operator said there was a five-hour difference."

"She was right. There is."

"Oh my god, it goes *that* way."

"As you say. That way. Clockwise. You're behind us. It's all part of a plan, a great plan that we are not given to understand."

"Oh lord, I *am* sorry. Goodness, how awful. No wonder they call it Greenwich mean time. I never heard of anything meaner in my whole life."

"OK. It doesn't really matter. But go easy, my head's not itself."

"What, other than obvious shortcomings we shan't go into now, is the matter with your head?"

10

"Can't imagine. The man said it was the best stuff since Acapulco Gold, but with an understandable vender's pride in his product he may have been—"

"Jane, really. No, I mean it. It's disgusting the way you live in that sordid factory and—"

"It's not a factory. How many times do I have to tell you it's a warehouse? And not just any old warehouse, either. We were in *House and Garden*."

"Whatever it is, it's sordid. And when people your age go around living in warehouses and smoking pot it says something, it definitely says something, about immaturity. I won't of course say *what* it says but it definitely—"

"Angela, knock it off. I'm not some downtrodden junkie, and anyway, since when does the kettle get to talk about the pot?"

"Not funny, darling. Too English."

"OK, not funny. Now tell me what you want so I can go back to sleep and forget about it."

"Ah, want. Want, indeed. What does anyone want? Love. Wisdom. The deathless light bulb. The return of Moxie in returnable bottles and no pigs' ears in hot dogs. Now that you ask, though, I really only wanted to tell you something while Aubrey's in the bathroom."

"Who's Aubrey?"

"Darling, really. Don't you have Suzy Knickerbocker in England?"

"No, thank god."

"Leonard Lyons?"

"No."

"Eugenia Sheppard, then. Surely you must. Everybody has Eugenia Sheppard."

"Not us."

"God, what a place."

"So who's Aubrey? Your paper boy?"

"No, he's a beautiful people. Aubrey Phipps Wetherby the Fourth. Not to be confused with old Aubrey Phipps Wetherby the Third nor, indeed, with old dead Aubrey Phipps Wetherby, Junior, who played first base for Harvard. And you know what?"

11

"What?"

"They say I'm going to marry him. I read it at the hairdresser's."

"Well, I hope you'll be very happy. First base is a nice spot. Of course I've never actually got there myself, but I've heard great things about it."

"Not that one, you idiot. This one. Anyhow, it's not true. That's what I'm trying to tell you: *it's not true.*"

"For this I held the lion? You couldn't. Not even you."

"Jane. You asked. Remember? You asked. God, that dreadful drug, it's mind-destroying. And that's not all. It's bad for the skin too. Did you know that? *Bad* for the skin."

"Oh for the God's sake, Angela. My skin's fine. Thick, maybe, but fine. And so if it wasn't that, what was it?"

"Guess. Come on, just you guess."

"Ophelia Griesecock has won the Miss Rheingold thing, and you voted for her."

"Darling, they don't even *have* that any more I don't think."

"You're going to study for a high-school diploma at home."

"Not even warm."

"OK, I give up."

"Well, with you in this terrible mood I just don't know that I'll tell you after all."

"OK, so don't."

"Well, maybe I will."

"Oh, jesus *christ*, Angela."

"No, it wasn't important. It wasn't ever important, and I was silly ever to think that just because *I* thought it was important that you would too and—"

"Angela, I—"

"No. No, don't apologize. It's all right. I understand."

"Angela, you don't understand."

"I do. I do too unders—"

12

"You don't, because there isn't anything to understand is what I mean. Now, what *is* it?"

"What is what?"

"What is it that you were going to tell me?"

"Do you really want to know?"

"Yes, of course I really want to know."

"Well, all right . . . if you *really do*, it's that I'm coming. To London. To—well, you know, where you—so to speak—live."

"Are you? How lovely! When?"

"Wednesday."

"How long for?"

"Don't know yet. For as long as it takes, I guess."

"As long as what takes?"

"The fascist hyena. He wants a cover story on the Labour Party. Background for the election. Something that catches all the fever-pitch excitement that the volatile British and their elections are so known for. Did you ever hear of anything stupider in your life?"

"Not lately. But why you? You don't like England. You don't like politics. You're no good at the lower orders. And you—"

"Darling, didn't you know? I got good at the lower orders. On that South American thing. I bet you've never been to bed with a Bolivian guerrilla with crabs. Not even with your catholic tastes and lifelong misuse of opportunities to better yourself, I bet you haven't."

"What in god's name was a Bolivian guerrilla doing even talking to someone who writes for the beast?"

"Ah. He thought I was from *Scientific American.*"

"What a funny thing to think. How come?"

"I'm afraid I told him so."

"Oh my god. No thought, of course, for his wife and twelve children or what the head guerrilla might say."

"He was the head guerrilla. And did he give a thought to my husband, or if I had one, or even to elementary hygiene? Jane, truly I don't exaggerate. If you could have *seen* those things ... It was too ghastly and would you believe it, before I even knew what they were I had them all over my—"

13

"OK, OK. I believe you. So what time Wednesday? Would you like to stay here? I've got a nice comfortable sofa that opens out into a—"

"Darling, I'd adore to, you know that. But I think I'll just rough it at the Connaught and get to know the real England and all that. Is lovely Mr. Gustav still there?"

"Gosh, I don't know. The Connaught isn't someplace I exactly hang around, you know. But I can find out, and what do you want if he is?"

"Well, him to begin with, and then maybe a—"

"No, come on, Angela. A room? A soote? You can press your suit better in a soote, I'd think, but all I don't want is to get it wrong and have you carrying on in the lobby and kicking at the rubber plants."

"Just a room, I think. A small something in the garret over the airshaft from the kitchen to get me in a Labour Party frame of mind. God, I can't tell you how I dread it. Do they still wear greenish tweed suits and pledge allegiance to the Red Flag in rooms that smell of sweat? It's the sweat I don't understand. How they ever get warm enough to."

"Well, you know the poor. They can always find a way to smell bad. They never miss a chance."

"Exactly. Why else would they always live around the gas works and sit in the third balcony at the opera?"

"Angela, you're so right. When she's asked them— *begged* them I don't know how many times to all come live in the garden at Buckingham Palace, and Windsor for holidays. But will they? No."

"You see? What can you do with people like that? But seriously, you wouldn't like to have a little party and ask a few over, would you? Nothing fancy, just high tea with bloater paste and a darts board. You know, whatever they're used to."

"Sure, if that's what you want. I'm short on guerrillas, though."

"So am I. He said he'd write, but I guess he meant learn to."

"I'd meet you, but there's about three shows on Wednesday, and all spread out."

"Darling, I wouldn't dream of it. Anyhow the London office has an awful old Rolls that only snorts all day in its stable and needs the exercise. What about lunch?"

"Fine. On the beast?"

"Absolutely. And you can order from the left-hand side."

"Where, then?"

"Where's good?"

"Lacy's. They have lamb with rose-petal jelly from Hungary that's unbelievable. God, you know what I had last night? Not at Lacy's. Here."

"What?"

"Battered fish fingers."

"Goodness. I didn't know fish had—"

"I know, but that's what it said on the packet so I guess they do. Pow! Right on the mitts. Like James Mason and Joan Fontaine in that thing where she's a—"

"Where she's an actress named Ann Todd? That one?"

"Joan Fontaine, it was."

"Ann Todd, darling."

"Christ, maybe you're right. Well, they're all poor soles, I guess, so what's the difference?"

"Now will you believe me that that stuff corrodes the cortex of the brain? But what else besides battered fish fingers? I don't mean for dinner."

"Not much. A new boy friend. New to you, anyhow. And right down your alley. He's a lord."

"A crummy life peer from the Rhondda in a greenish tweed suit, I bet."

"Not at all. Real. Poor, but real."

"I don't like a poor peer, real or not."

"Maybe you know his brother. He's a sort of semi-beautiful people and always in New York and Newport and places like that."

"Oh? Who?"

"Hugo Wiltshire."

"My god. Not that awful queer duke who sold the Caravaggio at Parke-Bernet only he didn't know it was one. Him?"

"Him. And Anthony says he probably would have known except he was too mean to pay to have it cleaned first."

"Oh dear, it's somehow awfully like you to wind up with the penniless younger brother of a duke who's not all there."

"I haven't wound up with him, he's just a—you know, a friend. Besides, he's got lovely upper-class hair and the most beautiful hands. I'm staring at them right now."

"And what does he do with his beautiful hands? Anything?"

"Well, that's one of the troubles. Not much, really."

"And I can tell you another one. Mama. They say she's worse news than big brother even."

"I haven't had that treat yet."

"Well, dearie, just you watch out. She's not going to like him falling in the clutches of a bolshy American who feeds him on fish fingers."

"She should talk. She never fed him anything at all. Do you know until he went away to school he never ate with anybody except servants? And you know what they used to give him when he was a baby to keep him quiet? *Brandy tits.*"

"Brandy *snaps*, surely. I've seen them in Bloomingdale's."

"No, *tits*. A finger from one of Mummy's old kid gloves with a tiny hole in the tip and filled up with warm water and sugar and brandy. Nanny did it, and that's what they gave him to suck when he cried. How about that?"

"You're making it up."

"Nobody has to make up things like that around here. They're thick on the ground."

"Is he an alcoholic, then?"

"No, but he's still pretty funny about gloves."

"Darling, how awful. Really, such people . . . I mean, all that and cold bathrooms too; you must tell me more the minute I get there, but Aubrey's on his third drink and looking cross. One-thirty?"

"Twelve-thirty, better make it. I've got a show at three."

"Not very chic, twelve-thirty."

"Not very chic being the lowly movie critic on a left-wing rabble-rousing paper, either."

"Perhaps Lord Right will take you out of all that."

"Mm, maybe. Anyhow, twelve-thirty. Lacy's. And Angela?"

"Yes?"

"I'm really awfully glad you're coming."

"It will be fun, won't it, darling?"

Jane hung up, pushed the button that closed the curtains on the skylight, and put Anthony's arm around her. He moved closer and kissed the back of her neck very sleepily. "What was all that?"

"Nothing. Old friend coming to London. Angela, her name is."

"That fragment had not eluded me. Angela who?"

"Van Schuyler. She's from New York and sort of plays for *News Views*."

"Plays?"

"Well, you couldn't call it work. Says she knows your brother. Knows of, anyhow. Didn't seem to like the sound of you, though."

"Whyever not?"

"You're not in oil. Angela likes men in oil. Besides, the rich never like the poor. Didn't you know that?"

"She likes you."

"Well, she knows me. They kind of forgive the poor they know."

"I'm not poor."

"You're not what the poor call poor, but Angela only goes for the big-time. Anyway, what's it matter? God, that stuff was awful, wasn't it? My throat's still burning."

"Mm. So's mine."

"Orange juice?"

"Is there?"

"Lots."

"Where?"

"Icebox. It's the frozen kind."

"That would be good."

"Mm, wouldn't it?"

She waited. She counted slowly by fives to two hundred. She tried to remember the capital of Idaho. Des Moines? Boise? She tried to put together the bit in *Antony and Cleopatra* about the crocodile. "It is shaped, sir, like itself; and it is as broad as it hath breadth: it is just so high as it is, and moves with ..." Well, with something. "... and the elements once out of it, it transmigrates."

Not bad.

But nobody can outwait an Englishman who doesn't want to get out of bed. She undid his arm from around her again and went to get the orange juice.

The London real-estate smoothies Jane had met when she was apartment-hunting, the ones who try to look like RAF pilots in movies about Colditz and wear double-breasted, double-vented blazers with Royal Automobile Club buttons, had all made it pretty clear that they didn't class Covent Garden as a desirable residential neighbourhood. Pushed, they granted it had the advantage of being central and, if you like garbage, even a certain apache charm. But to live in? No. People should live, or should anyhow want to live, in bijou mews cottages in S.W.3, all painted pink or blue and with a bay tree in a pot at the front door. The tree prudently chained and padlocked to the bootscraper, of course.

She couldn't do it. Where you had to have chains and padlocks on trees, she didn't want to live.

She was, she realized, a little matter of 350 years too late to catch Covent Garden at its best. Then, it must have been really something. Then, when S.W.3 was open fields and N.W.1 had nothing to boast about except that Dick Whittington had once walked by, Inigo

19

Jones had laid out the great piazza that was his answer to Venice, and Covent Garden had had its big moment. For a while it was the OK place to live.

It hadn't lasted long. By the eighteenth century the pace-setters who had kept up with that first great Jones were already chasing some other Jones westward in London, and Covent Garden started its slow downward slide. Graceful ground-floor rooms grew new glassy fronts and became shops. Coffee houses, whorehouses, theatres, and grubby lodging houses opened up. And in the nineteenth century Mr. Jones's dream received its coup de grâce. The carriage manufactories and warehouses went up. Printers and publishers moved in. The market was roofed over with glass and iron. Sheds for vegetables were allowed on the open spaces he had so carefully mapped out. Gin shops raked in the money, and as the right place to live, as even a place to live, Covent Garden was simply no longer in the running.

A lot of it is still very handsome; if the porticoes of Saint Paul's are filthy with grime now and dwarfed by oafish red-brick neighbours, it is still a church not to be sniffed at. And there are other survivors. The house on Russell Street where—or so they say—Boswell first met Dr. Johnson is still there. The house where de Quincey wrote the *Opium Eater* is still there. Nobody has yet knocked down the house on Henrietta Street where T.S. Eliot used to work after they turned it into a bank. Even David Garrick's early eighteenth-century house on Southampton Street still stands, and so does its almost-identical-twin neighbour. And even more miraculously there is a whole row of houses between Monmouth and Shelton Streets that have for more than two hundred years escaped everything from itchy town planners' fingers to German bombs. But of course how much longer any of it will be able to pull such a clever hat trick is anybody's guess.

Not even Jane would deny that Covent Garden is more utilitarian than beautiful. Newspaper offices, publishers, ballet-shoe-makers, costumers, pubs, and a lot of little old-established businesses are its mainstays—as well, of course, as the market itself—and there are no pretty back gardens or yellow front doors with brass dolphin knockers such as you find in Belgravia.

Which is not to say that no one lives in Covent Garden, because a lot of people do. They're poorish people—that goes without saying. Who else would live in grey Victorian tenements of the sort that, in England, are called Buildings?

Peabody Buildings. Throgmorton Buildings. Macclesfield Buildings. In all England there is no more socially damned address than a Building, and now that even council flats are called fancy names like Hill Terrace House and Birchwoods Hall, this is more true than ever.

Curiously, although they stand cheek by jowl with the Buildings, Victorian Gothic warehouses like the one Jane lives in are something else again. They have become OK. They convert into superb huge-roomed apartments that, once the oak floors have been scraped and bleached and a couple of details like doors, kitchens, and bathrooms added, make people say, "But how did you ever find it?" From there it only takes a couple of tubs of flowers—amusing tubs of flowers, as they say—and a bit of ivy and treillage out back to hide the drainpipes, and the next thing you know it's all in a glossy mag and your rent trebles.

Still, it suited Jane. She liked her huge rooms. She liked the unsqueaky solidness of the floors. She liked being able to walk to her office just off Fleet Street. She had even got used to the all-night noise of the market, and when the people who had started off saying, "But how did you ever find it?" stayed the night and ended up saying, "But how do you stand it?" she was very hurt.

They did have a point, though. Almost every apple and mango and every lettuce and potato that is eaten in England anywhere south of Hadrian's Wall passes through Covent Garden, and nearly every daffodil and

21

carnation likewise. Nor do they come in, or go out, on little cats' feet.

In-pulling trucks waiting to unload jockey for road space with other trucks that have loaded up and are trying to get out. Crates crash, and iron-wheeled barrows rattle over cement floors and cobbled streets. Drivers and loaders curse each other, and porters struggling with loads that would strain a horse curse everyone and everything.

Except for the script, which consists entirely of obscenities, it's a little like going to see *Hamlet* every night of your life. The plot's fine. The action is great. It's undeniably an exciting show. But sooner or later familiarity is bound to pull its dirty trick and push you to the point where you no longer want to watch it or hear it ever again. What's harder to get to is the nerveless nirvana of sleeping through it.

When the banana barrows started rolling out down below, Jane got up, took a bath, and got dressed. Anthony, who very coldly shared the estate agents' view of Covent Garden as a place to live, stayed in bed with a pillow over his head.

For all the difference that it could possibly make—which was none—Jane tried to be quiet and took her typewriter to the living room to finish her piece. At nine o'clock she let Mrs. Bush in, and with Mrs. Bush's arrival Friday got going in earnest. She even had her favorite scrap of news to deliver: that some layabout had gone off with the milk again.

"Oh dear, have they?" Jane was too busy to give the crime the attention that she knew Mrs. Bush felt it deserved. But Mrs. Bush was determined to have her say and she stood by Jane's desk to have it. "It's the principle, though, really, innit?"

Jane pretended to listen. Mrs. Bush was a real hair shirt, and her principles were the hairiest part.

However, as hair shirts go she was at least a clean one and no anile basket case who had to lean on the vacuum cleaner to stay upright. She liked things nice, said so often, and made them so. She believed in aired rooms, mustard poultices, the Tory Party, holidays in Britain at seaside boarding houses, turned mattresses, strong yellow bar soap, and distilled water for house plants. Tap water, she said, was all lime and chlorine. Poison, nowt but poison. It was death to pelargoniums and didn't do humans no good, either.

Every Friday morning Mrs. Bush snapped on her orange rubber gloves with the grim air of a surgeon in a field hospital and got at all that offended her. She blasted hissing foam at oven dirt. She hung chemical discs in the toilet that turned the water madonna blue. She boiled the dish towels, ironed, polished the floors, poured dreadful caustic things down the drains, and went at the paintwork as if she were afraid it might get her first. What she was really keen on, though, was killing rats.

With open murderous relish she squeezed her lips in a mean straight line and flung handfuls of deadly white powder into the garbage bins, and when Jane didn't have enough garbage to lure enough rats to death, Mrs. Bush would bring leftovers from home. The body count was a Friday high point.

"Two today," she said, coming back from her reconnaissance trip downstairs, "and big uns too. Leaders, I wouldn't wonder. They have leaders, y'know, rats do." She cackled her all-purpose substitute for laughter, and Jane knew a Mrs. Bush joke was coming. "Like *socialists* they are, my Alf says. With leaders and all. Like socialists."

The trouble with a good body count was that it set Mrs. Bush off on all the other areas where pain and/or death could improve the situation *if* the pain and/or death were painful enough. Unfortunately, no one had yet developed such foolproof punishments, and so the wicked always got off too easy with penalties that were too good for them. Hanging was too good for murderers. Castration was too good for rapists. Birching was too soft on thugs. Prisons were too soft on prisoners. A good whipping was less than what bad children deserved. Unmarried mothers had got what Mrs. Bush

23

called their "just deserts," but sinisterly she sounded as if they were only just.

As well as insufficient punishment, Mrs. Bush was in no doubt at all about what else was wrong with the world. It was them Jews and Catholics. It was lefties. Students. Unions. Long-haired so-called intellectuals. Demonstrators. Do-gooders. They were layabouts all and troublemakers, and now what with this new permissiveness and nignogs flooding in there'd be no end to it, and what they should do is bring back hanging and give some of them young folk a taste of the buckle end of the belt. There was no sy-ky-atrist as could tell her that *that* wouldn't work.

Jane was appalled by Mrs. Bush but so terrified of losing her that through hell and high water she kept a craven silence. Anthony, though, got on with her like master and dog and only had to say "good morning" or "thank you" to make Mrs. Bush—who liked gentlemen and liked lords even better—absolutely quiver with pleasure.

Jane would watch them sometimes: Mrs. Bush weaving through her awkward whooping-crane servile courtship and Anthony leading her on by taking an occasional neat step in his own icy minuet. And then she'd think how right Disraeli had been when he said that England was two nations—the privileged and the people. It hadn't really changed at all. "Wot a nice young gentleman Lord Anthony is," Mrs. Bush would say sometimes when Anthony wasn't around. But when Mrs. Bush wasn't around, Anthony never mentioned her. It was as if she didn't exist. And she didn't, not for him.

But if Jane was appalled by Mrs. Bush and Anthony simply conned her, it was Tom who saw her most clearly for what she was and hated her.

He hadn't always. Not openly, anyhow. At first— back in the days when Mrs. Bush had come on Tuesdays—Tom had reacted to her with nothing worse than flat, following eyes and a warily silent neutrality. He had always avoided her, true. If she came into the room where he was sketching or reading, he would simply gather up his pencils and books and go to another room.

They never spoke—obviously each of them feared and disliked the other too much to do that—and Tuesdays with both of them all day in the apartment had been pretty tense. But after a fashion their system of unadmitted, controlled hostility had worked. Worked, that is, until the Tuesday when Jane had come home from a morning press show and found Tom lying face down on the bed. He wouldn't open his eyes, and Jane had a feeling he'd been crying.

She lit a cigarette, gave it to him, and sat beside him, patting his shoulder. "What's the matter, Tom? What is it?"

He twisted out from under her hand. "Nothing."

"Come on, it must be something. Can't you tell me?"

"There's nothing to tell."

She lay down beside him, stroked his back, and waited. Finally he turned over. "That fucker. Christ, I hate her."

"Why, Tom? Did she say something nasty?"

"You ever hear that fucker even speak to me?"

"What, then?"

It took a long time.

". . . and it wasn't just a spiderweb. Well, all right, look at it one way and it was just a spiderweb. But it took that poor bloody spider all morning to build it, and I know because I watched. And you know—hell, I know it sounds crazy—but it was beautiful to watch, really beautiful. First he got the—I don't know what you call them, the sort of anchor places, doped out. Really scientific, you know what I mean?"

He opened his eyes and looked at her.

"Then he gets the spokes in, all as even-spaced as if he'd measured them. And then he went round and round. Not fast but not slow either, more just steady sure, like he really knew what he was doing. He did, too. You could see he did from the way he hooked each bit on with his back leg just where he wanted it to go."

He gave her the cigarette to put out, and put his arms around her. Then he took a deep breath, as if he were fighting off the tears again, and with his mouth against her hair he went on slowly. "Christ, it took him hours. Bloody hours. And then it's done and all in the sun by the window, where there'd be plenty of flies—or some, anyhow. You could tell he knew that too, that he'd picked by the window because it would be the best place. God, he was one smart spider, he really was. And so then he knocks off for a bit—you know, takes a rest like. And so he gets in the middle and sits there and every once in a while he'd give a little bounce. Like he was testing it."

This time there was a long silence.

"Well, there isn't much more, not really. He makes a couple of practice runs along the spokes. He wasn't after anything because there wasn't anything yet to be after, it was just more tests. And then—well, that's all. The fucker got him. She swoops in and with one jab of that fucking broom she rides around on she got him, and when he hit the floor and tried to run, she finished him off with her foot. I know it sounds nothing if you didn't see it happen. But Jesus, it was horrible. Horrible. And, Jane, there was no need for it. He wasn't bothering her. He wouldn't have hurt her. He wasn't after anything that's hers. He hadn't done anything to her. All he wanted was a corner by the window in the sun, and a few flies. Shit, she's always killing flies—and she doesn't even eat them. Though, christ I don't know, maybe she does. I wouldn't put it past her, anyhow. But why couldn't she've just left him alone and let him live? He could even of been a help to her—with the flies, I mean."

For a long time after that Tuesday, Tom's face would suddenly go hard, and Jane would know he'd thought of a new way to get back at Mrs. Bush. One time he was going to shove a cactus up her cunt and sew it in with a rusty needle. Then he was going to fill

26

her eyedrops bottle with vitriol. Or slice slabs off her ass and sit her in a pile of salt. Or tie her down in the path of some soldier ants. He had lots of final solutions for Mrs. Bush, but Jane stopped listening to them and almost forgot the ones she had listened to. Almost. Not quite.

The Tuesday when Mrs. Bush brought her spunglass boat to show, Tom's fantasies of revenge surfaced in Jane's mind.

The boat was Mrs. Bush's greatest treasure. Alf's nephew had brought it all the way from Venice, all packed in foam granules so not so much as a single thread of the rigging had been broken. At home she kept it carefully out of harm's way on top of the TV on a specially soft crocheted mat and dusted it only with a tiny sable paintbrush.

After it had been sufficiently admired, Jane had watched Mrs. Bush put her boat carefully on the carved oak chest. Right in the middle of the chest, where nothing could happen to it. Yet somehow it had fallen. Poor Mrs. Bush had cried as she swept the fragments into the dustpan—and Jane had almost cried too when she found out that a not nearly so splendid replacement boat was going to cost her £25.

She didn't say anything to Tom that time. Nor even the next time, when the heavy parsley pot fell from the kitchen sill and barely missed Mrs. Bush in the back areaway below.

"It must of been the cat," Mrs. Bush had said. "You can't never trust a cat." Jane wasn't so sure.

But then, a good two months after the spider murder, Mrs. Bush's flat was most thoroughly burgled, and Jane was sure.

"Tom, it was you, wasn't it?"

"What was me?"

"You that robbed Mrs. Bush."

"Me? Turn over that fucker's hole? What's she got I'd want? What's she got that anybody'd want?"

"Don't lie, Tom."

"Lie? Who's lying?"

"You are. You are and you know you are and I know you are. But never mind that, what you've got to do is take it all back. Just get it all together and leave it on her doorstep or something is all you have to do. But you have to do it."

"Get what all together, for jesus' sake? I don't know what you're going on about."

"Tom. Do as I say."

He didn't do as she said, though. Mrs. Bush never saw her mother's silver-plated cruet set again. Or Alf's watch. Or the gilt trinket box that played the Brahms lullaby when you opened the lid. Or the genuine musquash coat that she'd queued at five in the morning to buy in the after-Christmas sale at Barker's. Even her three plaster seagulls had been pulled off the wall and had gone with the rest.

Who else in or even on the fringes of London's criminal world would be caught dead stealing something so stupid as plaster seagulls? Nobody. It had to be Tom, and Jane knew it was Tom.

Jane typed away, and around noontime the market quieted down. Friday was in full stride now, and the piece she was working on was almost finished. She looked at her watch. It was almost time for Anthony to be getting ready to leave for the weekend at Cravenbourne.

She heard Mrs. Bush carrying his breakfast tray back to the kitchen, and while she jabbed x's through a line of her copy she thought how like Anthony it was to have had his breakfast in bed.

And yet why shouldn't he? If he liked breakfast in bed, and if Mrs. Bush liked giving him breakfast in bed, which she most certainly did, why shouldn't he? No reason at all, really.

Then why do I resent it? I don't. Not resent it. It's just that—well, it's hard to say, exactly.

So forget it. Anyhow, he's going soon.

Good.

Good?

No, not good, that's putting it too strongly.

28

But it was true that after long stretches with Anthony you got the feeling you'd been playing tennis against a brick wall. The ball came back each time you hit it—sure—and right there that's more than you can say about playing tennis with people. But when you play a wall the only energy in the game is your own. You have to begin it. You have to keep score. You have to decide when the game is over and who, if anybody, won. And it's only you that gets sweaty and tired.

What you can say in favour of playing with a wall is that it never says no or complains. And it never plays any better or any worse than the time before; you know where you are with a wall. The catch is, though, that the wall never really gives a damn. It's like children who go all limp and dull-eyed and say, "I don't care," when you ask them if they want an ice-cream cone. Except that with them it's probably only a primitive protective hedge against the possibility that the offer of the ice-cream cone may not be genuine. The wall, alas, really means it.

It rankled her puritan soul, too, that Anthony didn't do anything. It wasn't right for people not to work, and she had never known anybody before who didn't. Yet at the same time Anthony's nonaggression pact with life was one of the nicest things about him; in a world of hustlers, somebody who doesn't want to corner wheat or be first on Mars can be very attractive. He wasn't greedy. He wasn't competitive or achievement-minded. He didn't want to Amount to Something. All he wanted was to do—well, what he wanted to do. And he did it.

He read the books, not just the reviews. He went to openings of new galleries and plays. He went to lectures at the British Academy. He drifted in to auctions of Etruscan pots and things at Sotheby's, and if he wanted something he bought it. If Florence was where the best show of Henry Moores was, he flew to Florence.

Anthony wouldn't have lasted five minutes in a bank, say, and he couldn't possibly have told you what bus to take to get to Clapham Common, but there were some things he knew quite a lot about. Jane had found this out once when an art historian so famous that even she had heard of him came from New York and Anthony had taken her to his lecture at the Courtauld.

She'd tried, she really had tried. And it wasn't that she didn't understand the words, because the handsome Christ from Columbia used only simple words and never got pretentious. Nor was it that, most of the time anyhow, she couldn't grasp the ideas. But just when she thought she'd got it, really had hold of it and almost understood it, the great man put the one block too many on what was already a very wobbly tower in her mind, and it all fell down. Then, while she was trying to remember what it had been that she had almost understood, he flashbacked to Crete, jumped to troubadours and romantic love, and said something witty about some sixteenth-century Italian. He could have been talking Urdu for all she understood of any of it from there on. When he poised briefly on the towers of Chartres and spread his Superman cape to take off again, she knew she couldn't possibly follow him and so she had just sat there numb-minded, like a ninety-pound weakling who had crumped out in a snowdrift while everyone else pushed on to the Klondike.

She'd watched Anthony and the others. They understood what he was saying. Raptly intent, they followed every word, and when Art and Life had been wrapped up in a neat package that included God, Man, Whither? and even Why? they gave him a big hand. So did Jane; she clapped like mad. Except that—shove Chartres—what she was applauding was the man himself. She might not know much about Art, but she knew a fantastic man when she saw one, and she knew that that was what she liked.

But if Anthony's interest in things intellectual and aesthetic was real and admirable, so were his passivity and nonparticipation irritating.

Maybe he was out of his time. Maybe the heyday of Empire would have suited him better than the franticness of today with its smart bombs and dumb people.

India. Poona. The Bengal Lancers. Not lancing anyone —more just leaning around on silk rugs and cushions eating grapes with Madeleine Carroll.

Balls . . . balls, balls, balls at the Viceroy's palace. Wogs that knew their place. Pig-sticking. Brother-officers'-wives-sticking. Chota pegs. Polo. The fishing fleet of slightly overblown English roses who husband-hunted East of Suez. The posh life of Port Out, Starboard Home. An occasional uprising on the Afghan frontier to make just enough activity to keep the calf muscles from atrophying. But mostly a life centred around the arrival of packets of books from Heywood Hill and plenty of monsoon leisure to read them in. Yes, it would have suited Anthony down to the ground.

Before she'd known him she had never known anyone who had always been looked after by servants and who took it for granted that he was superior not only to them but to pretty much everyone else as well. Not that he lorded it over anyone nastily, in fact he was rather humble about it all—in that way that people who know they're superior, and who have never once questioned it or tested it, can afford to be humble. As Jesus was humble, those people are always humble—until the crunch comes, when they have their little ways of making it clear that dad was God and that they're God Jr. It was the quiet arrogance and occasional blank insensitivity to other people's feelings that were hard to take.

Anthony, for instance, didn't see anything wrong with there being a colour called "nigger brown," though even the cheesiest shoe stores had finally caught on and stopped using it.

Almost like Mrs. Bush, he believed that miners and nurses were more than adequately paid, and if miners and nurses didn't think so, then it was quite simple— they should get another job. He saw the welfare state, especially free medicine and free universities, as something that undermined the national character (whatever that was) by making things too easy for people.

In bed he was lovely. When not in bed, he was too English. He never helped do the dishes. He never

31

carried things, not even potatoes. If Jane started the *Times* crossword puzzle and put it down even just to answer the phone, he'd finish it. In ink.

If he took a shower he always let the curtain hang outside the tub and couldn't understand why it made her cross. If he took a bath he'd leave his facecloth unwrung-out and folded in a neat square on top of the soap, where they fused in a cold slime. He used her toothbrush, too. But this could have been a genuine cultural difference; she had known enough Englishmen to know by now that they all used whatever toothbrush happened to be there, even if it was a wet one.

What was really askew with Anthony was that on any level he couldn't quite see that what he liked was not necessarily what everyone liked. Mustard on steak was good; *he* liked mustard on steak, and so everybody must. How could they not? She had said, "No, thanks," a hundred times, but still whenever they had steak he passed it to her and said, "Mustard?" And he knew she hated cricket. But whenever he watched it on TV he'd call out to her in the bedroom or wherever she'd escaped to, "Darling, it's too exciting—three sixty-four for four, England not out, and Davis bowling."

She didn't very much mind his not seeing what was funny about the Reedmore bookstore, or the Wackett Brothers demolition business, or the little factory with a sign over its front door saying: MANUFACTURERS OF SCREWED PRODUCTS. But there was a lot about Anthony that she did mind.

Most of all she minded his being an assumer and assuming that, as she wasn't married, it didn't matter if he left things lying about. His squash racket in the hall. Bills from Turnbull and Asser on the bedside table. His Gucci diary by the phone. There always was something he managed to leave behind, and every Friday after he'd gone she had to go through the apartment with a fine-tooth comb and erase all traces of him. (POLICE COMB SHEPHERDS BUSH FOR MISSING GIRL. There, that was another thing that Anthony hadn't thought was funny.)

Usually Mrs. Bush caught it all and would leave Anthony's things in a prim pile on the oak chest, rather pointedly in the OUT basket. But even Mrs. Bush could fail, and one Friday evening Jane had found Franklin in the bathroom with Anthony's wooden bowl of shaving soap in his hand.

"Stephanotis? What's a stephanotis?" was all he'd said, but Jane had been very careful ever since. She had met enough Casanova men with motley collections of earrings, bobby pins, and left-behind lipsticks that were kept in cigarette boxes where other women would be sure to see them, and she didn't want to be the female equivalent. The simple truth was she very much liked having three lovers, but she didn't feel any need to show off about it. In fact, one of the reasons it all worked so well was, she was certain, because she kept them as scrupulously seperate as she did and never even hinted to any of them that another one, leave alone another two, existed.

On Fridays, then, Anthony was erased. On Mondays she wiped away all traces of Franklin, though there was hardly any need to, as Franklin was not a leaver. And on Wednesdays she did it after Tom. Except Tom was different; Tom was allowed to leave things because sometimes he really had to. And what he left—silver, pictures, typewriters, mink coats, jewellery, that kind of thing—was at least left out of sight. He was even more determined than she about that.

She had long since given Tom his own big cupboard out in the hall that connected the living room with the rest of the apartment, and he had put the lock on himself and only he knew the combination. To make it even more secret, he had brought from some unspecified somewhere a big gilt-framed mirror that covered the wall from ceiling to floor and hid the cupboard door rather more than completely. But if Tom's secret cupboard and the stuff in it sometimes worried Jane, a much bigger worry was Tom himself.

She had known him for about a year, and though in some ways she knew him very well—in bed he was lovely too—all she really knew about him was what she could guess at and piece together from the guesses. It added up to not much more than she had found out the night of the accident, when he had dropped, like manna, into her bed.

It had been a cold, rainy winter night, and she had gone to bed early to keep warm. Sound asleep, she hadn't even heard the skylight break. Then cold rain, wet, dirty glass, and a very wet, bony young man had all fallen on the bed at once.

He grabbed her wrist. "Shut up or I'll shut you up."

Somehow she knew he was too young, or too something, to be dangerous. "Don't be ridiculous, you silly boy. Let go."

He held on tight, and she could smell his wet leather jacket. "There an alarm here?"

"No, for the gods sake, there's no alarm. And now *let go*. You're"—thank god for lousy movies—"you're hurting me."

He let go, and she turned over onto her back. "Who the hell are you anyhow, and what were you doing on the roof?"

"Roof? What roof? I was going over in a helicopter and—*Get your fucking hand away from that telephone*."

"Ah, the world-famous jewel thief is nervous, is he? I was just trying to put the light on. OK?"

"OK. But that's all, see."

There was blood everywhere. On him, on her, on the pillowcases, the blankets, even the floor. "Hey, I think you're . . ."

He pulled a filthy rag from a pocket and wrapped it around his right hand. "It's nothin. What's down below?"

"Below here, you mean?"

"Below where the fuck else d'you think?"

"Hell. Where you're heading for."

"Don't be funny, lady. I want a straight answer."

"OK. Bananas."

"That all?"

34

"That's all. A large—a very large—number of bananas."

"Shit."

"Well, that's how it goes. Next week, the crown jewels. In the meantime, bananas. Now, come on."

"Come on where?"

"Bathroom. Water. Bandages. If you're good, maybe a celluloid duck in your bath."

He took her by the wrist again and let her lead him to the bathroom. While she ran the water and got the witch hazel, he leaned on the basin and looked at himself in the mirror. "Jesus, what a bloody mess."

The cut on the ball of his thumb was deep and jagged and needed stitches. "You'll have to get this one seen to by a—"

"Fuck that doctor bit."

"OK, it's your thumb. But this is my carpet, and you're not going to bleed all over it."

She got a very thin needle and silk thread from the sewing box, but the needle's eye was too small for hands that shook and thread that frayed. She went back to the sewing box, got the curved upholstery needle and threaded it with manageable cotton thread. It must have hurt a lot, but he never even said "Ow."

In the kitchen she poured him a brandy and made herself a cup of coffee. Her hands were still shaking, and now her teeth had started chattering. "Here," he said and took off the smelly wet leather jacket. "Put it on."

It was such a ludicrously chivalrous gesture that for the first time she took a close look at him.

He was even younger than she'd thought. Eighteen? Twenty-two? Tall for fourteen? At thirty-four she was no longer sure of anything about the young; all she could be certain of as she stared at him stupidly was that she had never seen anyone more beautiful in her life. His brown hair was wet and dirty, but it was wavy and thick; the straight nose, wide mouth, and dark blue eyes were as impossibly perfect as the features of the heroes in women's magazine stories. My god, what

35

a face, she thought, and, reading the thought, he began to smile a slow, crooked, gay-desperado smile that,
unfortunately for him, she'd seen in a million bad
movies ever since Errol Flynn had liberated Burma in
the worst one of them all.

Right. That did it. If he thought she was some sex-
starved, maternally thwarted, sleeping alone librarian
from Hixville who fell for pretty boys in leather jackets
and dirty jeans, he was making one big mistake.

"OK, Brando. You can go now."

"I can? Thanks." But his eye caught the remnants
of a lemon meringue pie on top of the icebox, and his
tough-guy act dissolved. In a real voice he said, "Jesus,
but that looks good."

She knew, she knew while she was doing it that it
was a mistake, but she made him bacon and eggs and
one mean little piece of toast, and gave him the rest of
the lemon meringue pie. Not even on a plate, just in
the pie pan it had been baked in.

While he ate she cleared the broken glass and filthy,
sodden leaves and the rain-soaked blankets and sheets
off the bed. But the bed was wet through and it was
still raining. She moved the bed over so it wouldn't
get any wetter and started down the hall towards the
living room with clean sheets and an eiderdown.

He followed her. "Listen, I don't need sheets. It's a
waste."

"You don't need what?"

"Sheets. Don't bother, I mean."

She opened the sofa out and flicked the bottom
sheet on angrily. With his one good hand he helped
her tuck it in and handed her the top sheet.

She snatched it from him. "They're not for you, the
sheets. They're for me. You're going home—wherever
that is." She stopped making the bed and shook one
cross finger at him. "And if I ever catch you around
here again I'll . . ."

He smiled the phony smile. "You'll *what?*"

"I'll . . ."

"Go on. I'm listening."

"I'll know who you are, that's what. I'll know what you're up to and I'll call the coppers."

"You're sure about that, are you?"

"Of course I'm sure about that. Now get out. Take off and don't come back."

She stomped across the living room, opened the front door, and held it open. He didn't move, except to sit down in the black leather chair and light a cigarette.

"Oh for the *chrissake*," she said and slammed the door shut.

She was undoubtedly a fool to have let such a thing happen, but when he left the next morning she was surprised at how sorry she was that she'd never see him again. She was even more surprised at how glad she was when he came back that afternoon with squares of glass, pieces of wood, putty, and the rest of the things it would take to fix the skylight. He'd even got the right kind of glass, the kind that's two layers with chicken wire in between. "Makes it stronger, see," he'd said. And he was right, it made it a lot stronger; nobody ever fell through it again.

Almost all she knew now that she didn't know then was that his name was Tom, that he was an uneasy mixture of violent defiance and sentimental gentleness, and that he had a hunger for knowledge that made him gulp down and ask for more of everything she introduced him to from Jane Austen to five-card stud. The only other thing she knew about him was that she had grown extremely fond of him.

By now she pretty much accepted his secretiveness—she didn't, after all, have much choice—and it had been all of six months since she'd said, "Come on, Tom, be reasonable. What if something terrible happened? What if you fell down foaming at the mouth and I have to call an ambulance?"

"Call it, then. They don't ask your bloody name before they'll come, you know."

"But what if you died or something? Who'll I tell? Who'll I say you are?"

"Were."

"Were. OK, were."

"Don't say. Let them find out. Make the fuckers earn their money for once."

"Tom, you're being childish."

"OK. So tell the simple bloody truth. Say you found me here. I'd busted in, with intent. You don't know my name. How would you know it, for jesus' sake? You're a nice girl and you never saw me before in your life."

"But some of that would be a lie."

"Fuck me, lie, then. It's not hard. There's no great trick about it that only geniuses can learn after twenty years trying. *Look*. Tell the simplest story you can. Use as few words as you can get away with. Just answer what they ask and *only* what they ask and don't dress it up with details like some goddam film. And then stick to it. Sticking to it is, believe me, the big how-to-do-it about lying."

She smiled at him and reached over to touch his cheek. "Why do all liars say 'believe me'?"

"They don't. Believe me."

"But people have seen you here. The banana people. Mrs. Bush. The man next door. The man from Harrods. Lots of people."

"Holy jesus, you can fix that broken-down tart with a fiver, and nobody—believe me, nobody—is going to ask Harrods. God, that paper you work for must be off its head. Every week, each and every week including holidays or even if you're off sick, they pay a hundred and fifty quid—I can hardly believe it, one hundred and fifty quid—to a clueless, gormless nut case like you. I don't know who's the craziest, I really don't—you or them."

"Still, it's worrying, Tom. Not knowing anything about you is worrying."

"Jane, leave off. There's nothing to worry about. Just because that squint-eyed old bastard next door has seen me? OK, he's seen me, and so what? I was checking the place out. I'm a peeping Tom."

He looked proud of his joke.

"Very funny."

"All right, I'm a knickers fan, then. A breather come to take a look, or a flasher come to give you a look. How would you know what I was? All you know is I came round a couple of times and said I was selling subscriptions."

"But what about your family? Your mother."

"What about her?"

"If something happened to you, she'd have to be told."

"And make her bloody day? Not fucking likely."

"Well, even if you think they don't care, I care. Can't you trust me enough to tell me anything?"

"I trust you. It's not that. It's that nothing is going to happen, and if it did it wouldn't be anything that was your fault. I don't want to be the cause of you getting mixed up in any mess. I don't want anybody getting at you because of me. That's why I don't tell you. You know you're the only person I—well, you know what I mean, and nothing is bloody going to happen to me anyhow, so will you please for the love of God leave off."

That was absolutely the last time she had ever brought it up.

Pulling on Hermès driving gloves with round holes cut out over the knuckles, Anthony came into the living room and stood behind her, reading over her shoulder. That was another thing she hated and that he knew she hated.

"Ready, darling?"

She stopped thinking about Tom, x-ed out another line, and rubbed the space between her eyebrows with one finger. "Almost."

"How almost?"

She didn't answer.

"Almost really, or almost almost?"

She still didn't answer.

"Ah. That kind of almost."

He took off his gloves, sat down in the playground swing that hung on leather-covered chains from a beam, and with a slight sigh he opened up a copy of *Elle*. Jane sneaked a look at him and saw he was—as she knew he'd be—reading his horoscope. "Your liver, Anthony. You must watch your liver."

"Not only that. I must disintoxicate my entire organism." He threw the copy of *Elle* onto the desk. "A tiresome people with, as is I daresay only to be expected, a tiresome language in which to say tiresome things."

"You want to know something really tiresome in French? Say 'At Roquevaire, the river flows towards the green worm's glasses.' "

"À Roquevaire, *la rivière*—What's the word for flows?"

"Verser."

"Ah, yes. À Roquevaire, *la rivière se verse*—"

"To yourself, darling. Out loud when you've got it."

There was a hurt silence. When she stopped typing and pulled the paper out of the typewriter, he said, "You know I'm no good at French. You say it."

"À Roquevaire, *la rivière se verse vers les verres du ver vert*. How about that?"

"At school that kind of nonsense was known as good confiture."

"Good confiture?"

"*Jambon*. Jam, *bon*. But isn't 'flows' *couler*?"

"Hey, that Eton. That's a school that really fixes a kid up for later life. I mean where else could you learn so many ways to put other people down?"

"Sorry, darling, but one's formative years die hard."

"Die? Listen, with some people their formative years never even fade away."

She picked up the typewritten piece and began to stuff things in her bag. "There. That's that. Another blow struck for the cinema as the art form of our time. Another onward and upward Sunday over the chunky-cut marmalade for the discerning readers of the *Orbit*."

Anthony had his gloves on again. "Off?"

"Off. Just must have a tiny word with Mrs. Bush first, and then—Oh god, what's that?"

"Doorbell?"

Anthony took off the gloves and sat on the swing again while Jane pushed the window open and climbed up on the sill. "Yes? No, up here. Who is it?"

"It's me, miss. Ron. Come to see to the windows."

"Oh, hi, Ron. But isn't it awfully soon? You were just here a couple of weeks ago."

"Me? No, miss."

"You mean to tell me it's six weeks? Already?"

"Oh, absolutely, miss. More like seven really."

"OK, if you say so. I'll be right down."

She jumped backwards off the sill, and one foot landed in Scat's saucer of milk. "Shit."

Anthony shut his eyes slowly. It was his must-you-swear? look. "Must you, darling?"

"Sorry. It just slipped out and it will never happen again. Honest. I promise. But do me a favour, will you?"

"Of course. Anything."

"Go down and let him in."

All the way down Bow Street in the slow traffic Anthony kept up a miffed silence and eased the red Aston Martin past barrows and trucks while Jane sat as far down in the leather seat as she could get so as not to see the venomous looks that she knew the car was getting. It was an embarrassing car, and she hated it. The vroom-vroom was embarrassing. The AF-1 number-plate was embarrassing. Everything about it was embarrassing. Anthony himself was embarrassing, come to that, and sometimes she couldn't think what she saw in him.

He was, if not out-and-out reactionary, very conservative in his views. He was idle. He was snobbish. He was self-centred. He was, he really was what she used to march from Union Square on May Day singing "We Shall Overcome" about.

Yet there was something about him that appealed to her; she had to admit it. Those classy good looks, for one thing, and if that made her the world's biggest sucker for good-looking men—well, that was true, that was what she was.

But it wasn't only that, and it wasn't only the way he scared the bejesus out of snotty headwaiters, either. Anthony had it all, and all that *Goodbye, Mr. Chips* bullshit about calm authority and natural leadership wasn't entirely bullshit. People like Anthony were taught from the cradle that they were the greatest, and so quite naturally, whenever there was a chance to, the Anthonys behaved like the greatest.

She had seen it once when a bad four-car pile-up had happened just in front of them on the motorway. She'd seen it again when, without even raising his voice, he had broken up a bad fight outside a very tough pub. He was, in his own way, the real McCoy.

He had, in fact, all the great English qualities. He was courageous. Tolerant, but not squishily sophistic. He was even sometimes funny—if you like wrought irony. He was never numbingly earnest, but he could be serious too. Also he was modest, and though it was true he had a great deal to be modest about, he was still an improvement on many people who had even more to be modest about and were not.

She suddenly remembered Ron and did some mental arithmetic. "Can't be," she said.

"What can't be?"

"Can't be six weeks. Last time he came I had . . ."

"You had what?"

"Nothing. I just had an idea it was more recent is all. But isn't it funny?"

"Isn't what funny?"

"How it . . . oh, you know, flies. And that reminds me. When's Mummy back?"

"In a fortnight, according to her latest letter. Not, to be sure, that my mother's letters are documents one may take as guarantees. Why? Oh, lord, you're not ratting again, are you?"

"Me, oh lord? Never. Tom Mix hates a quitter."

"Tom who?"

"Nobody. Just somebody I used to know. But Anthony?"

"Mm?"

"Can't I convince you how bad I am at it? Do you have to see my gold medals from the Chicago Exhibition, not to mention Vienna? I've got more than the mustard ever saw."

"Something tells me we've had this conversation before."

"I know. I know we have. But it will be hell, believe me. The horses will hate me. Everybody will hate me. And I know those houses. Sooner or later somebody will say how much the fox enjoys the hunt too, and I'll say, 'Which fox said so?' and your mother will look down her lorgnette at me, and the only one who won't hate me will be the fox—the fox who had such fun at the hunt that he died laughing."

"Darling, you're making a maudlin fuss about nothing. All that is asked of you is to behave civilly for a weekend in a house that is, if nothing else, extremely comfortable. There may well be dullish people there, but that is all they are—dull. Nobody will hate you. To be quite honest, I really do not see how anything so unchallenging can reduce an ordinarily level-headed girl like you to an hysteric."

"Jane-Ann Hysteric. I hate people who get my name wrong."

"You are, if I may say so, being quite extraordinarily tiresome."

"I am? Well, it's a knack. A small knack maybe, but death to hide. But honestly, Anthony, can't you see? They'll put their ears back and roll their eyes. Horses know, you know."

"What do horses know?"

"Plenty. A lot more than they say."

"Then you needn't go anywhere near a horse. We'll only do what you want."

"OK. I want to stay in London."

"We can watch television if you like—or play Scrabble."

"Right. So why don't we stay in London and do that?"

"Because, for one thing, I dislike weekends in London. For another, my mother has specially asked that I bring you down—"

"You bring me down all right. You don't need your mother for that."

"For a third, I very much want to show you Cravenbourne. And you—in a recklessly unguarded moment, of course—have even said you'd like to see it. Also, both least and last, Mother is expecting you, and she is not a woman who takes great pleasure in last-minute changes of plan."

"She isn't going to take one hell of a lot of great pleasure in me either. I'm the kind of plan I'm dead sure she'd never find it too late to change."

"You have only persuaded yourself of that."

"OK. But name, rank, and serial number is all they're getting out of me. Maybe I can dig me a tunnel out."

"Possibly. In that case, dig due south. It's only a mile to the road that way."

"How far's it the other way, for the god's sake?"

"Two—two and a half."

"God. Think of the poor old postman with shrapnel in his legs from Ypres struggling up that front walk. Twice a day, yet."

"The postman is neither poor nor old. He almost certainly never heard of Ypres. He has a van. And he comes only once a day—yet."

"Once a day? That's criminal. That's grinding the faces of the rich, and it's not a decent way to treat a duke. It's them Jews and commies and everybody having free orange juice and trusses that's at the bottom of it."

Anthony cut sharply in front of a bus, turned left off Fleet Street, and stopped in front of the grimy building where the *Orbit's* offices were. He was cross again,

44

and so far Friday had gone badly. She thought of the 4:15 from Cambridge and hoped it wouldn't be late. Somehow just the thought of Franklin made it easier to be nice to Anthony.

"I'm sorry I was Ann Hysteric. I'll try my very best at Cravenbourne, really I will."

He kissed her and patted her knee as if she were a slightly skittish gun dog that had finally obeyed and come to heel. "Good girl."

It was the last straw. Too much is enough. Did he really have to talk like that? Nigger-brown. Smart frock. Splendid chap. Long vac. And now, good girl.

"Bye-bye, Anthony. Cheers. Chin-chin."

Next to swearing, Anthony disliked non-U genteel-isms most. He put on his you'll-not-catch-me-that-way smile.

"Good-bye, darling. I'll read you on Sunday, if old Jamieson will lend me his *Orbit*."

Old Jamieson was the half-cracked gamekeeper at Cravenbourne, who was known for his mad Marxist views and also for the fact that he never washed and was so incontinent that—or so the Cravenbourne witti-cism went—he had never caught any poachers because they could always smell him coming.

She turned in her copy and sat on the features editor's desk, doing her nails, while he read it. Halfway through he frowned, reached for a pencil, and went back to the first paragraph. It was a bad sign. So was the brush salesman smile. She blew on one nail to speed up the drying, and looked at him.

He took off his hornrimmed glasses and leaned back in his swivel chair, polishing them. "Super." God, the creep had been in England twenty years—why couldn't he lose that Saskatchewan accent? "It's a great piece, Jane. I like it, it's got the old pizazz and lots of it."

Fulsome praise. Another bad sign. She started doing her right hand. "But?"

"But? Honey, there ain't no buts. It's from Goodtown Junction, I love it."

Lies. The worst sign of all. She deliberately made a mess of one nail and pretended to concentrate on wiping the polish from around the edge.

He tapped the lead paragraph with the pencil. "I just kind of wonder, though, if—well, if this Yugoslav movie isn't a little low-profile, a little, you know, esoteric to lead on."

She blew on her nails again and started on the second coat. "Do you think? It was the best movie this week, Jim. By a long shot."

"Oh, I agree. I can see it was. Easily the best. And don't get me wrong, Jane; I have the greatest possible respect for your judgment."

"Gosh, it's not just me. It won the big prize at Cannes and—"

"Of course it did. And it deserved it. I've got no doubt at all that it deserved it. But will it go down in—"

"I don't know. But does it matter? Karajevic is the best director working in Europe today. His last picture was *Exalted State*—do you remember it?"

"Of course. A marvelous film. Really great."

"I mean did you see it?"

"No. I wanted to, but . . ." The brush-salesman smile had faded. He meant business. "Now, Jane, let's not kid around. I agree with you one hundred per cent that Kara . . ."

"Karajevic."

"That's right, Karajevic—I agree he's a great director who makes great movies. But we have to turn out a newspaper that is read by—well, by a large but not necessarily very sophisticated cross section of the population. Will they like this subtle satire on communism? Will the people in the North like it? Will they even have the chance to see it? What chance do you think this movie has of getting distribution in Yorkshire, say? You get my point?"

"Bugger Yorkshire."

"Well, I know that's your attitude, though I wish it wasn't. But couldn't we—I'm only running this up the flagpole to see how it flutters, you know—couldn't we simply switch the order and lead on the thriller? Michael Baker is a big name, and it's a big picture. A British picture, too, and—well, I leave it up to you. What do you say?"

"I would think it's pretty obvious what I say, because I've said it. And I don't see why Yorkshire should influence what we lead on, anyhow. Not for the god's sake on the grounds that, as they prefer second-rate pictures, we should always lead on second-rate pictures. Nor do I care how big Michael Baker is, because for my money he couldn't act his way out from under a pile of wet leaves with a two-edged machete. Also I don't think we should push trashy sex and violence, which is all this Baker film is."

"I see. Yes. Well, let's put it to Mike, shall we?"

Mike Tyrone was an amiable man and a very good editor, but Jane knew for a fact that he hadn't been to a movie since Mrs. Miniver and that this week, with a printers' strike brewing and his deputy editor on holiday, was not the week to bother him about what film to lead on.

"No, it's not worth it. Have it your way."

"It's not my way, Jane, it's just that, all things considered, it may be the better way, that's all. Only maybe, and only marginally maybe, the better way. Anyhow, it's only a detail, isn't it?"

"Sure, Jim. It's only a detail. It doesn't make any difference to me."

It did, though, and he knew it. She knew that he knew it, and he knew that she knew that he knew it. It was an old fight, and not one that Jane won very often.

Back in her own cubbyhole office, Janet, her secretary, was caught up in one of her open-ended telephone conversations. Without even taking off her Burberry raincoat, Jane stood going through her mail and, as Janet showed no signs of stopping, finally shoved it all into the drawer on top of last week's letters and left.

At the elevator she ran into the sports editor, who was very drunk and leaning against the button.

"'allo, Miss America. What's up?"

"Us, Leo. Way up. Where's Mr. Otis's contribution to the greater comfort of mankind?"

"Down. Way down. I think ish dead."

She liked Leo Fraling. He was an agreeable, lost man who disliked all competitive sports with an intensity that could drive a man to drink and had. He kept a sullen little blond wife, whom he never called anything but "she" in a much-mortgaged mock-Tudor house somewhere out near Twickenham, and he'd play chess until closing time with anybody in the pub any day of the week rather than go home to face her. Their troubles were a small Fleet Street legend.

"I've had it, Jane. She's leaving. She says this time she means it."

"Gosh, Leo, that's tough. But she has said it before, hasn't she?"

"Yeah, but this time's different. I think she's got a chap."

"So? After all, you've got a girl. Several, so they say down at the village pump, anyway."

"It's different for a man."

"What's different for a man?"

"The whole bloody thing's different. A man doesn't get involved, not emotionally involved the way a woman does. A man can go to bed with anybody, and it doesn't mean a thing. It doesn't necessarily mean a thing."

"And why can't a woman?"

"She can't, is why. It's not in a nice woman—and she is a nice woman, no matter what I've ever said about her—it's not in a nice woman's nature to be promiscuous."

"No? Maybe it is, Leo. Why shouldn't it be? People—men especially—have believed a lot of things about women that were never based on cold fact, you know."

"Yeah? Well, the women I've known—not that it's been all that many—all get the cold fact of sex mixed up with some pretty fanciful notions about love. Now, men do a lot of crazy things, but they don't do that. Only women. And women always do it. Always. You show me the one that doesn't."

"Me."

"You? That's a bloody laugh, you're the completely typical example of exactly the kind of woman who does it most. Tough on the outside? Oh, yes. Independent? Totally. You're the career girl who doesn't need roses around some old cottage door—you think. No, you're a nice straight girl, Jane, but take it from old Leo, the bigger the nice straight girls come, the harder they fall. And they don't bounce."

She walked up Fleet Street, turned into Chancery Lane, and went under the old archway that led to Lincoln's Inn Fields. On the square some London School of Economics students were playing tennis and looking very chilly. Spring had bogged down, and Friday still wasn't doing much better. She'd have to placate the angry gods that controlled such things by doing virtuous deeds when she got home.

At home, though, there wasn't anything virtuous left to do; Mrs. Bush had beaten her to everything important, and there were only fritterings left to offer.

She made barbecue sauce. She set the table for two and shortened some sprawling yellow tulips to put in the middle. She washed her hair and wrote a thank-you note to a producer who had taken her to lunch. She poured Scat some fresh milk; Mrs. Bush had cleaned up the spill, but Mrs. Bush didn't like Scat, so the saucer had been washed and put away.

These were thin offerings, but they were of a kind the gods sometimes accepted. To bring up the weight, she threw in a little bit of mind-improvement as well and took *Religion and the Rise of Capitalism* to read in the bath.

When he came in, she heard his books hit the desk, and the icebox door open and close. As he came down the hall he slid farther down in the water so her breasts would float rather than droop. He knocked and came in. "Hi. Sorry I'm late, but the master race had a little trouble with their train set outside King's Cross."

"Oh. Ah'd begun to wondah iffen you all just couldn't tell tyum, like what us whyut folk can."

"Don' yo trouble yoself, missy, over ussens. We kin tell tyum. iffen it's writ big. It just don' mean nothin to us, is all."

He leaned over the bath, and she put her arms up around his neck to kiss him. "How's Cambridge?"

He rolled up his shirtsleeves and washed his hands in the bath. "Not so bad. I got a nice offer in the mail today."

"Did you? What of?"

"Dayton. They need an Assistant DA, and it's more or less in the bag if I want it."

"Ah. Offstage thunder, and enter the big-shot uncle. Well, there's nothing like a big-shot uncle, I always say—unless it's two big-shot uncles."

"You bet your ass, baby. A little nepotism never hurt a nepot."

"And so?"

"So I'm thinking it over, that's all."

"You must be crazy. You'd get back there and rile things up, and sooner or later some bohunk honky in the National Guard will get you."

"You see too many movies."

"Jesus, that's the truth. And I suffered another ignoble defeat at the warty hands of the Sage of Medicine Hat today, too."

"What kind of defeat?"

"Same old kind. Give the people what they want. Or, rather, what Jim boy thinks they want. But never mind, guess what's for supper."

"To hell with supper; let's go to bed."

"You won't want to when you hear."

"I will, but what?"

"Spareribs. And real spinach. Real spinach simmered gently in its own juices and served on a crunchy bed of real sand."

"You're lying. It's a low-down trick to preserve your virtue."

"White woman does not speak with forked tongue. Anyhow, what virtue?"

"Let's eat it in bed."

"God, spareribs in bed. That's a real idea. An even worse idea than Dayton."

Dayton didn't come up again until the next morning. While he made the coffee, she snipped chives into the scrambled eggs, and from the way he glanced at her once or twice she knew it was coming.

"It's not really such a bad idea, Dayton."

"What's good about it?"

"Well, I've got to go back sometime—nobody can life off the Ford Foundation forever. And it's a pretty good offer, all things considered. It's the kind of job where I can do, or anyhow start doing, some of the things I think ought to be done."

"Like getting yourself killed?"

"And the pay's not bad and—"

"But what about the law-school job? You don't have to be a cop."

"A DA isn't a cop."

"It's a sort of cop."

"Jane, face it. My brother, he thinks the world's going to turn into one big beige heaven now he's got tenure at Princeton, but I don't kid myself like that. It's not going to happen that way. And I'm not going to fool around in New Haven waiting for something that's not going to happen to not happen."

"You're not going to make it happen by remaking *High Noon*, either. Come on, why don't we make a new movie? Where the good law professor guy says to hell with cops and robbers and lives to be a hundred and three in the shade."

"Baby, it's no good. I'm thirty-three. That eerie wail you can hear when you tilt your head is time whistling by. There's a lot I want to do, and I've got to get going."

"The race isn't always to Tom Swift."

"It is when he's racing Jim Crow. And no race is won by somebody not running in it. I'd go crazy stuck in the law school. Jesus, I'll go crazy if I stumble

53

around much longer in the tall wet grass at Cambridge. Don't you see that?"

"Of course I see it. I also see you talking a lot about Wasp guilt when you're the biggest Wasp of all, and one dumb stuck-up nigger to boot."

"My mammy, she raised us to be proud."

"She raised you. Her and a governess, she raised you."

"Well, she was a busy woman, don't forget. Would you really rather I'd crawled out from under One Hundred and Twenty-fifth Street and had the rat bites to prove it?"

"Oh, for the chrissake. But Dayton? Why Dayton? Do you think we'd *like* Dayton?"

"We'd have to see. We can't do that from here."

"No. No, I guess we can't."

"And Jane?"

"What."

"You know what."

"Boy, don't I? Your family. What I don't see is why they're all going to fall in their vichyssoise and drown if you come home with a no-good white-trash female, but go mad with joy if the same female is a wife."

He poured another cup of coffee with exaggerated slow calm, but that had got to him and he was angry. "It's not like that, and you know it."

"Isn't it? Listen. We get along fine." She stopped. Something about the tone of voice didn't fit the statement. They both laughed.

"No, honestly, we do. We have for two whole years. I'm in love with you, whatever that is. I even like you, and I do know what that is. But to get married, to be foisted into getting married just to satisfy other people's sensibilities is too much. Can you think of a worse reason for getting married? This side of a shotgun?"

"It's old-fashioned, I know, but—"

"Old-fashioned? It's positively medieval."

"OK. It's positively anything you want to call it. But that's how they are, and I've always found it one hell of a lot easier to sort of string along than to rock the boat. Anyhow, what real difference could it possibly make? We'd be no different than we are now."

"I don't know. It scares me, that's all. Not just marriage, but everything. Them. Dayton. America. America scares me to death. You don't know that place the way I do, and so it doesn't scare you—but it sure does me."

"Baby, I know what you're thinking about. But that was twenty years ago. It's not that bad now."

"You're right. It's not. It's not that bad, because it's worse. Twenty years ago they were content with little things, like hounding my father to death. Now—well, you only have to read the papers to see what they're into now for kicks."

She ran water into the sink, squirted in the green liquid, and started on last night's dishes. "You're too swell, Franklin. You were brought up too gently. But America is a vicious place, and I don't trust it. I've seen what they can do. I saw them take a perfectly decent man like my father and—and kill him. For nothing except believing there could be such a thing as justice, and for making pictures that tried to tell the truth. He pulled the trigger himself, sure. But it was them that put the gun in his hand and the defeat in his heart that made him do it."

"Don't, baby. Please don't. It doesn't do any good."

She put the platter she was washing on the drainboard and wiped her nose with the back of her hand.

"And you're right, that was all years ago. That was back when they were saying nobody was poor in the land of plenty, while barefoot kids with big empty bellies died of pellagra and beri-beri and shitty diseases like that. That was when they were saying there was liberty and justice for all, and to prove it they bombed black kids in Sunday School and threw civil-rights workers into the soft cement of some lousy dam in Mississippi. That was when the American way of life and the miracle of science had made everything easy for everyone, except most people didn't dare go to a doctor when they were sick for fear of what it would cost. And they still don't.

"And you say it's better now. Jesus christ, now they're even shooting white kids—not just blacks, they've always shot blacks. And by now everyone is so used to violence, so used to thug police and corruption and drugs and murder and schools where kids learn nothing and prisons where people are treated worse than animals and cities that have gone to hell, that they take it for normal and hardly anyone can remember a time when it wasn't like that, or even if there ever was such a time.

"Even what they've done to Vietnam they take for normal. No, it's a country gone mad, Franklin. And in record time, too. God, these poor English loonies may not be able to make cars that go or telephones that work, but their crazy system has worked. For a thousand years it's staggered along, changing a bit here, smelling a bit of mothballs there, and never perfect, but it *has* worked. But America? With all that lovely room, all that lovely wealth, and all that lovely chance, they've loused up the whole works in less than three hundred years and will, if they get the chance, louse up the world as well. I tell you, if that's not a place to sort of think twice about going back to, then I'd like to know what is."

A bowl in her hand was dripping sudsy water on the floor, and he took it from her, set it on the dishrack, and put his arms around her. "Jane, stop it. It doesn't do any good."

She pushed him away and ran the water hard to wash out the sink. "It does too do good. It reminds me of what a rotten, lying, corrupt, hypocritical, synthetic-flavored tutti-frutti, homicidal nightmare that country is."

She blew her nose on a paper towel and laughed. "Wow. Send me in, coach, huh?"

Franklin heated up the coffee and poured two cups. "You put it like that, and what can I say? Maybe it *is* worse now, or anyhow just as bad. But don't you see, that's why I've got to go back. I have to at least try and do—oh christ, you know, my bit and all that baloney. If I can do anything, even just a little—well, fine. If I can't, then what the hell, at least I'll have tried. I know that's square and maybe even old-fashioned." He looked at her to see how the dirty word was going over. "But that's how I feel. All I'm not sure of is what's the best way to go about it. The Dayton job is one way. But there are other ways that might be quicker."

"Like?"

He smiled at her. "Ah, those are black secrets. Meet me on the ramparts some night, and I might tell you."

"I don't like heights. Send me a letter. But seriously, Franklin . . ."

"Yes?"

"Nothing. Except that I know how you feel, I really do, and I didn't mean all that stuff about *High Noon*, you know. I mean, I've got some idea of what it means to have to do something—even though I haven't ever felt it myself."

"I know, baby. It's all right. But you know what else I know? I know you've got to go back too. You can't hide here forever—Hey, how about that? You think I should write cowboy scripts?"

"No, because you believe it. It's against the rules to believe it."

"I only believe it because it's true. You know as well as I do that England is the bush league and finished. Even if it weren't, it's not home—not for me, and not for you either. It's not where anything's at."

"I don't know. It's hard, I guess it's always hard to leave a place that's easy. What's really happened is I've developed a kind of Gaza Strip mentality. I don't really feel at home here, but I don't want to crawl out of my tent and leave the soup kitchen— not, anyhow, for a back street in Cairo and that lousy deal they call real life. Can you blame me?"

"Not Cairo. Dayton."

"You're so right. Dayton. And maybe Dayton I

could take. But this marriage thing? I don't know—I just don't know. I mean, I'd like to be married, but I don't want to get married. Does that make sense?"

"Well, yes and no."

"Oh! Oh, you clever man, that's exactly it. More coffee?"

He looked at his watch. "No, it's late. What time does the British Museum open?"

"On a Saturday? England is closed on Saturday, you know."

"Oh jesus. No, they've got to."

"Got to? Got to, boy, is not something I'd toss around lightly about the British Museum, if I was you. Like be more British. Tug that forelock. Have that hard-won pass between your teeth. Kneel on the top step and say, 'Please sir. Please, nice sir, can I come in and look at your books? I've got very clean hands, sir.' "

"You know what Miss Johnson used to tell us when I was about eight?"

"What?"

" 'Always remember, children, that American ends in I can.' How about that?"

"I like it. It must have been a great rod and staff in Vietnam."

"It was. I assure you, it was. Right up to the day I suddenly thought of Siam."

"What bird can live cheaper than one?"

"A toucan?"

"Right. What river does a con man live on?"

"You got me."

"Ha. The Rubicon."

Like the people who go for spike-heeled boots or black rubber underwear, she couldn't resist something about his almost white trenchcoat. When he came back into the kitchen with it on, she felt a wave of pure lust undulate from just under her ribs clear down to her knees. She put her arms tight around his neck and breathed in the faint aphrodisiac smell of dry-cleaner's fluid from the shoulder of the coat.

"Don't go. Don't leave me for that germy reading room; let's go to bed."

"Can't. I hear the rumble of a distant drum."

"Heed it not, Lochinvar. You have in your arms a vibrant living creature, a soaring untrammelled spirit, calling out for human warmth and love."

"Call out about midnight tonight."

"My spirit will be all trammelled by then. Take off your clothes."

"What time's the theatre?"

"What theatre? Oh jesus, is that tonight? I'd forgotten all about it. Do we really have to go?"

"We said we would. I heard you say it. Right to his face you said it. I did wonder at the time just how drunk you were."

"Christ. Well, that's life, isn't it? Try to be nice, and you're bound to hate yourself in the morning."

"Shall I meet you there or come back?"

"What you mean is can you trust me to show up?"

"Well, can I?"

"Sure. What the hell—if you can't, who can?"

4

Waiting for Tom on Monday night, Jane lay on the floor in the living room and tried to imagine life in Dayton. God, it would be awful. The gracious-livers would have big banal colonial-style houses set well back from streets named things like Sunset Vista Drive. They'd be Republicans. Their station wagons would have genuine wood-grained polystyrene trim and enough lights to watch night baseball by. In flat Ohio voices they'd talk about persons being *real*—and the real persons would be involved in, concerned about, and fully committed to every half-assed thing from Girl Scout Cooky Week to the John Birch Society.

Picking up more hairs on her old Levis and T shirt from the white fur rug, which was shedding badly, she rolled over and poured herself another glass of red wine from the bottle on the slate-topped table. Leaning on her elbows, she sipped at it and let her imagination off its leash.

These real people would have real problems. *Prawblems*. What to wear on safari. Where to go this time in Yurp. How to fit a deer into the freezer.

Whether to buy more AT&T or wait for Conglomerated Aircraft to pick up. How to keep Jews and blacks out. Not Franklin, of course; a black tennis-playing lawyer in Savile Row suits would chic up the flagstoned patio no end.

Hidden under those American smiles, under the decorator-colour wall-to-wall broadloom, and way deep inside the French Provincial hi-fis that had never seen France, there'd be the truth, and when they were drunk or desperate it would come out. Money. Boats that were yar as hell but not paid for. Second mortgages that their wives didn't know about. Analysts' fees that had piled up. Bills from very select, very expensive bins.

There'd be drinkers. Secret, frightened homosexuals who got blackmailing calls at the office and jumped every time the phone rang at home. Tall, slouchy children who took funny pills and escaped from the frying pan of home into the fire of communes and talked pat, empty American jargon about meaningful life experiences. Impotent executive husbands who were all "Howzit going, Mac?" at the nineteenth hole, but whose last satisfactory sexual adventure had been with a hired eleven-year-old child in a Hong Kong hotel.

No. Jesus christ, she couldn't. The land of David Webb cufflinks, landscaped swimming pools, Steuben glass collectors' items, buttondown collars, and pent-up neurotic anxiety was not for her.

Who, then? What would they do for friends? Join up with the bestseller-reading, ecology-conscious, noisy minority who had majored in child psychology and once thought about joining the Peace Corps? Married, she and Franklin would be sitting ducks for them.

They were the ones who'd make their own bread from stone-ground, compost-grown whole-wheat flour. They'd sit on Environment Improvement Committees and be as involved, concerned, and committed as the other fools—except about different half-assed things.

They'd activate their leisure picking broken glass and tin cans out of vacant lots so underprivileged children would have a place to play—but they'd never

62

rebel against the system that had created those under-privileged children. They'd talk a lot about the vanishing Indian and what to do about the California grape-pickers and how to go on from where Head Start left off. In a state of beatified, earnest togetherness they'd sit around their outdoor barbecues and talk a great deal about these things. But would they ever do anything about them? She doubted it.

And, oh *god*, there'd be those Christmas cards. Greetings of the season were not all you'd get from "Bob, Alice, Bob Jr., Betsy, and our new arrival, Pavlov, who is really an adorable Sealyham but who thinks he is a people. . . ." Greetings of the season would be the least of it.

". . . and at this, the season of peace and good will, we sincerely hope that your year has been as full and as rewarding as ours. . . .

"Bob Sr. and Alice spent a most enjoyable and instructive two weeks in the summer on a refresher course in Advanced Handicrafts which has already paid great dividends at their Thursday evening sessions at the Boys Club . . . and Bob Jr., after some pretty fraught days of waiting, finally got the good news that he had passed his College Boards with flying colors . . . and to top it all off, he then got word that his application to Michigan State had been accepted, and so he is (do we have to say it?) one mighty thrilled guy. And so are we, for him.

"Betsy is still the real live-wire activist of the family, however, and not only did she skip the sixth grade (an event that is, as most of you will remember, a very unusual thing to happen at Beamish Country Day) but she also qualified for her Junior Lifesaving Certificate and, just as if all that weren't enough for one young lady's busy year, she now has her 'Maestro' rating at Miss Duff's recorder group.

"As for Pavlov, well . . ."

No. It wasn't possible.

Why not? Other Americans live in America. What's so special about you? Nothing. And I know they do.

Many Americans. Great unwieldy numbers of Americans. And maybe I could manage New York. New Haven, even. In a pinch, California again. But Dayton? Jesus.

You've never even been to Dayton. It may not be as bad as you think. No? I've seen Cleveland, though. Dayton can't be all that different. Anyhow, where's Tom? It's late.

You're dodging. Stick to the subject. Right. Dayton. Me. No, not me, us. No, him. Franklin. Franklin Rodgers. Franklin *Pierce* Rodgers. Who is thirty-three, six-foot-one, a lawyer, and an ex-Infantry lieutenant who got out of Vietnam OK, except for an elbow that is now held together with a cunningly fashioned metal pin and hardly gives him any trouble at all.

What else? Well, he weighs about 185 pounds, plays the piano, and, considering the elbow, is still pretty good at tennis. He's lousy at poker, but he dances better than any man I've ever known, and he makes love better than any man anybody has ever known, even Angela. No wonder white men are so scared of them. They have every reason to be.

The thing about Franklin, though, is he *likes* women. Really likes them. They don't even have to open their mouths for him to know what they're thinking or feeling. He just—I don't know—knows what they want. And not just in bed. Even in restaurants he knows what they want.

They? Who's this they? OK. Me. He knows what *I* want. I don't have to finish sentences with him. Sometimes I don't even have to start sentences with him.

And maybe it's true what they say about women and blacks, maybe they do have the same lousy row to hoe—and maybe that's part of the attraction. You know, mutual sympathy and all that. I mean it's obvious. They're both fed up with being second-class citizens and kicked around. Most of them, anyhow. Not so much Franklin. He's never been kicked around by anyone ever.

More? Well, he's pretty. He's very pretty. And you

64

see this room? How it's all black leather and white fur and white walls? I made it that way because he looks so great against it. Before I knew him it was all a mess of bloody old straw matting and Indian bedspreads and christ awful. But now it's all pulled together and looks like a room that's made up its mind, you know what I mean? Of course a lot of these crazy paintings are by Tom, so it isn't all Franklin. And Anthony gave me that Tiffany lamp that doesn't really go with the rest of it, but he'd paid so much for it at Sotheby's that I didn't have the heart not to use it. And Tom made that mobile too. So OK, it *isn't* a room that has made up its mind. But—it almost has.

Franklin's a Scorpio. One of those sexy ones that go for power. Not at all like me, I'm Aries, one of those dumb ones who take terrible chances. But him? I wouldn't be at all surprised if he doesn't see himself as the first Emperor Jones of New York or something, sometime. At the moment, though, he seems to be satisfied with sex, bourbon, the theatre, Buster Keaton movies, Chicago jazz, and shirts with his initials on them—providing he has enough of all of them and in roughly that order. And don't forget the tennis. Southern New England Champion. Singles too. I forget what year.

You're still dodging. What's the catch, the drawback in this schmalzy set-up? Right. Right on. It's his family. They're one of those families you have to live up to. You have to be perfect. You have to get all A's and be good at everything and be a *credit.* Just from what he tells me I can tell they're so Ph.D.'d and high-minded that if you're slow on the Latin you miss all the best jokes. His sister's a doctor but doesn't have to do with sick people or anything unwholesome like that. More your research.

She's very beautiful, the sister—I'll give her that— and she floats around in sort of noble-savage clothes from Eastern souks. You know, East 57th Street. She's a pretty big deal, too, in whatever it is that she does, and has as well—wouldn't you *know?*—two frighteningly well-adjusted children who do things like ride awfully well and sculpt.

I know they sound very great—and they are. What's wrong with them is they're exactly like any other well-off, intellectual, vitamin-enriched Americans. Too innocent. Too goody-goody. Too superior. God, they're like black Cabots or Lowells or something and—I don't know, maybe it would be better if he did come from 125th Street and *was* a Pullman porter's son who'd had to wait on table to get through school.

Better? Better for whom?

Well, it sounds silly, but better for him, really. As it is, he's always had everything made, without even having to make much of an effort. He's had it too easy—and I know that sounds like Anthony talking about the miners, but it's true. It's left him very smooth on the outside, but I'm not so sure about underneath. I don't think even he knows what's underneath.

Anyhow, that's them, and that's how it is. They got their start when some female ancestor was horse-traded to some other plantation-owner after she'd engineered a slaves' rebellion that didn't come off. I don't suppose the first lot of bastards who owned her ever told the second lot of bastards about her wayward ways, but she must have been really something, that lady, because it only took her a little while at the new place before she had the elder son completely in love with her.

There must have been a pretty spectacular family fight about *that*, but whatever else happened, at least the two children she had got to go to school. The little boy died before he was grown up, of malaria. But the other one, the girl, was Franklin's father's grandmother.

She must have been something too, because after the Civil War she moved North, where she married a black preacher and had three children, every one of whom she sent all the way through school. Jesus, can you imagine? It was all my grandfather could do—and I don't know any further back than him—to get out of some Estonian ghetto with a yarmulka on his head, a violin under his arm, and a future that turned out to be a lifetime in a garment factory down around 14th Street. And Jews are supposed to be so smart already.

So anyhow one of those three children was Franklin's grandfather, and when he grew up he married a half-Sioux lady who wasn't all that enchanted with life as it is stacked by white men either. Franklin can remember her. Dimly. Mostly only that she had bumpy veins in her hands and that he was frightened of her. But Franklin's father can remember the tent that her mother lived in—how about that? It was out in Oklahoma or someplace insane like that.

Franklin was born in Washington because Roosevelt—that's who he's named after—had talked his father out of teaching in some black college down South and had brought him to Washington to work in the Public Health Service. He's a doctor too, the father, except he's retired now. But when Franklin came along they were living in a big old house in Georgetown with a pink magnolia out front and slave quarters out back where—I like this bit—they kept the children's pony.

His mother—"Mothah," we call her—taught anthropology in those days and has since written some pretty big books that are all about South American Indians and how there's only fourteen of them left or something. Me, I should think fourteen South American Indians was plenty, but Mothah doesn't see it that way. Part of our precious heritage, she calls them. Part of our precious heritage, my ass. All they do is run around gibbering at each other and get stoned on some dumb drug that they blow up each other's noses through six-foot pipes.

Franklin had a pretty dull childhood—with a mother like that, who wouldn't?—and he can still remember looking out the window of the family Packard and seeing kids playing stickball in the street, and wishing he had high sneakers with big rubber circles on the ankles like theirs. He never got them, though. *Their* clothes came from Best's, and Best's was never big on slum sneakers.

So that's about all. After Roosevelt died, Franklin's father was sent abroad with the World Health Organization. To Geneva and Stockholm first, and then New Delhi.

India was a kind of shock to Franklin. No stickball there, just unbelievable filth and poverty. And it was there that he began to realize, too, that there was something wrong with being black. Like Jimmy Baldwin says, it's a big shock to find out that, in a world of Gary Coopers, you're the Indian.

He went back home to boarding school then, and then Yale, and then law school. He doesn't talk much about any of it and, worse—or it seems to me worse, anyhow—he never mentions anyone who was with him at these schools. No, that's not quite true; once he did say that somebody he had known at law school was one of the junior attorneys who had tried to help George Jackson, but it wasn't that he'd heard from the guy or anything; I think he only read about it in *Time*.

I'd never known, not really known, a black person before I met Franklin—not that there's anything so extraordinary about that. I mean, I've never known and still don't know anyone who's Chinese, even Chinese-American, or, for that matter, Swedish. And to me what colour he is doesn't make any difference anyway; in fact I'm so used to him I don't even see any more that he *is* black. Besides, he isn't very black, just an awfully nice brown, really, that's exactly the same colour people try to get at Saint-Tropez by lying on the beach all day.

It's other people who make me remember he's black. He slides over it with a lot of cool, but I've walked into enough parties and restaurants and things with him to know awfully well that first flicker of surprise in people's eyes and how it turns into a slow sideways stare. Or sometimes to real hostility, or that blank, lunatic look that's supposed to show they haven't even noticed. But he just takes it for granted, the slow stare

68

and everything. Even when they stare at the front of his pants—and you'd be surprised at the number of people who wouldn't say shit with a mouth full of it who do that—he doesn't pay any attention. And maybe that's not so strange, after all, he's been seeing that look and those flickery eyes all his life.

It does make you wonder about people, though. What are they frightened of? What do they think they're going to see by staring like that? What do they think is so different about him? You can see that something, some really crazy thoughts are running zigzag like a bunch of startled lemmings through their minds. But what? They can't all be thinking what one girl was thinking when she came up to me at a party and whispered, "God, he must be the best fuck in London." Can they? It seems extraordinary.

It seems extraordinary too the way everything important happens by accident. Not little things. Little things you can control. You can find the right pink sandals to go with the pink dress. You can test-dye a bit of your hair before you shove your head in a bucketful. You can phone for a weather report before you go out sailing. You can even wait for a better invitation before saying yes to the Creep-Bores' dinner party.

But with big things you don't get a chance or even a choice. It was only because he'd missed a train to Cambridge that Franklin was at that party where I met him. And I hadn't even been invited; I'd just gone with somebody who had. I still don't know whose party it was or what it was for, or anything, and yet those people and their party changed my whole life. If it hadn't been for them, I wouldn't be lying here on the floor now getting drunk and thinking about going to live in Dayton. Jesus. And some people believe in free will.

She couldn't drink any more wine. She knew she ought to get up and go to bed. But she didn't. Instead, she shut her eyes for that fatal pre-bed little rest, and when she woke up, cold and cross, Tom was lying on the sofa, reading.

"Hello, sneaky. How'd you get in without my hearing?"

He picked up the empty wine bottle and tilted it. "Easy when you know how. You OK?"

"Me? Sure. We also serve who only lie in wait."

"Sorry. I know I'm late. But I brought you a present."

She frowned. She wasn't fond of Tom's hot presents. She already had crested silver plates and a coffeepot she never dared use, and waffle irons and mixers she didn't dare have repaired because their serial numbers had been chiseled off.

He led her down the hall to the bathroom and pushed the door open. "There. Isn't it beautiful?"

On newspapers in the bathtub, leaning back on its heels with its eyes blearily half shut, was a baby pigeon. It wasn't any uglier than any other half-fledged pigeon, and quite pretty blue-grey feathers had almost replaced all the wispy, dirty down. But the corners of its beak were still yellow, its toes were all scaly and red, and it was not something she needed or wanted.

"Christ."

"Isn't it beautiful?"

Kneeling by the bathtub, he tried to pick it up, but it scuttled to the far end and opened its beak in a loser's try at being fierce. "See those wings? He'll be flying in a week or two." Tom spread one wing out and admired it. "And I'll make him a house out on the roof, feed him up a bit, and then when he's ready we can take him to the park and let him go."

He stood up. "You do like him, don't you?"

"Words, Tom, mere words aren't enough to express it."

"He's no ordinary pigeon, either. He's a wood pigeon."

"Is he? My. But what if ..." This was The Last Chance Saloon. "What if he dies?"

"Him, die? *He* won't die. Look at him. Never. The ones that are going to die, their hearts beat fast and they struggle; that's what they die of, I think, the fear and the struggling. But this one? When I picked him up in the road outside his heart never even jumped. He didn't even mind being in my pocket. He won't die, not him."

God. He was probably right. He almost always was about things like pigeons. She couldn't be nasty about the damned little thing any more. "OK. Even if he wants to die, we won't let him. We'll grow him up into the biggest, fattest pigeon in London, and then we'll let him go—we *will* let him go, won't we, Tom?"

"Sure. It's not right to keep them penned up once they're grown."

She shut Scat in the living room and fed Tom, and then Tom fed the pigeon, holding its beak open and poking in big lumps of brown bread soaked in milk. When its crop was nicely rounded and its eyes shut drunkenly, he put it back in the bathtub and they started to get ready for bed.

Jane was in the bathroom, brushing her teeth, when he called from the bedroom, "You know anything about Magritte?"

She reached over the tub for a towel, and the pigeon opened its beak ferociously. "Oh, shut up, will you," she muttered, and yelled back to Tom, "Not much. A surrealist. Belgian. Dead now, I think, but only recently. Painted sort of jokes, things like reverse mermaids—big fishes with women's legs. Why?"

There wasn't any answer.

Brushing her hair, she walked into the bedroom. "Tom, you leave anything by Magritte strictly alone. He's too well known to fool around with. You hear?"

He was flat on his stomach on the floor, pulling things out from under the bed. "God, you're worse than the bloody fuzz. I only like to look at his stuff, for jesus' sake."

"Well, there isn't any under the bed—I hope."

"No, but that *Twentieth Century Masters* book is here somewhere, because that's where I put it."

He'd pulled out a suitcase. A cardboard box of old

71

press clippings. A pair of tights. An apple core. "The fucker's a great cleaner, you can say that for her."

The jetsam pile was growing, and Jane stepped over it to get into bed; she was winding the clock when he reached up and handed something to her. "Here's a useful-looking thing. Wouldn't want to lose that, if I was you."

Without even looking at the squiggly length of plastic he put in her hand, she knew instantly what it was.

Jesus.

What must have happened ran through her head like a speeded-up film. She could see the whole thing as clearly as if she were drowning.

Mrs. Bush briskly turning the mattress on a Friday. But god, which Friday?

Ron's voice. "*Oh, absolutely, miss. More like seven, really.*"

The skirt that had shrunk at the cleaner's. The inexplicable lurch of nausea when she'd opened the can of paint to do the bathroom windowsill. Separately, they were all nothing. But together . . .

Staring at the treacherous little piece of plastic, she added it all up and said, "My god."

Tom had found the book and was lying on the floor, looking at it. "My god what?"

"Tom. Oh my god, Tom."

He got up and sat on the bed. "What? What's the matter?"

"I'm . . ."

"Mm?"

"I'm pregnant."

"What makes you think so?"

She handed him the plastic squiggle. "This."

"This? What is it?"

"It's a coil. An intrauterine device, they call it. Except it's no longer intra, as you can see."

"But how did it—"

"I don't know. I've heard that it can happen, though. Without your even noticing, it can happen."

As he slowly caught on, his dark blue eyes widened,

and she had never seen his beautiful face look more beautiful or more serious. "Are you sure?"

"Sure? Just look at Pakistan; it must happen the whole time there to everybody." She took it back from him and shook her head. "I never thought it could happen to me, though."

Nothing turned Tom on more than babies or any small, vulnerable creatures that needed looking after. He kissed her hands and stroked her face, and then he made love to her as if she were as fragile and delicate a holy vessel as Mrs. Bush's glass boat.

Afterwards, while he covered her carefully with the blankets, he said, "What are we going to do?"

"Not we, Tom. Me. It's not your problem, and you're not to worry about it."

"Worry? Christ, who's worried? I'm glad about it. I'm ..." He broke off and looked apprehensive. "You wouldn't ..."

"Wouldn't what?"

"Wouldn't—you know, get rid of it or anything, would you? You wouldn't want to do that, would you?"

"I don't know. It's complicated. There's a lot more to having a baby than—"

"Than what? Look at those Pakis—christ, anything they can do we can do better. It's not all *that* complicated. We can manage."

"I don't know, Tom. I just don't know. I'll have to think."

Tom went to sleep with his arms around her, and she listened to his even breathing that was like a child's. But her thoughts got nowhere.

Anthony's?

Tom's?

Franklin's? Oh christ, *Franklin*.

Black?

White?

Have it? Her heart said to, but her head said not to.

Another abortion?

If only she knew which Friday. Last Friday? The

Friday before that? No, it must have been before that, and what did it matter anyway? Even if she knew which Friday it had got lost under the bed, she still wouldn't know whose the baby was, would she? And there wasn't any way to find out, was there?

5

Angela had hit the Connaught hard, and when Jane
got there the ripples were still spreading. Baskets of
things from Fortnum's and flowers from Moyses Stevens
were coming in the way new oil wells come in, and a
cluster of matching leather suitcases stood snobbily
aloof in the lobby, waiting to be taken up.

The door to room 235 was open, and Jane walked
in. In a sable coat Angela lay across the bed, talking on
the phone, and Jane picked a black mink jacket off the
floor and put it on. In front of the long wardrobe
mirror she fluffed up her hair, sucked in her cheeks,
hiked her skirt up over her knees, and, leaning backwards, minced whorishly across the room.

Angela hung up and said, "Got it. Sadie Thomp-
son."

"Right. Right as rain."

The phone rang again, and the new caller got short
shrift. "Darling, how lovely—but call me back, will
you? Yes, that's right. In absolute knots. You will?
Lovely. Bye."

She kicked off her shoes, shoved a pile of empty

boxes and tissue paper onto the floor, and lay back on the bed. "Tell me something."

"Like?"

"Like how do you stand this withered walrus dug they call a country?" She fitted a cigarette into a long black holder.

"Oh for the chrissake, Angela, you've only been here an hour. Don't start that yet."

"Two hours, darling, and in some places two hours is enough. Two hours on the rack, say. Or, not dissimilar, two hours in that jumped-up trading post down the road."

"One goat, one wife. Two goats, two wives. The system's simple enough, once you get used to it."

"Would you believe it? All I wanted was a brown lace bra. One such as a lifelong stutterer could buy in thirty seconds in Ohrbach's. And do you know what this catatonic creature behind the counter *said?*"

"I can't imagine."

"She said, 'Sorry, moddom.' Without even looking. With that ghoulish smile the English put on when they haven't got what you want, she said, 'Sorry, moddom. There's no call for brown bras, moddom, and we haven't any.' This with me calling for one as if to a hard-of-hearing Iowa hog."

"So shop in Ohrbach's, why not? Come here for the peace of mind and *kulturny.*"

"How very like you to be the ever-sympathetic friend and true sister in Christ. I might have known. And no—I can see the little thought forming like a pearl in your mind, Jane, but don't say it. I, too, know full well that a bra is not what life turns on. But it's the not having it and being so *pleased* at not having it. It's *that* that is, as you well know so don't *lie*, what's wrong with this country in a nutshell."

"You may well be right. And how are things back home? How's Lieutenant Calley, for instance? Mitchell? Haldeman? Ehrlichman? All the old gang—how are they?"

"Oh shut up." Angela reached for a pile of tele-

76

grams and read them while Jane unzipped a suede jewellery pouch on the dressing table and went through it piece by piece. She held the earrings up to her ears, tried on the rings and bracelets, and very systematically made a little pile of the things she liked and dropped the others, one by one, into the wastebasket.

Angela looked up as a pavé diamond elephant disappeared into the basket. "My god, what are you doing?"

"Nothing. Why?"

With an awful little yelp Angela jumped off the bed and grabbed the wastebasket. "Good lord! Mother's engagement ring." She dumped the wastebasket onto the bed and, slapping at Jane's hand, she began to stuff her treasures back into the suede pouch.

"You're no fun any more," Jane said reproachfully, "are you?"

"No, I'm not," Angela snapped. "And neither are you. What's this surly little 'Miss Otis regrets' message that I got? A fine welcome *that* was."

"I'm sorry, Angela, I really am. But a one-o'clock appointment was all they had."

"All who had?" Angela had the long black holder between her teeth and was pencilling notes on the telegrams.

"Gynecologist."

"Ah. No worse, they say, than a bad cold, and, as they also say, there's a lot of it going around."

"Except that's not what I've got."

"No? It's what everyone else has. What makes you think you're different?"

"Don't make fun. It's awful."

Angela took the cigarette holder out of her mouth. "Really awful?"

"Well, it depends how you look at it, I guess. I just don't know if motherhood's my scene."

"Don't be ridiculous, darling. Motherhood isn't anybody's scene. Not any more. It's out, definitely out."

"So was the coil."

"Oh. Oh my god, how *awful*." She fitted another cigarette into the holder, lit it, and took a long, reflective drag. "Still, it could be worse."

"I don't see how."

"Darling, *think.* Think of it in its long, fancy christening gown, with the Fairfield crest on its ten thousand heirloom diapers and the tenants all standing with their caps in their hands outside the church. And just think, *I* can be godmother."

"But it may—"

"I'd like that. Being godmother. I really would."

"But it may be black, Angela. Will you like that?"

"Black? Darling, the Fairfields have won very few Nobel prizes, I admit, for sagacity, and perhaps not even for egg-candling, but I do know for a fact they're not *black.*"

"Well, it's not only him, you see. There's—"

Angela groaned. "Oh god, naturally. I knew it was too good to be true. How stupid of me."

"Still, whatever happens, I figure it's got a two-to-one chance of being white. That's not so bad, is it?"

"What do you mean, a two-to-one chance and that's not so bad? Let's get this straight now. There's the poor peer. Right?"

"Right."

"And somebody black. Right?"

"Right."

"Black American or black emerger?"

"American."

"And?"

"And another one. Tom, his name is."

"Tom who?"

"What does that matter, Tom who? He's a burglar, if you must know."

"A *Burglar?* Who are they? I've never heard of them."

"For the god's sake, Angela, you must know what a burglar is. Somebody who takes things."

"Oh my god, a *burglar.* Literally a burglar. Jane, how could you? A poor peer, a *nigger,* and a *burglar.* No, it's too much." She picked up the telephone. "Send up a

78

bottle of brandy, and please for goodness' sake make it fast."

Without putting the receiver down, Angela pushed the button to break the connection and reached for her address book. "Well, you certainly don't deserve such an act of selfless kindness, but I just happen to have with me this valuable hand-illuminated and quite unique book in which there is the name and tele—"

"No. It's no go, Angela. Remember what I said last time."

"Darling, you said that the first time too. Everybody says it. It's just a thing people say."

"No. Because last time they said it too. Not me, *they*. Strictly no more, they said. And anyhow—well, I'm thirty-five, aren't I? If I'm ever going to have a baby, it had better be soon, and when could be sooner than now? Who knows? I might even get married."

Angela closed the address book. "As a solution, darling, that has a certain classic ring, and you mustn't think I'm being indelicate or anything, but in this *particular* case you really couldn't get married until—well, until—"

"Until I know what colour it is. I know."

"Jane, be practical. If it's black, well, that's that. That most decidedly is that. But what if it's white? What if it's the burglar's? Darling, you can't, you really can't marry a burglar."

"He's only twenty-three, too. Isn't that awful?"

"Oh lord. Not just a burglar but a baby burglar. Happiness is a warm, cuddly baby burglar. Where *is* that brandy? What are they doing down there?"

"Will Saturday be OK?"

"Darling, even in England it can't take them till Saturday to get a bottle of brandy up two flights."

"Well, I hope it's all right because that's when I've asked people for."

"Oh, the party. Goodness, you've got me so addled I'd forgotten all about it. Yes, Saturday would be lovely. I'm off to the coal seams in the valleys on Monday, and then Clydebank and then—No, let's not even think about it." She shuddered and reached for her diary. "Saturday. And which of the proud daddies will be there? Or, as the latter-day Joan of Arc of the sexual revolution, have you asked all of them?"

"No. You see, they don't know about each other."

"Not yet they don't."

"It'll be Franklin."

"The poor peer?"

"No, that's Anthony."

"Ah. The Black Panther."

"He's a lawyer, in fact."

"Right. Black Panther with shoes on."

"And I've asked Gwyn Owens. You remember, he was Home Secretary in the last Labour government."

"I remember all right, and so, I'm sure, does Senator Bickell, as it was his wife that Mr. Owens laid all over Washington. They may not get to town often, your friends, Jane, but when they do, they certainly make the most of it. Tell me something. Do you think Labour politicians behave the way they do because they know they'll never get a second term in office? Or do you think they never get a second term in office because they behave the way they do? It's an interesting question, don't you think?"

There was a knock at the door. "I think your Saint Bernard's made it."

"Oh, thank god. Come in, darling." The frightened-looking boy stood there while Angela swept the tray with a very fast eye and took a pound note out of her handbag and tore it in half. "There. Half now. The other half when you bring the ice."

Angela shut the door after him. "Idiots. A whole countryful of idiots."

"What do you expect? You didn't say ice."

"You shouldn't have to say ice. Where were we?"

"And I've asked James Campbell. He's a humble crofter's son who edits the *Echo* and has, if he says so himself and he does, risen to that dizzy height on nothing but hard work, merit, integrity, and lifts in his shoes. That he also has a rich, well-connected wife is purely coincidental."

"Of course."

"And there'll be two seedy MPs because seedy ones are all you can get on the weekend, and anyhow ten's the most I can get around my table."

"Ten? That doesn't add up to ten. Oh—wives. I forgot."

"One of the seedy MPs doesn't have one, though. He's for you."

"Thanks."

"Don't mention it."

The boy came back with the ice, and Angela gave him the other half of the pound note. Jane tried on the sable coat and admired herself in the mirror. "How much did this small treat cost?"

"Fifty thousand."

"*Dollars?*"

"No. Fifty thousand ghastly hours of backgammon and boredom on my old harridan aunt's yacht. And not worth it, darling. Stick to your simple camelhair ways."

"About Saturday, though, Angela. Franklin doesn't know yet, so go easy, won't you."

"Darling, I'll be discretion itself. Did you think I'd come in my Norfolk jacket with a shotgun?"

"No, but—"

"But he's the one you want. Is that it?"

"Yes." Jane took off the sable coat and threw the paper airplane she'd been making out the window into Mount Street. "But I think I'd better hang on to Anthony a bit longer too. Just in case."

"You promise you won't marry that burglar?"

"I promise—except it's a pity in a way because he is really very, very nice."

"Now, Jane. Don't you go all willow-willow on me. Here, have a little more brandy."

"Can't. Got to go. Will eight o'clock be OK?"

"Eight o'clock will be lovely, darling." They walked out to the hall and towards the elevator. "Do you want me to bring anything?"

"No, but don't be too flash, will you? I mean, leave the sables here."

"Jane, I do know how to behave when I want to."

"Mm. Well, want to. Make sure of that. Oh god, Angela, what'll I do if it's twins and one's black and one's white?"

"Darling, I don't think that happens except with puppies."

"What if it's a mongol, then? I'm close to the age when you have mongols."

"Darling, it won't be a mongol. Any mongol has more sense than to pick you for a mother."

Out in the sunshine, Jane walked up towards Grosvenor Square. The daffodils were just coming out, and she looked at them for a long time before she walked down the centre path with the statue of Roosevelt at the far end.

How fantastic, she thought, looking at him. I never knew you. I never so much as laid eyes on you. And you certainly never even heard of me. And yet just because of one tiny decision you made way back in 1933, I'm maybe going to have a black baby and go live in Dayton. All because of you. How about *that*, Mr. Roosevelt, for making Yalta look like small potatoes?

When she left the doctor's office she walked to the top of Harley Street and into Regent's Park as far as the duck pond. There she leaned on the fence and watched fluffy yellow ducklings make small v wakes inside the mother ducks' large V wakes and wondered blankly what picture she was missing, and what Prairie Jim would say if he knew.

When it got cold and the flowers began to close, she walked back through the park and caught a taxi on the Euston Road. If anyone had asked her what she'd been doing all afternoon, she almost certainly would have said, "Thinking things out," or some lie like that, and as the taxi moved slowly from red light to red light she wondered if everybody not only told lies—she knew everybody did that—but told the same lies. She decided they did. They must. What other lies were there?

Anthony was furious. She could tell it the minute she opened the door and heard the decibel level of the Vivaldi on the record-player. But Anthony was the most practised liar of all and, smiling broadly, he stood up and opened his arms wide to her. "*Ecco. La bella signorina.*"

"Hello, Anthony. Sorry I'm late."

"Darling, it doesn't matter. It wasn't in the least important."

"What wasn't?"

"Oh, had you forgotten? We were to have a drink with Mark. To meet his new wife."

"Gosh, so we were. But why on earth did you wait? Why didn't you just go without me?"

Only when she'd said it did she suddenly realize that she'd walked straight into his favorite type of trap.

"Go without you? Darling, I couldn't possibly leave you dangling here waiting, not knowing where I was."

Touché. One bloody *touché* too *muché.*

"You could have left a note. I can read. You can write, can't you?"

That only got her deeper into the trap. He did the double-eyebrow-raise plus the palms-up gesture of well-I-*try*-god-knows-I-try.

She lay down on the sofa. "You wouldn't get me a drink, would you? My feet hurt."

"Certainly. Whisky? Gin?"

"Gin. No, whisky. No—oh, what the hell. Both."

He poured her a gin. "Ice?"

He was trying to get out of getting it.

"Yes, please, lots of ice."

She bet herself a pound he'd put two ice cubes in, and she won. "Thanks. And how was the ass-end of past glory?"

"I'm sorry?"

"The family seat. Still there, was it?"

"Oh. Yes, of course. We had marvelous weather and rather amusing people for a change. Old Hugo was positively genial, some of the time at any rate. He even roused himself so far as to play croquet."

"Gosh, what fun."

"I can't imagine why you don't like it, darling. It's a marvelous game, played properly."

"It's not the croquet I don't like, it's the people who play it—especially the people who play it what you call properly. I don't like the way it brings out the nastiness that hides about two millimetres under their civilized exteriors."

"I do think you exaggerate, darling. Both what it does, and what's there."

"The hell I do. Croquet is the British middle- and upper-class substitute for bank robbery, rape, and murder."

"What a ridiculous thing to say."

"Is it? For people so constipatedly dishonest about themselves, I don't think so. What better way to deal with nasty unadmitted festering fantasies? Where better than in croquet can they get all they yearn for, which is a chance to be vicious while seeming to be just playing a game?"

Anthony looked bored. "I sometimes wonder if you Americans will ever completely recover from that heady moment when Montgomery Clift played Freud."

"Nobody has to be Freud to figure out that a game where people use long, rigid sticks to hit balls through wickets, and in which the most skilful bit is lousing up other people's chances to hit their balls through the same wickets, is a game that is something else in disguise, and that is, moreover, bound to end in tears."

"I do enormously dislike glib generalizations, but if croquet is sex, violence, murder, and one hesitates to wonder what else in disguise, what then is American football?"

"Football is simple male aggression. Than which there is nothing simpler on earth."

Anthony got up and made her another drink. "Too easy, darling. Not worthy of your vivid imagination."

"Football, Anthony, is not worthy of anyone's imagination, vivid or not. It's a stupid, simple-minded, aggressive game, and admirably suited to stupid, simple-minded, aggressive men. It is only men who play aggressive games like that. Or hadn't you noticed?"

"Curious, in that case, isn't it, the rather widely agreed view of American women?"

"Curious isn't the half of it, you subtle creature, it's puzzling enough to make Occam cut his throat. But, right. Aggression. Let's take aggression. Not what men say about women, but real authenticated aggression. Crime, say. Would you agree that criminals are aggressive?"

"Certainly."

"Doesn't it strike you as strange, then, that in this country, which is roughly fifty-fifty men and women, there should be at this moment something like forty-five thousand men in prison—but only about one thousand women?"

"It was, however, American women we were talking about. Everyone knows the British female is a tame soul who likes the comfort and safety of her nest."

Jane walked across the room to shut the blinds. "I must say, Anthony, for someone who dislikes glib generalizations, you take the cake. But to hell with it; let's go out. I can't face cooking. Not tonight."

He came and stood behind her, his chin on her head and his arms around her. "Darling, forgive me. You're tired, and I'm sorry if I've made you cross."

"Cross? Who's cross? I'm just hungry. Didn't have any lunch, unless you count a brandy."

"No lunch? You silly girl."

"Couldn't. Had an appointment."

There. That was his chance. But of course he wouldn't take it; the English taboo on direct questions wasn't going to crumble that easily. What he would say was "Oh."

He said it, and she put her shoes back on and fed the pigeon and Scat in strict separateness, and they walked through the soft trying-to-rain drizzle to the restaurant that wasn't very good but was the nearest.

When they got back home she bolstered up the

wearing-off Valpolicello with a big scotch and poured an even bigger one for Anthony. He was, she thought, going to need it.

Lying on the sofa with Scat on his chest, he reached up and took the glass and said, "Why Scat, darling? For such a dedicatedly lethargic cat it seems hardly the right name."

She sat on the fur rug and leaned back against his shoulder. "I don't know. He was brought by somebody named Tom, and so for a long time he was called 'Tom's cat.' It just got shortened, I guess."

"How simple things are, once they're explained."

"Well, I hope you really believe that."

"Why?"

"Because I've got something to tell you."

"Jane, I am not going over that well-trodden ground again. Mother is back on Wednesday; I shall drive her down to Cravenbourne and be back in London the next day. On Friday we—"

"It's not that. It's something else."

"Oh. Well, whatever it is, so long as it's not that, I'm delighted."

"You sure?"

"Of course I'm sure. What is it?"

"I'm pregnant."

The dead silence lasted longer than she'd expected. He very slowly picked Scat off his chest, dropped him on the floor, and stood up. "You're what?"

"Pregnant."

"You couldn't be."

"Why couldn't I?"

"Good god. But aren't you on the pill or something?"

"I had a coil, but it . . ."

He walked across the room and leaned against the oak chest, swishing his drink around in the glass and staring at her. "Good god."

"You said that."

"Sorry. But it's—well, it's something of a shock, you know."

"I do know. It was to me too."

"You don't look pregnant."

"Don't I? Hang around."

"You can't be very pregnant."

"Not very, no. Just a little."

"I see. Well, there's really no need then for drama, is there? I'll get on to Pamela first thing in the morning; she knows the best abor—"

"No."

"No? What do you mean, 'No'?"

She picked Scat up for comfort, but Scat smelled tension and trouble and he struggled so hard to get free that she had to let him go. "I mean no. Just plain no."

"Jane, really."

"Sorry, but that's it."

"Am I allowed no vote at all?"

"You can vote any way you like and twice in Cook County, but it's mine, and I'm going to have it."

"Darling, be reasonable. It's not only yours."

"OK. You be reasonable. I'm thirty-five. I'm not dependent on you or anybody else. I earn my own living and I'll go on doing just that. But the first bloom is, as they say, gone—and it's not coming back. I wouldn't have chosen it to happen this way but—well, it has, and I'll go along with it. You needn't, of course. If it makes you feel any better, you can think of yourself as the Holy Ghost. Or, if you prefer, an AID."

"I feel extraordinarily unlike the Holy Ghost, but what's an AID?"

"Artificial insemination by donor. As opposed to artificial insemination by husband, which is AIH."

"Ah."

"Ah? Ah, what?"

"You'd rather I were your husband."

"Not specially, no."

"Jane. I don't like it."

"Anthony. That's obvious, and so OK, don't. Don't even think about it. I'll be all right, you wait and see."

"You're trying to make me look a shit, aren't you?"

"Who needs to try?"

"Darling, don't. Don't let's have an ugly scene. Let's go to bed."

"No, let's me go to bed; you go home."

He poured another whisky and held up the bottle. "Want one?"

When she shook her head he lifted both shoulders slightly. "Now you're angry, and frankly I fail to see why. If I reacted with—well, with surprise, it was only that, only purely and simply surprise. I don't propose to abandon you; I have in fact suggested you marry me, and, risking another not altogether polite refusal, I'll suggest it again. Will you?"

"Will I what?"

"Will you marry me?"

"Say 'please.'"

"Jane, this is not a time for childish games. Please."

"Pretty please?"

He was really angry now. His face hadn't changed, but she could tell it from his eyes. "All right. Pretty please. Pretty please will you marry me?"

"No."

He held the palms-up gesture as if for a time-exposure, and then he got his coat and put it on while Jane took a slow tour of the big room, turning off lamps and the record-player and putting the lid back on the ice bucket. When she'd spun it out as long as she could, she stood by the front door and he put his hands on her shoulders. "Darling, a good sleep will make a great deal of difference. Shall I call you in the morning?"

"I don't know, shall you?" She leaned against him. "Poor Anthony. I'm sorry it was such an awful shock and that I was nasty."

"Darling, don't. I understand, truly I do."

"Do you? You want to know a big secret, then?"

"I'm not sure I'm up to another one right now."

"Of course you are. You're the bulldog breed, remember? Anyhow, you'll like this one."

"Will I? What is it?"

"The baby. It may not be yours at all."

Except for another longish silence, he gave no indication that what she'd said was anything more serious than that his tie was crooked.

"I see," was all he said.

She smiled and patted his cheek. "Thought the sultry, scheming American adventuress was after the big title and the family emeralds, didn't you? Come on, admit it."

He almost smiled but thought better of it and, with the cool dignity that was his most trustworthy foil against the slings and arrows of vulgar life, he kissed her on the forehead and said, "Good night darling. Sleep well."

C

Angela obediently showed up unsabled, but the long coat of stiff black silk lined with nutria was worse. A sable coat can always be sneered at for being a showy piece of too conspicuous consumption, but this silk thing lying so smugly sure of its well-bred self on Jane's bed was unfaultable and could provoke nothing but naked hatred.

The maroon Rolls-Royce waiting outside was no popularity aid either. Neither was the black halter-neck Halston dress that boggled the men's eyes with tits and made the women's take on a mean *wot-about-us-workers?* glint. From the first olive Jane knew it was going to be a party no one would forget, or forgive.

As coldly as Harry Lime peddling watered penicillin, Angela had taken one squint down the concealed gun-sight of her long black cigarette holder, decided the women weren't worth even a warning shot across the bows, and glued herself to the men. The men were willing enough, but by the time Jane got them all to the table the women already looked as if they would like to run her—and Jane too, guilty by association—out of Dodge City on a rail and why wait for morning.

She rushed them through dinner, hoping that the mobility of after dinner and Irish coffee might make things easier. But Irish coffee is a fiddly thing to make, and making it took too long. Like a collie, James Campbell had already cut Angela out of the flock, and there was clearly a tacit agreement between them that she would sit in the swing laughing and letting him look down the front of her dress so long as he kept a steady stream of fact and gossip that would come in handy for the *News Views* cover story. It was a very workable *quid pro quo*, except for the effect it had on his wife, the Lady Philippa.

She was not a woman of great Last Night Out vivacity at the best of times, the Lady Philippa, and dining with Labour politicians, especially left-wing Labour politicians, at an American nobody's flat where another American nobody was snaffling her husband was not her idea of the best of times. Sourly superior, she sat apart from the others and responded to such conversational bones as came her way with a flat, "Really?" or, for rich variety, an even flatter, "How frightfully interesting."

Gwyn Owens had gone through Jane's last bottle of Jack Daniel's like a circus motorcyclist going through a burning hoop, and he grew more sonorously pompous as his sibilants began to slur badly. His wife and the MP's wife, upstaged by Angela, ignored by the men, and rejected by Lady Philippa, talked to each other about children and schools and the appalling cost of train fares to their husbands' constituencies.

Franklin had spent the evening on the receiving end of all of the some-of-our-best-friends-are-black clichés in the book. Now, dutifully handing round more whisky-laced coffee, he was followed doggedly by the unmarried MP, a young and deadly serious exschoolmaster who was relentlessly explaining the significant contribution to racial harmony made by a recent Fabian Society pamphlet.

Jane stuck Gwyn Owens with the Lady Philippa—who said, "Yes, I've met Mr. Owens before," with exactly the same enthusiasm with which she might have said, "I've had bubonic plague"—and rescued Franklin. When she got him in the kitchen she whispered, "We've got to do something. It's awful."

"Well, now you mention it, there is a kind of palpable lack of togetherness. Your friend, she's a great mixer."

"I know, and I'm going to kill her."

He unbuttoned the top two buttons of her shirt and kissed her neck. He was down as far as the fourth button when Angela appeared in the doorway. "As indeed I suspected. Necking in the kitchen and missing all the fun."

Then, in a stagey whisper: "Darling, I wouldn't leave anyone, especially you, alone with these gunslingers, but I've got to be up at the crack of dawn. Will you ever forgive me?"

"Sure. I don't know what went wrong."

"Don't you?" Angela sat down on the table and pawed through a dish of nuts, picking out all the cashews. "I do. Those third-rate evangelical saviours of the world in there are a haunted house divided against itself. In a word, they loathe each other. Not to mention you and me, which really is a waste of energy. And, worse, they loathe each other more than they do the enemy."

She chewed on the cashews and finished off a half-full glass of wine from the cluster of glasses at the sink. "Always fatal, that. No wonder they can't stay in charge long. What beats me is how they ever get in charge."

Jane looked nervously at the door, and Franklin shut it. "Oh, come on, they're not that bad. They're just not very svelte, is all."

"Not very svelte? Listen. In one room as drafty as but not as big as the Hall of Mirrors you've got one pompous drunken ass who shoots with the high and mighty, not at them. You've got one amiable, utterly

93

corrupt newspaper editor who hasn't seen Wigan Pier since the tide went out, and not only because his wife won't give him the carfare to get that far away from her. Plus a couple of men who would be overextended as dogcatchers, whose wives—underneath all the egalitarian talk—are primarily interested in a) money, and b) maneuvering their children into Oxford. A place that, as we all know, is the real springboard to real socialism."

She finished another glass of wine. "Didn't you hear the one who was saying how she only has a twin-tub washing machine—whatever *that* is—and not some better kind that she says everybody else has. *Everybody?* Where does she get that everybody? It is not a gem of information so fascinating that I bring it up often, god knows, but I do just happen to know for a fact how many people in this country haven't any washing machine. And if you don't find that riveting enough, I can tell you how many houses haven't got a bathtub and how many people haven't even got a house to put a bathtub in if they had one. Furthermore, a third of the people in this country over the age of sixteen haven't so much as one of their own teeth left. And—"

"Oh, Angela, shut up for a second. Franklin, be lovely and get in there and sort of dance around, would you?"

She turned back to Angela. "So what do you expect? You didn't exactly knock yourself out to put them at their ease, did you?"

"Darling, I'm sorry. I really am. But don't fuss, I'll phone you—no, I'll send a runner with a note on a forked stick, it's quicker—the minute I'm back."

When they'd gone, Jane washed the dishes and Franklin took the empty bottles and garbage down. When he came back he said, "You know, I'd have bet five bucks even money that nobody could drink so much without laughing. Now I know better."

She let the water out of the sink. "And that son of a bitch drank all the Black Label Jack Dan—Oh god. I think I'm going to be sick."

With one hand he held her hair back and held her forehead with the other while she knelt on the bathroom floor and vomited into the toilet. But even after she'd brushed her teeth and splashed her face with cold water she still felt rotten. "How about a little brandy for the world-famous party-giver?"

"Baby, you need a brandy like I need suntan lotion."

"Please? Just a tiny one."

While he got it she took off her clothes and looked at herself sideways in the mirror. No. If you didn't know, you wouldn't know. She put on a long pink Indian cotton nightdress and walked slowly down the hall and got into bed. He was getting undressed, and she watched him. If he was pretty in clothes, with them off he was sensational.

Standing with his back to the window he rubbed his elbow. "You OK?"

"More or less. Is it hurting?"

"A little. It looks like I might wind up one of those boring old bastards that can tell you when it's going to rain."

"Darling, it's been raining for hours."

He bent down one of the metal slats and looked out. "God, so it is. Well, I'll be the other boring old bastard who tells you when it's going to stop."

She patted the pillow. "Mr. Watson, come here; I want you."

"Sherlock Holmes."

"That's Dr. Watson. You've got cultural lag, that's what you've got."

"Ah, too true. OK. It was Alexander Fenimore Cooper who said it over an early walkie-talkie as he beat the ass off the British Navy on Lake Erie. And that reminds me."

"I know. Ohio. But not now."

He got into bed and leaned on one elbow, looking at her. "God-damn it, but your feet are cold. You wouldn't slide into an alcoholic coma on me, would you?"

"Not on you. Under you. I'm too tired to be the dominant female tonight."

Kneeling, he pulled the blankets back and rubbed her ankles. "Know what? You're dead."

He lifted her feet up and held them against his chest. "No, you can't be dead. Dead people don't get sick on two small whiskies."

"Dead people don't have babies, either."

He slid her feet down to his thighs. "So. You know."

"So I know? I was telling you."

"I knew last week."

"Last week? My god, how?"

"Black magic. Nobody can fool a four-time uncle."

"What a creepy kook you are. No, honestly, how?"

"Little things. Funny, sleepy eyes. I don't know—it's just a look. And even though I love you primarily for your mind and fine character, of course—"

"Of course."

"I couldn't help noticing the altogether more voluptuous bosom. I felt, too, that perhaps the deep friendship we share might now develop into a finer and more permanent—"

"Why didn't you tell me?"

"And do you out of the knitting scene? I'm not that creepy a kook."

"My god, with a talent like that, why don't you work in a lab and save the lives of many innocent frogs and rabbits? Or dress up in a turban and do it in a tent at fairs? 'Step right this way, madam, and avail yourself of the opportunity to let Snake Oil the Swahili Seer gaze into your . . .' "

She was a woman with all the mystery of a bucket of lard, and now the tears were running out of the corners of her eyes into her hair. A leg on either side of her body, he leaned over her and licked them away. "Don't, baby. It's nothing to cry over. Sooner or later everybody gets trapped. You had a good long run, and now it's over, that's all. You don't mind, do you?"

"Me? No. I was afraid you would, though."

"Do I look like I mind? Now, quit it. Smile."

She tried.

"Oh jesus christ, not like that. It's not National Lockjaw Week."

Her nose was running and it blew a big bubble. He went and got the Kleenex. "God, women."

She pulled out three and blew her nose. "God, women? God, life."

He knew more about women than Tom and didn't make love gently, as if she were a sacred vessel. But afterwards she lay there for quite a while, not able to sleep for wondering how she was ever going to tell him the truth.

On Monday morning a case of Jack Daniel's came from Angela with a fortune-cooky slip taped in it: YOU ARE RIDING A TIGER—BE CAREFUL WHEN THE TIME COMES TO GET OFF.

"Now what the hell can that mean?" Franklin asked and handed her the bottle.

"Who knows? Angela eats in some pretty inscrutable restaurants."

"And there's something else I'd like to know." He took off his glasses and tipped the typewriter up to look at its underneath. "How do you get along without a 'g'?"

"I et alon fine. God comes out od, but what's in a name? Tell me more about Dayton."

"Ah. Well, Dayton, folks, is a scenic paradise situated on its own limpid sewer somewhat to the north of somewhat less beautiful Cincinnati in the majestically beautiful state of Ohio, and has many interesting features. There is not only the Fire and Brimstone Rubber Company, a breathtaking sight if ever there was one, but there is also the post office with Doric pillars that, legend has it, were hewn from the living rock by Doris herself. Not more than a dead-cat-throw away from the nuts-and-bolts factory considered by many to be the purest example of nineteen-oh-five pre-Bauhaus functional architecture this side or, possibly, either side of Steubenville there is a fine early ranch-type house completely furnished from the rugs on the wall to the pictures on the floor, and people. Three. Two big and one small."

"So it's on."

"Yes."

"Gosh."

"You got any stamps?" He opened the top drawer of the desk. "Od, what a mess. You hoard junk like an old pack rat."

She sat on the desk, reached across her typewriter, and picked a book of stamps out of the marmalade jar the pencils stood in. "Here. Where's it for, England or America?"

"America. I'm telling my mother she's not so much losing a son as gaining a pack rat."

Jane had the stamp half torn out of the book. "Oh."

"Oh? Oh, what?"

"Nothing—except do you think you ought? I mean do you have to do it this minute?"

"Seems as good as any other minute. Sooner's better than later, things being like they are."

In her right mind or given any choice at all, she would probably have not picked a Monday morning as the ideal time to shove bamboo slivers under the fingernails of someone she loved. But she didn't seem to be getting the choice.

She told him only part of it, of course. She was quite truthful about the coil, but Anthony and Tom were amalgamated into an old almost-forgotten boy friend who had unexpectedly turned up a couple of months ago. She didn't know why she'd been so silly as to get drunk and go to bed with him, and she wished she hadn't. But she had.

As a good lawyer should, he listened without interrupting or even moving, and when she'd finished he tore up the letter to his mother and dropped it in the wastebasket. He rubbed his jaw and opened his mouth once or twice as if he were going to say something. Then he stood up, shoved his hands in his trouser pockets, and walked to the middle of the room. "Jesus christ." He looked at her and shook his head. "Jesus h. christ."

She wanted to put her arms around him and say she was sorry, but she'd already said that several times. "Franklin?"

"Yeah?"

"I can always—well, you know, have an ab—"

His face clouded and he jerked his chin up. "And how many would that make?"

"Only four. Four's not many. I know somebody who had—"

"Four's too goddamn many and you know it. They said after the last one—"

"Doctors always say that. It's just something they say, that's all. But he was wrong, wasn't he? I mean obviously he was, because here I am, pregnant."

"No. You can crowd your luck just so far."

"Please. I'm willing."

"Well, I'm not."

They had a grim little lunch and missed the 1:30 to Cambridge. To catch the 2:45 he got Jane's mini out of the garage on Endell Street where she kept it, and they drove in strained silence to King's Cross. After he parked the car, he handed her the keys and she walked with him to the gate and leaned her forehead against it. "Oh god, Franklin, how could I have done such a stupid thing?"

He smiled. "I told you. You're a pack rat. You can't throw anything away, not even people you don't really want."

She nodded and blinked. A speck of train-station dirt or mascara had got in her eye and was starting to sting.

"Come on, don't dissolve. Figure the odds. Chances are everything'll be all right."

"What if it's not, though? I'm no born gambler."

The train had come in and he kissed her. "Gamblers aren't born, baby, they're made. To coin a phrase."

"Don't be horrible."

"I'm sorry. I didn't mean it. When do you get back from this crazy weekend?"

"Monday, I guess."

"I'll be down Monday night, then. OK?"

"Stay Tuesday too? Please?"

"Right. Tuesday too."

She watched him get on the train and then she walked slowly back to the car and started home. Stopped at a red light, she shut her eyes and said, "Dear god, if there is a god, please god let it be his and I promise cross my heart and hope to die that I'll never say another word against you or Dayton or anything else ever again."

She hadn't mumbled it quickly but said it slowly and carefully syllable by syllable, and she hadn't seen the light change or the young policeman who now stood leaning in the car window. "Are you feeling all right, miss?"

She was on the prayer second time around, but turned it off. "Me? Yes, I'm—oh goodness, I am sorry, I didn't know." She shifted into first and let the clutch in too fast. The car took one lurch and stalled. "Oh dear, I—"

The light was red again, and the young policeman kept a very wary eye on her until it turned green and she finally made it across the intersection.

7

Tom didn't show up that night or Tuesday, and that worried her. It meant, too, that, as he hardly ever phoned, she'd have no chance to break it to him gently that he wasn't to come next Monday or Tuesday either.

Anthony wasn't coming on Wednesday because he had to meet his mother's plane and drive her to Cravenbourne, but then on Thursday, when he was to have come, he phoned to say he couldn't make it and was it all right if he came Friday instead. Jane said of course. But of course it wasn't all right, it wasn't all right at all. She hadn't spent a week alone in a long time, and every day that went by the apartment grew bigger, and emptier, and quieter.

Without even a token struggle, she slumped very quickly into a listless, staring depression that made even minimum movement exhausting. She didn't make the bed or wash the dishes, or her hair. She fed Scat canned food, and the pigeon on stale bread. She drank milk out of the bottle and ate cornflakes out of the package while she watched TV. She went to bed early and compulsively read every scrap of every magazine in the house, even the ads for garden sheds and radial ply tires, and went to sleep with the light on. Twice she had bad dreams about the tarantulas that someone had told her came in on the bunches of bananas and that clung with their hairy legs all over the walls downstairs, slowly dying of the cold. She didn't really believe in the tarantulas any more than she believed in the twelve-foot alligators that people said lived in the New York sewer system—but all alone in the middle of the night, she couldn't be sure, and after four nights alone she began to believe in them.

Wan efforts to get hold of people came to nothing. Some were away. Some had children with measles. Numbers were busy. Other numbers didn't answer. By Tuesday she had felt like the girl in *Butterfield 8*; by Friday she felt like the girl in *Repulsion*. Like blue sky at the top of a deep well, even the prospect of Cravenbourne began to look good. At least there'd be people and the sound of the human voice.

On Friday she bribed Mrs. Bush to come in and feed Scat and the pigeon over the weekend, and then she wrote a piece with no possible fights for Prairie Jim to pick. It was a lousy piece, but there was, she knew, no better route to instant acceptance than lousiness. She had discovered that just about the same time she had discovered that inoffensive agreeable blandness was the route to social success and that she was never going to be one.

Waiting for Anthony in the *Orbit* office, she sat on Leo Fraling's desk. "She go, Leo?"

"Yeah, she went. But then she came back. It's funny how people can't ever really leave what makes them miserable."

"Not very funny. Where else could they get such kicks? Where else could they get such an excuse for not being a world-famous ballet dancer? People need a scapegoat. That way they never have to face that pretty nearly everything bad that happens to them is their own fault. Not many people can face that."

"You know, you may be right. She says if it wasn't for me she could have made something of her life."

"Naturally. It's an old, old script, Leo."

"Speaking of old scripts, I saw a great old film last night on TV. Cagney. In—"

"Mm. I know. I saw it too."

"You? I thought you were out every night whooping it up in trendy discothèques with the swingers."

"Did you? Didn't you know that what people think about how other people live is almost always wrong? And that eight times out of eleven everybody is just home watching Cagney, worrying about their income tax, picking at their hangnails, and waiting for the frozen chicken pie to do its thirty minutes?"

"I thought you were different."

"I am. I'm the live-close-to-the-edge type, so I only give the pie *twenty-seven* minutes."

In his loud check tweed coat that had not one cape but two, as well as a round beaver collar, Anthony walked into the newsroom and down the long line of green metal desks. "Darling, I'm on a double yellow line and there's a traffic warden prowling about. Are you ready?"

"Hello, Anthony. You remember Leo, Leo Fraling."

"Oh, sorry. Yes, of course. Nice to see you again."

The Aston Martin had to be held on a short rein through London, but when it hit the M-4 it took off. And Franklin had been right, she was sleepier than usual. They were past Salisbury when she woke up, and half an hour later, deep in picture-postcard territory where villages were called Biggling Bottom and Elf-ton-on-Avon, Anthony turned in at tall open gilt-tipped gates. Another mile on, after they'd gone through a rhododendron tunnel, over cattle grids, and past cottages, estate offices, and stables, she got her first look at Cravenbourne. It stood on the far side of a pond that had swans on it and a round Greek temple at the edge, and in the pale spring sunset the huge stone house glowed opaquely honey-coloured like a marzipan mirage. Deer chewing on the lawn lifted their heads and twitched their tails, and when Anthony, without even slowing down, drove past a PRIVATE NO ADMITTANCE sign onto a crunchy white gravel forecourt she began to feel like the girl in *Rebecca* but didn't dare say so.

Stone steps slightly less wide than the New York Public Library's led up to a long many-windowed façade. From the ends of the seventeenth-century central part of the house, two long early-Georgian wings stretched back, and at each end of the wide, shallow steps were huge stone flower urns. Over the front door a gently curved stone eyebrow had something carved on it in Latin with, over that, a square worn-away stone plaque of a man on a rearing horse skewering some even more worn-away creature that lay on its back by the horse's front legs. A peacock posing on the steps was not pleased at their disturbing its narcissistic daydream and, dragging its bronze and green tail behind it like a heavy train, it took its unhurried leave and disappeared around the corner of the house.

"Well, I see what you mean," said Jane. "It's not much, but it's home."

Anthony was getting her bag out of the car. "You see? There was a time when the English knew how to live."

"Mm. Some English. The catch was the other ninety-nine per cent weren't doing so great."

"Darling, please. Not straight into the plight of the rural labourers in eighteen-fifteen. A drink first. Agreed?"

"Sure. I can do it even better on a drink."

The butler opened the door, and Anthony said, "Thank you, Parkes," and introduced her. Not knowing if she should shake hands or not, Jane avoided having to decide by holding her handbag in front of her with both hands on the handle and smiling a smile that was meant to be neither offensively matey nor stand-offishly distant. "Hello," she said.

Parkes could smell a vulnerable unimportant outsider a mile off with the wind in the wrong direction.

He bared yellow ferret's teeth at her briefly and, turning back to Anthony, he said in a nasal toastmaster's voice, "Her Grace suggests, Lord Anthony, that you and Miss Cornell join her at seven for cocktails in the long library."

He disappeared with Jane's suitcase and when he was out of earshot Jane whispered, "I've seen that character before. *Dracula. The Fall of the House of Usher. The Cabinet of Dr. Caligari.* He gets around, that guy. Why don't you get him a toothbrush for Christmas or, better, shove a pointed stick through his chest and plant him out under the rhododendrons where he belongs?"

They were in a round and echoing marble entry hall, and Anthony wasn't listening to her but was leafing through messages and letters that stood in a rack on a circular table. She looked around at the pink pillars that held up the domed ceiling, where bosomy goddesses in trailing cheesecloth draperies sprawled on painted clouds against an unnaturally blue sky. Floating around these apparently stoned ladies were overweight hydrocephalic babies playing with cornucopias of fruit and flowers, and other more serious babies who pointed chubby fingers upward at a young man tearing through the clouds in a chariot pulled by two horses. Way at the top, peering over the edge of the highest cloud, a cross-looking old man—God?—looked as if he was going to beat the hell out of all of them as soon as he could get them behind the barn.

From two sides of the round hall, pink marble stairs curved up, and at the far end, where there were no stairs, a larger-than-lifesize marble lady stood in a scalloped niche, leaning on a sword as if it were a 1955 Dior umbrella. She was naked except for a visored helmet and what looked like football shoulder pads.

Anthony headed for the right-hand staircase and, still looking up at the ceiling, Jane followed him. "Mother has put you in the yellow room. It's very like a can-can petticoat, I'm afraid, but for goodness' sake at least pretend you like it."

She caught up with him and grabbed his arm. "Can't I sleep with you? I'd rather."

"Of course. The yellow room is only part of the game."

"What game?"

"Darling, you're being deliberately obtuse."

"Deliberately, what do you mean deliberately? I was born obtuse."

"You were not, however, born yesterday. So stop it."

"OK. But how will I ever find you in this huge place?"

"I'll find you. That's part of the game too."

They walked down a long red hall with ancestors on the walls and sheafs of firmly disciplined flowers in vases on chests and tables, and then they turned a corner and went down a shallow flight of stairs and along another long corridor. Just opposite an enormous painting of the Armada ·formed up in crescent shape for battle in the Channel, Anthony opened a heavy door and stood aside for her to go in.

Dark oak Elizabethan panelling had been recut to fit the room, and three heavy faded tapestries covered the stone walls that the pannelling hadn't stretched to. The carpet was an antique dark red-and-green Persian thing that once must have been magnificent but had also been vandalized and cut to fit the room. Beyond the carved four-poster bed grey *pointe d'Hongroise* curtains hung at leaded diamond-paned windows, and opposite the foot of the bed was a wide fireplace with logs laid on andirons that were lions sitting up holding shields, with their tongues hanging out.

"Yellow? This is yellow? I want my money back."

"This is my room. I thought we might have a little talk before drinks and baths and dinner and people get in the way."

He took off his coat and opened a window while she prowled around the edges of the room like a cat, picking things up and looking at them and putting them down again. "I'd forgotten that bit about country

106

houses. About taking a bath every time you turn around. Actually"—she looked at both sides of her hands—"I'm quite clean."

She threw her coat and handbag on the bed, and he took her hand and led her to a windowseat. "Darling, relax. There's no need to be prickly; nobody is going to force you to bathe. I only want to tell you how sorry I am about—well, about last week."

"So am I. I was awful to you and I'm sorry."

"Not at all. You—"

"I was. I was foul. I was a horror. I *am* a horror."

"You're not a horror. You're not at all a horror. But I did rather think you might not feel it unreasonable if I were—were to ask—well, not *ask* but . . ."

". . . but tell you where you stand in the stork stakes."

"That puts it baldly but—well, yes."

Anthony was not the kind of man she could explain Franklin to, or Tom. She could have taken twenty years to do it, and he would still never understand her attachment to either. So she mixed a new amalgamated man, and as seniority was a concept Anthony respected, she made the new amalgamated man senior in every way. He was forty-five. He had been her lover for four years. He was an American. A painter. Very talented too. Anthony nodded understandingly, and she made the liar's fatal mistake of getting carried away on her own lie. Not only did she begin to believe it herself, but she felt stirrings of righteous indignation. Why should she have to sit here explaining her every move? Who was Anthony that she had to tell him whom she went to bed with? She didn't ask *him* things like that, did she?

It was thin ice, but she sailed out onto it. "You know? It's a dirty trick. For fifty thousand years men have had it their way. They've had other men's wives, mistresses, pick-ups, secretaries, and anything else female they could grab, and they've run two, three, or god knows how many simultaneous affairs as if it was meet, right, and their bounden duty to do so. Yes?"

"Well, perhaps not all men."

"Perhaps not. The point is they could if they chose to. But it's only recently that women—and it's still only a few women who manage it—have begun to get even half the leeway that men have always had. It's late in the game, of course, but it's right, don't you think, that women should have their innings?"

"Of course."

"But it doesn't really work out fairly, does it? Because the poor idiot woman can still be betrayed by her extremely treacherous physiology, and when she is, we're right back to the same old scene. Him booming, 'Explain.' Her down on her knees, hanging her head and sobbing like a goosegirl."

"There are, I think, some slight exaggerations of detail here. For example, you—"

"Never mind me. It's all women I'm talking about. And the point is that for the fifty thousand years when men had it their way they blithely planted babies on women and then just as blithely disappeared. Did they care that fatherless babies and husbandless mothers might have a tough time? Did they stay awake nights feeling bad about having made some girl's life a misery? Did they give a damn that some other guy might get stuck with a baby that wasn't his? In a pig's eye they did. If they lay awake at all, it was only because they were busy doing the same thing again to another woman."

She stood up and started on another cat prowl around the room.

"It does seem curious to me, Anthony, that after such a long and conscienceless tradition of being casual about fatherhood, men can suddenly get so uptight about whose baby is whose. I mean, no man seems to mind the other guy getting stuck with his, but they're all awfully determined not to get stuck with the other guy's. And that just isn't realistic, is it? It's just about as crazy a piece of male behaviour as those cretins who spend every Saturday night busting virgins in the village—yet still insist that the girl they marry has got to be one, and, what's more, that she's got to come from that village."

Wrapping her arms around one of the carved posts on the bed, she looked at him and smiled. "Cuckoo, that's what men are. Cuckoo."

From the bed she wandered over to the windows and looked out over the wide green lawn. "Still, who knows? Maybe men have been right all along. Maybe who a baby's father is isn't important. Maybe all that's important is that babies should be welcomed and loved and looked after properly. Preferably by two people, of course, because that way it's easier on everybody, especially the baby. But does it really matter which two?"

She had flown so high on fine oratory that she didn't even see the hole she'd left until Anthony made for it.

"Darling, it's a strong case you put. Men have undoubtedly been pigs for centuries, dishonorable liars, exploiters of women, and everything you say. It is quite right that women should now have their innings, and not have to explain, and not have to marry someone whom they don't want to marry."

He put on his Ronald-Colman-as-Sydney-Carton look.

"And though it makes me very sad, of course, I have for some time now had a feeling—only a feeling, mind you—that there might be someone else to whom you were more attached than to me. Now that you've told me about this American painter friend, I see that—well, that what I feared is true."

He switched from Sydney Carton to gentlemen-we've-lost-India. "If that is, in fact, the case, I have no right to—"

She'd followed the wronged goosegirl too far out on the thin ice. Swiftly and ruthlessly she married the American painter to a Catholic and gave them three small children, one of which was a spastic.

"Oh dear," said Anthony sympathetically. "That is difficult. Poor darling, I am sorry."

The long library was very long. A huge marqueterie partners' desk stood at the far end, two big leather chesterfields flanked the fireplace that was in the centre of the long wall, and in a large L-shaped area to the right of the double doors were several deep, square, comfortable chairs around a low square table on which rows of magazines overlapped each other like a giant's game of solitaire.

From above tall bookcases dark portraits of hard-looking men and menopausal ladies stared down. Over the fireplace was a Devis painting of a family group with a big country house far in the background, and scattered about the room were Queen Anne chairs with needlepoint cushions, an enormous yellowed globe that stood on rosewood legs inlaid with ivory, and several glass-topped display tables crammed with small, precious objects. Opposite the fireplace long windows opened out onto a balustraded terrace and stone steps that led down to a lawn geometrically crisscrossed with gravelled paths. In the middle of the lawn was a big round pool with a stone swan in the centre, its neck stretched out and water gushing from its beak.

Her hands behind her back, Jane leaned over a round, many-colored *pietra dura* table to look at a Book of Hours that lay open on a wooden stand. Anthony turned a page for her and was saying something about its being a slightly earlier one than the Duc de Berry's when the door opened and two fat smelly spaniels flumped in. Behind them came a tiny kewpie-doll figure in a black sidesaddle riding skirt and jacket with a neatly folded white stock at the throat, and on her head a minute bowler that rested on but did not muss her blond figure-eight chignon.

"Darling Ants!" The doll figure unpinned the bowler, flung it on a chair, and advanced on them, arms wide open. In her shiny little black boots she stood on tiptoe to kiss Anthony and then grabbed Jane by both hands. "My dear, can you forgive me? I foolishly told Parkes to tell you six-thirty because I so wanted to meet you and I was determined, absolutely determined, not to be late, but those tiresome people from that Italian magazine insisted on picture after picture after picture. Stand here. Stand there. Now, one in the ballroom. As if one would *be* in a ballroom in these ridiculous clothes!" She laughed a little tinkly laugh. "No, it was *too* tiresome. And then their flash things went wrong and—well, there it is. One agrees to do these things in a moment of weakness and . . ."

Jane got one hand free, but the minute Duchess held onto the other one as stubbornly as a ringmaster triumphantly displaying a captured Amazon, and led her towards one of the sofas. "You'll forgive me, won't you, my dear, even if that naughty Anthony won't?"

Jane nodded and tried to smile. "Of course. We only just got—"

"Splendid. Oh, I'm so glad. Did you hear that, Ants? Your nice Miss Cornell has forgiven me, and now we can have a dear little chat before Hugo bursts in." She lit a cigarette, and her voice took on an emery-board edge. "Did you know, Anthony, that he'd asked that odious Charles again? I didn't, I fear, and I rather fear too that Miss Cornell will find him as tiresome as we do." She patted Jane's hand and switched back to the honey voice. "But there it is, my dear. Consideration is really not something one can expect to be treated with by one's children. One learns that, my dear, and one learns, too, never, never to complain."

The voice switched again, and now the meticulously made-up doll's face looked into Jane's, as eager as a puppy. "Now. Now, tell me all about yourself. I want to know everything. Anthony said, I think, that your home is Boston—or was it Connecticut?" She clapped her hands and tinkled with laughter again. "It's too appalling, I can no longer remember anything important at all. It is Boston, isn't it?"

"No, I'm afraid not. I was born in New Boston, but that doesn't have anything to do with the real Boston, it's only a small town in New Hampshire. And I never really lived there at all. I grew up in California."

"Oh." In a nicer woman the small pause wouldn't have meant a thing. "I'm afraid I've never been to California. But I once had a very dear friend in Boston and I had rather hoped ..." Her voice dwindled just enough to make the point.

"But how foolish of me. One always forgets, doesn't one, that Americans come from all over America? And California is such an exciting, fascinating state, they say. And you write. I know I've got that right, haven't I? Such a marvelous thing to do, writing. It must be such fun!"

"Well, I don't really write. What I do is review films for a newspaper."

"Oh, *heavenly!* Anthony, why didn't you say?"

"I think I did say, Mother."

"Did you, darling?" The Duchess tipped her head prettily and pressed her fingertips against her temples. "You see? Nothing. Nothing is retained. But what a *clever* thing to do, my dear. I so envy you. In my day—alas, such a long time ago, my day—one was never allowed to do clever things. Which newspaper?"

"The—"

"No, let me guess. The *World.*"

The *World* was such a reactionary Tory paper that Jane almost smiled at the bizarre idea of her working for it. "No. The *Orbit.*"

"The *Orbit?* Is that the one that—yes, of course it is, it's that frightfully exciting one that comes out on Sunday, isn't it? I'm afraid we don't take it in and so I don't often see it, but I understand it's an extremely popular newspaper. Perhaps we could get it. Anthony, do you think old Mr. Watkins could get us the *Orbit?*"

"I daresay he could, mother. The *Orbit* has been coming out every Sunday for forty years and sells four and a quarter million copies a week. It shouldn't be beyond even Mr. Watkins's capabilities to get us one."

"Darling, then we *must.* We must, starting this very

112

Sunday. And with Miss Cornell writing in it I'm sure I shall become—what is that word? Hooked?"

Jane looked nervously from one to the other. "No. Gosh, no, don't bother. It's a rotten paper really. I only work for it, I don't have to love it."

"But my dear, four and a quarter million. That is a lot, and Anthony is quite right, it's time I was more— more with it. And it does make the World look a bumbling old slow coach, doesn't it? I really must remember to tell Michael Wentworth when next I see him that he had best look sharp and pull his socks up."

"I suspect, Mother, that Lord Wentworth already knows the Orbit's circulation. It's the kind of thing newspaper proprietors tend to know about other newspapers."

"Is it, darling? Then I shall tell him we know a most clever and charming American from Connec—no, from California, who makes his Ronald Melly look very drab indeed."

"George Melly, Mother. And he writes in the Observer."

"Does he? I thought it was that awful Kenneth Tynan who wrote in the Observer." She glanced at a tiny carriage clock that stood on the table. "Darling, do ring for Parkes. He's got as doddery as I and may have forgotten we're having drinks in here and not the morning room."

She turned back to Jane. "What a nice talk, my dear, and we must have another one very soon. Shall I show you the stables in the morning? Would you like that? Hugo has the most splendid new Arab horse and if you're very, very nice to him he might even let you ride it. Did someone tell you I've put you in the yellow room? I do hope you find it comfortable."

"I'm sure I will."

There was a silence. The Duchess was clearly waiting for something more.

"It's—it's very pretty," Jane said.

"My dear, I'm so glad you like it. This gloomy old

house very badly needed a pretty room, and we had such fun doing it up, didn't we, Ants? It took months, of course—so exhausting, isn't it, getting a room just right? But so rewarding too, of course, don't you think?"

Jane nodded and thought, Holy christ. Then the door opened and Parkes pushed in a noisily rattling trolley loaded with bottles, glasses, ice cubes in an open, cut-crystal bucket with silver tongs hung over the side, and a silver cocktail shaker that was as whoop-de-do! a relic from the 1930s as an Astaire-and-Rogers musical.

Parkes made a great Dr.-Jekyll-and-Mr.-Hyde production of pouring jiggers of gin and other things into the shaker, and while he was shaking it two more spaniels slopped into the room, followed by His Grace, Hugo, Seventh Duke of Wiltshire.

"Darling!" shrieked the little Duchess. "Those tiresome Italians, have they gone?"

"Think so," Hugo said. "'Lo, Anthony."

"Jane, this is my brother, Hugo. Hugo, Jane Cornell."

They shook hands. "'Lo. Do you ride?"

"No."

"Oh. Pity. Need someone for the morning. Charles's got a poisoned foot."

A tall chinless young man came hobbling up behind Hugo and held out a long, limp hand. "Stepped on a carpet tack. Silly, wasn't it? How d'y'do."

Sipping the nasty frothy and opaquely white drink that Parkes had made, the Duchess allowed Charles to kiss her cheek. "Dear Charles. How nice to see you again and so soon. But how perfectly dreadful about your poor foot."

"Mm. Bore, that."

One of the spaniels very insistently nudged its wet nose up Jane's skirts, and she gave it a couple of shoves she hoped no one saw. When it clamped its front legs around her leg, she stood up abruptly and accidentally stepped on its back paw. The dog let out a yip as shrill

114

as if it had been scalded, and immediately everyone, even Parkes, turned and stared at her. The spaniel cowered behind Hugo and stared around his legs at her with its runny eyes, and Jane began to wish she was back home in bed with the ads for radial ply tires.

Left alone in the yellow room, she had just begun her detailed examination of it when the amorous spaniel tracked her down and started whining and scratching at the door. She opened it, took a quick look left and right down the hall, and gave him a sharp kick on his fat behind. "Git. You I don't need."

The room wasn't, in fact, so bad. No one could totally ruin a room that was so perfectly proportioned, and though a pretty determined ruiner had obviously tried, the attempt had failed. They could have gone a little less hog-wild, she thought, on the chintz with yellow roses the size of lettuces all over it, but, even so, the room had emerged merely a good, not a four-star, example of the Clarissa-it's-heavenly school of English country-house interior decor.

The walls had been painted yellow on white and then dragged, an extremely expensive treatment that produces a not altogether beautiful look of hair soaked in setting lotion and combed. The ceiling was paler yellow. The woodwork, white. Two very good Barbizon School landscapes and three big oval gilt-framed pastels of eerily ethereal Victorian children were very pretty against it, but they hung on too visible wire from that curse of any room, a picture rail. And, very Englishly, they hung eighteen inches too high.

Everything that could match, matched. The curtains matched the bedspread. The bedspread matched the dressing-table skirt and bench. Even the headboard of the bed had been upholstered in the chintz and then covered again with a sheet of clear, icy plastic. This was an excess of caution Jane had never seen except with people who keep the cellophane on new lampshades, or their lighters in the chamois bags they came in, and she touched the plastic wonderingly.

The carpet was a very practical dark green, and yellow enamelled roses twined with green ivy leaves on a sort of birdcage chandelier that hung from not quite the centre of the ceiling. Directly under it, craftily placed to do maximum injury to anyone foolish enough to take a step without the light on, was a round table with a chintz cover that hung to the floor. Like the dressing table and the two bedside tables, it had a protective glass top, and scattered about on it were a lot of little enamel boxes, some articulated silver fish, a silver candle-snuffer (but no candle), and a squat Lalique vase with yellow roses in it. In the middle of this carefully arranged clutter was a superb Art Nouveau silver-and-sharp-yellow cloisonné inkstand and a dark green leather folder with, inside, a yellow blotter, several sizes of CRAVENBOURNE ABBEY writing paper, and a British Rail timetable of the trains from Froynton-on-the-Marsh to London. There weren't many.

She sat down on the magnificent down-cushioned Louis XV chaise loungue that, like a Hindenburg Line, was clearly intended to stop anyone who had got past the table alive from actually getting to the bathroom in the dark. Her bag had been unpacked and everything in it hidden, and she still hadn't found her shoes. But she couldn't resist the cloisonné inkstand and the CRAVENBOURNE ABBEY paper. While the bath that anyway she wasn't going to take got cold, she sat down and wrote a note to Angela.

Chère Amie:
　　I don't know how it is with you in Tonypandy or Sheffield or wherever you are and where you so richly deserve to be but it is the nicest time of the year here at home where the hearth is and if you go for a stirrup cup of Drano before dinner lots of fun too, and not at all like all those bleak years on the upper reaches of the Orinoco with only piranha fish for company. Mumsy is, you will be glad to hear, well and looks only slightly younger than you or, in a bad light, me, but she is very petite I think the word is and does not look strong though you never can tell. She of course over-taxes herself cruelly by letting wop photographers have their way with her, and running this huge house, a structure that had not Engels feared to tread would now be the Froynton-on-the-Marsh mental home and, now that you mention it, is. But that's Mumsy all over and there's no stopping someone who is always think-ing of others' happiness and how to get rid of it, is there? She has even in her characteristically kind way promised to break the news to Lord Wentworth that some papers sell more than others and so perhaps she *is* stronger than she looks, everywhere except in the head.
　　My room is a veritable Easter Bunny bower and so far I have spent many exciting happy minutes in it looking for my shoes. I have not yet found them but have certainly found within me a new, awed respect for Mumsy's practical side. *Every possible surface is covered with glass.* To the point where one suspects she either collects fingerprints or has shares in a glass factory. And you should see the *butler.* Ima tellink you he's not just any old mock-up of Bela Lugosi but is Vlad the Impaler himself, back by popular demand from a five-century run in a Rumanian freak show, and there is already a current of affectionate warmth and mutual admiration between us that truly lightens the

step and gladdens the heart or, indeed, vice versa. But my it seems a long ways to Sunday, though that may well be only an irrational feeling stemming from nothing except living on the wrong side of the International Date Line. If you do not hear from me again you can have the record-player, one speaker, the left side of the amplifier, and my corneas too if you promise to look after Scat. And so, farewell. We who are about to dine with no shoes on salute you. See that the messenger takes some refreshment and the 4:30 back (no dining car, buffet off at Swindon, does not run Sats Suns or hols.) There'll always be an England. In these dark hours, remember that at least.

Hugs and kisses from your pal.

Mary Wortley Montagu (Lady)

In the bathroom she let the water out of the yellow tub, hung up the big yellow towel, and sat on the edge of the bath looking at the two Marie Laurencin girls who hung on the wall staring moonily into each other's dark eyes. Her shoes. Where the hell could they be? She wandered back to the bedroom and ate a couple of the tiny cherry-topped macaroons from the silver biscuit box on the bedside table while she wondered if she dared call Anthony.

She looked at her watch. 8:20. *Jesus.* She picked up the yellow telephone and pushed the button next to a little slot where it said Lord Anthony.

"It's me. I mean, it's not so much me as my shoes. I can't find them."

"Don't be silly. Have you looked in the wardrobe?"

"Don't who be silly, of course I have."

"Darling, they must be there. Ask the maid. After all, she unpacked."

Jane pushed the button next to another slot that showed a little female figure in an isosceles-triangle skirt, and she had just bitten into another macaroon when the knock came at the door. She pushed the bitten macaroon under the pillow and, brushing the crumbs off the front of her sweater, said, "Come in."

The shoes, stuffed with yellow tissue paper, were lined up under an insane sliding false floor in the wardrobe.

"Gosh, I'm sorry," she said. "I got you all the way up here for—"

"Not atall, miss. But I'm afraid I couldna find yer klusekawver."

"My what?"

"Your *klusekawver*, miss. I couldna find it."

"Oh. That's funny. But never mind—I guess I forgot it."

The girl looked startled and as if she were used to dealing with an altogether better class of maniac. "Very well, miss. Will that be all, then?"

Jane pushed Anthony's button again. "What's a klusekawver?"

"A what?"

"A *klusekawver*. It's something I should have had in my suitcase and didn't."

"Oh. A *clothes* cover."

"OK, but what is it?"

"Darling, it's a foolish thing that women put over their underwear."

"What do you mean they put it over their underwear? Is it something they wear?"

"No, not wear. They put it on a chair. After they take their underwear off, they put the clothes cover over it on a chair."

"What for?"

"I told you, it's foolish. It's nothing to worry about. It's just a thing women do."

"I don't do it."

"Darling, it's not worth—"

"But why do they do it? Who are they, anyhow? I've never seen anybody do it."

"I don't know why, and nobody really does it anyhow, but what I do know is it's late. Have you got your shoes?"

"Yes."

"Put them on, then. And come down."

The soup had been brown, the fish white, and the main course tiny little birds with empty, charred eye-sockets, bones like matches, and so small that everyone got two. Jane couldn't even look at them, much less eat them, so she simply dissected them very amateurly and spread them around on her plate, hiding as much as she could under the piece of toast they had come on.

But now it was almost over, and ever since the hot apple tart and cream so stiff it had to be spooned out of the silver jug she had been waiting tensely for the moment when the ladies would suddenly stand up and troop out like offended delegates from some banana republic. The signal for the walk-out would be, she knew, almost undetectable, but it wouldn't do to miss it and be still sitting there while they stood like sheep at the door and the men began to look uncomfortable.

She thought it would happen before the coffee was served, but it didn't. Everyone had coffee at the table, and Parkes followed the footman around with a tray of liqueurs.

"Kirsch, please," she said when it was her turn, and he filled the tiny glass so full that only surface tension kept it from spilling, and waited evilly for her to pick it up. While Parkes made a big thing of wiping up the few drops that spilled on the table, Jane kept her eyes steadily fixed on Hugo, who, on her right, was telling how it was the fresh fall of powder snow that had covered the crustier snow underneath and been responsible for someone named Bumbo breaking both his legs at Klosters.

She relaxed. She had behaved beautifully, and Anthony had been right; they weren't anything worse than deadly dull.

With queenish Charles on her left she had made the required bland, no-talk talk. She had listened animatedly to Hugo's horse talk and hunting talk. Even when he explained to her how the gamekeeper kept careful count of the fox cubs born in the spring so they would know exactly how many there would be to hunt that winter, she didn't let it show on her face what she was thinking.

She was very pleased with herself for having done so well, and while she finished her yellowy-white dessert wine she allowed herself a slow look around.

The four spaniels lay asleep in front of the fireplace, where logs burned and made the red damask curtains and the colors in the big Persian rug glow as brightly as if they too were on fire. On the dark panelled walls were huge paintings of earlier Fairfields and Dukes of Wiltshire in ermine-trimmed coronation robes, and much earlier ones in velvet bloomers slashed with brocade insets over long white tights. Down the center of the table almost-life-size silver grouse and pheasants stood separated by four tall silver candelabra with many arms that twisted out and up like branches of well-tended trees.

It was as splendid a room as she'd ever been in and even very beautiful, but somehow the people didn't measure up to it. On Hugo's right was Lady Whyteclyffe, a blotchy blond frump all gone to bosom and fat bare arms, with not-right twin diamond clips at the corners of the square neckline of an even less right electric-blue satin dress. In a very carrying voice she had talked, mainly to Hugo, about a holiday in India that had been made unpleasant by being constantly pursued through the streets by verminous beggar children wailing for baksheesh.

Next to her was Colonel Braithwaite, who, sixtyish and silver-haired with a mustache and very taut skin, looked like an elegant whisky ad and was, Jane gathered, a neighbouring landowner. Until Lady Whyteclyffe had drowned him out with the rigours of tourism in Bombay, he had attempted to say some quite sensible things about a country as small as England not being able to afford to lose year after year the thousands of acres of land that were being turned into highways.

Next was a pink-cheeked, very healthy-looking girl named Fenella, whose gums showed when she laughed and who knew apparently no verbs at all. But she did know an astonishing number of names of horses that might, or might not, do well at the Badminton Trials. When Hugo, who was not perhaps very forceful but did try his best, had introduced Jane to her as the film critic on the *Orbit*, all that had come back from Fenella was, "I say. Lucky old you. The *Orbit*. Madly good racing page."

Then there was handsome Anthony, who didn't seem to go much for Fenella either but concentrated instead on the very pretty girl on his right. Her name was Catherine Pennycuick, and before dinner she had told Jane she worked part time in an antique shop and would love to do it full time but there was so much else to do wasn't there and one couldn't do everything could one. Anyhow what she *really* wanted to do was drive across the Sahara with some friends in a Land Rover that Daddy had given her, and was leaving next month.

Beyond the hard-pushed-for-time Miss Pennycuick it was the Duchess's territory, and the names were a blur. But from the merry laughter and general noise level at that end of the table, Jane had a sneaking idea that Her Grace had creamed off the more amusing people for herself.

Or maybe she was just better at it. Certainly, unlike easygoing Hugo, she dominated them like a vigorous little gym teacher. Her tiny hands fluttered out tirelessly from a brilliant, busy swirl of long-sleeved green-and-blue chiffon, and she tilted her head prettily towards everyone in turn. Confidently she squelched the too talkative, pulled in the too silent, and like a candy-floss pied piper she got them all in line and led them down the conversational alleys that she chose for them to take.

At Jane's end, Hugo and Lady Whyteclyffe were talking about his new horse, and everybody else was listening to something funny that Charles was saying. As she'd heard about the horse several times already, she tuned in on Charles.

"... my dear, you're so right, and that's what's so awful, isn't it? One plucks one's courage up. One ventures out on a filthy night and almost drowns in Sloane Square, struggling to get a cab, to go literally miles across the river to queue up at that cramped, nasty little cinema to be—one hopes—entertained. Perhaps even amused. And what did one get? A dreary, mouldy old thing about some coal strike. No, it was, I swear it, it was about absolutely nothing except a coal strike. Can you imagine? 'Well, really,' I said to Freddie, Freddie Langton, who was with me, 'what do they take us for? We could get all this, if we wanted to, every morning in the papers.' And do you know what we did? We walked out. We did. Right out. And of course by the time we got another cab and were back across the river, it was far too late to do anything but go and bore each other to death at Crockford's."

Everyone found Charles's little story too amusing. As the laughter broke around her, Jane felt her heart speed up and her hand tighten on her wineglass.

She knew the picture this idiot meant. It was *Black Fury*. Made by Michael Curtiz. In 1937—no, 1935, at Warner Brothers. It was, indeed, about a coal strike. It was also about all men everywhere and any time who had ever lived at the mercy of smug mine-owning, factory-owning, land-owning employers.

It was about Harlan County, South Wales, and Detroit. It was about the poor gormless fools that had been murdered at Peterloo. It was about the Dorset farmers at Tolpuddle who had dared ask for wages enough to live on and had been sent to Botany Bay for their impertinence.

She was almost trembling with anger. Who was this castrate in a frilly shirt that he dared make fun of men like those? She'd show him—she'd show him right now. But then she saw Anthony's pretty head nodding politely at some verbless something Fenella had said, and he looked so relaxed and unaware, so much like the baker at Pompeii ten seconds before the eruption, that she swallowed her anger down with the Kirsch.

125

Now for the first time the whole table was united in common conversation, and, spurred to anecdote by Charles's success, everyone had something to say about films.

The Duchess said how tiresomely dated old films were and that if she ever had to see *Casablanca* again she didn't think she could bear it. Sorry, Mr. Curtiz, Jane thought. Not your night.

Fenella said well, mostly that was true, yes, but not entirely because *National Velvet* was so super. Everyone agreed that *National Velvet* had been and would forever remain super, and then Lady Whyteclyffe said she really didn't know how she felt about old films because it was all she could do to avoid new films, most of which were out-and-out filth.

Catherine Pennycuick didn't agree. Well, she agreed, but it wasn't so much the sex that was disgusting, though that was bad enough and there was no need for it, it was the violence really that was worse. It was so ugly. It really had—she was sure of this—a very bad effect on everyone, especially the young.

Nice old Colonel Braithwaite tried to get a word in about a jolly French film he'd seen once that was all about a little chap who'd got a balloon. But everybody else talked over him and around him all at once, and he gave up. Fenella started to tell about a film she'd missed but that was quite, quite beautiful and all about the white horses in the Camargues, when, beyond Charles on Jane's side of the table, Lord Whyteclyffe raised his plummy voice. It was an interesting question, films, he said. There were important issues involved.

The important issues were an extraordinary mishmash of how long-haired so-called intellectuals not only had a lamentable influence on the young at the universities, but also had infiltrated the press, the BBC, and the film industry. All of which was one of the reasons, of course, for the flagrantly left-wing bias currently rampant in the communications media, and if that were all, well, that would be bad enough, but that was not all. The real trouble was, in point of fact, well known, and it was that the film industry was and always had been in the pockets of foreigners, not all of whom were Christians by any means and some of whom undoubtedly got their orders straight from Moscow. That much was obvious. What was not quite so apparent, except to the expert eye, was that these chappies, quite content, of course, to make their fat livings in Britain, were tirelessly engaged in turning out propaganda. Yes. That's what it was. When you got right down to it, it was propaganda. Disguised as entertainment, of course, but basically and fundamentally propaganda. With, as its real purpose, the deliberate undermining and destruction of all that Britain stood for both morally and politically.

The table fell into a respectful silence as Lord Whyteclyffe toyed with his liqueur glass and warmed to his subject. Her Grace's little hands were still as she listened, and her pretty little face gazed admiringly at the jowly ruined mass that was his. "Do go on, Francis. We're all fascinated."

Lord Whyteclyffe was only too willing. What he'd just said was, he said, only the tip of the iceberg. There was more, much more, underneath that he was not at liberty to—uh—divulge. And of course filth and pornography were the least of it. British justice was still British justice, and these lesser evils were relatively easy to deal with; one could still have faith in British judges and British juries to see to that. The political poison, however, was far trickier, and so far no government—least of all the socialists, who, after all, stood to gain from left-wing bias—no government had had the courage to put its foot down. Until such a day came, the BBC would continue to display its contempt for both good taste and public opinion, and so would the press. As for the film industry, it was a hotbed of undesirable elements and would remain so, so long as no one had either the courage or a clear plan as to how to turf them out.

Lord Whyteclyffe set his many chins firmly and

went on. In that respect, the weeding out of undesirables, there was a lesson to be learned from the Americans. Some years ago, in a roughly parallel situation, the Yanks had quite simply grasped the nettle and rather effectively ridded Hollywood of a goodly number of—to put it mildly—suspect people.

He wasn't, of course, suggesting that that particular era in American politics, or McCarthyism in any form, was an entirely good thing. But there are many means to an end, and, say what one would, the action taken in America had been effective. A number of people had gone to jail, and quite right that they had. Others had been boycotted by what was, fundamentally, a decent industry. As for that chap Chaplin, he had turned tail, fled the country, and . . .

Jane could suddenly see the studio projection room where, when she was ten, her father had taken her to see *Black Fury*. She could see her father's face, and she could hear his voice—it had been such a nice voice, too, always saying serious things laughingly and silly things seriously. It was all as clear as if it had been yesterday. And then she heard her own voice.

"Lord Whyteclyffe, may I . . ."

He hadn't heard, but the rest of them had. Heads turned towards her, and she tried again. "Lord Whyteclyffe . . ."

The jowly silver head swung round in her direction, and she wished she had a custard pie. "Lord Whyteclyffe, I apologize for interrupting, but I must. First, though, I'd like to say something to Charles, something I want you all to hear."

Campily jabbing his chest with his finger, Charles mouthed a "Who, me?"

"Yes, you. That picture you were just so killingly funny about is, as it happens, one of the great pictures of the thirties. The dreary, mouldy coal strike it was about was no drearier and no mouldier than the lives that many people led, and what that picture tried to do was to show the misery and poverty and futureless, powerless limbo that those people lived in and

128

that, moreover, too many still live in. That picture set out to wake complacent fools up to reality. And it did—some. That it did not do it for you is sad, but I can't do anything about that. I only thought you ought to know what it was really about, that movie, and if I've given you any idea at all, that's all I ask."

Charles's pink mouth hung open. Jane didn't dare look at the Duchess, but she saw that Anthony had one elbow on the table and was masking his eyes with his hand. She felt sorry for him, but there was no point in quitting now. The rope around her neck would be just as rough for the lamb as for the sheep. She turned to face the sheep.

"As for you, Lord Whyteclyffe, I don't know what your experience of the press, or the BBC, or the motion-picture industry is and I don't claim mine to be wide. But I grew up in Hollywood. My father worked at the same time as that chap Chaplin, at the old United Artists studio and later for Warner Brothers. At both places he wrote and directed some very fine pictures—and so did Michael Curtiz, who made the picture Charles was talking about."

Nervously she reached for a cigarette and lit it.

"I remember very well the 'weeding out,' as you call it, and though I can't speak for all the people it happened to, because it would take too long and, unlike you, I know only some of the facts, I can speak for my father, who was one of them. He was not a Jew, Lord Whyteclyffe, or a foreigner. He was half Jewish, yes. But he was born in Salem, Massachusetts—a small irony that I'm sure you will appreciate—and he was a completely loyal American. All his life he voted the straight Democratic ticket, and he most certainly never took an order or even a hint from Moscow. Yet my father was one of those nettles that was grasped. He was grasped, uprooted, hounded to Washington—where he refused to turn informer—and then he was fired. Two years later, when he knew he would never work again in the industry that he loved and that had been his life, he put a revolver in his mouth and shot himself.

129

He was thirty-nine years old, and he was—or so some people say—the most talented man to work in Hollywood since Irving Thalberg."

She looked around the table, but no one would look back at her. "While we're at it I think you ought to get it straight about Mr. Chaplin. He didn't flee the country. He was out of the country at the time and he simply didn't go back, out of, I would think, heartbreak and disgust and fear for America's sanity. But that's a detail. What's important is that, whether or not they weeded out any really guilty people, the witch-hunters destroyed other people as well. Innocent people.

"They're embarrassed now about this time in America. Oh, they say, that was then. That was McCarthyism and the cold war and maybe some of it went too far and maybe all of it was a big mistake. But that doesn't undo what happened, does it? That doesn't give men their jobs back, or bring my father back to life, does it? No. And underneath that thick layer of whitewash the injustice is still black.

"If this is what you admire and call 'action,' if this is a remedy you seriously recommend for whatever ails the British film industry, then I say you are wrong, Lord Whyteclyffe, and not only that you are wrong but that what you propose is evil. It was evil when it happened in America, and men who feared the same phantoms you fear carved themselves a very ignoble niche in history. I saw that happen, and I would not like to see it happen here. But so long as there are people like you, and other people so foolish as to be persuaded by people like you, there is always the dreadful possibility that it could."

She lit another cigarette and thought, Jesus christ, I've set a new world's record. And maybe she had. It's not everyone who, on one weekend and before midnight on Friday, can violate every British commandment from "Thou shalt not ever make an angry fuss about anything" to "Thou shalt not attack anyone directly and/or personally." She had done it all. In one swell foop she had shot the rapids, and she was glad she had, and fuck them anyhow.

Very twitchily the dolly Duchess stood up and smiled at the ladies—the other ladies, that is—and as they filed out they began to chatter vivaciously.

Jane hung back. Nobody was chattering to her, nor was anyone likely to. Even Anthony didn't risk more than a quick half-smile at her, and Jane heard Lady Whyteclyffe's grating voice saying, "No. No, my dear Hugo, it's quite all right. In one's position one is used to . . ." The rest of it she couldn't hear.

When Lady Whyteclyffe caught up with the others and left the room, Hugo gave Jane's arm a little squeeze and whispered, "I say. Well done. Pontifical old bore, Whyteclyffe."

She smiled gratefully and said she was sorry. Then she walked alone out of the dining room and, trying to look purposeful and as if she had forgotten something upstairs, she took the long, lonely walk to the yellow room, where she sat on the chaise lounge and—just as if she were timing a hard-boiled egg—stared at her watch for fifteen minutes.

When the fifteen minutes were up and she trailed back downstairs, she met Anthony in the hall. "Well, that certainly socked it to them, darling."

"Sorry. I wouldn't have done it if I'd thought. I mean, I didn't even know I was doing it until I'd got really started."

"Darling, it doesn't matter. Truly it doesn't." He smiled a shade too forgivingly just so she'd know it did matter. "Come on downstairs. I'll teach you snooker."

"I like that. Me that was shooting eightball when you couldn't see over the table. Who is that purple-faced old schmuck, anyhow?"

"Whyteclyffe? Don't you remember? He was an MP for donkey's years. You know, one of those backbenchers who always manage to get in the newspapers."

"Was he? I can't remember him."

"His name was Burton-Glover then. As soon as they decently could, they pushed him upstairs into the

Lords, and he's a most frightful old dinosaur, darling, so don't worry about it. I did think you were a bit hard on poor Charles, though. He's an awfully good sort underneath all the nonsense."

The snooker lesson was not a success. They quit and rejoined the dinner party in the long library, where the Whyteclyffes, Colonel Braithwaite, and the Duchess were playing bridge and the others were deep in Catherine Pennycuick's Sahara trip.

"Camels," Fenella was saying. "Don't really fancy 'em. No stamina."

"But think of those marvelous Arabs." Charles rolled his eyes ecstatically. "The desert isn't *all* camels, y'know."

Fenella sniffed. "Better Arabs over at old Mrs. What's-her-name's in Kent."

"Not the horses, you ridiculous girl. The men."

Jane stayed just long enough to give everyone a chance to pretend that nothing unpleasant had happened, and just long enough to establish clearly that she was not upstairs sobbing her eyes out in her room, and then she said good night and went to bed.

Upstairs, whoever had turned down the bed had carefully rescued the bitten macaroon and had put it on a little plate on the bedside table.

That was bad enough, but about three o'clock the deep black country quiet waked her up, and on one of those coltish impulses unsuitable for anyone past the age of fifteen she decided to visit Anthony.

It wasn't as difficult as she thought it would be. Silently barefoot, like little Puma Paw the Indian Boy, she went along the carpeted corridors and down the marble stairs, then up the other stairs and along the corridors that led to Anthony's door opposite the Armada picture.

She put her hand on the doorknob and had even turned it when something stopped her. Quietly she turned the knob back, hoping it wouldn't click, and put her ear to the door.

There were three voices—no, two. One was Anthony's and that figured. But the other? She could make out only a few words. "... most ghastly mistake, Anthony ... awfully dishonest, really ... yourself, of course, but not ... really must say ... long run ... bound to, my dear, bound to ..."

It sounded like a woman, but it wasn't a woman. It was Charles.

Anthony and Charles?

Not possible.

Charles was Hugo's. Anthony was hers.

What the hell kind of a crazy world did these people live in, anyhow?

She made the return trip to the yellow room in even faster time and, leaning against the icy-clear plastic on the chintz bedhead, she ate every macaroon in the silver box. There were fifteen—she counted them—and by the end her mouth was so dry that she unscrewed the top from the mineral water by the biscuit box and drank the whole bottle. Then, still hungry, but drunk on defeat, she went to sleep.

9

Time passed. Some of it went fast, some of it dragged; sometimes there were shuddering pauses like the lift-off moment of a moon shot. But even if it was in fits and starts, with all the grace and dignity of a sack race, the next six months went by. The lovely sodden spring turned into the statutory week-long English summer in June, and on the surface Jane's life was very little changed.

As she did every spring, she sponged the soot off the ivy that straggled reluctantly up the trellis, planted nasturtiums in the tubs, and bought her one scientific gardening aid, a package of Lux. Right on schedule the blackfly appeared and, sluicing them off with the warm soapy water, she wondered, as she always did, where they came from and how they *knew*. How could the brainless little things know that in mid-July on a roof in the center of London there'd be nasturtium buds ready for eating? How? What told them? What guided them to the roof? It was the kind of thing that occasionally tempted her to believe in God. Who else was nasty enough to think up a thing like blackfly?

She had her hair cut short and, as always, instantly regretted it. She went, as always, to a couple of film festivals. Anthony took her to Ascot. And because Tom had never been to a zoo she took him to Whipsnade. Her hope was that by doing ordinary things, either things she'd always done or things that were in no way far out, she'd be able to keep everything as it had been. But the more everything masqueraded as normal, the more it was all different and getting more so every day.

Franklin still came every weekend. They still went to the theatre and they still played tennis, but not very often because he had now got down in earnest to writing his paper on civil rights. Saturdays he wouldn't leave the library even long enough for lunch; Sundays and Mondays he spent doggedly at the typewriter.

He flew to Dayton to talk to smoke-filled-room people about the job, and then spent a few days in Washington with his family and a few more in New York with friends. Not long after that he got a letter in Cambridge offering him another job running a ten-lawyer poverty law office in North Philadelphia, and so in August he went to the States again to see people about that.

Maybe it was two trips home in such rapid succession that did it, but each time he came back he was much more American than before. His American accent was heavier. He used new slang that Jane hadn't heard. He had been to plays and restaurants in New York that she didn't know existed. He talked about court cases and legislation that she hadn't known were happening. And though it was impossible to pin down the exact moment when he had changed, from then on he never seemed really content in England again.

He'd suddenly go silent and sort of stare, and then just as suddenly he'd be his old self again and pound up twenty-thousand ice cubes to make mint juleps with Angela's Jack Daniel's and the mint that tasted slightly of Lux, even when you washed it.

Little things, though, had begun to irritate him in a

136

way they hadn't before. The door handle came off the Mini, and wasn't that just what you'd expect from a limey car? He couldn't get a book he wanted. His telephone bill was all wrong. The man didn't come to fix a sashcord when he said he would, and absolutely none of these things could have happened anywhere except in half-assed, fucked-up England. He'd had to wait twenty-five minutes for a bus. How about *that*?

"Oh, come off it, Franklin. That happens everywhere."

He put his long legs up on the desk, tipped back in his chair, and, for a moment, tipped back to his old, unserious way. "Not in Dayton it doesn't. In Dayton buses come every thirty seconds. They're all free. There's seats for everybody. And they all go nonstop to the Big Rock Candy Amusement Park."

She was on her knees on the floor, hunting fleas on Scat's belly. "What about the people at the next bus stop? Can't be much fun for them watching buses whizz by every thirty seconds."

"Well, everyone in Dayton, see, has his own bus. Mine stops for me; theirs stops for them. Why don't you leave that poor cat alone?"

"If I leave him alone, I leave the fleas alone too. To get them, I have to bother him. He understands that. Don't you, Scat?"

"You do, of course, realize that it was on exactly that same fink-false principle that the United States bombed the hell out of a small rice-growing peasant country? That, on the same principle, people used to swing witches, remove the bad spirits from the mad by beating them, and pull other people's arms and legs off in Inquisition interrogation chambers? Is this really the gang you want to travel with?"

She let Scat go and stood in back of Franklin, her arms around his neck. "And what about you? What if somebody doesn't want to go to the Big Rock Candy Amusement Park?"

He took her hands and slid them inside his unbuttoned shirt. "Nobody in Dayton's that crazy. They always want to." He turned his head against her breast, and she felt the muscles tighten in his shoulder. "So do I. Let's go to bed."

Slowly she massaged the back of his neck. "What about the big opus? The life's work? The revised and improved Rights of Man?"

"To hell with it."

"What about the Marshalls? You told them we might see them."

"I only said might."

"Still, you'll have to call them and say."

"You, baby. You call them."

"OK. Shall I say something came up and you're in a tight spot you can't get out of?"

"Right. I'll call them myself. And tell them you're in bed with a very rapid pulse and breathing funny and seem to have a foreign body lodged in your esophagus."

"Foreign? You're not foreign. You're just a nice clean-cut homegrown sex maniac."

In the end they never even got as far as the bedroom and didn't call the Marshalls at all.

The pigeon changed fastest of everything. By May it had a beak like a vulture. By June it was more than fully grown but was so completely hooked on the soft, freeloading life it led that it obviously hadn't the slightest intention of leaving. It didn't even want to learn to fly.

Patiently, Tom taught it to. He'd sit the gentle, overweight, and totally sedentary creature on the clothesline out back and walk away from it. It hated that. It hated being left alone ever. But it hated even more the effort of flapping its wings, and as Tom moved farther and farther away from it, you could almost see the terrible choice roiling in its transistor-sized brain.

Panic won. Teetering back and forth on the line, it had to spread its wings to keep its balance, and then very awkwardly it would take off and fly to his shoulder. But it only did it as if flying were some parlor trick that idiot humans—for no known reason or sensible purpose—expected it to do, and it never did it at all when Tom wasn't around.

The day Tom and Jane took it to the park to let it go, it showed off its trick as frantically as a vaudeville act auditioning to play the Palace. When they put it on the ground and walked away, it took off like a bomber on one engine and flew straight to Tom's shoulder. When they ran, it chased them. When they hid behind trees, it found them. When they made a final dash for the car and tried to hide under the dashboard, it sat on the hood looking at them through the windshield reproachfully as if the stupid game, which it had never thought much fun anyhow, had gone on long enough.

And all the way home it perched on the back of the seat between them, with its eyes shut, making tired-but-happy throat noises about its day in the park.

Softhearted Tom was all for letting the pigeon live in the whisky crate out on the roof forever, but Jane had had enough of it coming in the bedroom window every morning and cooing in her ear until she got up and gave it breakfast. There had been, too, a taut little scene with Anthony the morning when, unwilling to wait any longer, it had gone foraging in the kitchen and shit in the sugar bowl.

"Darling," he said as he stirred his tea, "has the milk gone off?"

"Shouldn't think so. It's brand-new fresh this morning."

He took a cautious sip. "Tastes horrid. Looks strange, too."

She'd put down the *Times* and knew immediately. "Oh my god. It's the pidge."

She got him a clean cup and everything, but Anthony was too shaken to be soothed and went off saying he'd have breakfast at his club. The next weekend she and Franklin took the pigeon to the big park at Richmond.

They drove around and around, looking for what she

called "a good place," but finally Franklin just slowed down and said, "Here," and so she gave it a last kiss on the top of its bony head and held it out of the car window on her wrist until it took off. Flying with much more determination than it ever had before, it chased them desperately for about half a mile, but when Franklin shifted into top gear and drove faster, the pigeon fell farther and farther behind until they couldn't see it any more.

Out of the park, they stopped at a pub by the river to celebrate having got rid of it. It took only two small gins before Jane began to cry about having treated it meanly and said they had to go back to the park and get it. But Franklin wouldn't. He took her drink away from her, finished it, and with one hand firmly under her elbow he got her into the car and headed back to London. That was the end of the pigeon. And things were changing so fast now that it seemed almost like the end of an era, too.

In a way Tom grew up with, and as fast as, the pigeon. Like a speeded-up film of a water lily blossoming, his beautiful, boy's face began visibly to become a man's face, and slowly, gradually, feeling his way like someone coming out of a cave into sunlight, he dropped the artful-dodger façade that had served him so well and so long. For a while, out of habit, he'd still duck behind it occasionally, but the new grown-up, serious Tom was stronger, and little by little the flippantly defiant tough-guy boy disappeared.

With energy that seemed to increase the more he used it, he began to do some of the things he had always said he wanted to but had shied away from. He joined an English Lit class at an adult education centre. He bought, or anyhow got, a *Teach Yourself Algebra* book, went through it in a month, and then started on *Teach Yourself Geometry and Calculus*.

As he changed, so did his taste in what he stole. He was still far from being a smooth Raffles, but the pictures he put in his cupboard now were no longer sunset scenes of Highland cattle by Loch Schmoch, but Gwen John drawings, a couple of Picasso sketches, and, once, even a small, muddy early Corot landscape.

Worse, he developed a very worrying taste for small Fabergé animals and rare and probably extremely traceable, identifiable books. First editions of Trollope and Oscar Wilde. A signed copy of the *Joan of Arc* with the Boutet de Monvel illustrations. A whole set of leather-bound Dickens with someone's *ex libris* stickers in them. And, like people who buy books for Christmas presents and read them before they give them away, Tom read them all. This meant they stayed in the apartment—not just in the cupboard, either—far longer than was good for Jane's peace of mind, and though she was delighted Tom had taken to reading in such a big way, it did seem a very dangerous way to get an education.

After dinner one Tuesday, when she thought he was working on his geometry, she brought coffee to the living room and found him staring at one of his own bright, crazy paintings on the wall. He had his lower lip between his teeth, and very slowly he half bit it, half rolled it, released it, and then went through the same painful looking process again.

"Tom. Coffee."

Either he hadn't heard or he didn't care. Still biting his lip, he cracked the knuckles on his left hand.

She took her coffee to her desk and put a piece of paper in the typewriter. "Tom. Cut it out."

"Cut what out?"

"That horrible noise. Your coffee's getting cold."

She had taught him to like black coffee, or maybe he had only learned to drink it without liking it, but he still put three spoonfuls of sugar in. She listened to him stir it and thought that, wherever it was he'd spent his childhood, it certainly hadn't been a candy store.

"I've been thinking," he said.

"And?"

"And I'm packing it in."

"What, thinking?"

She turned around, and he smiled his nice smile, his new grown-up smile. "Yeah, and thieving too. Oh, I could go on. I'm not chickening out, I could go on easily. But, like you say, it's a mug's game really, and I'm finished with being a mug."

She hid the relief she felt, because approval and praise were not things Tom would accept. Once, before she'd learned that, she had too enthusiastically praised an almost finished drawing, and he had torn it up slowly in front of her. Another time a house of cards had been destroyed with one flick of his finger because she'd made the mistake of saying how pretty it was. Even the pigeon—and he had dearly loved the pigeon—had never got its elaborate pergola cage, because she'd encouraged him to build it. This time she wasn't taking any chances, so all she said was, "Oh? What do you figure on doing instead?"

"What I'd like is to get out of London and ..."

"And?"

"No. Fuck it. It's too early to talk about. If you talk about something too soon, sometimes the talk is all that happens."

She was finishing a piece on Russian films for an American magazine and pretended to be more interested in it than in what he was saying. "Gosh, did you know there was a Russian general named Timoshenko?"

"The bloody Irish, they'd join anything to get a uniform. But Jane?"

"Mm?"

"Now don't go mad, because I don't mean it in a nasty way, but this baby—is it mine?"

God. Everything you dread happens. She got up, made herself a whisky and water, and said, "Want one? A drink, I mean."

"No. You know I hate that stuff." He went to get her some ice and one by one he dropped four cubes into her glass. Without looking at her, he said, "Is it?"

"I honestly don't know. I wish I did."

142

He sat on the desk and touched her cheek gently with the back of his hand. "Yeah." His voice was low, and the new seriousness was heavy on him. "That's about what I figured. All I wanted to know for was . . ."

Whatever was coming was too much to say while actually within sight or reaching distance of another human being, so he got up and walked behind her. "I know I've got no claim on you—how the jesus could someone like me have a claim on anyone, or anything, come to that? But if somebody lets you down or—well, I wanted you to know you can—you know, count on me. I know that's not much to offer, being like I am. But I don't always have to be like I am. I can change. I want to change." He came back and sat on the desk again. "You don't think that's crazy, do you? I mean, don't you think people can change if they want to?"

It was the most overt declaration of love he had ever made, and she knew what admitting it, and making the offer of commitment, must have cost him.

She led him over to the black leather sofa and held onto his hand while she tried to think what would hurt him the least. Finally she said, "I don't know what's going to happen, Tom, I truly don't. I don't think anybody will let me down or anything, but there's a lot more to it than that."

She told him the truth. Franklin. Anthony. Everything. At first, being truthful felt as strange as walking after taking off roller skates. But as she got used to it, it came easier.

". . . and so you see even if it's white and even if I knew, really knew, it was Anthony's, I still don't see me in that world. It's not only that they're different from us—and I don't care what Hemingway said, all that money does make them different—it's more that they're so second-rate. They're frivolous but not funny. They're vain but not clever or beautiful. They're educated but dumb. They live in a closed-off world and they don't want to know any other." She hunched her shoulders and shuddered. "God, they're awful."

"OK, but a whole lot of people who aren't rich

aren't all that fucking marvelous, you know. I've known some who didn't own a pot to piss in, but that didn't stop them being the biggest bastards on earth."

"Sure. But it's easier to understand how people who have nothing can be lousy. If life has been hard and lousy to you, if you've never had any kind of a break and have never known or even seen kindness and generosity and things like that, it must be pretty hard to learn to be nice. But these people have had the works. They've had all the treats and goodies and privileges there are. And they're still cruel and selfish and shallow and—well, rotten."

"They can't all be. Not every single one."

"No, I don't suppose they can. There must be some nice ones; I know there are. I've read about them and heard about them. But I honestly think there are more of the crummy kind. Not all madly rich. Just—as they say—comfortable. It's them, the placid, unquestioning, accepting, smugly comfortable ones I hate the most. The bloody arrogance of them. The stupidity. The greediness. The way they grab all they can get, and to hell with anybody who can't grab, or won't."

She finished her drink, and he got up to make her another. "You know, Tom, even when they're making their best effort to be lovely, they're still awful. Take those charity balls, when they all turn up to show off their social conscience and generosity and best diamonds and all buy raffle tickets in the hope of winning another Jaguar. Only after all the champagne and strawberries and lobster that they guzzle has been paid for do the starving people eating rats in some godforsaken country even see a penny of it. With the rich, it's first things first. And so what if each balloon they pop with lighted cigarettes costs the same as feeding a hungry child for a day?"

"OK, they're lousy. But look at it this way: maybe they just don't know any better. Maybe if you joined up with them you could—oh christ, you know, change it a little."

"I bet you a lot of people have thought that, Tom.

But I bet you those people have pretty soon learned that if you join them you can't fight them. You're outnumbered. You're on their territory. And you're done for. Anyhow, I doubt if anybody could last against that mother. She's young, too, only just turned sixty and far too nasty to do anything nice like die. She could live another thirty years easily. And probably will."

"Let her. What harm can she do?"

"I don't know. But do I want to live hemmed in by people like that? Who don't like me any more than I like them? Who maybe even more don't like me than I don't like them?"

Tom paced the floor and then leaned against the oak chest, frowning. "You can't not like them all. What about him? You must like him."

"Well, he's different from them mostly. But I don't think he has the courage to kick them, or to kick the system, either. I think if I married him and started to go the full fifteen rounds with the rest of them, he might watch in an amused sort of way for a couple of years—or maybe not even that long—but in the end he'd get bored with it as entertainment and with me for making the kind of trouble he's always avoided. Mumsy would see to that."

"You worry too much about her. Why not just stay out of her way? Christ, you know how those fuckers live, always off to jolly Monte to rest up at the chemmy table from doing nothing, and then old Blotto gets a bright idea and they're all off to Africa to shoot themselves a couple of tigers. You could stay clear of them easy."

"Tigers live in India."

"What tigers are left are bloody lucky to live anywhere, the way those guys go after them. Jesus, you know what I did once?"

His face lit up. Telling her things he'd done was a nice part of the new Tom.

"I came across this bloody great tiger rug in a pad on Eaton Square—near busted my leg stepping in its mouth in the fucking dark, too. And it was a good one. I could have got a hundred quid for it easy. But I couldn't do it. I've got no right to sell the skin of some tiger that never did nothing to me, and they'd got no right to have it on their floor, either. So you know what I did? I took a razor blade and I sliced that tiger up until if you'd held it up to the light you'd of sworn it was a venetian blind. I never made a single quid out of that whole night. But I did that to them and I was glad."

She looked at him and shook her head slowly. "You'll never get them that way, Tom. Don't you see you never will? You slice up their tiger—OK. Big gesture. But what do they do then? They collect the insurance and go out and buy another one. Or maybe this time they go for something more colorful. Something from Morocco, say, or East Afghanistan. Handknotted and all that."

"So what? I don't give a damn what they do."

"No? Did you know that children work on those rugs? That seven-year-old kids work a ten-hour day tying those knots? What's worse? That, or the tiger?"

"Christ, I don't know. Put it that way, and everything stinks."

"That's right. That's why it's no use cutting their rug to ribbons. It doesn't help the tiger. It doesn't help the kids. It doesn't even help Eaton Square idiots to learn that it's wrong to use tigers—or children—that way. All it does, in fact, is to make them absolutely certain that they're right to hate people like you."

Tom looked uncomfortable. He had very clear ideas of right and wrong and didn't like them being messed up with complicated moral issues or shades of grey. "Yeah. Well, I was only young then and—so the hell with it. Let's get back to what we were talking about."

Now she looked uncomfortable. "Well, the awful thing is I haven't even told you the worst bit yet. You see, there's another—"

"Another guy? Jesus, you get around like a top."

"It's not that. For the god's sake, I do get out of bed once in a while, you know."

146

"Yeah? Well, watch it. Stand up too much and you'll get a rush of blood to your feet that'll flatten your arches."

"Tom, I don't believe it. You're *jealous*."

Three months ago he would only have smiled the gay-desperado smile at such a mawkish impossibility. Now he looked her straight in the eyes and said, "Of course I am." As he said it the whole balance of power shifted; you could almost hear it creak as it did, like ice breaking up on a lake. He was the grown-up one now, and she—she was the one with the phony smile on her face.

"OK, so never mind that. What I was going to say is the thing about Anthony really is—well, I don't know for sure, but I think he's queer."

"You mean . . . ?"

"Mm."

"But he makes it with you."

"I don't think that means much by itself. Some people are sort of both, you know. When they're young, anyhow. But I've got an awful feeling that as they get older they get—I don't know, just more whatever they are that's different."

"Jesus god almighty, you can't marry a queer. You'd go off your head."

"Would I?"

"You think you wouldn't? You? I've never known a woman who liked sex the way you do. A lot don't, you know."

"Don't they?"

"Oh, maybe they like it. But they're not really into it. They don't think about it. Or talk about it. Or say honestly what they want or anything like that. But you? Married to a fag? It'd be murder."

"Oh, come on. I could get off with manslaughter."

"It's not him, it's you that couldn't take it."

"Oh. Well, I could always have—you know, *friends*. I mean what the hell."

"That'd make a bloody change."

"I know, and that's the trouble. I mean it may

sound funny, but sleeping around is not what I like. If I get married, I want to get really married. But the longer I stay in this country, the more I think Lawrence hit his head right on the nail about the English and their coldhearted fucking."

"You hang around with half-queer teasers, and what can you expect?"

"I thought teasers were girls."

"Nah. A teaser's a second-rate stallion the horse-breeders send in to warm up the mares for the first-rate stallions. The minute she's all worked up and ready, the poor old teaser's pulled off and the one that's worth money gets her."

She was amazed and looked it. He leaned over and kissed her on her half-open mouth. "That's how it goes, love."

"What extraordinary things you know."

He was too fast on his feet to fall for an obvious lead-on like that; just because he'd told her about the tiger didn't mean he was going to tell her everything. "Fantastic," he said flatly, "isn't it?"

"The thing is, though, its not just the half-queers, it's the straight ones too—the stiff-upper-lip, old-school-tie ones. You know, it only dawned on me recently, but Englishmen don't like women. It's not British reticence or any of that baloney at all; it's that they plain don't like them."

"No? From what I've heard they can't get enough and would shove it in a cottage cheese if they had to."

"That's it, they would. They do. And who wants to be a cottage cheese?"

"Not me."

"No, nor me either, but that's how too many of them treat women. To them, women are the enemy. Crazy things you have to humour along, like drunks or village idiots—and that you escape from every chance you get. That's what soccer games and pubs and men-only colleges and those dirty old clubs on Pall Mall are for. And even escape isn't enough; women have to be made ridiculous as well, and despicable. You know, dirty jokes. Mother-in-law jokes. Women-driver jokes. Strip shows. Bunnies. Tarts. Why have Englishmen always been so dead keen on tarts?"

"Don't look at me. It's against my policy to pay for anything I can get for free. You know that."

"Mm. But ask them why, and they'll say it's because what a man wants is a good fuck. Right? And OK, if that's what they got, fine. But they don't. What they get is a half-hour with a creature who hates them and whom they use the way they'd use a spittoon."

"You think that's by accident, Tom? All those dirty jokes? All that hostility? Oh, they marry women, sure. Who wouldn't, if it got you an unpaid sock-washing, shirt-ironing slave? But who wants to be in one of those marriages where they call each other 'dahling' and hate each other's guts and he screws her once a month with his pyjama top on? I don't claim it's an exclusively English thing, all that, but just like you're more likely to get typhoid if you live downstream from Typhoid Mary, if you marry a certain kind of Englishman you're more likely to get that kind of marriage."

"Marry me, then. Go on. Why not?"

She smiled gratefully at him, but shook her head. "Tom, be sensible. I'm a hundred years older than you. When I'm a raddled old hag you'll still be young. I'd be a drag, and you'd hate it. Sooner or later you'd hate me too, and I couldn't bear that."

The dark blue eyes went hard and searched out the lie behind the smile. "It isn't that, and you bloody know it. You won't because of what I am."

"No, honestly. It isn't that."

"It is that. Don't lie."

"I'm not lying. Believe me, I'm not lying."

For a moment he regressed, and for just about the last time she saw a hint of the old self-protective look. "Why do all liars say 'believe me'?"

"Just because all liars say it doesn't mean that all people who say it are liars."

"OK, but make me a deal. If I can change and be more—well, less dodgy and all, and if the baby's mine, or even if it's not, but something doesn't work out with—with whoever—how about then? Would you marry me then?"

"Tom, I told you. I'm too old for you. You wait, you'll meet some—"

"Oh, jesus. Right. I'll meet some nice girl my own age at the Saturday-morning kiddies' show. *Fuck that.* Will you or won't you?"

"All right. If, like you say, you change, and if it's yours I'll—well, I'll think about it. *Then* I'll think about it. Not now."

"You promise?"

"I promise."

Angela's cover story in late July pulled no punches in taking the Labour Party apart for Luddite mulishness, self-destructive infighting, incompetence while in office, and when out of office an apparent determination to do anything and everything necessary to prevent its ever getting back in again. She called the left wing "chiliastic dreamers steeped in Keir Hardie and stewed in tannic acid" who would, among other things, "let a newspaper die, or a mine close, or an entire industry cripple itself before they will give up overmanning or any of the other ancient, restrictive practices that lie at the bottom of much of Britain's economic trouble."

The right-wing Labourites were "schizoid pseudo-socialists who live affluently and pay lip service to an egalitarianism that they scrupulously avoid practising."

She even got in a dig at the MP's wife who wanted a better washing machine.

More out of automatic sympathy with the underdog than any real conviction, Jane cabled: WHEN PULITZER UPCOMES HAVE SUGGESTION WHERE UPSHOVE. NO LOVE. JANE.

She'd barely hung up the telephone when the answering cable came back: AS SOMEONE NOT WHISTLING DIXIE SAID A PARTY THAT IS CONSTANTLY SWINGING TO AND FRO ON A BROKEN GATE NEVER ACHIEVING NOT

REALLY PURSUING DESERVES AND GETS AN AWFUL FATE.
WHAT MEAN NO LOVE? SURELY OPPOSITE ABSOLUTE ROOT
OF PROBLEM WHICH MORE WAYS THAN ONE MUST BE
OBVIOUS BY NOW. MUCH LOVE. ANGELA.

10

While everything was changing, what changed most of
all was herself. She wasn't one of those women who
are unobtrusively pregnant and suddenly produce with
a modest little flourish an eight-pound baby from what
was never more than a modest little bulge. Nor was
she the kind who radiated a glowing inner serenity
from behind a Mona Lisa smile. She was the other
kind. She looked pregnant from the very beginning,
and from the sixth month on she looked so much as if
she would give birth at any moment that people got
up and moved away from her in buses. Her legs swelled,
her hair turned lank and limp, and what glow she
had was the red nose and puffy eyes that followed sudden, unpredictable, uncontrollable bouts of crying.
Pregnancy was clearly not her forte.

She also made the three classic mistakes. She ate
too much and put on too much weight. She bought
too many maternity clothes and wore them all too
early, until, with still two months to go, she was sick
to death of all of them. And she read all the books.

From breech presentations, spina bifida, umbilical

hernias, projectile vomiting, infanticide during postnatal depression, and stress situations in the preschool play group, she plowed on through sibling rivalry, autism, and the problems of puberty, and got more rigid with fear as she went. There were moments when, if it hadn't been too late to quit, she would have.

Friends were hardly any help. All they wanted to know was whose it was and was she going to get married. When she dodged the questions, it only unleashed bitter speeches and dinner-table fights about marriage as an institution and how this was her enviable chance to avoid the institution and strike a blow for Women's Lib.

The Harley Street doctor was useless. He had babies every day and was monosyllabically offhand about the whole process. She asked a lot of questions, but he had obviously no intention whatsoever of sharing hard-won and exclusively professional information about childbirth with a fool mother-to-be who was in a stew from reading books she had no business reading. Also thoroughly masculine, Franklin and Tom didn't like speculating about and flatly refused to worry about dreadful things that only might happen. Anthony only looked wild-eyed at any mention of the baby at all. There was no one she could talk to.

Even Mrs. Bush would have been better than nothing—although she had, as she put it, "buried" two of her three—had she not stubbornly refused to acknowledge that Jane was pregnant. She knew—of course she knew, it wasn't possible that she didn't—but she didn't want to know and therefore she didn't. Even when painters and carpenters came in to work on the two unused back rooms and she had to carry skis and other spare-room junk down to the back-yard shed, she kept up the pretence that she had no notion whatever what the rooms were being readied for. It was not an attitude that encouraged girlish confidences.

At Jane's office, too, no one said anything. Jim got more nervously jumpy each time she came in, and sometimes she could feel eyes following her as she passed the desks in the newsroom. But the omertà was as solid as in a suburb of Palermo.

This heavy charade of tact pulled her down. She felt more alone than she would have believed possible, and very sorry for herself. Nobody was making a fuss over her the way people did over other pregnant women. Nobody cared. Nobody at all. She felt cheated— cheated out of what, she didn't know, but cheated.

She felt especially cheated that, after having paid for five years an income tax approximately the same size as the gross national product of a small but copra-rich archipelago, she wasn't even going to get the chance to recoup some of it by having the baby free on the National Health. But that would have meant a London hospital, and a London hospital was too close for comfort. Whatever else happened, she wasn't risking the possibility of low-grade farce scenes with Tom and Anthony and Franklin colliding in swinging doors or coming face to face with each other across her bed. She would have the baby privately, in all senses of the word, in a maternity clinic the Harley Street ghoul ran near Brighton.

She would, that is, if the Harley Street ghoul still trusted her that far.

She wasn't sure he did. Even as she moulded the third amalgamated man—a Mr. Cornell, John Cornell—the doctor had looked flatly sceptical. While she padded Mr. Cornell out with details—he was an electrical engineer more or less permanently in Africa, where he was working on a dam—the doctor's eyes had stayed polite, but the lids had drooped just enough to make her think: My god, he doesn't believe me.

It had been pretty easy to persuade herself that that had been only her new paranoiac imagination at work. But then she had phoned to break an appointment, and had told his receptionist it was because she had to go and visit her husband in Nairobi. On her next visit to Harley Street, she blew her cover completely.

"Awfully warm, I expect, in Kenya this time of year," the receptionist said, and Jane looked up stupidly

155

from the old copy of *Punch*, not even sure it was her the receptionist was talking to.

"Kenya? Gosh, I wouldn't know."

The few seconds the receptionist spent in the doctor's office before Jane was ushered in had clearly been long enough for her to tell him that Mrs. Cornell was either mad, or a liar, or quite possibly both. As Jane sat down, he took a pen and a blank form and wasted no time on small talk.

"It's purely routine, of course, Mrs. Cornell, but we must have your husband's address. Simply for the record, you understand."

She understood all right and mumbled something about how he moved about a lot. It wasn't, you see, just one dam he was working on but—well, several. And mail deliveries in those hill stations, especially those hill stations on the river, could be erratic. It wasn't easy to say just where he'd be at any given—

The doctor's pen stayed mulishly steady over the blank line. "His firm's address will be sufficient, Mrs. Cornell. The head office is, I assume, in Nairobi?"

"What? Oh—yes, Nairobi."

Such crass, money-grubbing callousness on top of not being believed and nobody caring or making a fuss, was too much. So was her story.

Mr. Cornell had, she said, left her. That was why she'd had to go to Nairobi. He was living with another woman and had been for some time, and now he wanted a divorce. She didn't have his address any more; the last two letters she'd sent had come back. He had quit his job too. So it was no good trying to get hold of him through the firm.

The doctor looked as if she'd told him that stump water cured cancer.

"I see. How very unfortunate. However, we must, as I said, have this information for the—uh, record. Is there perhaps another close relation you would like to name as next-of-kin?"

He wasn't sold on Jane's sister. Maybe he'd already had experience of next-of-kins whose checkbooks were as far away as California. But with moderate good grace he settled for Mr. Wilkinson, her bank manager.

As soon as she had done it she tried to blot it out of her mind, but she couldn't blot out Mr. Wilkinson's face. Mr. Wilkinson's blameless pink face, even pinker with sleep, and with Mrs. Wilkinson's rollered head beside his on the pillow, when the 3 A.M. phone call came from the clinic saying unfortunately they hadn't been able to save the mother, but the black twins were fine and as he was down as next-of-kin, would he pick them up or should they send them?

Except for having dragged poor innocent Mr. Wilkinson in and except for the embarrassing easy tears, Jane rather enjoyed the last weeks of being pregnant. She looked with new and real interest into occupied baby carriages, and she fluctuated between feeling as strong as a gorilla and leadenly sleepy as a sloth, both of which were sensuously satisfying feelings. She even enjoyed the nest-building instinct that occasionally drove her to get out of bed at first light to make soup or clean out the broom cupboard or polish things.

It was about 4:30 one of those mornings when Anthony woke up, found her gone, and tracked her down in the kitchen, where she was maniacally scrubbing with an old toothbrush and pink silver polish at the ridged edge of a big round platter. It had been one of Tom's earliest presents to her and was black with tarnish.

"Darling, what are you doing?"

"Nothing. I couldn't sleep is all. And there were a couple of things that needed cleaning."

"Needed it now? This minute?"

"Mm. Why not?" She rinsed the platter and started to polish it dry with a clean dishtowel. "See how pretty it is when it's clean?"

He took the platter from her and admired it. "Very. Very pretty. But I still—" He had slanted it at an angle that caught the light dead on the center. "I say— how extraordinary. That's the Bessinghome crest."

157

She felt tiny jets of adrenalin hit her bloodstream, and her heart jumped. "Is it? Who are they?"

"Cousins. Filthy rich—live on Chester Square." He held the silver platter at arm's length and shook his head disbelievingly. "Strange, I wouldn't have thought they'd ever in their lives parted with a piece of silver that wasn't a coin, and only most reluctantly with as few of those as possible. I am aston—" He looked at her quizzically. "Wherever did you get it?"

Almost snatching, she took the platter from him and shoved it back into the cupboard. "Goodness, isn't it silly? I can't remember. Some junk store I guess. Would you like a Coke?" That was a mistake and brought on his look of kindly-indicate-the-way-to-the-British-consul's-office, and she quickly added, "I mean tea. Would you like some tea?"

The adrenalin must have waked the baby up; it was thrashing about wildly. If it had been Tom and not Anthony there, she would have taken his hand and, with fingers as light as a safecracker's, he would have followed every move it made—but feeling an unborn baby move, particularly one that might not be his, was not Anthony's bag.

He got up and changed the enamel mug she'd put in front of him for a proper cup and saucer, and she watched him pour the tiny drop of milk into his tea that was so little it always made her wonder why he bothered with milk at all. "That reminds me," he said, stirring it. "Mother rang. She's coming to London tomorrow and I gathered she'd like to see you—if it's convenient, of course." Spoon in mid-air he hesitated for a moment before he put it down on the saucer. "And Jane—I'm afraid she knows."

Jane stopped spreading blueberry jam over peanut butter on a thick piece of bread and pointed the knife at him. "Anthony, you didn't. You didn't tell her. God, I thought I made it clear that—"

"Darling, don't bridle so. Of course I didn't tell her. I don't, I grant you, understand why you're so adamantly determined she shouldn't know—after all, there's very little she can do about it one way or the other—but I certainly didn't tell her."

"Then how did she—"

"I haven't the faintest idea. I daresay someone simply saw us together somewhere—noticed and then couldn't wait to get the news back. That's how these things usually happen."

"God, how awful. But—well, it can't be helped, so to hell with it. But what does she want to see me for? I thought I slightly outranked Blackpool as something to be avoided."

"Darling, how often must I tell you you've got it completely wrong? That nonsense with Whyteclyffe has been totally forgotten and, in point of fact, Mother always asks after you and speaks very fondly of you."

She marvelled at his lack of guile but knew better than to try and persuade any man that his mother was a monster. "OK. If that's what she wants, it's fine by me. Are we summoned to S.W.1, or will she come here?"

"As you choose. She's dining somewhere, so it can't possibly be a lengthy ordeal."

"Well—a drink then. I can't manage much else; it's a rotten busy day."

"I'll ask her to come here, shall I? About, say, seven?"

"Yes, here. Better here than there. What would be really better is—well, neither here nor there. She won't tear her hair and gnash her teeth, will she?"

"Mother? Tear her hair? Extremely unlikely. It's not her way. I rather imagine she wants nothing more than a cosy heart-to-heart. She doesn't of course know ... the complications, and whether to mention it or not I leave entirely to you. I did gather, though, it's only you she wants to see, not me."

"Did she say so?"

"Of course not."

"Then how do you know?"

"Darling, when one knows Mother as well as I, one simply senses these things."

"Jesus. It's a great way to—as we gauche Americans say—communicate."

Anthony looked smug. "It has its advantages. No fine high drama or Comanche whoops, of course. Nonetheless there are certain small, almost imperceptible advantages."

He poured another cup of tea and added the precise three and one-half drops of milk:

"Why don't you put the milk in first, like other people?"

"What other people?"

"The other fifty million who live in these parts."

"I don't know. It's just one of those impossibly ridiculous things. One simply doesn't."

"Does one ever think one might be just plain buggy?"

He wouldn't be baited; he considered the question for a moment and, having weighed the evidence, he shook his head. "Not really. Odd, possibly. Buggy, no."

Anthony's mother was almost as embarrassing a guest as Angela and left a large sleek car parked in the narrow street smack in front of the warehouse door, just where the banana people would hate it most. Then, in shiny knee-high black boots and a black divided-skirt gaucho suit of very hard-edged chic, she burbled her way up the stairs.

"My dear child, how very kind of you to let me come. And such an *enchanting* place to live. One never knows, does one, until one opens one's eyes and *looks*, what magic lies tucked away on these curious old streets?" She caught Jane's hand in both of hers and trilled a breathless little laugh. "Poor Thomas totally lost his way! I fear we are such sticks of country cousins that the Opera is really all he can find in this fascinating neighbourhood—too ridiculous, isn't it? And such a to-do we had! Shouting questions to persons on the street! Plunging blindly down one-way streets the wrong way! It was too exciting, my dear, and so frightfully amusing, don't you agree, to be lost like simpletons in dear cosy London."

Jane looked as amused as she could and stood aside to let the Duchess go through the door. Inside, the Duchess stopped so abruptly that Jane almost walked up her heels, and then she clapped her hands together and did a pretty little pirouette.

"My dear, it is charming! Utterly charming. Such heavenly space." She flung both her hands up and sort of waggled them at the whitewashed beams. "And such amusing pictures!"

On tiptoe she spun in another half-pirouette away from the Kathe Kollwitz drawing of a ragged woman and child scrounging in a garbage pail, and gazed at one of Tom's big, bright, do-it-yourself Matisses. "Brilliant! Quite, quite brilliant."

Jane maneuvered her towards the sofa, and she shrieked, "Oh, how divine. A pussycat!"

Scat fled embarrassingly fast, and Jane said, "Can I make you a drink? I'm afraid there's not much choice, only whisky or gin, or not very good sherry."

The Duchess undid the big Georgian paste button on her jacket, fluffed out the lace ruffles of the silk blouse underneath, and catching sight of Scat's muddy paw marks on the sofa, edged away from them. "Nothing, thank you, my dear. I must, alas, face a wickedly fattening dinner and so daren't." Rooting about in her black, baby-alligator bag, she brought out a green-and-yellow woven gold case, from which she took an oval Turkish cigarette. Jane struck a match from the big kitchen box on the table, and while it burned down, the Duchess waved the cigarette about.

"My dear, these white walls are too perfect! It is the only possible colour, isn't it? And the texture of the bricks! Oh, it's all such fun, and what a clever girl you are to—"

The flame had almost reached Jane's fingers. "Oh, my dear, how kind." She took a long drag on the foul-smelling cigarette, and Jane made herself a whisky and water and sat down on the leather chair facing the sofa. The Duchess had fallen suddenly silent, and Jane tried frantically to think of something to say, something safe that didn't say anything. "It must be very beautiful at Cravenbourne this time of—"

"It *is*, my dear. It is quite, quite heavenly and you must come very soon again so you can enjoy it with us. Will you? Do say you will."

Jane nodded and smiled the lie, and there was a small awkward moment before the Duchess drew a breath through slightly flaring nostrils and dived in. "Shall I come straight to the point, my dear? I think we understand one another well enough for me to do that, don't we?" She tilted her creamy gold head and smiled confidently.

"Yes, of course," Jane said.

"Good." The spikily mascaraed china-blue eyes closed for a moment of what Jane guessed was supposed to be either gratitude or girls-together rapport, but when they opened again they were as flat and cool as a postcard fjord. "One is of course not unaware of how presumptuous it is to intrude on a situation that ordinarily would concern only Anthony and you. And for that I must ask your forgiveness. However, I wish, as I'm sure you know, only great happiness for both of you, and that being so, much as one would want to wait until together you had reached a decision ..." The eyelashes fluttered. "Perhaps you have reached a decision."

Jane didn't like the general drift of any of it, but she wasn't going to be dog-in-the-manger about the not quite asked question. "No, we've made no decision yet."

"In that case, my dear, I shall pay you the very great compliment of being utterly direct and straightforward and lay my cards on the table." She paused, and the nostrils flared slightly again. "I have no way of knowing, of course, what you have told Anthony or what you have not told Anthony, for naturally I have not

162

asked. However, several rather distressing things have come to my notice from—from another source, and much as one dislikes having to mention them, I fear I must tell you that I know perhaps more than you would wish me to know."

The expert-interrogator pause worked, and Jane heard herself saying, "Do you? About what?" For a ridiculous moment she thought the Duchess would answer, "Ve ask der questions." But Her Grace had a different movie cliché in mind.

"You must not think, my dear, that it has escaped my notice that manners have changed or that I am unaware that situations once mal vue are now only too commonplace. I accept this. And all things being equal, I would not dream of interfering with Anthony's private affairs. Unfortunately, in this particular situation, I feel . . ."

She paused again, but this time Jane saw the trap and waited.

". . . I feel I have no choice. You see, I know that Anthony is by no means your only—what shall I say?—your only friend. I understand there are two other gentlemen, at least two others, of whom one is American and, I believe, black." She did a fastidious eyes-shut-double-eyebrow-raise that was so like Anthony's must-you-swear? look that it almost made Jane smile.

"As well as the black gentleman there is also, it appears, a much younger man who—unless my information is inaccurate, which I think is unlikely—follows a not altogether law-abiding occupation and is, moreover, not unknown to the authorities at Scotland Yard as well as to those in Glasgow, which is, or was, his home."

It was the way she said Glasgow. The way her prissy-mouthed ruling-class accent made it sound like a dirty word. Jane tried to fight down the anger, but she couldn't. No. No sandpaper doll was going to sit there and get away with snotty sneers at Tom.

"Who told you all this?"

163

"Surely, my dear, that is unimportant. What I feel we must—"

"You're wrong. It's very important, and you're going to tell me. Right here and now you're going to tell me, if I have to pull it out of you with tweezers."

The Duchess pushed one eyebrow up into a mean inverted V and stood up. "I do not take that kind of order from anyone, my dear," she said softly. "Nor, frankly, do I consider you to be in a position to issue any order whatsoever. It was perhaps a mistake for me to have come here, and if so it is not something that need be pro—"

"Look. Just shut up a minute. And stand up or sit down or chin yourself on a red-hot poker, it's all the same to me. But I assure you—I lay it on the line with a double-your-money-back guarantee that unless you tell me, and tell me now, where and why you have dug this stuff up, I will marry Anthony tomorrow—and I mean tomorrow. He knows as much as you do. In fact he knows more than you do. But he will marry me, if I want him to. I wouldn't want you to be in any doubt about that."

The Duchess put on a civilized half-smile that didn't match the cold blue eyes and sat down. "Very well, if you insist, I shall tell you. I cannot imagine what difference it can possibly make, and I would of course much prefer to shield you from an unnecessary unpleasantness, but—"

"Never mind all that. Just tell me."

"As you wish. I have been given this information by an extremely respectable and, I believe, reliable investigator who—"

Jane nodded and, like Tom, half bit and half rolled her lower lip. "Given? You've hired some crummy private eye and paid for it. Isn't that more like it?"

"If you choose to put it quite so unattractively, there is very little one can—"

"Oh, I choose, lady, I choose. But why?"

"Surely it's obvious. We know—or rather, we knew—very little about you and it was painfully clear

164

that Anthony was becoming more and more infatuated. That, to be sure, perhaps might not have lasted."
She smiled openly nastily this time. "But with word of
this somewhat unfortunate pregnancy, we felt it would
be as well to find out precisely what he was—if I may
put it bluntly—letting himself in for. We had no idea,
of course, there would be so much. We very much
hoped, in all truth, that there would be nothing. But
there it is, one—"

"Who's we?"

"Hugo and I, of course."

"Whose idea was it?"

"Really, my dear, this—this bullying is tiresome.
Nonetheless I am quite prepared to acknowledge that
the idea was initially mine. Hugo and I discussed it
quite frankly and openly and agreed it was undoubtedly a prudent course to take, and that no one with
nothing to hide could possibly—"

"So Hugo agreed, did he? Fancy that. But of course
the poor bugger has always agreed, hasn't he? And so
now what are you—you and Hugo, that is—agreeing to
do about it?"

"Do, my dear? Why—nothing. I think we rather
wondered what you were going to do."

"Me? Well, to tell you the honest-to-god truth, I
don't really rightly know what I'm going to do. Cross
my fingers and wait is what I had in mind."

"Ah, yes. Yes, I see. The black gentleman does perhaps rather complicate it for you."

Sipping her whisky, Jane stared at the Duchess over
the rim of the glass until she was absolutely certain the
picture had sunk in of Hugo dying childless and Anthony having legally adopted a black baby who could
then become the next Duke of Wiltshire.

"You mustn't, you know," Jane said quietly, "make
the mistake of thinking I'm too stupid or have lived
here too short a time to know when you fancy-talking
bastards are being insulting, but the black gentleman,
as you call him, is something I doubt you'd understand. He is, however, about the nicest and most civi-

lized man I know—and you can shove that in between the strawberry leaves on your coronet or wherever you've got the most room for it, because it happens to be true. What is also true is that every time I draw breath I hope and pray the baby is his. If it *is*, I'll marry him and we'll all go home. That's what I want, and that's all I want. I don't want a lousy title. I don't want a piece of that big compost heap you've got, or any part of the gangrene you're all up to your chins in. I've seen it. And, just like the Bay of Naples, it looks great but it stinks."

The Duchess clicked her bag shut and stood up, a new and very thin nasty-nice smile on her face. "In that case, my dear, do believe me when I say that our hopes and prayers are joined with yours."

"I believe you. Don't think I don't. But what else has your sleazy creep told you about Tom?"

"Tom? Oh, of course, the very young man."

"His name, for instance. Did they tell you his name?"

"His name? It may have been mentioned—I really can't remember. But what a curious question. Surely you know his name."

Jane had had enough. Enough of the trilling little voice, enough of the tiny square-toed boots, and enough of the cold, cruel little mind underneath the neat blond chignon. "Never mind. Forget it."

The Duchess did up the glittery button and sighed. "Ah, if only one could."

Jane crossed the room and held the door open for her. There was no effervescent chat now about the amusing pictures or the texture of bricks. Her Grace didn't, as a matter of fact, even say good-bye.

11

The Duchess could have had a phone in the car, or else that ESP she and Anthony used really worked, because when he came in, not long after she'd gone, he seemed to know the cosy meeting had gone badly. Maybe he'd just figured the odds.

Jane wasn't exactly drunk, but she'd had a nerve-steadying whisky or two and wasn't exactly sober either. Anthony had been to see the Acapulco Gold man and pulled out of his pocket a block of hash and some American grass in polythene bags. "Thought we might have a little party," he said, "to celebrate."

Sitting on the floor with her elbow on the slate-topped table and her chin cupped in the palm of her hand, she said, "Celebrate like what?"

He smiled and shrugged his shoulders and set out the pot-ritual equipment. Liquorice cigarette papers. A couple of saucers. A knife. Filters. While he charred a corner of the hash over his lighter, Jane, still leaning on her elbow, carefully sifted through the grass, picking out the round brown seeds. They wouldn't grow; they never did. Not even sessions under the sunlamp could make them grow properly. But she always planted them anyhow, and hoped.

Anthony rolled an enormous hash joint for himself and a smaller, thinner one of grass for her and said, "How was it, Carruthers? Rough?"

"Not so bad, sir. A bit of flak at Bremen, and Jerry very active over the channel. But nothing extraordinary. A few exhilarating moments, that's all."

"Your head, Carruthers, it's gone. Had you noticed?"

"Sorry about that, sir. Happened over Ramsgate."

"Ramsgate, eh? Haven't been there in years. Used to be quite jolly, Ramsgate. Donkey rides on the beach, that sort of thing. Still—never used it much anyway, did you?"

"Never used what, sir?"

"Your head, Carruthers. Your head."

"Oh. No, sir. Hardly at all, sir. Very clean head. Top gear like new, sir."

"But your arm, Carruthers. That's gone too."

"Awkward, that, sir. Reached out to touch the stars as you said to, sir. Next one knew, the old arm had bought it."

"Yes—well, can't be helped. May mean grounding, though. Only until the stump heals, of course."

"Grounding, sir? Oh I say, sir, not that. Please not that. Only a *left* arm, sir. Usually kept it tied behind me, actually. Couldn't find the string tonight, that's all. Careless, that, I know."

"Now look here, Carruthers—"

"Can't, sir. No head. Remember, sir?"

"Not funny, Carruthers. Switch on your radar."

"Can't, sir. Only the one arm now, sir. The one I'm saluting with, sir."

"Your foot, you clot. Use your foot. *Improvise.* Britain's secret weapon, the ability to improvise."

"No foot, sir. Had them both in my mouth when I lost my head."

"Mmm. Difficult, that, Carruthers."

"Not really, sir. Double-jointed knees. Runs in the family, sir."

"Yes. Quite. Seen your sister lately, Carruthers? Jolly good sort, your sister."

"Not lately, sir. Saw your mother, though."

"Ah. Not quite the same thing, that. Not the same all-pervading atmosphere of fun and fiesta."

She took a long drag, and the end of the joint burned bright red and made little popping noises. "You can say that again."

"Was it awful?"

"Awful? Whatever gave you that idea? Like you said, all she wanted was to be cosy."

"Why so down, then?"

"Well, her idea of cosy is a little what you might without exaggerating call strange."

"Such as?"

"Such as she's had a cosy little private detective on me for god knows how long."

Making another joint, he was just about to lick the edges of the cigarette paper. "She's what?" He leaned forward and stared into her eyes. "Are you sure?"

"Well, she said so and she didn't smile when she said it."

His face barely changed, but his fingers shook as he finished making the joint and lit it. He smoked it quickly, and it burned so hot he had to keep switching it from one hand to the other. When he finally spoke he sounded completely defeated.

"Jane, I cannot tell you how sorry I am. She— No, it's inexcusable. It's insane. She is a—"

Whatever it was he couldn't say it. Pitying him, she switched back to Carruthers. "Right, sir. She certainly is, sir. I say, sir, you do have a way with words, sir. A real gift is what I'd say it is. Not many people have that gift, sir."

He managed a small one-sided smile, but he wouldn't play. "What else did she say?"

"Not much. Stuff about it being a prudent course because of your being infatuated with me being—you know, pregnant and nobody knowing who my grandfather was and all that."

"Good god."

"Oh come on, it wasn't that bad. So she's a nut. So what does it matter she's a nut? What real harm can she do?"

He reached for her hand and with the exaggeratedly intense concentration of the slightly stoned he opened her fingers one by one and looked at the little round seeds. "They never grow, do they? I wonder why."

"You limeys maybe should have asked for the Tropic of Cancer instead of the Gulf Stream."

"Sun."

"Yes, dad?"

"A curious thing, the sun. Did you know? There used to be a tropical garden at Cravenbourne."

"A tropical garden? Down there in Nanook of the North country?"

"It's all overgrown and gone to jungle now, but when I was small there was an old gardener who tended it, and it seemed to me the most astonishing place on earth. Bananas grew there. One couldn't eat them, of course, but they grew. Orchids—tiny little greeny-bronze orchids not much bigger than honeysuckle. And fuchsia; even in January, fuchsia. There were palm trees. And pineapples and frangipani. Bougainvillea, too. And bamboo. Great forests of bamboo—or what seemed like great forests then; really only a couple of smallish clumps, in fact. Even papyrus. What a curious thing memory is—I'd forgotten it all, really, but now I can remember every detail, even the gardener's name. Burgess. Yes, that was it. Burgess. He could have made these grow." He closed her fingers around the marijuana seeds and smiled at her.

It was such a touching, pot-happy smile that she put the seeds on the table and knelt beside him on the sofa, her arms around his neck and her forehead on his shoulder. "Why couldn't you?"

He stroked her hair slowly and turned his head so his mouth was close to her ear. "Why couldn't I what?"

"Eat them."

"What, the bananas?"

"Mm."

"Don't know. Couldn't eat the pineapples, either. Or the papy—what're those things, those other things?"

"Nobody eats papyrus. Not even Egyptians."

"Not papyrus. Yellow things."

"Canaries?"

He unbuttoned her dressing gown as far down as the top of the bulge and pushed it back off her shoulders. "Not canaries. Fruit." Sliding his fingers under the bra strap on her shoulder, he eased it down her arm. "It's made a mark." He rubbed the strap mark with his thumb.

"Lemons?"

With a finger he traced the network of blue veins on her chest and breasts down to the dark brown circle around her nipples. "Extraordinary, the female body."

He turned to pull her closer, but the bulge was too big. "Carruthers, I don't like to have to say this, but you're putting on weight. A little exercise is what you want."

"Right, sir. How about a game of squash?"

As she stood up he let his hands move down from her breasts to the great mound of stomach. "Are you sure it's not for another month?"

"Positive. It's what the man said."

"What man?"

"Don't be nasty."

"Papayas," he said and stood up. "That's what they were, papayas."

Pot may be bad for the skin and for conversation, but sexually it has it uses. It can also loosen the mental logjam in people who ordinarily shy away from revealing anything.

In the safe dark, in flashbacks and flashbacks within flashbacks, Anthony talked more—and more openly—about himself than he ever had before.

It wasn't a pathetic story of an isolated and lonely

171

child, because he hadn't been aware of being either. It wasn't a list of screaming rows, anxieties, and traumas because that hadn't been the way they had lived. It began as roses, roses all the way and even when it turned into a murder story it was such a quiet, gradual, and civilized murder that even now he seemed only half aware that it had been he that was murdered.

In the background was all the paraphernalia of richness. Shelves of books and toys. Donkeys and ponies. Swings. Sandboxes. Birthday parties. Christmas puddings with sixpences in them—and the Christmas tree in the nursery almost as big as the grownups' tree downstairs.

Cousins came to stay. There were picnics. Hamsters and dogs; no special dog, but many dogs. Tea by the nursery fire. Games of dominoes with Nanny. And, as if they were scenery painted on the farthest-back backdrop of a very deep stage, there were a hazy, almost ectoplasmic father and the incredibly beautiful, gay, laughing young mother. Hugo played only a walk-on part as the Genghis Khan of the holidays because by the time Anthony was two, Hugo was seven and already away at school.

The Duke and Duchess's timetable had been as inexorable and as unchangeable as the wondrous pattern of the seasons in a Walt Disney nature film. In the spring it was London, with weekends at Cravenbourne. In early September they went for a month to the South of France. Back from France, they took a house party to Scotland for the grouse and partridge. From November on it was foxes.

Even when they were at Cravenbourne, Anthony had seen very little of his father, but every afternoon Nanny brushed his hair, dressed him in a silk shirt that buttoned inside the waistband of short velvet trousers, and took him by the hand for the long walk downstairs to spend his half-hour with his mother. Sometimes he even stayed longer, to watch her have tea. And once, when Nanny was ill and there was no nurserymaid to pinch-hit for her, he had spent the whole day with his mother. Not mealtimes, of course, those he'd had in the kitchen, but other than that, the whole day. She had even given him his bath and put him to bed.

From Nanny he had learned the Rules. It was better to lie than be impolite, and untidiness was bad. All toys had to be tidied away at bedtime, even if the fort wasn't quite built or the battle the soldiers were all in place for hadn't yet started.

Disobedience was bad too. If one cried at having to destroy what it had taken so long to build, one's teddy was taken away and put on a high shelf, where one could see it from bed but was forbidden to try and get it back. *Boys didn't cry.* That was almost the most important Rule of all.

Boys didn't tattle either. One was not allowed to tell the truth when Hugo stole one's pocket money or broke one's toys. Yet, curiously, one was always expected to own up and tell the truth when one had done wrong oneself; telling on oneself wasn't tattling. The built-in defect in the system was obvious, but it never seemed to occur to the Rule-makers, neither Nanny nor headmasters, that those most likely to do wrong were also the least likely ever to own up. It was a cruel one-way justice in which the innocent and honest suffered and the guilty almost always got off.

All pleasures were not only booby-trapped with Rules but also surrounded by a minefield of penalties. If you played with yourself, it would, Nanny said, come off in your hand and your brain would go soft and you'd be blind. If the thank-you note for a present had not been written by a certain, not always specified, date, the present vanished and never reappeared. And food was the biggest minefield of all.

If you had been allowed to hold the long fork and toast your own crumpet over the nursery fire and the crumpet fell in, you did not get another.

If Mummy had curvy almond-paved tuiles for tea or the shiny chocolate cake with "Sacher" written in icing on the top, you had to sit quietly and watch her eat it. To ask for some was Rude; the one time he had asked, poor Mummy had been dreadfully shocked. "Darling, no. This is Mummy's tea. You'll be having yours in the nursery presently." Which was perfectly true—except of course there wouldn't be *tuiles* or *Sachertorten* but only yellow cake with no icing and plain biscuits.

If you had been allowed the treat of lunching with your parents, it was absolutely against the Rules to show either pleasure or displeasure at what you were given. If you hated it, you couldn't say so, and you had to eat it all. If you liked it and said, "Hurrah, ice cream!" the punishment was you got none and had to sit without fidgeting while the others ate theirs. If you fidgeted, you were sent upstairs to Nanny, who would then tell you what a naughty, ungrateful boy you were.

If you had a peach you had to peel and quarter it with a knife and fork and eat it slowly and tidily, bite-size piece by bite-size piece, with the fork. Bowls were not allowed; all puddings, even ice cream and fruit salad, had to be eaten from flat plates with a spoon and fork.

Away from Cravenbourne, food was even more perilous ground. When he was ten and at a boarding school where the meals were both bad and skimpy, he had sometimes walked to the village to buy tuppence worth of greasy potato chips. Such voluptuous living was not allowed, and sooner or later he was, as he knew he would be, caught and caned for it. It wasn't by a long shot the first time he had been caned, because it was the kind of school where you were caned for anything, but what really hurt was he'd been caught before he was even halfway through the newspaper cone of chips. Ever since, he said, whenever he ate chips, or even passed a fish-and-chips shop and smelled them, his mind automatically would dip back through the almost twenty-five years and he could see them—the beautiful, golden, crisp chips all lying every whichway in the gutter where the prefect had thrown them.

He told it with no self-pity and no resentment—none that showed, anyhow, and he called the Rules discipline. Nothing, he said, could run smoothly without discipline. If it now sounded too starchy—well, it hadn't seemed so at the time and was simply the way things were. There were the Rules. There were the Penalties. And there had been no appeal allowed against either. If anything had been wrong about his childhood, it must have been—he said this several times—his own fault.

He was seven when, in his new grey flannel uniform and the cap that was too big for him, he had waited alone in Cravenbourne's big domed entry hall for his mother to come and take him to boarding school. When she had left him that day in the cold Victorian dormitory that was to be his home for the next five years, he had wanted to cry—but boys didn't.

He was nine when on Sports Day he missed being in the one race he had a chance of winning, because when the run-off heats were held he was still at the gate watching for his mother's car. It was strange, he said, but he'd remembered that day only recently when she'd been late for a concert he had promised to take her to and had said, "But darling, when one knows it's going to be tedious and one doesn't want to go, one can at least be late, can't one?"

He was ten and home for a holiday when he had knocked at her bedroom door, walked in, and found her in bed with a man. He hadn't any idea who the man was or what they were doing in bed in the afternoon, or even why his coming in had made her so angry. But he had never forgotten the terrible voice, quite unrecognizable as his mother's, that told him to get out and stay out.

He hadn't realized how central a figure Nanny was in his life or how much he loved her until, when he was thirteen and at Eton, she died. She was very old, of course, and had long since been pensioned off to a cottage on the estate, but that she could die had simply not occurred to him. He hadn't cried, because boys

175

didn't, and he didn't in fact even tell anyone it had happened for fear of being called soppy and babyish— to be thirteen and still attached to your nanny wasn't done. And so he had even missed her funeral. Nanny had been taken back to her village in Dorset to be buried, and though he'd been meaning, he said, ever since to go sometime and put a bunch of flowers on her grave, he never had.

That same year at Eton he had learned about the other kind of love when he was taken up by one of the school gods, Forbes-Osgood-Hanbury, who was seventeen, captain of everything, and already in Pop, the one club that really matters at Eton.

Almost overnight Anthony's life changed. He had been a little nobody, but as Forbes-Osgood-Hanbury's friend he was suddenly somebody. Little boys like himself looked on him with new awe. Bigger boys left him alone. For a whole term he wasn't beaten once, no matter what he did, and he had never been so happy in his life. It was like being wrapped in your own private sunshine.

Then his sun had gone down on him. Literally. And that—well, that wasn't serious because he had learned by then that Nanny had been wrong and that it didn't fall off in your hand and you didn't go blind. He still felt guilty, of course. But what's a little guilt when you're in love?

What Anthony hadn't been prepared for was buggery. He knew it existed; even at prep school it had existed, or so other boys said. But buggery wasn't love; it was something shepherds did to sheep, or tramps and gypsies did to boys when they caught them. It was a violent, shameful, dirty thing that you could go to jail for, and what possible place could such a thing have in what he felt for Forbes-Osgood-Hanbury or in what Forbes-Osgood-Hanbury felt for him?

The first time he had tried, Anthony fought him off and got back to his own room before the tears came. That boys *didn't*, didn't matter that time. When true love is trampled on, even boys can cry.

And so his life changed again. Forbes-Osgood-Hanbury no longer spoke to him. Worse, he simultaneously transferred the private sunshine to a little boy named Asherton and launched a vendetta against Anthony. That very first week Anthony was railroaded on some phony charge and beaten so viciously by Forbes-Osgood-Hanbury that the cane broke. After three weeks of it, he ran away.

He spent the night in the waiting room at Charing Cross Station and the next day, hungry and without a penny left, he hitchhiked home. His mother was appalled, but he couldn't tell her what had happened; that would have been tattling, and anyway it wasn't done to mention sordid things like sex to one's mother. Sent straight back to school, he was beaten again for having run away. But this time by the headmaster and with the full, solemn rigmarole that goes with an important Eton beating.

The next night, with the cuts on his bottom still raw, Forbes-Osgood-Hanbury and another older boy had held him head down in a toilet with his face almost in the water, and both had buggered him.

That had been Anthony's introduction to sex. He knew nothing about girls. He had never seen a live female naked, not even a little girl. He had lived segregated at boys' schools since he was seven, and all he knew of heterosexual sex was from looking up words like "intercourse" in the dictionary. It had sounded a pale enough thing there, but he knew it wasn't—he had seen what went on in the fields when the bulls and stallions were let loose, and he had heard the screams of mating cats and even more terrible noise that sows make. Whatever was happening to them could not be pleasant or normal, and the dictionary must have got it wrong. There were, too, terrible diseases that men caught from women and that could start with a tiny pimple you might not even notice. And there was a servant girl that one of the footmen had told him about who had hanged herself because she was pregnant. That had made no sense at all.

177

Whenever his mother's friends were pregnant, she always said, "Darling, how exciting. What marvelous news!" Totally bewildered, he had decided that, whatever this sexual love was, it was not for him.

Pain, punishment, and humiliation became synonomous with sex in his mind. When he was beaten at school or when he watched other boys being beaten, his whole body would go rigid with fear and anticipation and guilt and sexual excitement, and it had all plaited together so strongly in his mind that it had been years before he could separate them. Even now—well, even now there were moments.

"Extraordinary, isn't it? I hated what he had done to me. And yet I still wanted to be with him, I wanted it to be me and not Asherton who was with him and pleasing him and loving him. I even wanted him to call me a filthy little beast and to hurt me." He stopped talking for a moment, and the conflict inside him was so great it made him clench his fist. "In a way," he said quietly, "sometimes I still do."

Jane thought of the night she'd heard Charles in his room at Cravenbourne. "And what do you do about it, these sometimes?"

He smiled his slow one-sided smile and kissed her shoulder. "Very little." The kiss turned to a bite. "Rape you is what I do."

"But Anthony, it isn't important, is it? I mean, surely adolescent homosexuality is as common and normal as—well, as anything? It doesn't mean much, does it? What I really mean is, you don't still want that in preference to this, do you?"

He got out of bed and put on the black-and-white silk paisley dressing gown that she'd bought for all of them and that was too short on Franklin, too loose on Tom, and too big all over on Anthony. "Is there anything to drink?"

"Coke. Or grapefruit juice."

He came back with two glasses and the can of juice. "I don't know. Sometimes I want him, figuratively speaking, very much. But I don't do anything ridicu-

178

lous like falling in love with stable boys or picking up guardsmen in the park, if that's what you mean. If I have to, I can get along without any of it. Sex isn't enormously important to me."

"Gosh. Thanks."

"No, don't. Don't make fun. You're important to me. I'm happy with you, and you're the only woman I've ever really loved. You're not the only woman I've ever been to bed with, but you're the only one I've ever felt sure of—No, saying that won't make me popular either, will it? The only one I've felt sure *with* is what I meant."

"But Anthony . . ."

He put down his glass and took off the dressing gown. "Mm?"

"Well, you know all that old stuff about men who make love to their fat, dreary wives and pretend it's some glamorous movie star. Do you ever . . ."

He got into bed and put out the light on his table. "Pretend you're a boy?"

"Something like that."

"No. No, honestly, I don't. I have done—not with you, but before. Once—this was a long time ago, mind you I even bought a bottle of some kind of brown stuff that was supposed to make everything all right."

"And did it?"

"Don't be ridiculous, of course not. All those things keep up is your hope. But it was called something revolting like 'Stiffacock' and it tasted so nasty that when it was gone I never bought any more."

She laughed. "Darling, you are silly. You never needed that. It's crazy to think you ever even thought you needed that."

"Are you sure? One never knows what ghastly comparisons may be gliding silently through the twisted channels of the female mind."

"Of course I'm sure. My god, men. Always standing around in locker rooms pretending not to look but eyeing each other's the whole time and wondering if theirs is OK. Is it as long as his? As big around as *his?*

179

Jesus, they're all bigger than mine, and she must have been faking it all along. She'd much rather have him. Or him. Or maybe an electric vibrator and two guys and a side order of Shetland pony." She kissed him slowly. "Gosh, don't men know that sex is all between the ears? Don't they know that it's what's in her head about a man that turns a woman on?"

"They come to know it. It takes a bit of time."

"But it's all so crazy. I mean, men don't go around staring at other men's tongues and hands, do they? And yet all men must know that tongues and hands are just as important. More, really. Don't they take that into account? That knowing what to do and knowing lots of ways to do it is what matters?"

"Yes, sooner or later they find these things out— usually later. That's what is so ill-arranged, isn't it? When a man's at his peak sexually he's too young and inexpert to know what to do with it. By the time he learns, he's already so far downhill, sexually speaking, that—"

The baby gave such a hard kick that it made Jane jump, and Anthony went very tense. "What is it?"

"Nothing. Poor little thing's pretty cramped in there, I guess, and it wants out."

For the first time he gave in and felt it. He put on the light, uncovered her, and felt it with both hands. He even put his ear to her stomach. "Good god. No— lie still. I think I can hear its heart."

Lying back, she shut her eyes, and he stayed so quiet for a long time, stretched out between her legs with his head on her stomach and his hands on her shoulders, that she was sure he'd gone to sleep.

She tried to pull a blanket over him without waking him, but his fingers dug into her shoulder hard and he lifted his head. "Jane, marry me. Please marry me."

Tears were running down his face, and she felt them cold and wet on her neck when he moved up and lay beside her. "You were right; it doesn't matter whose it is. All I know is I don't want to lose you." She turned towards him and put her arm around him and licked the tears away, the way Franklin had done for her. With his hand on her cheek he pushed her face back gently and looked at her. "Please say you will. I've never wanted to be married before—but now I do. I want it more than I can possibly tell you."

"Don't, darling, please don't."

"Don't? But I want to marry you. Don't you understand? I love you and I want to marry you."

"I know. But I can't."

"Don't be silly, my darling. Of course you can. That mischief of Mother's is—"

"It isn't that."

"What is it, then?"

"Anthony, I lied to you. I lied about the whole thing. There isn't just one other man—there's two. And one of them is—"

"Darling, I told you, it doesn't matter. You don't have to tell me anyth—"

"But I do. You see, the baby is—"

"Is what, darling? Good Lord, it's not even born yet. How do you know what it is?"

"That's it. I don't. And it may be black."

"Black? What do you mean, black?"

"Darling, I'm sorry. I truly am." She watched the disbelief on his face turn to unvarnished horror. "I love you dearly, Anthony, but I—"

"Sorry? You're sorry? God damn it, but there are things that 'sorry' doesn't quite cover, you know." He flung back the covers and stood up. Trembling with anger, he started to speak but couldn't, and when she reached out to him he hit her hand away.

He put on the dressing gown and walked as far away from her as he could get. "Is this what my mother found out?"

"Yes."

"I see. Otherwise you wouldn't have told me. Is that it?"

"I didn't know what to do, Anthony. I just—I mean, until it happened, I didn't know how much in love with him I was. Now I do know." She stretched out

181

her hand toward him again. "Please don't be angry. It just is like it is. I didn't choose to be in love with him, it just happened. And I—"

"Don't be angry? What the hell do you expect me to be? Pleased? Delighted?"

"I'd hoped you'd—"

"You hoped I'd what?"

"Understand?"

"Understand what? Understand the pretty speeches about sex being between the ears when all the time you've been having it off with some greasy, shiny buck nigger with a cock as big as a—"

He caught himself, but too late. She had had no idea the fear was so near the surface or that the prejudice was so bitter and deep. For a long moment they stared at each other while the words he'd said filled the space between them.

"OK. That's enough. You can go now."

"Thank you for your permission." He said it ludicrously pompously for someone who was stark naked and feeling around on the floor for his socks. "That is precisely what I intend to do."

She listened for the slam of the front door and the vroom-vroom of the Aston Martin's engine. When the noise dwindled away she turned to put out the light and saw on the table under the lamp his watch with no numbers and the lapis-lazuli dial.

Now what, she wondered, would Dr. Freud make of that? Watch my dust? Or, dust my watch because I'll be back?

12

When the phone rang early the next morning she picked it up and said, "No, Anthony, I haven't hocked it. Not yet."

There was a pause, and a cold puzzled voice said, "Jane?"

"Oh. Oh gosh, it's you. I wasn't ex—"

"Clearly. I'm sorry to call so early, but I had to get you before you went out to say I won't be able to get down tonight."

"Oh, Franklin, why not? What's happened?"

"Have to dine with my leader. You know, High Table and the whole white-tie bit. Seems it's one of their little gestures towards departing visitors. They are, as I've told you, a real chummy bunch."

"White tie? What are they, crazy? Why not be chummy right back and not go?"

"That's what I figured on doing, but there've been some pretty leaden hints dropped lately that my week-end disappearing act hasn't gone—as they say—unnoticed. 'Not seen a great deal of you this term, Rodgers old chap. It is Rodgers, isn't it? Yes, thought so.' But the bastard has made a point of asking some Professor of Jurisprudence too, so I've really got to."

"Oh. Well, if that's it, that's it. But when will you come? I miss you."

"Tomorrow morning. If they don't zonk me with too much panther-piss port I'll catch the nine-fifteen. Are you OK?"

"Me? Sure. I'm fine. Nothing else is, though, is it?"

"Why? Like what?"

"I don't know—everything. I can barely bloody move, for one thing. No, honestly, we've all seen pregnant women before, but this is ridiculous."

"How long is there left?"

"God, twenty-nine days or something. And, Franklin?"

"What?"

"I'm scared."

"Come on, baby, don't be like that. There's nothing to be scared of, *nothing*."

"It's all right for you. It's not you that has to waddle. It's not you that has to—oh, hell, what's the use of even saying it?"

"It's very far from all right for me, Jane, but jesus christ let's not—what I mean is we've come this far without fighting, so let's not begin now. OK?" She didn't answer. "Hey," he said. "You still there?"

"No, I'm not. *I* thought it would be nice to have a little fight."

"Later."

"Tomorrow?"

"Tomorrow."

"OK. Bye."

"And Jane?"

"What?"

"Nothing. Just—you know, keep your chin up."

Keep your chin up. *Jesus christ.*
Keep smiling. Keep right on to the end of the road. Keep your pecker up. Keep your powder dry. Keep your nose clean. Keep a corner in your heart for the

184

Lord. Keep on your feet. Keep your balance. Keep well. Keep right. Keep left. Keep your hair on. Keep your pants on. Keep your shirt on. Keep your promise. Keep it under your hat. Keep house. Keep your wits about you. Keepsake. Keep time. Keep going. Keep a disorderly house. It'll keep. Keep a secret. Keep trying. Keep a dog. Keep this in a safe place. Keep an open mind. Keep the change. KEEP OFF THE GRASS.

God, I'm cracking up, going off my head. Angela was right, that stuff rots your mind.

She took a bath, washed her hair, cleared away all the evidence of pot before Mrs. Bush arrived, fed Scat, finished her piece, and went to the office. It was a mean, cold, rainy day, and while the bus jerked along Fleet Street in second-gear spasms, an inspector got on to check tickets. She couldn't find hers, and he waited stolidly while she went through every pocket and every corner in her bag. "Sorry, it's not anywhere. I don't know what I did with it."

"You did have one, miss?"

"Yes, certainly. But I'll pay again if you like."

He called the conductor, and everyone stared at her with ox faces while she went through her bag again and the terrified little Pakistani conductor scrabbled around under the seat, picking up old tickets and Mars Bars wrappers. "I know have ticket," he kept saying. "I give. At Strand, I give."

"Look," she said to the inspector, "there's no need for all this fuss. I'll pay again. Here." Her eyes blurry with tears, she tried to give a coin to the conductor.

The inspector snapped an elastic around his notebook as wearily as if he'd been questioning Pepe le Moko for twelve hours and still couldn't pin a thing on him. "It won't be necessary, miss. Not *this* time."

It wasn't until she looked at the calendar on her desk that she remembered today was the first of November and that she hadn't said, "Rabbits, rabbits" when she'd waked up. That explained everything. Calling Franklin Anthony. The bus ticket. The scene with Anthony. And now the whole of November was doomed. Nothing good could happen, not even by accident. Of all months, what a one to goof on.

She went along to Prairie Jim's office, and while he read her piece she sat quietly and thought about nothing. It wasn't any fun torturing him with her embarrassing condition any more. Anyhow, she'd been pregnant so long he'd got used to it.

"Fabulous." He swung round in the swivel chair to face her. "Lots of good wry bite. I like it. That's great about Westerns having degenerated into amorality plays." He gave her an admiring wink and clucked his tongue. "I wish I'd said that."

"You will, Jim. You will."

The Oscar Wilde was lost on him, and he looked uneasy. "But Jane . . ."

Godalmighty, there couldn't be a "but." It was his type piece. It was hand-tailored facile gibberish that she'd written specially for his *Reader's Digest*, Medicine Hat mind. There wasn't a "but" in it.

"Well—uh—naturally I hate having to bring this up, and to be absolutely frank, Mike and I had kind of agreed to wait until you—uh—brought it up yourself. But without being indiscreet and with no notion of prying—that goes without saying, of course—we—uh— —nonetheless thought it wouldn't be entirely out of line to—uh—"

She put him out of his misery. "Find out when this baby's due. Yes?"

"Uh—yes."

"Jim, I do apologize, I really do. I should have told you ages ago but—well, I kept putting it off and that was stupid."

"My dear Jane." He made an expansive two-handed wave. "Don't think for a moment that we care—that is to say don't think it *matters* in the least." He seemed to realize he wasn't quite getting across what he meant and quit trying. Again she put him out of his misery.

"I know what you mean, Jim, and—well, anyhow, according to the doctor it should be the end of this month. What I'd like to do, if it's OK by you and

Mike, is to work for the next two weeks and then take December off. Do you think that would . . ."

He reached for his calendar and carefully selected a thick black pencil from a chromium mug full of absolutely identical thick black pencils. "Let's see. A month. That brings us past Christmas and into the New Year."

"Is that OK?"

"Oh, absolutely. Certainly. No trouble at all; we can easily get Philip Worth to—uh—that is, you will be coming back, won't you? You aren't deserting us permanently?"

There was so much naked hope in his voice that she smiled. "Not yet. I may be soon, but don't worry, I'll give you lots of notice when I do. Not like this time."

"Great." He fixed his smarmiest smile on. "Not great to lose you, of course, but great that—uh—well, it goes without saying, but we certainly hope everything comes out all right. I mean, that it turns out the way you want it."

Back in her office she found a note saying that Anthony had telephoned twice and would she call him. Jane scribbled "Tell him to drop dead" across the bottom of the scrap of paper and left it on Janet's desk. Then she shoved the week's letters into the drawer on top of all the other letters and left.

In the lovely suspended-time, mindless limbo of a long bus ride she went clear across London to Knightsbridge and, going by a list she'd got out of one of the books, dived into an orgy of baby-clothes buying. Then, buoyed up by such purposeful efficiency, she walked around the corner towards Sloane Street and into a domestic-employment agency that one of Anthony's friends had once said was very good.

Bravely she walked up to the tiny white desk where the woman with blue-rinsed and lacquered shredded-wheat hair was writing.

"Can you help me, please? I've come about a nanny." The blue head didn't look up, but a painfully

Kensington voice came from somewhere underneath the hair. "Take a seat, moddom. Ai'll be with you in a moment."

It was a lengthy moment before she clipped some papers together, daintily wiped her fingers with a Kleenex, took off her harlequin glasses, and, finally, looked at Jane. "A nanny, did you say, moddom?"

"Yes. A nanny."

"And what precisely are your requairments?"

"Well, just a nanny really. Someone experienced and nice. Not too old but not too—"

"Ai see. The child is under fayve, moddom?"

"Under what?"

"Under fayve. With children over fayve we're really more into the governess category, aren't we, moddom? Ai merely want us to be quaite clear on the point."

"Oh. Yes—yes, it's under five. It's under here in fact." She made an idiotic gesture at the bulge, and the Kensington mouth twitched an anaemic smile. "Ai see. Shall we have the particulars, then, moddom? You keep other staff, of course."

"No. But there's a cleaning lady who comes."

"Comes how often, moddom? Daily?"

"No, only once a week really. But she probably could co—"

"Ayo. That does make it most fraightfully difficult. You see, moddom, our nursery staff are all fully trained and qualified persons, and naturally they cannot be expected to undertake domestic jooties as well. I'm afraid, moddom, we have to make that quaite clear to all prospective employers."

"That's all right. I hadn't expected her to. I really want someone only to look after the baby. I work, you see, and so I've got to have—"

"Yes, moddom. Quaite." With a gilt pen she wrote "mother working" on a slip of paper. "Now, accommodation. Nanny will, of course, have her own room and television, we assume that. Staff kitchen, moddom?"

"What?"

"Is there a staff kitchen?"

"No. No, there's only one kitchen. It's a flat—quite a nice flat, but there's only one kitchen."

"Ayo." She wrote "no staff kitchen—flat." "Which floor, moddom?"

"Second. No. No, first."

With a malevolent parody of patience, blue head waited. "Have you decided, moddom, which it is?"

"First. I get mixed up because it's what we call second in America."

"Ai see. There is a lift?"

"A lift? For the first floor?"

"For the pram, moddom. It's extraimly difficult negotiating a stairway with a pram."

"Oh. No, there's no lift."

"Ai see. And which pock, moddom?"

"Pock?"

"Yes, moddom. Hyde Pock? Kensington Gahdens? Regents Pock?"

"Oh. Well, none really. I live in Covent Garden."

"In Covent Gahden? Do you mean the *mahket?*"

"Yes."

"Ai see. Now, the day nursery. Would Nanny be in full charge there as well?"

"As well as what?"

"The point is, moddom, Nanny would expect to tend the *night* nursery, but if there is no nurserymaid—well, you appreciate the difficulty, of course. Nanny really could not be expected to tend the day nursery as well."

"I don't think there'll be any problem; there isn't a day nursery."

"No day nursery?"

"No day nursery."

"Ai see."

"There is a nice flat roof, though, with lots of room for a playpen and all that. In good weather I thought we could—"

"On the *roof?*"

"Oh, it's got a wall around it, quite a high wall—

high for a baby, anyhow. I thought we could rig up some wire or something that would—"

She wasn't even listening. Her lips moved slightly as she wrote "no other staff . . . no park . . . no garden . . . no day nursery . . . roof."

"What wages had you in maynd, moddom?"

"I hadn't really thought. I'd rather pay more than the going rate, though, if that way I could get someone really good."

"And taim off? Taim off is most important, and while we don't of course prayzoom to make a hard-and-fast rule, we do recommend a day and a half a week, alternate weekends free, and a full four weeks' paid holiday annually. Is that what you had in maynd, moddom?"

"Yes, absolutely. If that's normal, that's what I had in mind."

"May I ask, moddom? Is it a first baby?"

"Yes. Yes, it is."

"And your husband? What is your husband's profession?"

"I haven't got a husband. I'm not married."

The Kensington mouth went into a tight, wrinkled little circle like an asshole, and next to "roof" she put "N.M." and, when she thought Jane wasn't looking, underlined it twice.

With an expression of brave martyrdom on her face, she took down Jane's name and address and the date the baby was due. "There we are, then, Miss Cornell. It won't be easy, but just leave it with me and we'll—we'll be in touch."

It was don't call us, we'll call you. As Jane walked slowly up Sloane Street to the bus stop, she knew she'd never hear a word from them. And she was right; she didn't.

Next morning, in the full grip of compulsive nest-building, she got up very early and walked down to the flower market, where because everything was so cheap she spent far more than she would have in a flower shop and had to get a taxi to lug it all home. With the taxi man helping, she got the pots of chrysanthemums as far as the downstairs entryway, and when he'd gone and she'd more or less dealt with all the cut flowers, she gave the long, shapeless velvet tent that was now almost worn out a going over with carbon tetrachloride. Then, clean in thought, word, deed, and even dress, she walked to the garage, squeezed herself behind the steering wheel, and went to meet the 9:15 from Cambridge at King's Cross. It never crossed her mind that it could pull such a dirty trick as to come in at Liverpool Street.

Caught in the Saturday-morning traffic that was as thick and unarguable with as Nile lettuce, she drove back home wishing she'd remembered to say, "Rabbits, rabbits," and by the time she got there Franklin was already at the typewriter. He took off his glasses as she came in, kissed her on the cheek, and said, "Baby, you look beat."

"I am. Like an idiot I went to King's Cross to meet you and—well, I know it sounds crazy, but I think I'll lie down for a little while. How was it?"

"I don't honestly remember a lot about it on account of I took the coward's way out and drank myself blind."

"Did you bring me the menu?"

"What the hell for?"

"I don't know, it's a thing men do. I know an English wife who hasn't been out to dinner in ten years, but she's got a whole big box full of menus that her husband's brought her from that kind of party."

"I guess I'm not the thoughtful type."

"I asked her once why she didn't type out what she'd had to eat when he went out and give it to him to keep in a box. You know: *Oeuf à la quatre minutes. Sardines en boîte. Sandwich de jambon bonne femme.* I don't think she ever did, though."

He had brought champagne and, lying on the bedspread with their shoes on like travelling salesmen in a fleabag hotel, they drank it half and half with Guinness.

"OK. Tell me."

"You won't like it."

"So think of me as a doctor. A priest. A fact-finder for Oxfam."

"No wonder that poor son of a bitch brings her the menus."

"Come on."

"Right. We had oysters."

"Christ, men."

"A whole dozen each."

"Naturally. And?"

"And then pheasant. It smelled like low tide to me, but those who know their pheasant said it was very great, and I guess if pheasant's what you go for, it was. Then we had some crazy lemon sherbet."

"What's crazy about that?"

"Nothing. Except that I thought it was dessert, but after it we started all over again."

"More oysters?"

"No. Saddle of lamb. About five kinds of potatoes. Vegetables. Salad. Chocolate soufflé. And then some unbelievable limey thing on a piece of toast that so far as I could make out was skinned field mice, each one wrapped in bacon like a little mummy. And just in case anybody was still hungry, they brought on bananas and apples and tangerines and—well, you know, a lot of stuff like that and little candies, all piled on big three-story plates."

"You ate all that?"

"Me? No, I quit just the other side of the field mice."

"God. And here I thought it was the finer things in life that Cambridge went for."

"You thought right, baby. There was so much Mouton Rothschild around it looked like sheep-dip time down on the old Bar R."

"Well, I think it's disgusting."

"I kind of had a feeling you would."

"Hogs. Fascist pig grunting-snout chauvinist hogs."

"Right on, baby."

"No, you don't take it seriously, I know, but I—well, I'm full of—"

He rolled over and put his arms around her. "You're full of champagne is what you're full of. I know the signs."

"I'm not. I just think—"

"Take that revolting sack off."

"Revolting? This is revolting? You wait till you see how it is underneath. But tell me one thing."

Unbuttoning his shirt, he walked across and closed the blinds. "What?"

She let the velvet tent fall onto the floor and stepped out of it. "How come they never had a revolution in this country?"

Naked, he stood behind her and undid her bra. "They did."

Without turning around, she reached for his shirt to cover her grotesquely enormous breasts and belly. "It didn't stick, though, did it?"

He got the shirt before she did and threw it out of reach. "No. No shirt. No wasp seemliness." Gently he turned her around and kissed her. "Of course it didn't stick. Wasn't British," he said into her shoulder. "Frightened the horses."

She wanted him so much that her knees went wobbly and she had to sit down on the edge of the bed and, frightened by wanting him so much, she couldn't stop talking. "Do you think they'll ev—" He pushed her back gently until she was leaning on her elbows, and he knelt on the floor between her legs. "—ever have another one?"

She had got the question out more or less in one piece, but she didn't get any answer.

When she woke up she reached out for him sleepily, but his side of the bed was empty and his pillow was cold. She lifted her head and listened for a sound, any sound, but the apartment felt silent and empty in a way that it wouldn't have if he'd been anywhere in it.

At first it only puzzled her, his not being there. But

then, as if she'd stepped on a loose plank in the barn floor, the truth came up and hit her in the face. He'd gone. He'd gone for good.

That was why the champagne. That was why the shoot-the-works lovemaking. It had been the kiss-off. The swan song. The fireworks finale. Obviously. He hadn't had to go to that thing last night at all—he just hadn't wanted to see her. He wouldn't have come today, or very likely ever again, if she hadn't made such a fuss.

And you couldn't blame him, either. Not really. What other man would have stayed around this long on nothing but the off chance that a baby might be his? *Tom?* Well, Tom, yes. *Anthony?* OK, even Anthony. But how many others would have? How many black men would have? They were different, black men. Rednecks and sniffy social workers had always *said* so, and—well, they ought to know.

Maybe they'd been right all along. Maybe it was true that blacks were cop-outs and quitters, and that it was just something programmed into them, the same as sickle cell anaemia, that made them like that. Wives. Kids. Jobs. Schools. Whatever the long-term responsibility or commitment was, maybe if it hung too heavy they simply sloughed it off like a snake's skin and left.

And so that was that. It should have been absolutely predictable. If she hadn't been such an idiot, it would have been.

She struggled into the huge cotton bra with the ridiculous flaps in front like children's dropseat pyjamas, and pulled the velvet tent on.

In the bathroom she peed noisily. What difference did it make how things sounded when you were alone? Making ghastly noises was almost the only compensation there was. Numbly she brushed at her hair, but there were so many tangles she finally had to take a comb and pick at them. It was a metal comb, too, and hurt. *His,* the lousy carpetbagger. The comb made pinging noises at each pick and hurt so much that it, or something, brought tears to her eyes.

She splashed cold water on her face and leaned towards the mirror. Her mouth was bruised and her tongue couldn't stay away from a swollen cut on the inside of her lower lip. She pulled the lip down and looked at it. Jesus. Then she turned her face sideways and ran her fingertips over the red bristle-scraped patch on her cheek. It hurt too. You'd think a man who was about to walk out on you would at least have the decency to shave.

As she put the jar of moisturizer back on the glass shelf, she saw his toothbrush standing in a mug. She picked it up, held it and the metal comb over the waste-basket for a moment of silent exorcism, and dropped them in.

The living room was dark, and she switched on lamps that made laser-beam shafts of light but didn't really light anything. Outside, fog muffled the noise of the traffic, making the apartment even quieter and reducing the street lights to fuzzy orange spots that didn't light anything either. The new restaurant across the street was open, and its big window glowed yellow, but the storefronts either side of it were black. She couldn't tell if it was seven o'clock or eleven. And what did it matter anyhow what it was?

She found the note propped against the ice bucket on the slate-topped table, and without even unfolding it she squeezed it into a tight ball and threw it across the room. For maybe thirty seconds she sat on the sofa, staring at nothing in particular, before she got up, walked heavily across the room, and got the ball of paper out from under the oak chest.

Baby: Couldn't bear to wake you to say but have to pick up some books and will be back around 7:30. There's another bottle on the ice but don't get too paralytic as we've got a reservation at Rule's for 8:30. Love, F.

195

Jesus. She'd been wrong before but never like this. And she was the one who'd taken that huffily high moral tone with Anthony. She was the one who was slightly more noble, a lot fairer, very much less prejudiced, and immeasurably nicer than anybody else. She was such a pile of driven-snow-pure principles that she could be shocked by Cambridge dons eating oysters. *What a laugh.* It had taken two minutes and one fit of self-pitying panic to show her up as just as shoddy as most, and shoddier than many.

Paralyzed by the horror of herself and the things she'd thought about him, she sat on the sofa without even moving until the front door slammed and he started up the stairs two at a time. Then she ran for the bathroom.

She listened to his footsteps come down the hall and turn in to the kitchen. The icebox door opened, and an egg fell out and broke. "Goddamn" he said under his breath and, over the sound of paper towels being torn off the roll, he called, "Hey, what's the matter? You haven't even opened the bottle yet."

Standing at the washbasin, smearing last year's suntan makeup on her face, she reached over and flushed the toilet to show where she was. "Just coming," she called back in a two-tone doorbell voice that felt as phony as it sounded, and, squatting down, she felt in the wastebasket for his toothbrush and comb. Very carefully she pulled the hair combings from the bristles, rinsed the brush under the faucet, and put it back in the mug on the shelf.

"Wow," he said when he saw the Tru Tan face. "Look who's muscling in on the act."

She put her arms around his neck and hung onto him tight while a mixture of tears and makeup spread over his shirt front. While he held her close and wondered at the mysterious hair-trigger emotional instability of pregnant women, it crossed his mind that it was the only clean shirt he had with him. But he didn't say so. He was far too nice a man to do that.

196

13

The waiter was hovering, and Franklin smiled at him. "Sorry, I guess we're not ready yet. Do you think we could have a bottle of Veuve Clicquot while we're deciding?"

When the waiter had gone, Jane leaned across the table and whispered, "Franklin, this is too expensive a place to go crazy in."

He smiled at her. "Can I help it I've got a sense of history. See that door?" He pointed across the restaurant. "I only have to walk through it and I can see it all."

"See what all?"

"Them, baby, them. Lily Langtry and whatshisname, the portly Prince. Not down here with the rabble, of course. Upstairs. A purple sofa with fringe. Her flat on her ass, if flat's something she could get on an ass like hers. Him on his knees with his hand up her skirt and breathing hard. Can't you see it? 'Dining together' it was called, and one way or another I bet you they really got it together. How many oysters you reckon it took to fill her up?"

"Which end?"

"You see? You too have the inquiring mind of the born historian. Together we could go far."

The champagne had come, and he touched her glass with his. "Come on, cheer up. This is a celebration."

"Of what?"

"It's done. Where the con man lives has been crossed."

She'd known it would be that. "Oh? Ho! for the Monongahela, then."

"More your Chesapeake Bay, actually."

"Philadelphia? What happened to Dayton?"

"I want to be where there's oysters."

"Oh, shut up about oysters. I thought there was a Wyatt Earp in you struggling to get out. Wasn't that the idea?"

"Yeah, it was. For a long time it was, and it fitted right in with a living-colour vision I had of me in politics." He looked down at the table and smiled as if he were remembering something, and then his eyes looked up into hers. "Did you know about that? The vision?"

"It had once in a while half struck me there might be one."

"Well, it figures, doesn't it? Our generation—and we're the last generation that fell for it—was brought up to believe in nonviolence and ballots not bullets, and all that. And even though it hasn't worked out the way we thought—well, it's hard—real hard—to stop believing in something you want to be true. It was because I couldn't stop that I saw the Assistant DA job as—well, as the first step towards the vision."

"And what was this vision?"

"Oh, nothing lurid. I was just going to take the state capitol first, clean up the Mafia and pollution, make Senator, and then be the dark horse—hey, you like that?"

"I like it."

"—that won the New Hampshire, Florida, and California primaries, after which I would modestly accept the Presidential nomination, which was bound to come through on the first ballot. That's only a rough idea, but that's the picture."

"I remember it well. Maybe this time we could call it 'Mr. Rodgers Goes to Washington.' "

"I had in mind 'Rodgers the Great.' How does that grab you?"

"Why not just 'R'? Subtle. Restrained. Not pushy. You wouldn't want to be a pushy President, would you?"

"Now, though—now I'm not so sure. I'm not so sure politics is the way to do it. Takes too long, for one thing. And for another, the smell that hangs over every state capitol, and Washington too, can't be all gasoline fumes and uncollected garbage. No, there's one real crooked dice game going on, and too many politicians are in it. Not that that's news; hell, nobody could grow up in Washington and not know that since forever. But now—now I think there are better and faster ways of getting things done."

"Like?"

"Well, I'm not sure yet. I'm not sure just how rough it will have to get."

He had got solemn, and he wasn't going to let himself be solemn. He grinned. "So anyhow, one way and another the vision faded out and I—I cut bait, that's all. It was no great loss. In fact I was amazed at how little I missed it. And what the hell, I can always go back to it later if I want to."

"But Philadelphia's no rose either, Franklin. There are things in Philadelphia that could make even uncollected garbage smell good."

"Sure. But in a law firm in Philadelphia I won't have to make the kind of compromise I'd have to if I used the Dayton job as a springboard and got into the political scene seriously. I'll be freer, with more room to manoeuver. I won't be beholden to anyone. I won't have to kiss anybody's ass come election time like I would in state politics. And if—it's a big if, but if—I decide someday to branch out, well, I know I'm being modest again, but lateral entry fairly high up appeals to me one hell of a lot more than swinging like a gibbon on the bottom rung of the ladder."

"Oh god, you're in your manic mood. I can tell."

"Not really. It's just I liked everything about the Philadelphia job better. It's an old firm, rich as anything, and with direct pipelines to the most loaded foundations. Better even than that, they've got a big endowment some crazy old liberal millionaire came across with to finance this free office in North Philly. The money has been, as we say, wisely handled, and now there's enough to expand some and—I'm not as manic as you think—open a couple of small offices in third-floor walk-ups in Pittsburgh and Harrisburg. I know that doesn't sound any big deal. But you wait, baby. You wait."

They ordered, and the waiter went away again. "The guy running the North Philadelphia office now, Otis Vickery, is an old friend of my father's and he's a very nice guy but he's one of the ones who came up the old hard way—summers he picked cotton in Oklahoma to put himself through college, and after college he worked days in some lousy job in the post office so he could go to law school nights. I'm not knocking him or anything—jesus, who am I to knock a guy like that?—but it's hard for him to see that times have changed and that nobody's willing to put up with that kind of shit any more. And they're not. There's a whole new mood shaping up. You might not notice it at first glance and, sure, the bastards are cutting welfare and shoving people around the way they always have, but people are wising up."

"Praise de lawd."

"Anyhow, that's it. It's a rundown old building off North Broad Street, and they work like baying hounds were after them in a swamp. But I think it's right— right for me, anyway, and right for a couple of years while I figure out the next step. And you'd like them, you really would."

Would. Not will. Would.

When he stopped grinding pepper over his smoked salmon, she reached out for his hand and thought that if she held on, really held on, he couldn't go without her. He leaned forward and kissed her fingers, but she could tell he did it automatically; it was only his reflexes that were still in London. His head was already in North Philadelphia.

"I don't kid myself that a free law office in North Philly is going to do it all. But what are the choices? Some people still talk about direct confrontation, and that's crazy. They've got the pigs and the tanks and the National Guard and the gas and the guns. And what've we got? Nothing except a lot of people to fill up a lot of jails. Some people, like Vickery, still talk about education. But that's not going to do it either. Even if it worked, it'd be slow, and it doesn't work because the kids who need education the most get the least. No, the way I see it is we've got to go for power, and the only way to get power—power that will last and that nobody can break your head and put you in jail for having—is to get it legally. And that means organizing people, getting voters registered, and getting registered voters to vote, and showing them they've got rights that they needn't be afraid to use. Christ, there isn't a city or fair-sized town in that whole goddamned country where people aren't screwed and fucked around their whole lives for nothing except lack of enough places they can go to for real help. And call that being manic or call it anything you want, that's something that's got to change. I don't care whose front yard gets the railroad shoved through it, it's got to change."

He pulled his mind out of North Philadelphia for a moment and looked at her. "But there's another thing, baby. Not such a good thing."

"Like?"

"I've got to go back. Not for good or anything, but I've got to go back next week. Vickery is going on a lecture tour the end of the month and wants to see me before."

Holding on to him hadn't worked. Not even for five minutes. Already he was going. She felt the first sharp jolt of fear and put down her fork. "Oh god—how long for? Will you be back in time for—"

"Baby, of course I'll be back in time. Those big silver birds, they go every day now, you know, both ways. And this time they're paying, so it's no fly-by-night charter snow job."

"But what if you're not? What if—"

"Come on now, cut it out. 'I shall return.' Think. Who said that?"

She blew her nose. "MacArthur," she said through the Kleenex.

"Right. President Chester A. MacArthur, the least pushy President ever. A man right after your own heart, and I'm another." He winked at her. "OK?"

She took a deep breath and held it for a second. "OK," she said and tried to smile.

"That's better, that's the real Miss Ash Can Ozzie. Now, when are you going to—to wherever it is?"

"I don't know exactly. I'm working two more weeks, and then I'll go to—well, to near where it is. Clammy Hands still says the twenty-eighth, but I don't honestly think he knows his ass from a hole in the ground."

"I wish you'd tell me where it is."

"What, his ass?"

"No. The other."

She shook her head. "No. Like I told you before, it's much better I be by myself with nobody getting at me."

"I wouldn't get at you. I'd just like to know where you are. Please?"

"No."

"OK. If you're sure that's the way you want it."

After the velvet-womb warmth of the restaurant, the November fog was as cold as pulling on a wet bathing suit. "Jesus," he said. "England. You wait inside; I'll go get the car."

She watched him disappear into the yellowish-grey swirling stuff and, still caught in the remnants of the

202

despair she'd felt in the afternoon, she tried to imagine what it would be like if one day he did disappear forever. But no picutre of it would focus, and so she leaned against the wall, watching the people eat and wondering how long a man and a woman had to be married before they ate together without talking to or even looking at each other.

He leaned across to open the car door for her. "But you never said what you thought about Philadelphia."

"Didn't I? I meant to. I meant to say I was glad for you and that you were right to take it. Surely I said that, didn't I?"

"What about as a place to live? Better than Dayton?"

"Oh, miles. Also a better job. A better kind of job."

"You wouldn't mind living there?"

"Me? No. Goodness, no. But I—"

"But you what?"

"But I'm not counting on it or anything, that's all."

They were only a few blocks from home, but he pulled in to the curb, shifted into neutral, and turned to put his arm around her. "What's this about not counting on it?"

She escaped from the softening-up intimacy of his chin against her cheek by turning her head away, and then his mouth landed on her ear, which was even more softening-up. "Come on," he said. "I asked you a question."

She tried to sound briskly no-nonsense matter-of-fact. "Franklin, you know as well as I do that if this baby's not yours I can't possibly marry you."

"Why not?"

"Lots of reasons. Your family, for one. They'd go mad."

It was a while before he answered. "Now let's get it straight. My family isn't any problem. With them we could do it the never-apologize-never-explain way—which I admit might be a little rough. Or we can dress it up respectably. Like saying you were married before.

To somebody who went out blueberrying and was got by a bear."

"Great. Except your sister knows I've never been married. She asked, remember?"

"That was getting on to two years ago. You could have got married to somebody else since. Last fall—last winter."

"Got married to somebody else? While I was living with her irresistible baby brother? You'll need a long runway to get a granite glider like that one off the ground."

"So to hell with my sister."

"OK. To hell with your sister. But sooner or later, and I'd put my money on sooner, she'd tell. And then where'd we be? I can guess what those high-class Holy Rollers feel about lies. Especially that kind of lie."

"They'd never say anything. I know them, I know they wouldn't."

"They wouldn't have to. Anyhow, there's you too. How would you—"

"I can take it. I want you and I'm willing to take whatever comes with you."

"You could take it now, but could you always?"

"Why not? You were no trembling virgin when I met you, and did that worry me? Look, I'm not just asking for a short-term high-interest loan. I want to marry you."

"It's not the same. Me not being a trembling virgin is not the same as being landed permanently with the breathing, squalling evidence—and highly visible evidence, too—that I'd been—Oh god, what's the word? Disloyal? Unfaithful? Promiscuous? Jesus, already it sounds like a divorce case."

"Listen. Those words only mean what you choose them to mean. I don't own you; nobody owns anybody. That you went to bed with whoever the hell it was doesn't make any difference. Not to me. It just isn't important."

"No? How much would you give to make it so I hadn't?"

Again he waited an honest, longish moment before he answered. "OK. Now you ask, I'd give quite a lot. But only because of how it's affecting us—or rather of how it might affect us."

"Right. That's exactly what worries me too, so where's the argument?"

"All right. Let's take it from there. Now, either the baby is mine, in which case there's no problem. Right? Or it isn't. In which case we have two choices. Either we go on together, or we don't. If we don't, it means— well, you know what it means. I go. You stay. And it's finished."

He reached around her neck with his right arm and rubbed his elbow. "Well, that's out. It's not what you want, and it certainly isn't what I want." He switched on the heater. "So it would be idiotic not to."

"Not to what?"

"Jesus christ. Not to get married."

She turned her head towards him. "Don't be cross. I only wanted to hear you say it."

Smoothing her cheek with his hand, he said, "Sorry, baby. I didn't mean to sound cross. But if what's eating you is that ten years from now I may turn mean about it all, I can only tell you I won't. After all, if you'd been married before, or for that matter not married before, and had the baby then—well, there wouldn't be any question of me, or my family, getting uptight over what color it was, would there? It would just be part of what came with you—like, for instance, that indescribably elegant cat. Right?"

"Mm."

"OK. You're not convinced. So you tell me the difference."

"I don't know. I know there is one, but you bamboozle me so much I don't know what it is."

"I bamboozle you? Baby, you don't need me to bamboozle you, you take care of that all by yourself. You and your all-purpose, economy-size Old Testament guilt bag."

"It isn't guilt. It's conscience."

205

"Take it from me, one leads to the other. You know, the trouble with you is—"

"Oh christ, sentences that begin 'the trouble with you is' I don't need."

"OK. Not you. Women. Liberated women. The trouble is you've kicked one set of unfair rules. And so now you get educated. You vote. You work. You're independent. You sleep around. Just like men, you are. But what's the good of having done all that if when the going gets rough you build another set of unfair rules to clobber yourselves with? God, you don't even really change the rules; the price is still an eye for an eye. And, according to you, whose baby is whose still ranks high enough in the female mind to bust up a good going concern over."

"It's not that. It's more that no matter how liberated anybody gets there still have to be boundaries about what is acceptable behaviour. People have to treat each other decently. Nobody is ever going to get liberated from that, and it wouldn't be right if they did."

"But don't you see? 'Decently' is just another of those goddamned words. It doesn't mean the same thing to everybody. It doesn't, apparently, even mean the same thing to us. I say it would be decent for you to marry me no matter whose the baby is. You say it wouldn't. And where does that leave us except up shit creek without a Roget?"

"You're bamboozling again."

He took his arm from around her shoulder, shifted gears, and pulled away from the curb. "What a fucking mess. And you know? If you hadn't got—I mean, if things hadn't turned out the way they have, you'd probably never have told me you'd gone to bed with somebody else. And you'd have been right not to."

"Would I? I thought you were supposed to tell. I must say I never have—but I did think you were supposed to."

"Why?"

"I don't know. It's a kind of apologizing, I guess."

"To what end?"

"For the god's sake, I don't know. Expiation of sins? Forgiveness?"

"You see? You're right back in that Old Testament bullshit again. 'I have sinned. I admit it. I did it. Lousy me. Now, you fogive me.' Who wins in that loaded dice game? You get the sin. You get the forgiveness. What's in it for the other guy?"

"I never thought of it like that."

"Few do, baby. But when somebody goes to bed with somebody else and then tells the one person it might hurt, do you think they're doing it to make that person feel good? Like hell they are. They're doing it to make themselves feel better. To get it all off their own chest and onto somebody else's. And be forgiven to boot.

"And that's all supposing they're halfway nice. If they're not, they do it not only to relieve their own little pangs but also to give the person they're telling great big ones. Haven't you ever run across people who cheat and who can hardly wait to get home and tell the loved one? That's because slipping the icepick between the ribs is such fun."

"Aha. You admit it's an icepick."

"It's only an icepick if you see it as one or use it as one."

"What about the person you're telling? What if he sees it as an icepick and you don't?"

"If you're nice, you keep your mouth shut."

"What about the other way around? He doesn't, but you do?"

"If you're out to hurt him, it's tough luck on you and you'll have to find some other way. If you're not, you keep your mouth shut."

"What if you both see it as an icepick, and you've both got something to tell?"

"That's the meanest and the commonest combination of all. That way you've got the Old Testament, the New Testament, and the divorce laws that star adultery all rolled up into one big shark fight. But there's still no need for it to be a shark fight, *if* you both keep your mouths shut."

"And if it isn't an icepick to either?"

"That's where we came in. That's why you wouldn't have told me—if this other thing hadn't happened."

He parked the car in front of the warehouse, with two wheels on the sidewalk so the banana trucks could get by. "Got it?"

"Got it."

"OK. Bed. Jesus, I'm tired."

14

She was tired too, and when she saw the grubby brown envelope on the mat inside the front door she stepped over it and said, "Leave it. It's only the milk bill." But Franklin picked it up and handed it to her. She stuffed it in her bag, and very slowly they climbed the stairs.

He hung up their coats and said, "Brandy?"

"God, no. You have one, but me, no. Bed. Lovely bed."

She went on to the bedroom and with a glass of brandy in his hand he followed her. He helped her off with her clothes, and she exchanged the velvet tent for a red flannel one, got into bed, and leaned back against the pillows. "Lord, but that feels good. You know, children must be mad. How can they not want to go to bed? I'd go any chance I got. I'd go to bed in a hammock with a drunk orangutang with long toenails, if I had to."

His back to her, taking things out of his pockets and putting them on the chest of drawers, he said, "Work that act up a little, baby, and I can get you second billing in any club in Copenhagen."

"Second? Who gets first?"

"The orangutang."

His voice dropped to an angry mutter. "Now where the hell has it got to?" He opened her bag. "Ah, thought so. The pack rat got it." He held up his pen triumphantly.

"The pack rat didn't get it, she rescued it. From where the ex-President of the United States left it on the restaurant table."

"Don't you want to open this?" He pulled the brown envelope out of her bag.

"Told you. It's only the milk bill."

"Since when does the milkman call you Jane?"

"He doesn't. He calls me twenty-eight. Which is, god knows, kind of him, and I am, god knows, grateful."

"It says 'Jane' on the envelope."

She opened her eyes, and he handed it to her. A single sheet of cheap blue-lined paper was all that was in it.

Dear Jane, please come if you can and bring some money. I am at 47 Clabbard Street which is a right turn off Cable Street past the Tower. I wouldn't ask but it is urgent and so I hope you can make it but if you can't don't worry it's alright and I will understand.

It was signed "Tom," and there was a P.S.:

Third floor back. Please don't leave this note laying around where somebody could see it.

"Jesus christ." She jumped out of bed and started pulling on the clothes she'd just taken off. "Where are the car keys?" she called.

"The what?" He was taking a shower; she could hear the water.

"The car keys," she yelled. "Where are they?"

He came out of the bathroom and stood naked and dripping in the bedroom door. "What the jesus do you want with the car keys?"

"Somebody I know is in trouble and I've got to go. Right away I've got to go."

"Baby, be reasonable. You can't go off in the mid—"

She was counting the money in her wallet. "No, honestly, I've got to. God, only twenty-three pounds. Have you got any?"

"It's there on the dresser. But Jane, can't it wait?"

"No. He says it's urgent, and he wouldn't say that if it weren't."

Franklin went back to the bathroom and got a towel. "Well, whatever it is, you're not going alone." He pulled on his trousers and sat down to put on his socks and shoes while she yanked open a drawer and emptied a jewellery box onto the bed. "Now what the hell are you doing?"

"My twenty-three and your seventeen makes forty, but I've got a bracelet somewhere that's got a fifty-dollar bill in one of those stupid little glass—Here it is. Hell, it's soldered on. What'll I do?"

He got pliers from the kitchen and snipped the little gold link, and she stuffed the money and the bracelet charm into her coat pocket. "It's somewhere off Cable Street. Which way's Cable Street from the Tower of London?"

"Christ, I don't know. Where's a map?"

She ran and got it, and he opened it out flat on the kitchen table. "Let's see. Bank. Monument. Tower of London. Right. Got it. Cable Street runs east of that. What's the other turn we want?"

She unfolded Tom's note. "Clabbard Street. A right turn off Cable, it says."

He drew a circle on the map and she said, "Oh jesus, hurry, can't you?"

"Keep your finger right here. Right here in the centre."

It was still foggy, but some wind had come up and

was blowing the fog away. The streets were shiny, slippery black ribbons, but there was no traffic and when the Tower of London loomed up in front of them like a great white ghost of Camelot, Franklin stopped under a street lamp and took the map. "OK," he said and handed it back to her.

The bomb damage in Clabbard Street had never been repaired, and the houses that still stood sagged against each other, propped up by huge timber buttresses that arched across the sidewalk. Almost all the street lights had taken more recent direct hits from rocks, and only two were still working. It was almost impossible to make out the numbers on the dead, derelict houses.

Franklin drove very slowly. "That's thirty-one over there. What's the next one?"

"Can't see. No—wait—I think it's thirty-three."

"OK, the numbers run that way. That must be forty-seven there. That one just past the bombsite." He pointed at a house with the ground-floor windows boarded up and a front door that hung from one hinge and slightly open. "That's it, baby. Jesus, what a dump."

"OK. I'll be back in a—"

"You think I'm crazy? You think I'm going to let you go in a place like that alone?"

"Why not? It's only a house."

"So was Christie's place only a house. So was Landru's place only a house. Don't be so stupid."

They crossed the potholed street and went up low front steps that had shallow, worn scoops in them filled with water. More water dripped from a broken drainpipe into a big black puddle beside the steps, and the windows behind the rotted iron balcony on the second floor had caught whatever rocks had missed the street lights. Somebody had painted BLACKS—OUT beside the hole where there once had been a doorbell.

On its one rusty hinge, the front door pushed open easily but noisily, and inside they paused. The bare boards of the hallway floor were littered with empty bottles, and from the front room came the sound of snoring. As they moved farther down the hall, broken glass crunched under their feet, and the reek of cats, stale vomit, beer bottles, and mildew got heavier.

Some of the stairs had rotted away or been ripped up, and between the second and third floors, where the stairs were narrower, the banisters hung crazily out into space and they had to hug close to the greasy, dirty wall. Jane clung to Franklin's hand and fought down waves of vertigo.

At the top they inched their way along the hall towards the back of the house. The wall indented suddenly, and Jane touched what she thought must be a door. She knocked softly, and when there was no answer she put her mouth close to the crack and whispered, "Tom? It's me."

He must have been standing there listening to their slow progress up the stairs, but it was only when he heard her voice that two bolts scraped back slowly and the door opened just enough for them to squeeze in sideways. It was even blacker inside, and she put out her hand to feel her way. "Tom?" she whispered again.

He stepped from behind the door and touched her hand, and she jumped. "It's OK," he whispered. "Don't be scared." Then he put his arms around her and his head down on her shoulder like a very tired boxer who had given up any thoughts of winning and only wanted the fight to be over. "Jane. Jane, I—"

The tiny noise of the door shutting jerked his head up. "Who's there?"

Her heart turned over at the fear in his voice. "It's all right, Tom, it's all right. It's only Franklin."

Slowly his body relaxed. "Anybody see you come in?"

"I don't think so. The street was empty, and there's no lights in any of the houses. But what's happened, Tom? What are you doing in this awful place?"

He led her over to a corner of the room, and she sat down on an iron cot that was covered with a rough damp blanket. He squatted on the floor in front of her, holding her hand in both of his. "I can't tell you now," he whispered. "There's no time."

Next to the cot on a broken wooden chair there was a candle stub standing in a hardened pool of wax. She touched it. "Can we light it, Tom?"

"You got a match? I'm out."

He took the boxes of matches from her, and when he lit the candle she saw his face. Not sure if what she'd seen was true or just a distorting trick the candle-light played, she touched his cheek and felt the rough dryness of caked blood. "Tom. Oh, Tom," she whispered. "What happened?"

One eye was black and almost closed. His bottom lip was split open and still oozing blood, and more blood had run down the side of his face from a cut over his eye. His nose, his beautiful nose, was swollen and purple with bruising, and she couldn't speak for horror as she held his face in both her hands and looked at it in the candlelight.

He tried to smile the gay-desperado smile, but his cut lip couldn't make it. "It's nothing. But I've got to get out of London for a little while. That's why I had to ask you to come."

She reached in her pocket. "It's only forty pounds, Tom. That's all we had. But there's this." She put the square glass charm in his hand. "It's got a fifty-dollar bill in it, folded up. It ought to get you about twenty pounds at a bank."

He held the little glass box close to the candle and looked at it. "Christ, but the rich are crazy."

"Tom, can't you tell me at least some of it? Where are you going? And why, Tom, why? Why not come home with me now and let me look after you?"

"No. Fuck me, no. Not there. No, Glasgow's the only place I can go. And don't worry. I'll be all right once I get there."

"But Tom, I could help if you'd just—"

"You have helped. You brought the money." He cocked his head and looked at the glass-sided charm

214

again. "And this crazy little thing. There's nobody could do more than that."

He stood up and pulled her gently to her feet. "Try and make sure nobody sees you go out, and don't shut the car doors or put the lights on till you're out of the street. OK?"

"Tom, I can't leave you here like this. Won't you let—"

"Yes, you can, Jane. You can and you've got to. And if—"

"If what?"

"Nothing. Just if you don't hear from me for a time, don't worry. I'll be back as soon as I can—maybe a week, maybe two or three. If it looks like being longer, I'll let you know."

"Promise?"

"Promise. And when I come I'll bring a silver spoon for you to swallow, so it can be born with it in its mouth. OK?" He wiped the tears off her cheeks with his thumb. "Now go. And mind you do like I said."

He let them out, and the bolts scraped shut again. The stairs and floorboards were too waterlogged to creak, but in the downstairs hallway Jane's foot hit a bottle that was lying on its side, and it skittered across the floor and crashed into the wall. They froze where they stood, and waited, but the snores from the front room never even changed rhythm.

Outside it had suddenly turned colder; the fog had gone and it had begun to rain. The broken pipe wasn't just dripping now but gushing noisily into the black puddle.

When they had turned the corner, Franklin switched on the lights and leaned across her to shut the door. "Jesus, Jane, what was all that about? Who is that boy?"

Her mind was still too frozen with shock for her even to try and dress it up. "Tom? He's somebody I know, that's all. I don't know what trouble he's in—I mean, you heard me ask, but he never tells me things like that. Or anything, really."

"What about his family? Couldn't they help?"

"I don't think he has any family. And I don't even know his last name"—she bit her lip to keep from crying—"so I wouldn't know how to look for them if he did."

"You don't know his name? How can you know him so—so well, and not know his name?"

She turned her face away from him so he wouldn't see the tears. "I don't know. Knowing people's names doesn't mean you know them. Christ, how can anybody ever know anybody else anyhow? People keep all the important things hidden, and so what's the use of knowing paltry things like names? They're no help, not really."

"Names are more help than no names, and in a situation like this names can be a lot of help. Couldn't you find out?"

"No. I don't know anybody to ask."

"What does he do? Where does he work?"

"He doesn't work. He does—I don't know—this and that, but I don't know where he does it."

"Christ."

It was a lot slower driving back in the pelting rain, and when they got home one of the banana trucks had taken over the parking place.

15

The next week Franklin went to Philadelphia, and in London the days got shorter as the year nosedived towards the semi-permanent twilight of winter. It was, the weatherman said, somewhat cooler than average for November, and the weatherman did not lie, it was cold as hell. Outdoors an east wind straight from the Russian steppes blew viciously, and indoors a heavy sewer-like chill sat in every room and wouldn't budge. For all the good they did, Jane's double-bar electric heaters might as well have been neon lights.

In the long hallway a kerosene stove managed—so long as it stayed lit—to melt a hole in the iciness. But when she forgot to refill it the flame would turn from blue to yellow while the heat died a slow, stinking death that filled the hall with black, greasy smoke. Even keeping the gas oven on all day and all night, although it very successfully dried and de-oxygenated the air and made the windows run with rivulets of condensation, didn't much help.

More given to dramatic statement than the TV weatherman, the newspapers kept insisting it was a freak cold spell and most unusual for the time of year, but it was, in fact, no freakier and no colder than any other November Jane had known in England. The only truly unusual thing about this November was that she was sleeping alone and was coming perilously close to freezing to death doing it.

She plodded through grey days that held nothing but long movies and long waits in bus queues in the biting wind. No word came from Tom. She had no nanny lined up. And now even Mrs. Bush was quitting. Two Fridays in a row she didn't show up at all, and when she came on the third Friday, it was only to say that she couldn't come. It was, she said, Alf. He had the gastric.

Jane knew Alf's gastric from way back. Each November it struck, each May it vanished, and while it was on he was sometimes so ill that he could hardly get to the pub by opening time. This was the first time, though, that Mrs. Bush had used Alf as an excuse for not coming, and Jane saw the writing on the wall.

There was a postcard from Anthony. He was in Paris, where the weather, he said, was bleak and miserable and so was he. He would be back next week. He was dreadfully, dreadfully sorry for having behaved badly and would she forgive him? Please would she forgive him?

Jane turned the card over and looked at the picture. It was an old one, one of those old jokey ones they sell at Left Bank quayside bookstalls, of a man and a woman in bed with a bawling baby between them. The punch line was "Jamais deux sans trois" and as Anthony liked puns she could see why he thought it was funny. But she didn't, and it wasn't.

There were bills. The car insurance was going up again. A magazine wanted a piece on Luis Buñuel. She was invited to judge a competition for the best ten-minute film script written by the girls in the sixth form at the Theodora Boynton Grammar School, Newcastle-on-Tyne.

There was a cable from Angela: ARRIVING 22ND WITH

There was the Christmas catalogue from Neiman-
Marcus. There was a sour-mouth letter from her sister
in La Jolla, who if Jane would forgive her saying so,
thought it very rash to have a baby without being married, not so much because of the unconventionality of
such a step, as she well understood such conventions
no longer applied in large cities like London (though
they tended still, in her opinion rightly, to be respected in humdrum La Jolla), but more because a child
needed the basic security of ... *blah blah blah* ... But
it was Jane's own life, of course, and Jane was not to
think she was being censorious or disapproving in any
way, shape, or fashion ... *blah blah blah* ... and she
and George sent much love and would keep their fingers crossed.

But there was still nothing from Tom.

On buses she'd take out Franklin's letter—always
trying to make it look, as if it were a letter that had
just come, and that this was the first chance she'd had
to read it—and reread it over and over.

Dearest Jane,

Never go jumbo or you will find yourself in a hereto-
fore undiscovered circle of an extremely crowded hell
that even Dante would have left alone. The stew-
ardesses all flunked-out drum majorettes. The food
plastic that may *trompe* the *oeil* but doesn't fool the
estomac for a minute. The fellow rovers all retired
hardware merchants with merry yarns of Senior Citi-
zen fun cities in Florida, and wives who say you're as
old as you feel. Now I know why hijackers let the pas-
sengers off before heading for Havana.

Philadelphia is, loosely speaking, fine. All bright-
blue-sky football weather, new and baffling thruways
and Wm Penn still there with that great erection on. I
am staying with the Vickerys out in Chestnut Hill and
am pretty much cocooned off from contact with harsh
reality (except oysters, which you will be glad to hear

are very expensive) in a house that is a weird marriage of the miracle of electronics with the ye olde Currier & Ives look. Natural pine garage doors polyurethaned just like Dan'l Boone's that open by remote-control magic. Any cooking smells from the pumpkin pie eliminated immediately by the air conditioning that they tell me (and I believe them, I believe them) launders and changes the whole atmosphere every 30 seconds. And a genuine hound dog that sleeps on a hooked mat in front of the also genuine wbf. Real lawgs and real dawgs. I tell you it's too much.

The work, though, makes a great deal of sense and I have a pretty clear idea already about a couple of things that I think need doing. For instance about 95% of the problems they deal with, from murder to eleven-year-olds ripping off five-year-olds, stem directly from bad family situations, and whether you label this behavior as "disturbed" or "criminal" or something entirely different it seems only logical to help not just the guy in trouble but the whole family concerned. It's not a new idea, of course, but it's one that—around the places I've seen, anyhow—hasn't been given much of a chance so far to prove itself. I'm amazed that it hasn't—it doesn't, after all, take much imagination to see that it's better to try and keep people from getting in trouble in the first place, rather than waiting until they're up to their eyeballs and then trying to pull them out of it. Anyhow, even if fitting a couple of psychiatric caseworkers into a law office is a crazy thing to try and do, and there are certainly those who think it is, I have a date to see a Dr. Collins at Johns Hopkins who is, they say, the big deal. She sounds formidable as all hell over the phone and is, it seems, very hot on Women's Lib as well, so I really don't know what kind of female dragon I'll be up against. That's tomorrow. Afterwards I'm going home for the weekend—my mother has dreamed up some kind of a pre-Thanksgiving reunion and my sister is flying in complete with kids and Johnny is coming down from Princeton. I could live without it myself but it will please the family, and will also get me off that particular hook for another 10 years so what the hell.

I think a lot about you and I miss you and hope you are not still sweating over the Great Problem in that honky racist way of yours. If you are, I can only say again that it is not a problem. If it's mine, I shall instantly feel all the things that new fathers are supposed to feel and that are far too complicated even to try and explain to women whose brains are, as is well known, as smooth as ping pong balls and only slightly heavier. If it is not mine, the process may take a little longer, but that's all. Either way, I haven't the slightest doubt that we belong together, all three of us. Please believe me. I have never wanted anything in my life as much as I want you.

                                                    F.

P.S. Could you pick up my suit from the cleaners? The ticket is in a book I left on the desk. I have a flight back on the 27th but if anything happens and you want me to come sooner I can change it.

On the 22nd she left a key hanging on a string on the inside of the letter slot, and when she got home it was no longer there, so she knew Angela must be. And she was. As Jane shut the front door and yelled, "Hey, the British are coming!" the signs of Angela's presence were unmistakable. Mitsouko hung heavy in the air, the trusty address book lay open by the phone, her sable coat and one of the pigskin suitcases were on the floor by the sofa, and Scat was fighting the tissue paper in an open Henri Bendel dress box.

In a long silk thing that was a jungle of bright pink and orange and yellow flowers, Angela appeared from the direction of the kitchen. "Darling! How lovely you're back. I was just fixing our cocoa and baked beans. Are you starving?"

She kissed Jane on the cheek and stepped back. "Let me take a—" Jane's new Tawny Chestnut hair wiped the smile off her face. "Oh my god."

221

"Nice, isn't it? Doesn't wash out, either."

"And that horror—what's that horror?"

"What horror?"

"That horror you've got on. Have you been out in that? Out in the street? In public?"

"Of course. This is my best dress, and what's the matter with it, anyway?"

"Well, of course if you feel like that about it, if that's your *attitude*, then nothing's the matter with it—nothing at all." She picked a bottle of hock out of the ice bucket and poured two glasses. "Here. Maybe we can blur it a little."

Jane sat down and took a sip. "Fantastic cocoa, Angie. How's Washington?"

"Fine. Just fine. The rape capital of the world, we're known as now. Not that you'd know it by me; I've been working terribly hard."

"What at?"

"Oh, darling, I can't remember what at for goodness' sake, I just know I have been, that's all." She disappeared back down the hall. "Now get that—that *thing*—off."

She brought back an armful of soft pale blue wool, heavy with rows and rows of tiny little pearls at the neck and on the cuffs of the long loose sleeves. "Like it? It was in Bendel's window and I thought I couldn't live without it, but I see now that I can."

"Oh, Angie, it's beautiful. But it'll never fit. I mean look at me."

"It'll fit, darling. It's full as anything."

Jane put the pretty blue dress on and stood in front of Tom's mirror. "God, how marvellous, how absolutely marvellous. Oh my, I *do* look nice, don't I? I'd forgotten what it was like, looking nice."

Angela picked the velvet tent off the floor and dropped it into the big green metal wastebasket by the desk. "There. Now, food. Thank god for Fortnum and Mason, the last bastion of sanity in this whole septic isle."

"Who was it that said no, he wasn't sure he'd die for England, but for Fortnum and Mason certainly?"

"Don't know, and that's an English vice, asking who said things, and you mustn't get like that. But why is Flaming Locks all alone? Where are the three bears?"

"You may well ask. Blown—all blown. One's in Philadelphia. One's in Paris—or was. And the other's in—well, Glasgow, I think. But it's all all right. They're coming back."

"They said."

"What do you mean, 'they said'? Of course they are."

"Of course, darling, and anyhow what I really want to know is the schedule." Angela brought in coquilles St. Jacques and a poussin stuffed with foie gras and opened another bottle of hock. "There *is* a schedule, isn't there?"

"Of course there's a schedule. A very fine schedule. A gemlike schedule that is the veritable zenith of the schedule-maker's art—Hey, where's my parchesi board?"

"Your what?"

"You said you were bringing me something useful, and it couldn't have been the dress because you let slip that you had bought *that* for your mean selfish self, and so if it's not a parchesi board what is it? Where is it?"

"Ah. Down the hall."

"Here?"

"Where else?"

"You're lying. I saw down the hall. There's nothing."

"How much?"

"Ten pounds. No. Fifty."

"You're on, but come quietly."

"Why quietly?"

"Gone bye-byes."

"*What's* gone bye-byes? Angela, you haven't smuggled in some damned dog or something, have you? Not even you'd do that. Not at a time like this."

Angela stacked the dishes on a tray. "No dog. Far from." She opened the door to the hall, and at the door to one of the back rooms she put a finger to her lips. "Shh."

Jane put her head inside and looked at the bed. "You idiot. I knew it. I knew you were lying."

"Not there," Angela whispered. "There."

On a woven straw mat on the floor something rolled up in a blanket was breathing the deep, slow breathing of something very soundly asleep. "My god, Angela, what is it?"

"Ssh."

They tiptoed back to the living room.

"That, darling," Angela said when the door was closed, "is your nanny."

"My nanny? Where'd you get her?"

"Him."

"Him?"

"Him. He wears a long silk sarong, but he's definitely a him."

"A man in a sarong who's a nanny? I don't believe it."

"Another fifty?"

"No."

"Wise girl. And it's not a sarong really. A longyi, he calls it. Though it is, I must say, very, very like a sarong, if what I've been seeing in the National Geographic all these years is anywheres near the truth. Which, of course, it may well not be; I've never really trusted the National Geographic, have you?"

"Well, that sure explains everything. Stupid of me to have asked."

"Wasn't it?"

"Oh, come on. Don't be bloody."

"Well, if you're still that childishly addicted to irrelevant details, all right. His name is Tun Maung, and he's Burmese. You know, the old Moulmein pagoda and the Burma girl a-waitin? There. Where they had that road. He had five little brothers and sisters and knows more about babies than, thank god, you or I ever will, and he needed a job while he does a course here in London. And—well, that's it, really. His English is, I'm afraid, sketchy but his heart is pure and he had the strength of ten. He also has the wish to please of twenty. Years, that is."

"Angela, you are something else, you really are." Sitting on the fur rug, Jane leaned on her elbow and shook her head blearily. "The whole nanny bit had defeated me totally, but totally, and— But where'd you get him? They don't, I know this for a fact, grow on trees."

"But, darling, they do. That's exactly what he studies. Trees. I found him languishing at the Burmese Embassy, tutoring the Ambassador's son and saving up to get to London—the poor fool—to study these silly trees. When I heard *that*, I just grabbed him, literally grabbed him. He can cook, too. And drive. And eats rice. You know, cheap to keep."

"God, I wouldn't care if he had to have caviar flown in fresh for breakfast. But does studying trees last long? I can't see how it could, really."

"Darling, with his English, small acorns will be mighty oaks by the time he's through. It's a graduate course, too, so he only has to get to the occasional lecture and one seminar a week. Isn't that lucky? But we're straying. Tell me the schedule."

"Tun what?"

"Tun Maung."

"Goodness."

"Jane. The schedule."

"Well, there isn't one, really."

"I *knew* it. I said to myself before I left Washington that there was no possibility whatsoever of your having org—"

"Except I thought I'd go to Brighton in a couple of days."

"Brighton? Why Brighton?"

"The doctor has a sort of nursing home there. And I'm down, as they put it, for the twenty-eighth. But you know babies, so what I thought was to go a couple of days in advance."

"Very right. What hotel?"

"Hotel?"

"You know, those big buildings where everybody's named Smith."

"I hadn't thought. Any old hotel."

Angela fitted a cigarette into the long black holder. "Really, Jane, you are impossible. Impossible, do you hear? *Impossible*. You can't really propose to wander around Brighton with a baby two inches away, carrying a cardboard suitcase and looking for a—" She crossed the room, looked up a number in the address book by the phone, and dialled it. Jane watched, mesmerized, while she reserved two bedrooms, a drawing room, and a bath at the Pavilion Vista Hotel for the 24th.

"My god, Angela, you don't want to—I mean, it won't be your type thing at all."

"Don't be silly, I wouldn't miss it for the world. Brighton in November? What could be lovelier? It'll make Marbella look like Oak Bluffs."

"You'll be sorry, you wait."

"Nonsense. But it still does slightly puzzle me, darling, if you'll forgive me dragging it up again so tactlessly, why none of them is *here*."

"I told you, it's OK. Franklin's seeing a man about a job that he's taken in Philadelpia. Anthony turned ornery, and I threw him out. And Tom—" Her voice dwindled off.

"Go on, darling. Tom is . . ."

"Well, that's what I don't know."

She told Angela about the night that Tom had called her to Clabbard Street, and about the beating up he'd had, and how she hadn't heard from him since.

"Good lord, Jane, what a dreadful story. Did you go to the police?"

"The police? Are you kidding? For all I know it was them that beat him up."

"Do you want me to get hold of the magazine's Glasgow stringer? He's no fool and knows the ghastly city like the palm of his hand."

As she'd told about Tom, Jane had pulled all the petals off a chrysanthemum, one by one. Now she squared them up into a neat pile and said, "What'd be the use? We haven't so much as a name to give him to go by."

"What about that fool Stewart? He's not right in the head, but he *is* Secretary of State for Scotland."

"Him? You think he's going to break his Tory neck looking for a boy he never heard of and wouldn't like the sound of if he had?"

"You've no idea what the trouble is?"

"None."

"Do you know anybody else he knows?"

"No, nobody."

"Does anybody you know, any of your friends, know him?"

"No. Except for Mrs. Bush and the banana men and that kind of people, nobody has ever even met him. He would never let me take him to parties or anything like that."

"And you don't even know his *name?*"

"No."

"Well, you are something, Jane. I have to hand it to you, you really are something."

"Oh christ, don't rub it in."

They went to bed, and at exactly six o'clock the next morning Jane woke and knew with a sudden hyperclarity that what she'd said wasn't quite true. There was someone else who knew about Tom. There was the Duchess's private eye. She could hear Tom's voice saying, when she'd asked him to come back to the apartment with her, "No, *fuck me*, no. Not there. No . . ."

16

She lay wide awake for an hour before she dared go wake Angela. And waking Angela wasn't easy.

"Angie?"

The body under all the spare blankets and the eiderdown on the sofa bed moved. "Uhm?"

"Angie, wake up."

"No. Go away."

"Come on, you've got to."

There were more groans. "What time's it?"

"Never mind. Wake up."

"Why?"

"I know what happened to Tom."

Angela stuck her head out. "So do I, if this is a true sample of the boot-camp regime he led around here."

"No, Angela. Seriously."

Angela sat up and, hanging her head forward, gently massaged her temples. "My god but it's cold in here. It's like being on a duck shoot."

Jane switched on the electric heater and brought it closer to the bed. Leaning back against the wall with the eiderdown around her shoulders, Angela said, "Right. You know what happened. What happened?"

When Jane finished telling her about the Duchess's visit, Angela reached for the phone. "What's the number down at the ducal acres?"

"No, wait, Angie. Let me think what to do."

"*Think?* What's there to think about? You've got to get the name of whoever Her Gracious Grace has hired. You then have to find out whatever it was they found out about him. After that you've got to get somebody who can help. Which brings us, I need hardly point out, right back to where we were last night, with the choice between the police and that baboon Stewart. I don't know about you, but with a choice like that, me, I'd take the police. They're incompetent, but they're not, they cannot be, as stupid as he is."

"OK, maybe you're right. And if Anthony's there, the first bit is simple. Even if he's not, I think Hugo will scare easy. But if *he's* not there, it means I'll have to deal with Mummy, and I'm not so sure she'll play. And even if we get the name, what do we do then? We can't just grab these detectives by their shoddy lapels and say, 'Did you shop Tom?' "

"True. You know, there's more Nancy Drew in you than you'd think."

Jane had forgotten about Tun Maung and was not used to half-naked cinnamon-colored young Buddhas knocking on the door and standing there smiling. "My god, who's *that?*" She clutched at Angela.

"Good morning, ladies." The silver tray held out in front of him, he came in and bowed. "I bring coffee. Hot coffee. Or you like tea better?"

"Thank you, Tun Maung." Angela was very *grande dame* about it. "Not tea, no. Coffee is right. Could you put it here?" She waved a hand at the table and let the same wave take in Jane. "This is Miss Cornell."

"Hello." Jane held out her hand.

He took it and bowed again. "How you do. I very glad be here."

He smiled a very wide white smile, and through the worry and fear Jane smiled back. "I'm glad too. I really am."

The coffee pot he'd brought was the Georgian silver one that Tom had given her because while making its abrupt exit from its previous home it had got a bad dent when he'd slipped coming down the drainpipe and dropped it. She never used it, but now she watched the steaming coffee pour from its spout, and as the level of black liquid rose in the cup, black anxiety churned in the pit of her stomach.

"Thank you, Tun Maung," Angela said.

"You want more, you call. I be there."

Jane dialled Cravenbourne. No, Lord Anthony was not there. Yes, His Grace was.

With no preliminary small talk, she asked Hugo what she wanted to know, and he caved in instantly. She wrote down Tom's last name—Gregory—and the name and address of the private eye. "Thanks," she said and hung up in the middle of poor Hugo saying how good it was to hear her voice.

"And now?" Angela asked.

Jane looked at her watch, "I've got an idea, but   "

"But what?"

"But it's still awfully early to phone anybody English."

"Don't be an idiot, it's almost eight and high time the slugs got up. Maybe if they got up by eight a little more often, they too could make Toyotas."

"Mustn't be aggressive, Angie. It's not done here."

"I tell you it's not done here. Nothing's done here; that's the trouble."

"Right. Let's get them up."

Jane called the *Orbit* and got Leo Fraling's home number.

"Leo? It's me, Jane."

"What's the matter? Have the drums stopped beating?"

"Worse. How long would it take to get hold of the best crime reporter in London?"

"Blimey, I don't know. Fifteen minutes? Fifteen hours?"

"Go for the fifteen minutes. Take second best if you have to."

"I'll call you back."

Ten minutes later the phone rang and he said that Joe Leverson would see her if she could be at the *Post* office within an hour.

"Thanks, Leo. Tell him twenty minutes."

"Done."

She got the velvet tent out of the wastebasket, and when Angela opened her mouth to protest she said, "Shut up."

The taxi dropped them at the c. 1924 bronze and mosaic extravaganza that is Lord Forrester's monument on Fleet Street. They walked through the garish lobby, and Angela looked up at the mural of His Lordship standing like Christ at the Last Supper, holding his hands out in the direction of Industry, Trade, and Communication.

"Looks like a muleskinner," she said. "Was he as awful as I've always heard?"

"Much worse. Used to boast that one of his ancestors was a highwayman. It must have run in the family."

Joe Leverson was a squarish, slight little man with a hawk-nosed face, steel-rimmed glasses, and bushy black hair. He stood up as they came into his office, shook hands with them from behind the desk, and asked them to sit down. "Now, what can I do for you, ladies?"

Jane told him about Tom and the Duchess's private eye and the night she'd gone to Clabbard Street, and then she handed him the slip of paper with Tom's name and the detective agency's name on it.

"McNaughton and Cook, eh?" He looked thoughtful. "Dicey lot, them. But we'll have a go."

He flicked the intercom switch and asked his secretary to see if there was anything in the cuttings library on a Tom Gregory, and to bring the file on

McNaughton and Cook. He flicked the switch up again and looked across his desk at Jane. "What's this kid do?"

"Do?"

"What's his line?"

"Oh. Mostly house robbery, I think. Pictures. Bad pictures, mainly. Silver. Jewellery. That kind of thing."

"London?"

"Yes. But maybe other places too, I don't know."

"No drugs or anything like that?"

"No. Gosh, no. I know it sounds crazy, but he's very moral, very puritanical."

"Horses? Gambling?"

"He's never mentioned any."

"Anything big? Banks? Cigarette lorries? Whisky warehouses?"

Jane thought of the night Tom had fallen through her skylight. "No, nothing big. He doesn't go as small as bananas, say, but nothing big."

Joe Leverson nodded and forced a little smile at the limp little joke. "Associates? Mates? He work for anybody?"

"No. I mean he's never mentioned anybody."

"Phone calls?"

"None. Not in, or out. No, I'm sure he worked alone. He's an alone type."

"Pictures, you say. Bad pictures. Silver. Odd bits and pieces. In other words, no specialization."

"That's right."

"He ever mention how he got rid of it? Who took it off him, or where?"

"No. He never told me anything, really. He didn't want me mixed up in it."

"Any idea of a neighbourhood? Not where he worked, but some place, any place at all, he went?"

"No. I've never seen him anywhere—except for at my flat, I mean. And that room on Clabbard Street."

Joe Leverson wrote "Clabbard Street" on the piece

of paper. "Which direction would he go when he left your flat?"

"God, let me think. North, I guess. Mostly north. And once I gave him a lift to a tube station—but I can't remember now which one."

"Try."

"Let me see. I was cold. I remember that, and I was going to a cinema on Leicester Square and we went up Charing Cross Road and—yes, I remember now. I let him off at the corner of Charing Cross Road and Oxford Street."

"Tottenham Court Road, then, most likely. The Northern Line."

"I guess so."

He wrote a couple more things down, and then his secretary came in. "There's nothing on Tom Gregory, but here's the other."

"Thanks, Rita. Now go back, will you, and get me the cuttings on the Sullivan brothers. Not the whole thing; this year's will be enough." He picked up the phone and said, "Get me Chief Inspector Jones at the Yard."

Waiting for the call to go through, he took the receiver away from his ear and said to Jane, "This is only a hunch, mind you, and a very long shot in a very dark alley. But if this kid is the amateur you say he is, if he works alone, and if—when he's in a tight spot and scared—he fetches up in the East End, then my guess is whoever he's scared of is not in the East End. Stands to reason, wouldn't you say?"

A light flashed to show the call had gone through, and he put the receiver back to his ear. "Davey? Joe Leverson here. Yeah, fine. And you? ... Good. Glad to hear it. ... Now, what I want, Davey, is just a little information. ... Yes, off the record, certainly. It's for myself, not the paper."

The conversation that followed was almost entirely grunts, monosyllables, pub names, and a few dates mixed in with unlikely-sounding people named Mick the Mouth, Fat Ella, Paddy, and Bruce Sullivan. Jane wrote "Please don't mention Tom's name" on a scrap of paper and pushed it across the desk.

Joe Leverson winked at her and shook his head. "Thanks. . . . No, that's plenty, and very useful too. . . . Yes, we must soon. . . . And thanks again."

He picked up a long plastic ruler. "That, Miss Cornell, was a very rudimentary check on who's doing what, where, to whom, and for whom." He swung around in his swivel chair and tapped a map of London on the wall. "We will now have a little geography."

He tapped another part of the map. "Cable Street. The East End, right? Over here, Soho. Right?"

Jane nodded.

"Now, as I said, I don't think he'd go to the East End if it was an East End gang he was mixed up with. Nor do I think your boy is a Soho type. Soho is Greeks and Eyeties. Heavies. And the trade is girls and drugs. Other things too, of course, but knives, not black eyes, is more the style."

He moved the ruler over the map again. "Mayfair. Yes? But Mayfair is big stuff. Gambling. Funny import-export. Pictures, yes, but good pictures. Silver and jewellery, certainly, but—well, he just doesn't sound like Mayfair to me."

Now he touched several more places on the map, and frowned. "Without going into the subdivisons and overlappings and all that, frankly I think a nonspecialist would most likely be dealing with the people up here." He moved the ruler north. "Camden Town. An Irish no-man's-land, and a good ways from the East End. It's still a very long shot, but it could be it's the Sullivan brothers he's on the run from."

Jane's voice deserted her and she could only whisper. "Who in god's name are the Sullivan brothers?"

"They are, Miss Cornell, two extremely nasty customers. Psychopaths. And if you were to have the misfortune to meet their mum and dad, I think you'd see why. At any rate, the brothers Sullivan run a crude but highly effective organization that deals in everything from protection, running guns for the IRA, and armed robbery, to knocking off little old ladies' sweet shops and occasionally the little old lady as well. There's nothing fancy about them, and that, frankly, is why I think this friend of yours might be in with them. No offence intended, of course."

His secretary brought in a bulging file, and Joe Leverson went through it. "Yes, it could be. It just could be."

He scribbled a couple of names and picked up the phone again. "Give me an outside line."

With a pencil he dialled the number Jane had got from Hugo. The number rang a long time before anyone answered, and then a tough voice yelled, "Yeah?"

In a better stab at an Irish accent than a lot of actors can manage, Joe Leverson said, "Hello. McNaughton there? . . . No? . . . Oi'll have a wurd with Cook, then."

He handed Jane an extension, and she covered the mouthpiece with her hand to mask her breathing. Angela crossed the office and leaned over the desk, her ear close to Jane's.

"Yeah? Cook here. Who wants him?"

"It's Mick Brophy. Terence said for me to let McNaughton know that Bruce wants anything new yuv got on Tom Gregory."

"On who?"

Joe Leverson crossed his fingers, looked across at Jane, and winked again. "Gregory. Tom Gregory."

"Oh yeah, him. OK. Hang on a minute."

It was a long minute.

"You still there?"

"Oi'm here."

"There ain't nothin new. According to what's here, McNaughton ain't seen him for three weeks or more."

"Where's he gone to? You know?"

"Listen. We'd of knew that, we'd of told you. Anyways Bruce Sullivan told Mc—" The irritated voice became a suspicious voice. "Say, who is this anyway?"

"Oi told you. Mick Brophy. Oi'm calling for Terence. He said fer me to."

"Yeah? Well, I ain't ever heard of you and, like I said, we got nothin new on Gregory and there ain't gonna be nothin new till we see some bread. You tell Terence I said so."

"Sure. OK, Oi'll tell him—but like it may've slipped his mind, how much's he in fer?"

"Don't give me that slipped his mind bit. It's fifty, and he bloody knows it's fifty."

Cook hung up, and so did Joe Leverson. He reached over, took the extension out of Jane's hand, and hung that up too. "I'm sorry, Miss Cornell. They're bad news. Very bad news. But that fifty is hopeful."

Jane stared at him and tried to get a sound past the lump of fear in her throat. "Hopeful?"

"Very. If he's only worth fifty quid to them, it can't be anything big they're after him for. If it were, McNaughton and Cook would have smelled it and held out for more."

She absorbed the sense of this and said, "But Mr. Leverson, I don't understand."

He waited patiently. "What don't you understand?"

"I don't understand how come—I mean it was the Duchess who *hired* these detectives, and so how come these brothers in Camden Town have got the—"

"The information on him?"

Jane nodded.

"Very simple. McNaughton and Cook obviously do—well, let's say *jobs* for the Sullivan brothers, and it may even be the Sullivan brothers supply them occasionally with a list of names of people they're—uh—looking for. Oh yes, it's not uncommon, that. A simple crosscheck is all that's needed and then—well, then it's two fees with one stone. You can take my word for it, McNaughton and Cook wouldn't say no to that."

"But what do you suppose it's all *about*? What do you think they want him for?"

"Hard to say. Impossible to say, really. Terence Donnelly works for the Sullivans on a fairly wide

237

front. But my guess, for what it's worth, is that this boy's in trouble with a fence. You know, I assume, what a fence is?"

"Yes."

"But as I said, that's only a guess." He lifted his shoulders and spread his hands.

"Would going to the police help?"

His face was thoughtful, and he bit on the ruler while he considered it. "Possibly. It depends how much *they*—the police—want him too. If it's enough to make them really go after him, they might find him." He rubbed his jaw and frowned. "But if the police want him that much—well, it's six of one and a half dozen of the other, isn't it? He might be better off as things are. I'm awfully sorry, Miss Cornell, but, knowing nothing whatsoever of the circumstances, I'm afraid I can't give you a better answer than that."

"If you were me, though, what would you do?"

"I'd let it ride. I'd let it ride for a bit, anyway."

Jane didn't want to go; this little man was now her only link with Tom, and she wanted to hang on to his presence. But she saw his eyes take a quick, secret glance at his watch, and she stood up. "Thank you very much, Mr. Leverson. I can't tell you how grateful I am. It was good of you, and I appreciate it."

He stood up and came out from in back of his desk. "Don't mention it. I've owed Leo a couple of little favours for a long time. Glad to have been of assistance."

They shook hands, and she and Angela were almost out the door when he said, "Miss Cornell?"

Jane turned around. "Yes?"

"You won't go asking funny questions in Camden Town, will you? I really wouldn't advise it, you know. It's not at all like in the films."

"Yes, I understand. I won't."

"Good."

Neither of them even glanced at the muleskinner this time as they crossed the lobby, and out on the sidewalk Angela nimbly stepped between a young reporter and the taxi he had just flagged. "Thank you, sonny. The lady's in the second stage of labour, and I'm sure you know what that means."

The poor young man let out a squawk, and Angela bathed him in her most dazzling smile. "It's really awfully kind of you. Are you sure you don't mind?" To the driver she said, "St. Agatha's Hospital. Fast."

The taxi man pushed the meter flag down and pulled away from the curb. "What was that hospital again?"

"Claridge's."

"Claridge's Hospital? Where's that at, then?"

"Brook Street. Where it's always been at."

"Lady, that's a hotel, not a—"

"Don't be silly, it's one of the finest hospitals in Europe. I had my left breast off there. Would you like to see the scar?"

He pulled the taxi around in a wild U-turn and headed up Fleet Street towards Trafalgar Square. Sliding the glass partition shut, Angela said, "Very well. Another time."

Claridge's was polite but firm; no drinks could be served before ten-thirty unless madam was staying in the hotel. Was madam staying in the hotel? Madam wasn't? In that case—

"In that case we'll have a pot of coffee. And at ten-thirty on the dot, four double old fashioneds."

The coffee and all the drinks arrived at exactly the same time, and the little round table was very crowded. Jane pushed the coffee aside and took a sip of the old fashioned. "God, Angela, what do I do now?"

"I think, darling, you do as the man said and let it ride for a bit. He'll be all right, don't you worry."

"But what a ghastly world for him to be mixed up in." She stared into her glass. "I had no idea. I should have—I see now that I should have—but I didn't. Not any idea at all that it was so—so serious. The way he was about it, it always seemed—I don't know, like only a game."

"Jane, please don't. Don't torture yourself; it doesn't do any good."

"But it wasn't a game, was it? It was real. And now ... Oh, Angie, Angie, he's not *like* that. He shouldn't be anywhere near that world. He's gentle and kind. He likes to read. And draw—he loves drawing. And he's so young. God, he's so young. There must be something I can do. But *what?*"

"Darling, I know how you feel, honestly I do. But I really think the best thing you can do is—"

"You know? When I first met him I thought: God, he's so beautiful he really ought to be in pictures. And I almost did something about it, I really did. It wouldn't have been hard. They were making a lot of pictures that year, and I know hundreds of people who could have fixed it for him—if I'd asked. But I didn't ask. And you know why?"

Angela looked resigned to her fate. "Why, darling?"

"It's crazy. It sounds crazy now. But it was because I didn't want anything bad to happen to him. You know what a lousy, cheesy world the movie business is, and what it can do to people. I've seen too many people who were beautiful and innocent like him and who'd been sucked into it because they were beautiful and innocent, and then been turned into less nice people by making it. Or by not making it. And so I didn't. I didn't do anything. I just kept him to myself like—like a dog or something. And now, because I didn't, he—"

"Jane. Now *stop* it, Jane. It's not your—"

"But it is. It's all my fault. I didn't do for him what I should have done, and now through me, directly through me, he's in trouble."

"It's not through you. It's—"

"Angie, cut it out. If I hadn't had Anthony as well, and if I hadn't made an enemy of that awful mother, none of this would have happened."

"Maybe not. But none of that would have even mattered if he himself hadn't—Oh, what's the use? Why try to reason with somebody like you? Do you want that other drink?"

"No."

"Well, I do, so hand it over."

Jane pushed the old fashioned across the table, and a little bit spilled. "Sloppy *fool*," said Angela.

"Stupid drunken cow."

17

Jane had still heard nothing from Tom, so she left the number of the Pavilion Vista Hotel and of the maternity clinic with the answering service, and said that if Tom Gregory called they could tell him where she was. But only Tom Gregory. No one else. Did they have that clear? They did.

Scat was left with Tun Maung, and on the morning of the 24th she and Angela started for Brighton in the *News Views* Rolls-Royce. Nosing across the Strand in front of Minis and even Rovers, the chauffeur took the left turn onto Waterloo Bridge with the unhurried air of a man who knew nobody dared run into a Rolls, and they began the long crawl through South London.

Jane watched it go by. Kennington Oval, as dull and lumpen a place as the cricket matches that were played there. Brixton and its fortress prison. A Streatham that Dr. Johnson and Mrs. Thrale would never have recognized. Everywhere, besieged and crumbling terrace houses with only an occasional sturdy little stone church to remind you these built-up streets had once been village lanes.

But even the churches couldn't stop what was happening now. The yellow bulldozers and tyrannosaurus-jawed things on caterpillar treads had surrounded them like wolves waiting just beyond the perimeter of a campfire, and pretty soon all of it, even the churches, would be eaten. Poor old London, she thought, they're really wrecking it.

Angela read through a stack of mail the chauffeur had brought her, and the great maroon ark plowed along as steadily as the *Flying Cloud* making for home in a fair wind with all sails set. "Hey, Angie, this really is the life, isn't it?"

Angela didn't even look up. "Watch it. Remember what happened to Pinocchio."

"But *he* fell in with bad companions. Remember?"

"Well, you aren't exactly what you might call choosy, are you?"

"OK. Be disagreeable. I can get another godmother anywhere."

The Pavilion Vista Hotel was a blinding white Victorian palazzo that sprawled along the seafront and that, inside, was crammed like an overdone movie set with fountains, french windows, fake marble pillars, fake tapestry upholstery, balconies, niches, Palm Courts, and Winter Gardens. The bellboys and porters were so old they looked like the carved Quasimodo-uglies on corks, and two of these bottletop gnomes scurried off with the suitcases while Jane and Angela followed a third one, an altogether sweller one in a black jacket and striped trousers, who walked backwards towards the desk. If *Last Year in Marienbad* had been made by Jean Cocteau, Jane thought, it still couldn't have been as weird and surrealistic as this.

One thing you could say about Angela, though, was that she knew how to make a hotel work, and the printed notice that said "The Hotel Where Nothing Is Too Much Trouble," which Jane found very funny, Angela took quite literally. First, she sent the television back to be changed for a color set, and then she peered around for other little improvements that could be made. She began to sound like someone who had learned her English from a particularly terse and nasty phrase book.

"Could we have some ice, please? Could we have some more ice, please? Is there any ice water? These towels are too small. These towels are a satisfactory size, but there are not enough of them. We will need additional coat-hangers. The rooms are too cold. Please send up a menu; the lady is tired and wishes to have lunch in her room. Thank you. Thank you very much. Yes, that is all. Yes, for the moment that is all."

"Jesus," Jane said. "Would someone please ask Miss Gotrocks to refrain from beating the natives?"

"Darling, it's the only way. Hotels are exactly like horses. Once they understand who's boss and that there's to be no nonsense, everybody has a lovely time."

"The horse too?"

"The horse too."

"My. It must be marvellous to be so—so confident."

"All right. Just for that, the fence goes up another notch." She picked up the telephone and asked for a portable typewriter and the *Herald Tribune*. "And now," she said to Jane, "stop trying to pick fights."

For all the luxury of floating along in Angela's wake on a syrup river in a Never-Never Land where anything you wanted could be had for a phone call and a tip, Jane could not quite relax, and nothing quite smoothed over the tension she felt. If she was alone for even an hour, anxiety about Tom and countdown anxiety about the baby would surface, and then she couldn't even move—not even walk out on the pier or along the little lanes where the junkshops were and she would just sit. When it was really bad she couldn't even do the *Herald Tribune* crossword puzzle. She had never known that real depression and hysteria were such tight, quiet feelings.

Twice a day she forced herself to pick up the telephone and check with the answering service, but, except for messages from Anthony saying for her to call him, there was nothing. Then, on the 26th, the answering service called her. It was the first time it had, and her heart beat hard as she took the phone from Angela's hand. But it was only a call from Franklin in Philadelphia saying he sent love and was catching the morning flight.

After lunch the answering service called again, and this time it had to be Tom. But it wasn't. It was another call from Franklin. There was an airport strike in Philadelphia, and the morning flight would be nine hours late.

The baby, however, was not late. She and Angela were halfway through a tour of the Prince Regent's fantastic playhouse, the Pavilion, when she suddenly grabbed Angela's arm. "Oh lord, Angie, something's happening. It's all running down my legs."

"What's all running down your—Oh my god, I see what you mean."

"What'll we do? How are we going to get out of here?"

"Don't ask me, lady. I never saw you before in my life."

"Angie, this is no time for kidding around. Do something."

While they were hissing at each other, the guide finished his spiel and shepherded the group towards the door. "And now, ladies and gentlemen, we will move on to—" He glanced back at Angela and Jane. "This way, ladies, please. We are now going—"

"So," said Angela, "are we. But we are going this way."

She put a hand under Jane's elbow. "Come along, Prunella. Time for tea." Haughtily she swept Jane past the gawking crowd and back the way they'd come.

The taxi waited at the hotel while Angela went up to get her bag, and Jane sat stiffly on the edge of the seat, counting. She counted the seconds between pains. She counted the people who went into the hotel. She counted the people who came out. She counted the sea-gulls. She counted the number of times she'd seen *Le Jour Se Lève*. Twenty minutes later, and she knew be-cause she counted them too, they were following a starchy nurse down a shiny linoleum-covered corridor in the clinic.

She lay on the bed with both hands on her stomach and listened while Angela unpacked and put things in drawers and other clinkier, noisier things on the shelf over the basin. Crepe-soled shoes squidge-squidged along the corridor, and once the footsteps came into the room and somebody wound a blood-pressure thing around her arm.

When the pains hit their top level she tightened her fingers on Angela's hand and said, "Oooh." After there hadn't been one for a long time she opened her eyes. "Angie?"

"Here, darling."

She had to refocus her eyes to take in Angela's white cotton jacket with the high fencing-master col-lar. "What in god's name are you doing in that?"

"Like it? It's my Instant Obstetrician kit. Borrowed it off my dentist."

"But why?"

"Darling, it's Saturday and I know doctors. On Sat-urday they play golf. He'll never show up, and if he doesn't *I* am Doctor van Schuyler, personal physician to crowned heads in Europe and elsewhere. If he does, I'm just a friend of the family with funny taste in clothes."

"My god."

Another pain had begun its slow rollercoaster climb.

Almost all she could remember afterwards were flashes of Angela hamming her new role to the full A-to-B gamut in the delivery room, but carefully avoiding any of the actual rubber-glove dirty work or being caught too centre stage where it would have been obvi-ous that about obstetrics she didn't know beans.

"God, I've seen kittens born, who hasn't?" Angela said later. "But honestly, Jane, there were moments when I thought I'd faint. It was awful and thank god I flunked biology when I did. And when one of them sort of leaned on your stomach afterwards and out came that other thing—oh, you were asleep, you'd had an injection of something and you were asleep, but I wasn't, and you are never, never to do this to me again, do you understand?"

Jane could only remember a blinding overhead light in her eyes and thinking that maybe natural childbirth was like pot and something you had to try more than once before it really worked. But in fact it had all been so much less bad than in any movies except ones about stoic Chinese peasants that she was amazed. And she did remember more. She remembered someone saying, "It's a little boy," and then someone else had wiped the stinging sweat from her eyes and she'd looked at the slippery, wet, and still slightly bloody baby they held in front of her.

Its head was a mass of greasy black curls. Its mouth was an angry red hole in a dark, livid face, and its eyes were two tightly closed slits with black stuck-together eyelashes squeezing out from along the centre line. She had had only the quickest look before they snatched it away and put it in what looked like an aluminum roasting pan on the far side of the room.

But she hadn't needed more than that quick look. She would have known that chin and forehead anywhere. And though he was such a really terrible colour and much, much darker than seemed right, he looked exactly like his father. He was an uncannily perfect replica-in-miniature of Tom.

When she woke up, Angela was sitting in an armchair, reading, and Jane's mouth was so dry she had to lick her lips before she could speak. "Didn't know you were still here," she whispered.

Angela closed her book and got up. "My god, you're awake. How do you feel?"

"Fine. Awfully thirsty, though."

She helped Jane to sit up and held the glass of water to her mouth. "Not too much. Just little sips."

248

"Sips, schmips." She tried to get the glass away from Angela, but Angela moved it out of reach and put it back on the table. "There, that's enough."

Jane leaned back on the pillows. "Christ, you're a pain. Dress you up like a doctor, and the next thing you know you're acting like one."

"He's very pretty, your tiny boy."

"Is he all right? Where have they taken him?"

"Nursery. They said they'd bring him in when you woke up. Do you want me to ring?"

"Gosh, yes. What're we waiting for?"

"Well ..." Only very rarely did Angela ever look anything except crisply definite.

"Well what?"

"I think perhaps you ought to know first—I mean you may change your—"

"There's nothing wrong with him, is there? He's not ..."

"No, darling, he's perfect. It's just that—well, one of his daddies has shown up and is waiting outside."

"Oh jesus."

"And Jane—"

"What?"

"It's not the right one."

"Anthony?"

"No. The other one."

"Not Franklin?"

"I'm afraid so."

It wasn't fair. She couldn't. Later, maybe, but not yet. Not this very minute. How the hell had he found her, anyhow? No. She couldn't. She wouldn't.

"What time is it?"

"Just past two."

"Two in the morning?"

"Yes."

She leaned back and shut her eyes.

"Jane?"

"Mm."

"He's been waiting an awfully long time. What shall I tell him?"

"Oh *jesus, jesus, jesus.*"

"And then?"

"Tell him to come in, I guess."

"You sure?"

"I'm sure."

Angela was just going out the door when Jane called her back. "And Angie?"

"Yes?"

"Tell them to bring the baby too, would you?"

In his almost white raincoat he stood in the doorway and said, "Hi."

"Hi."

It was an awkward moment, and, rather too loosely cool, he came across the room and stood by her bed. "You all right?"

"Who, me? Gosh, yes, I'm fine. It wasn't nearly as bad as they make out."

"And the baby?"

"Fine. It's, I mean *he's,* fine, too." There was a little silence. "They're bringing him in in a minute. I told Angela to tell them to, anyhow."

She could tell from his eyes that he'd guessed, and she looked away. He sat down on the side of the bed, brushed a strand of hair away from her face, and said, "It's all right, baby. Don't be jumpy; it's all right."

He moved up and leaned his face down next to hers on the pillow, and she didn't know how long they stayed there like that, not saying anything, but he lifted his head only when the door opened and a nurse wheeled the baby in. It lay on its side, wrapped and shrouded like a tiny papoose, and was sound asleep. With one finger Franklin moved the edge of its flannelette wrapper away from its face and looked down at the small sleeping thing.

"He isn't very beautiful now," Jane said, and the words spilled out nervously, "but he will be. He's going to look just like his father."

From the other side of the baby's bassinet, Franklin looked across at her; he was still leaning over the baby, and his face was almost on the same level as hers. "Not now," he said. "Not yet."

She broke away from his eyes by burying her face in a pillow. "Why not now? If not now, when then?"

"Later."

She lifted her head and looked at him. "How did you find me, anyhow? I told them not to tell anybody."

"That's not quite what you told them."

"I did. I told them not to tell anybody except—"

"Except Tom Gregory."

"All right. Yes. Except Tom Gregory."

"And so when they asked me if I was Tom Gregory, guess what I said?"

She couldn't help it, she had to smile. The best-laid plan of the best-laid woman had ganged agley. "The One Great Scorer will get you. He hates a liar, the One Great Scorer does."

"Did you ever find out what his trouble was?"

"You said 'later.' "

"Later for the rest of it. Did you?"

"No. I haven't seen him since that night. I haven't even had a—"

"Nothing?"

"Nothing."

The nurse came in, her shoes squidging and her skirt swishing, and pointedly shook a thermometer rather longer and harder than any thermometer needs to be shaken. "I'm sorry, Mrs. Cornell, but it's very late and we'll have to ask your visitor to leave. As a rule, only fathers are permitted to visit at odd hours and . . ."

Franklin said, "Right," and kissed Jane on the forehead. "I'll be back in the—" He turned to the nurse. "What are the visiting hours?"

"There are no set visiting hours, as such," she said. "But after nine p.m. we do have that one little rule of fathers only." She gave a small but definite push at "fathers," and Jane thought: That's twice, the bloodly little beast.

In an imitation of the voice Angela used to get what she wanted in the hotel, Jane said, "Thank you, Nurse.

251

Mr. Rodgers will be leaving shortly." The voice wasn't coming over too well from around the thermometer, so she took it out of her mouth and put it on the table. "And as I haven't got a temperature, perhaps we could leave this until he has gone."

The nurse tossed her head and flared her nostrils like a horse and squidge-squidged out the door. "Bossy creep," Jane said, a fraction too loud and just as the door was closing.

Franklin grinned. "Bulls-eye. There's another friend for life."

"It works when Angela does it. Why doesn't it ever work when I do it?"

"God, I almost forgot. I brought you something." He felt around in his raincoat pockets and held his hands out to her. "Which one?"

She touched his left hand. "This one."

He smiled at her and opened his right hand. She took the walnut and looked at it. "All for me? You shouldn't have."

"That's all right. I was feeling generous."

She knew she was missing the joke, but she'd be damned if she was going to ask what the joke was. "Well," she said and stared at the walnut, "it's lovely, really lovely. Thank you."

"You're welcome. It is quite a nice one, isn't it?"

"Oh, marvellous. You'd have to—well, you know, get up early and look for a long time to find another one like it."

He kissed her on the forehead again and left. Just as she was beginning to realize how very, very tired she was and was almost asleep, the nurse came back and shoved the thermometer into her mouth.

18

For all the frilly, cottagey curtains and textured reproductions of Van Gogh sunflowers on the wall, it was, underneath, just like any other hospital. Reveille was at 6:45, and after that, except for a lot of hurrying White Rabbit footsteps in the hall, nothing happened. Unless you count nearly starving to death as something.

She had never been so glad to see a bowl of cornflakes in her life and was only halfway through them and loath to stop, when she heard Angela's voice coming closer. "That's right, darling. That's the room, that one there."

A red-cheeked bellboy from the hotel came in, pushing a trolley loaded with baskets of fruit and flowers, glossy magazines, a portable TV, a gardenia tree with shiny dark leaves and flat waxy-white blossoms, bottles of champagne that jiggled against each other and, sitting in the middle of it all, an enormous white teddy bear with a blue satin ribbon round its neck.

"Ah, motherhood!" Angela flung her arms wide and dropped her handbag in the armchair. "The end result of the awesome mystery of Nature and her great Design. And not only that, but also the answer to the question, the one great unanswered question of our time."

"What's that?"

"Ah. It is 'After the Multiple Orgasm, What?' Would you believe it, there was a piece called that—and not in any low-key soft-porn rag, either, but right in one of our most hoity-toity intellectual publications. I was astonished; you'd think mad physicists and nuclear reactorists would have more weighty things on their mind than that, wouldn't you? Even *I've* got more on my mind than that." She put a cigarette in the long black holder and said, "How'd it go?"

"Not so bad. He didn't put the back of his hand to his forehead and gasp 'Good-bye forever' or anything like that."

"Excellent. Very good sign, that."

"Mm. A very good sign that he's saving it up for today."

"Not necessarily, darling. Now, where's my godson? Has he grown? Any teeth yet? Good marks at school? They change so quickly at this age that I—" She picked up the walnut. "Ooh, a goody."

"How about that? A present from Franklin, yet."

"And what was it?"

"What do you mean, what was it? It was a walnut. It still is a walnut."

"The trouble with you is not only are you half-witted and disagreeable, which is an extremely undesirable combination of undesirable qualities, but you also know nothing about men."

Jane was brushing her hair. From the nape, the way it said to in magazines, and, sitting up with her head bent forward, she said, "Maybe not. But I have a very clear näive realist's knowledge of walnuts. I mean I know one when I see one."

It chipped Angela's fingernail polish, and that made her say "Hell," but she got the glued-together walnut shell open. "Goodness. I wouldn't have thought a Black Panther lawyer knew about such things."

"Eighty-five, eighty-six—yes, well, he's smart, though, probably even knows about pistachio nuts as well— eighty-seven, eigh—"

"French, I'd say." Angela held the ring out and looked at it thoughtfully. "No, quite possibly English. Much as I dislike having to credit them with it, they did make some very pretty things in those days. Yes, I'd say English. Early Victorian English."

"What are you gibbering about?" Jane raised her head and swept the hair out of her face. "My god." She took the gold ring with the heart-shaped amethyst outlined with tiny pearls. "Was this in that walnut?"

"This too." Angela held the folded scrap of paper just out of Jane's reach. "Shall I read it to you, darling? Wouldn't want you overdoing it on your first day of being where the multiple orgasm leads."

"Angela, you give it to me this second."

"I found it. You'd abandoned it, and I claim salvage rights."

Jane took a quick grab, got it, and got way on the far side of the bed to read it.

I am writing this before I see you so that when I say everything I said before still goes you will believe me. Have also found a hse. with a w.b.f. as well as dble gge, swmg pl, wdlnd frntge, nr schls and shpg cntr. Wht more cld anyone wnt?

She handed the note to Angela and with tears in her eyes she said, "Oh, Angie, it happens every time. Every time I think I'm insane to be in love with him and that he's nothing but a no-good, sportin-life callous black son of a bitch, something like this hap—"

He came through the door. "Who's a callous black son of a bitch? No—no hints. Let me guess."

Even a Doris Day movie would never have risked such a scene. Franklin kissed Jane. Jane wept. Angela laughed and opened a bottle of champagne and poured it out into tumblers from the medicine chest, and a nurse brought the baby in. If it had been a musical, it would have been the moment for the first reprise of the sentimental love song.

After the nurse went, they unwrapped the baby a little and looked at his ears and his eyelashes, his fingernails and toenails, and his scrawny little wrinkle red arms and legs. With hesitant fingers they touched his feet and his knees as if he were a transistor radio and they were Stone Age people in a New Guinea valley who'd never seen one before.

"I never can believe these things grow up and go to Harvard and get drunk and have acne and lay girls," Angela said. "It isn't right, is it?"

"Not right at all," Franklin said, "because this one's going to Yale." The baby closed its small fist around his finger. "You see that? He likes me."

Angela held the baby, and Franklin held Jane's champagne while she undid one of the flaps on the nursing bra. Angela leaned over the bed and put the baby in Jane's arms, and the minute his cheek touched her breast he turned his head and made frantic snuffling sounds. "He's got the idea all right," Jane said, "but he's—"

The baby began to cry. "Oh, poor little *thing*," Angela cooed. "For the god's sake, Angela," Jane snapped back, "stop trying to make it sound as if I'm beating him. I'm only—"

"Ladies, please. It's a very simple problem, really." Franklin put down the glasses, took her breast in his left hand and the baby's head in his right hand, and with great concentration brought them together. Once the desperate little mouth had got it right, it clamped down hard and held on like a snapping turtle.

"Ow!"

"See? He likes you too."

While the baby sucked hard and made glukking swallowing noises, he kissed her long and slowly on the mouth. "There. How about that for the all-time great double female sensation?"

Jane opened her eyes and smiled blearily. "Gosh, it's like an orgy must be."

"It *is* an orgy," Angela said. "And just as much fun as I remembered." She put on her sable coat.

Angie, you big liar, you've never been to an orgy. I bet you twenty bucks you haven't."

"I *have*. And the memory of all those men stumbling around looking dazed in their blue shorts and garters is not an easy thing to live with. I hadn't known that so many men wore blue shorts; it really isn't the kind of thing you notice when it's only one man, is it? Still, it's an ill wind and all that, and if orgies really catch on and blue shorts stay in—but not on—it ought to be a great shot in the arm for Mr. Cash and his name-tape business."

"Don't go. Have some more of this lovely champagne somebody brought me."

They drank another bottle. A nurse took the sleeping baby back to the nursery, and Angela left.

"Do you really like it?" Franklin turned the ring round on her finger.

"I love it. It's beautiful."

"You want another one?"

She spread her fingers and looked at her hand, the way women do when they have a new ring.

"Just like it, you mean?"

"No. Plainer."

She played for time. "Mm. Yes, that might look quite nice."

"It would look very nice."

"Are you sure? I mean I know it would look very nice, but are you sure?"

"Sure I'm sure. Aren't you sure?"

"Who, me? I've always been sure."

"That's funny, because you look just like a girl I used to know who sometimes said things that—"

"Oh, her. She's some kook who goes around saying she's me. But don't you worry, they got her and locked her up."

"They throw away the key?"

"Right in the moat, a crocodile swallowed it."

"What are you going to name him?"

"I hadn't really thought."

"You're a great liar. You know that, don't you?"

"Well, now that you mention it, I guess I had sort of toyed with the idea of calling him Tom. It's a nice name, Tom."

It was another awkward jump, and one that even a very foolhardy chamois might have thought twice about. But they made it. "It's a great name, Tom," he said. "Tom Rodgers."

"Tom Rodgers on the White Water of the Colorado."

"Tom Rodgers With His Flying Machine on the White Water of the Colorado."

"Tom Rodgers Saves the Day With His Flying Machine on the White Water of the Colorado."

"But Jane."

"Mm?"

"You'll have to tell the other Tom. You'll have to tell him what you're doing and why. It's only fair."

"I know. That's why I'm going to get out of here and go back to London tomorrow. He'll have called—I know he'll have called, but seeing as you told the answering service you were him, they're probably giving him the brush-off. And even if he hasn't called, he'll have left a note at home for me. He's bound to have."

"Isn't tomorrow awfully soon?"

"Not really. Oh, the doctors will look long-faced and as if they were the Microbe Hunters about to stamp out yellow jack in the Canal Zone, but if I promise to stay in bed for a couple of days and not try out for the football team or anything, it'll be OK by them. And Angela's promised to line up a nurse to come and stay for the first month."

"You sure you're not lying?"

"Why should I lie? It's only an hour's drive in the Maroon Ghost, and I can go to bed the minute I get there. With you."

"Jesus christ, Jane, you—"

"Well, all right, not with you exactly. But with you. With you there, I mean."

"Oh. OK, that's it, then." He looked at his watch. "I can call the airline from the hotel."

"Airline? What airline?"

He looked uncomfortable. "Baby, I didn't want to tell you before we'd talked about other things, but I've got to get straight back."

"Already? But you just got here."

"I know, and it's crazy, but I've got to. I had a seat for tomorrow, but I'll switch it to Tuesday. That way I can take you to London tomorrow and be with you tomorrow night."

"Oh god, how awful. How long for this time?"

"I'm afraid this time it's for good. Things have moved much faster than I'd figured on, and so . . ." He put his raincoat on. "What about you? When can you come?"

"Gosh, any time, I guess. As soon as . . ."

"As what?"

She was thinking about Tom, and about being alone again, and about there still being some sort of epilogue to get through with Anthony, "Well, as soon as I can," she said blightly. "As soon as I can clear it with Prairie Jim and get my severance pay firmly in my hot little fist."

19

The chauffeur drove stodgily carefully, and, sitting directly behind him where he couldn't see, Jane mimicked his cautious, wary movements. "Who'm I?"

"My grandfather," said Angela, "making for Bar Harbor in his nineteen-thirty Bugatti."

"No, it's a truck. Nitroglycerine aboard. A rough track through the jungle and—"

"*The Wages of Fear*," Franklin said.

"That's the picture, but who'm I?"

"Well, let me see. Knowing how your mind works, you won't be the star—who was it, Yves Montand?— because that's too easy. On the other hand, you won't be the ugly little fat man either, because that's too hard, and you don't remember the name any more than I do. So you're the other one. What's his name, the German—Peter Van Eyck? Right?"

"Right. Gosh, you're clever."

Jane put her head on his shoulder and went to sleep. The baby slept too in its carrycot beside the chauffeur, and it was past noontime when they drew up at the

Connaught. "Thanks, Angie, for—well, you know, everything."

"Nothing, darling. I'll come see you before I go, and—depending on how the diving goes, of course—you should have the pearl by late afternoon."

"Lovely. Don't get a bossy creep, though, will you?"

"Of course not. Good-bye, Franklin." Angela kissed him on the cheek. "Look after them, won't you?"

At home Franklin carried the baby up the stairs and came back down for Jane. "Hey, your description of the new nanny didn't do him full justice. He's something else, he is."

"I know. Trust Angela to find something like that. At a party, yet."

"Some party. I bet Sabu there is as at home on a waterbed as he is on an elephant."

"I don't think it was that kind of party. God, men. You're all impossible. White men say nasty things about black men, black men say nasty things about brown men, and for all I know brown men say . . ."

Slowly she swung her legs towards the open door and felt with her feet for the curb, but it seemed an awfully long reach down. She gave in and let him lift her out. "Come on," he said. "Brown man him wait top stairs door open, and black man him plenty hungry."

"Oh shut up." She leaned for a second against the open door. "Black man like kaoshway, I hope."

"Cow what?"

"It's our national dish. Noodles." With his arm around her she walked slowly across the sidewalk and said good-bye to the chauffeur, who stood holding the door to the stairway open. Then Franklin carried her up the stairs and she undressed and went to bed.

Scat jumped up and lay on the pillow close to her head for a welcome-home purr, and, scratching his battle-notched ears, she thought of Tom. But all she could concentrate on was that she was very happy. She'd had the baby. She was home. Franklin was there—for a little while at least, Franklin was there.

She fed the baby and went to sleep curled up beside it.

When she woke, the baby was gone and Franklin was lying beside her, reading a book called *Theory of Justice*.

"What time is it?" she asked.

"Five-thirty—six."

"Where's Tom?"

"Angela's Miss Fletcher has him."

"What's she like?"

"Blond. From Devon, she says."

"Nice?"

He took off his glasses, folded the dust jacket in to keep his place, and turned towards her. "Haven't found out yet."

"Come on, you must have been able to tell something."

"Well, she's clean. She looks honest. She doesn't trust that cat, though. Threw him out."

"I'm hungry."

"Right. I'll tell Gunga Din." He got up and went to the door.

"And Franklin?"

"Yes?"

"See if there's any mail—or messages. Would you?"

"Sure."

There were only three or four envelopes, and none of them was from Tom. She ran her eye quickly down the list of phone calls. Anthony Fairfield ... Mrs. Phillips ... Mrs. Spencer ... Anthony Fairfield ... Miss Bailey ... Anthony Fairfield ... Mrs. du Bois ... Mike Tyrone ... Joe Leverson ... Anthony ...

Her eye went back.

Joe Leverson?

She dialled the number, and a woman answered.

"Mrs. Leverson?"

"Yes."

"This is Jane Cornell from the *Orbit*. Can I speak to your husband, please?"

He was a long time coming. Long enough for Jane

to cover the back of an envelope with neat little interlocking hollow squares.

"Miss Cornell?"

"Yes. Did you call me? I've been away, but there's a message here that—"

"I did, yes. It's about your—uh—friend. The one you came to see me about."

"Really? *Honestly?* Oh, I'm so glad. I knew if I came back there'd be some word from him. Where is he? In London?"

There was a silence that lasted so long she thought they'd been cut off. "Mr. Leverson?"

"Could I come and see you, Miss Cornell? It really isn't—What I mean to say is, discussing it over the telephone isn't a—"

"Of course." Jane giggled. "Vun neffer knows ven der enemy iss listening, duss vun?"

"Sorry? I didn't quite catch that."

"Never mind, it wasn't worth catching, it was just me being silly. But when can you come? Tonight?"

"I could, yes. Where do you live?"

She gave him the address, and he said he'd be there in a couple of hours if that was convenient for her.

"Oh, my, yes, Mr. Leverson. That's convenient. But hurry, won't you?" She ate her own pheasant and half of Franklin's, and when Tun Maung brought their coffee to the living room she smiled at him from the sofa and said, "Delicious, Tun Maung. That was absolutely delicious."

"Ah, good. You like. I no know what is, but him look like jungle fowl and I know cook jungle fowl, so I buy. Is called how?"

"Pheasant."

"Fez-unt. Good. I buy now on much."

"Well, not too much, Tun Maung; it's very expensive, fez-unt. Only for parties. You know, nice times like now. Celebrations."

"Silly brayshuns." He laughed happily. "Fez-unt for silly brayshuns."

"That's right."

They'd finished their coffee, and Jane was with Miss Fletcher in the baby's room when the doorbell rang. "Gosh, that'll be Mr. Leverson." She handed the sleeping baby to Miss Fletcher. "I'll finish feeding him when he wakes up. OK?"

The nurse followed her a little way down the hall. "You wouldn't prefer that baby go on a regular four-hour schedule?"

"I don't think so," Jane said very lightheartedly. "Why should he? Why don't we just let him eat when he wants to? It's kinder, don't you think?"

Thinking, especially thinking about what might be kinder, had not played an enormous part in Miss Fletcher's very conventional training. She looked flustered and retreated down the hall with little Tom.

"Hello, Mr. Leverson." Jane smiled and held out her hand. "It's nice to see you again. This is Franklin Rodgers." To Franklin she said, "Darling, this is Joe Leverson, the man from the *Post* I told you about."

They shook hands, and Joe Leverson's sin-accustomed eyes took it all in at a glance but looked as if they'd seen nothing. "Can I fix you a drink?" Franklin asked.

"No. No thanks, I—well, possibly a whisky. On the rocks."

"Right. What about you, Jane?"

"Why not Angela's champagne? Wouldn't you like some, Mr. Leverson? Oh, *do*. Change your mind and have some. It's awfully good champagne."

"No. No thanks."

"All right. You're making a mistake, but it's all the more for us. Now, do sit down, Mr. Leverson and—oh, a cigarette. Would you like a cigarette?"

"No thanks. Gave it up." He suddenly looked very small and shy in the big black armchair, and even when Jane smiled a bright, encouraging smile he didn't smile back.

"Miss Cornell, I'm afraid I have bad news for you."

"Bad? But you said—"

Franklin had already handed him his whisky; now he

265

put the unopened bottle of champagne down and stood listening.

Jane's voice was very small. "Really bad?"

"I'm afraid so, yes."

Her heart began to beat so that she could hear it. "He's not—"

Joe Leverson nodded an almost imperceptible nod, and Franklin sat down on the arm of the sofa and put his arm around her. She turned her face against his chest.

"Can you tell us how you know?" Franklin asked.

"I can, yes. If Miss Cornell is—"

She pulled her head up and ran a hand through her hair. "It's all right. You can—"

"Are you sure, baby?"

She hung on to Franklin's hand hard, and nodded. "Yes. I'm sure."

"Well, after I saw you that day in my office, Miss Cornell, I put one of my boys onto it. Really just to— He's a new boy, you see, and it was to give him some practice in tracking things down. Naturally I didn't want to give him anything too easy, but at the same time he's too inexperienced to put onto anything im—"

"Important," Jane said. "It's all right. I understand."

"I'm afraid that's how it seemed at that moment in time, yes."

"Go on."

"I didn't—to speak frankly—think he could do it. But, he's young and dead keen; his first job on a national paper, and all that. And—well, he asked around, not that he found out anything much that way, and I knew he wouldn't. But he stuck with it and went— well, pretty much everywhere you would go if you were looking for somebody. Unfortunately he drew a blank every time. Nobody anywhere had known, seen, or ever heard tell of a Tom Gregory."

Franklin glanced down at Jane's face and said, "Mr. Leverson, can you just tell us how you're sure?"

"Yes, certainly. Sorry to have digressed. I merely

thought it best that you know the—uh—background. But, to make a long story short, when the police take a body out of the river—" He paused. "Are you certain you want me to—"

Jane nodded. "Please. I must know."

"—they make a minutely detailed inventory of every article of clothing and so on that they find on it. Usually it doesn't amount to much, but, as I'm sure you know, even laundry marks and dental work can help with identification."

He looked longingly at the glass of whisky, which he hadn't even touched, and Jane said, "It's all right, Mr. Leverson, drink it."

"Thank you." He took a discreet sip. "In this particular case, however, the police had in their possession the body of a young man that they had, frankly, given up on. There were no laundry marks. No surgery scars. No dental work. Nothing. There had been nothing in his pockets. They had, however, found in the lining of his jacket—aparently it had slipped through a small hole in the pocket—a very small glass-sided gold object."

He took another sip of his whisky. "They had listed it as a box, but when I saw this inventory—it was one of several that this boy I'd put onto the job had copied out and brought back to the office—I recalled Miss Cornell mentioning she'd given Gregory an American note in a glass-sided gold bracelet charm. I didn't think it could be coincidence, so I got onto the job myself."

Jane leaned her head down on Franklin's knee, and he smoothed her hair with his hand.

"I checked first where this body had been taken from the river, and when. I found that it had been just three days after the date that Miss Cornell had visited her friend near Cable Street. I also found that the spot where the body had first been sighted was approximately, give or take reasonable variations in the current, where a body that had entered the river due south of Clabbard Street would have drifted to in thirty-six to forty-eight hours. These two factors—in addition, of course, to the object found on the body—convinced me."

"How did he die, Mr. Leverson? Could they tell?"

"He drowned, Miss Cornell. There was extensive bruising of the face and body, and whether that was the same bruising you described to me or a new lot, there's no way of knowing. But he was alive when whoever—that is to say, he was alive when he entered the river."

She couldn't take any more. Leaning on Franklin, she stood up and said, "Thank you. Thank you for coming to tell me."

"Don't thank me. It was the least I could do, and I'm sorry to have had to."

"I'll see you to your car," Franklin said and opened the door.

"Thank you. But Miss Cornell, I'm afraid the police will be wanting to see you. They'll require a formal identification, and you are, so far as anybody knows, the only person who can supply it."

"Yes—all right. What do I have to do?"

"You just sit tight; they'll be in touch." He moved towards the door. "Oh, one more thing. What or how much you tell them is, of course, entirely up to you. I've mentioned nothing of the—uh—circumstances."

When Franklin came back, she was sitting on the bed with the baby in her arms, rocking silently back and forth while tears ran down her face.

"Jane . . ."

She looked up at him, still rocking, but said nothing.

"Jane, come to bed. You shouldn't be up anyway, and so now let me take the baby back to Miss Fletcher, and you come to bed."

She didn't resist; she let him take the baby out of her arms, and when he came back she was in bed. He undressed, opened the window a little, pushed the button that closed the curtain over the skylight, switched off the lamps, and got into bed beside her. She was facing away from him, her knees drawn up and her arms around a pillow. He moved close to her and put his arm around her. She moved out from under it and farther away from him. "No, please. Leave me alone."

He waited. After a long silence he said, "Jane, it—"

"No. Don't talk either."

He waited much longer this time, and then he put his arms around her again.

She stiffened. "Goddamn it, I said to leave me alone."

It was the worst thing she could have done. For a black American, he knew very little about rejection. He had carefully, if not consciously, constructed for himself the kind of life where there was almost no likelihood of its happening. Because he knew he was vulnerable, and because he knew he had no defence against it, he—like an alcoholic who never orders turtle soup for fear there might be sherry in it—never let himself stray into situations or territory where it happened. The few times he had made a mistake, he had felt a rage so intense that all the confidence he ordinarily felt in himself, and all the trust he had placed in other people, disappeared.

He lay there and felt like that now, and all the hatred and fear that he ordinarily kept under icy control broke loose and swarmed over him like maggots.

She lay there too, as alone as he, and not even aware of how badly she'd hurt him. All she could think of was what had happened to Tom, and that she was responsible.

Franklin was right, of course, when he called her Miss Ash Can Ozzie and Phyllis Stein and said she had an Old Testament mind. But guilty was something she only played at being; it was a white-mice bath she took an occasional dip in and that made her squeal and wriggle and say, "Oooh, stop." But that was all it was. Real guilt she knew very little about.

Even to have caused a stranger's death in a car accident that was not her fault was something she would have got over only very gradually. To have been the direct, underlying cause of the death of someone she loved and whose baby—a baby he would now never even see—was sleeping peacefully only a few yards away was unbearable.

Only a few inches apart, but locked in separate, private, watertight compartments of misery, they went to sleep.

A few hours later, when Miss Fletcher waked Jane to feed the baby, the crisis seemed to be over. They laughed at the piggish swallowing noises he made, and how the effort of eating made a vein on his temple throb and bulge. Jane said, "Darling, let Scat in, would you? He's out on the roof taking flying leaps at the window." And everything was normal again.

In the morning when Franklin got up and started through the minor flurry that goes with someone catching a plane, there seemed to be no residue of anger or hurt at all. She got Tun Maung to cook him his favorite scrambled eggs, and when he was ready to go she got out of bed and went with him to the door. He kissed her very convincingly, and when he'd run down the stairs to the cab he looked up to see if she was at the window and waved and blew her another kiss. He didn't usually do that, and so it was certainly a sign that everything was all right again.

But it wasn't all right, really. It was a lovely, sweet, smooth crème caramel that had a trace, just a few slivers, of broken glass in it.

20

The police didn't waste much time. Two days later she had a call from a Sergeant Dodds, who suggested—that was the way he put it, but she knew what he meant—she call in at her convenience. Like that afternoon, say.

She said she was sorry, but that afternoon wouldn't be convenient. Tomorrow morning, then? No, that wouldn't be convenient either. His flat policeman's voice took on a now-let's-get-it-straight-who's-in-charge-here edge of irritation, and in her own by-all-means-let's-get-it-straight voice she explained that she had just had a baby and was still in bed.

That got to him. He was obviously one of those simple-minded men who, doggedly against such things as "abortion on demand" (what, she had often wondered, would the fools prefer? abortion at random? abortion by lottery?) are always just as doggedly for motherhood. His flat voice changed to deep-toned idiot awe. Could she possibly manage next Tuesday? Was she sure that was all right? Would she like him to send a car?

On Tuesday she stood between a policewoman and Sergeant Dodds in an icy basement room that smelled of disinfectant and formaldehyde. Her throat was dry, her knees were weak, and the waiting seemed interminable. She watched the white-coated attendant move a dirty fingernail very, very slowly down a list on a clipboard. My god, she thought wildly, he's dead too; he's a trusty they thaw out every once in a while to do the jobs nobody else wants to do.

The trusty hung the clipboard on a nail and shuffled across the room, sucking a troublesome tooth as he went. Unceremoniously he yanked open a big metal drawer and stood aside, still sucking on the tooth.

Except for a small sheet, he was naked. His face was more battered than she remembered, the features were distorted and puffy, and a post-mortem incision stretched almost the whole length of his body.

But it was unmistakably Tom. The wide mouth was slightly open, the way it had been sometimes when he was asleep. The dark blue eyes were open too, but now they were dull and blurred. His long, wavy brown hair that had shone so prettily when she shampooed it lay stringy and dirty around his head like a sick-joke halo.

It was Tom, she knew it was Tom. And yet it wasn't Tom, too. This poor naked dead body had no connection at all with the Tom she'd known. None. Maybe, she thought, that's what they mean really when they say you can't take it with you—not your gold at all but the look, the thing inside you, whatever it is, that makes you something more than just recognizable.

He had taken one thing with him, though. He had taken with him one small victory that no one could take away from him. He was still beautiful. Not the dirt and slime of the river, not the mottled bruises, not even the awful grotesque indignity of being naked and dead had been able to make her Tom ugly.

She nodded. "Yes," she said and turned away. The policewoman took her arm gently. "That's all, dear. Not to worry. Come along. That's all."

But of course it wasn't all. Sergeant Dodds had a few questions. There was something to sign. Would she mind coming along to his office? It wouldn't take but a moment and there'd be—as if this were the inducement no one could resist—a nice cup of tea.

How long had she known Tom Gregory? *About two years.*

Had she known him well? *Yes, fairly well.*

Did she know where his home was, or where he came from? *No. She thought it might be Glasgow, but that was only a guess.*

As she had known him well, wasn't it somewhat curious she didn't know? *Not really. They had simply never talked about it, was all.*

What could she tell them about him? *She was afraid almost nothing, really.*

Yet she had known him well. *Yes.*

What exactly had their relationship been? *They had been friends.*

Not more than friends? *What was there more than friends?*

Had they been—er—intimate? *If by intimate he meant sexually intimate, she did not see what bearing that had on anything.*

Was she aware that it was an offence to harbour a real or suspected criminal? *Yes, she guessed so.*

Had she known that Tom Gregory was engaged in criminal activities? *No.* Had she known he was a thief? *No.* Had she suspected he might be? *No.* Had she ever wondered how he made his living or what his source of income was? *Not really.* How had he made his living? *She had no idea.*

Had she ever seen in his possession objects that she might have had reason to suspect had been stolen? *No.*

Did he ever have large sums of money? *Not that she knew of.* Had he ever bought her gifts? *No, never.*

Was she aware that it was an offence to receive or conceal or handle goods knowing or suspecting them to be stolen? *She had never thought about it, but she had probably read that somewhere, yes.*

273

Had he ever given—or sold—her anything? No, absolutely never.

She was quite certain about that? Would she like a few moments to think? There was nothing to think about; she was quite, quite certain.

Did she know of any possible enemies he had? No.

Could he swim? She didn't know.

That, then, would be all. They appreciated her cooperation and were sorry to have had to subject her to an unpleasant experience. Would she care for another cup of tea? No, thanks.

Sergeant Dodds heaved himself up out of his chair and, taking the brown pottery teapot with him, left the office. Jane sat with her hands very still and a blameless, innocent look on her face, but her mind was racing like a squirrel in a wheel.

Had she made any mistakes? No. Had she made the right choice? Yes.

If telling the truth would have undone Tom's death, she would have told the truth. If bigger lies would have, she would have told bigger lies. As it was, she had told precisely the right-size lies to stop any further investigation. The police had nothing to go on and, without her, they wouldn't get anything. It would be "death by misadventure," and that would be that.

It hadn't been a difficult choice to make. This way, whoever had killed Tom would get away with it—but they would have got away with it anyhow. It was extremely unlikely the police would have unearthed whoever it was, even if they had tried. It was even more unlikely that they would have tried very hard. What was it to them that a small-time thief had been roughed up and had fallen—or been pushed—into the river? Were they going to do a Maigret and spend cold December nights trudging around Camden Town looking for a haystack that, if they found it, might, only might, have the needle in it that had done it? It seemed the unlikeliest thing of all.

Sergeant Dodds came back, poured himself a mug of tea, and, smiling a frank, open, all-American smile at him, she thought: *Got you, you idiot; you'll never find out now. Tom will be left in peace. Me and little Tom too. No policeman will paw over the stuff in the cupboard or take away the coffeepot Tun Maung thinks is so nifty.*

There won't be any stories in the newspapers about a cache of stolen goods in a Covent Garden love nest for some hawkeyed well-wisher to spot and send home to Franklin's sister. Or for that bloody mother of Anthony's to use to justify her rottenness. It was finished. She had remembered Tom's lesson about lying. ". . . answer what they ask and only what they ask, and stick to it . . ." And it had worked.

Now the last thing and the only thing she could do for Tom was to take little Tom home. There, in America, with a wbf and swmg pl and wdlnd frntge, she could bring him up to expect—and get—more out of living than his beautiful father had ever had a chance of.

She asked Sergeant Dodds what would happen now, now that she had identified him.

Ah well, now they would get cracking and locate a next-of-kin.

As you couldn't lay it on too thick for a copper, she said, *Goodness, how clever*—but how would they ever do it?

The Glasgow police would be contacted. Wheels would be set in motion—there was a very efficient machinery for the whole process—and they'd trace it all back. Oh yes, she could be certain of that.

It did sound most frightfully difficult; did he really think they would be successful?

He couldn't guarantee it, of course, but yes, the chances were very good. There'd be a record of birth somewhere . . . school records . . . medical records. Bound to be. Just routine, really.

Could she ask him a personal favour?

She could ask, certainly. Whether or not it could be done depended on what it was.

If there was no next-of-kin, could she be allowed to arrange the funeral?

Ah. That might be a little difficult—but not impossible. Again, it all depended on a number of factors.

She flashed the all-American smile again. She'd be most awfully grateful.

Yes, well, as he'd said, it all dep—

Could she ask just one more tiny thing? When he got the information about Tom, would he let her just have a peek at it? Or anyhow tell her what it was?

He might be able to arrange that, yes.

Could he ring her, then, please, when he got it? If it wasn't too much trouble, that is.

Well, now, owing to pressure and volume of work, he doubted he could do that—but if she'd care to check back in a fortnight's time or so, he might have some news for her.

She thought: Pressure and volume of work, my foot—and stood up. "Thank you, Sergeant Dodds," she said. "You've been marvellous, simply marvellous."

He walked with her as far as the front desk and opened the swinging gate. "Thank you again, Miss Cornell. You've been of considerable assistance."

It was all very "Absolutely, Mr. Gallagher. Positively, Mr. Shean."

Oh god. Anthony's Aston Martin was parked outside her door. She was tired. She was cold and wet. She was shaken. She had just told enough lies to be put in jail for. And now, Anthony. It was too much.

"Darling!" He held her shoulders and kissed her on both cheeks. "You look absolutely, devastatingly splendid. All slim and pretty again."

"Anthony, at the moment I look like hell. I know it, and you know it, so let's not kid around. Would you like to see the baby?"

"Seen it, darling, and he's too perfect; I fell for him immediately. But—I say, you're not angry, are you? At my popping in like this, unannounced and all?"

"Of course not. Delighted. Do you want a drink?"

"Love one."

She got one of the endless bottles of champagne out of the icebox, but Tun Maung came padding down the hall and took it from her. "I do. You sit. I do."

Anthony had a nonfading, too-cheerful leer on his face and seemed much queerer than she remembered. When Tun Maung had poured the champagne and gone back down the hall, the leer got even brighter. "My dear, what an exotic creature. Where *did* you get him?"

"Angela—you remember, my crazy friend from Washington—she got him. He's the nanny really, but he rather enjoys pouring drinks, so what the hell."

"The nanny, darling? How extraordinary."

"Isn't it? But then, isn't everything? And what have you been up to?"

"Nothing. Absolutely nothing but moping around White's trying to get you on the telephone. You have been most uncommonly elusive, haven't you, darling?"

"I wouldn't have thought so, no. I've been busy, that's all. And having a baby kind of—you know, takes it out of you."

"Darling—"

"Mm?"

"I've been miserable."

"Have you?"

"Say you've forgiven me."

"I've forgiven you." She said it as coolly and flatly as she could.

"Not like that. Say it nicely. Say it as though you meant it. I can't bear it if you haven't."

"Anthony, I'm sorry. But I've just come from a morning with the police and from the morgue, where I had to identify a body."

"A what? You're joking."

"I was never further from joking in my life."

"But a *body*, darling? What body? Whose body?"

"Well, I don't want you to tell your mother—you'll have to promise me that."

277

"I promise. Of course I promise, but what has my moth—"

"That boy her private eye told her about is dead."

"The black man?"

"No, there were two. This is the other one."

"Two? Good god, how frightful. How frightful he's dead, I mean. What was his name?"

"Tom. Tom Gregory."

"But whatever happened? An accident?"

"It was no accident."

"What do you mean?"

"I mean that whoever else your mother's detective sold the information to about him killed him. But you are not to tell her. You've promised, and I will not have her feeling the satisfaction of—"

"Now, Jane." Indignation always made him pompous, and he was pompous now. "Whatever you may think of my mother, and I can well understand why you are not friendlily disposed towards her, she would never feel satisfaction at such an unfort—"

"Well, whatever the christ she would feel, I don't want you to give her the chance to feel it."

Miss Fletcher knocked and came in, carrying little Tom. "Oh dear me," she said, jiggling him up and down, "baby says where's my mummy and my din-dins. Baby ever so hungry. Goodness me, yes, ever, ever so hungry."

Miss Fletcher's burblings had brought on Anthony's Saint Sebastian look, and Jane smiled at him evilly. "Would Uncle Anthony like to watch? He doesn't have to, but he can if he wants."

"Well—well, yes, I don't mind. If you don't, of course."

"Me? I don't mind."

Anthony poured himself more champagne and sat down and looked everywhere except at her milk-swollen breast in the baby's mouth. "What are you calling him?" he asked too chattily.

"Tom," she said and raised her eyes to meet his straight on. "His name is Tom."

278

"I see."

"I thought you would."

"I don't suppose, in view of what's happened to his fa—or rather, in spite of what's happened to his—that there's a chance you might reconsider and mar—"

"No, Anthony. Not the slightest chance."

"Perhaps later. In a few months' time. When you've got over the—"

"When I've got over the what?"

"Perhaps 'got over' is not quite the phrase. What I mean is—well, the acci—"

"It was not an accident, Anthony. Please get that through your head. I would never be able to prove it wasn't, and I won't even get the chance now, because I lied to the police so there won't be any investigation. But it was not an accident, it was murder. I want you to know that, and I want you to remember it every time you sit at that dinner table and hear your mother laugh."

"Jane, I—I don't know what to say."

"Don't say anything. I'm not blaming you for it, because none of it was even remotely your fault. It was mine. Mine, and your mother's. But I don't want you ever to forget it happened. Murder shouldn't be forg—"

She couldn't go on, and why should she, anyhow? It really wasn't poor Anthony's fault, he was as much a victim of that filthy woman as Tom. Except he was still alive, and Tom wasn't.

"Then you—we—are—"

"Yes."

"What will you do? You really can't live here alone, with a baby."

"Do? I'll quit work and go home. I'm going to marry Franklin."

"Franklin?"

"Surely you remember? He's the greasy, shiny buck nigger with a cock as big as—you know, you never finished that bit. What were you going to say?"

"I don't know."

279

"Oh. Well, it doesn't matter really. Except there's one more thing I'd like you to know, and remember."

"What?"

"Just that his cock is, in fact, exactly like anybody else's. It's the rest of him that's bigger."

Anthony got up and put his two-caped coat on and pulled his Hermès driving gloves out of the pocket. "I shall miss you, darling."

"Will you? That's nice, but please don't be sad. It was honestly none of it your fault."

He smiled a wry copy of his mother's winsome, one-sided smile. "Ah, but that's not quite true, is it? I failed you. I said things you will never forgive."

"Anthony, we all of us fail everybody else. Always. And I have forgiven you, I told you that."

"I wish I could believe it."

"So all right already. Believe it. It's true."

He leaned over and kissed her on the cheek and touched the baby's face with one finger. "Good-bye, darling. Good-bye, baby."

"Tom," she said.

"Yes—good-bye, Tom."

When he got as far as the door, she dredged up a last smile and said, "Anthony?"

"Yes?"

"Nothing. Just, so long. So long is nicer than good-bye."

He nodded and smiled back at her, but he didn't say anything, and she never saw him again.

It seemed, afterwards, a long time afterwards, when she thought about it, absolutely crazy that in a tiny little country like England—where she often bumped into people she hadn't seen in years and who were only there for a week—she could say "so long" to someone she'd known so long and so well, and never ever see him again. It just didn't make sense. But, making sense or not, that's the way it was.

21

There is, she found out pretty quick, almost nothing to be said in favour of living a chaste life except it cuts down the housework. Food is bought in smaller quantities and lasts longer; you almost get to know the eggs before they're eaten, and the butcher no longer greets you as cheerily as he did. Laundry diminishes. Everything stays so presentable for days on end that if even the Ministry of Morals (Undesirable Aliens Department) were to drop in unexpectedly, there'd be no need to run around shoving things under the sofa cushions as the jackboots clumped up the stairs.

The bed, now a single-purpose thing meant for sleeping on and nothing else, becomes much easier to make. You pull the top sheet up. You smooth the blankets and pat the pillows. You unfold the primly neat bedspread, put it on, and, as the English say, Bob's your uncle. Which may or may not be true, but if your bed can be made in one minute flat and without starting from scratch, Bob is certainly not your lover.

There were no longer Anthony's scatterings to hunt

down; the watch with the lapis-lazuli dial was the last of them, and that she sent on to him at Cravenbourne. Tom's oily pastel crayons no longer got left on the floor to be stepped on and ground into the rugs. Franklin's T shirts and tennis shorts were no longer something about which she had to shout down the hall, "Oh, god, I'm sorry—yes, they *have too* been washed; they're just not dry yet."

The new strength-and-health-through-clean-living regime was thin, lonely stuff. She'd look at the lonely lamb chop in the icebox or the small morning-after still life of one glass, one coffee cup, and one cigarette butt in the ashtray on the slate-topped table and would wonder not so much where the snows of yesteryear had got to, because she knew exactly where they had got to. But, like a child in a mild winter with a new Flexible Flyer, she did sometimes wonder when—or if—it would ever snow again.

She knew it would, of course. There wasn't, in fact, anything holding it up at all except the things she had to do before she could pack up and go. So she started doing them.

She bought a jigsaw and a lot of little steel blades with mackerels' teeth, and on Miss Fletcher's day off she knelt on the floor in the hallway and sawed through the lock on Tom's cupboard door. Inside there was less than she'd thought. Getting rid of it wouldn't be hard at all.

With a razor she cut the labels out of the mink coats, an ermine jacket, and a couple of stoles, squashed them into a huge cardboard box, and addressed it to the East End church that always had an ad in the *Times* asking for warm used clothing.

She tore up some pale eighteenth-century watercolours and burned them in the sink. The small Rembrandt etching of a carcass hanging in a butcher's shop she slid behind a Bachrach photograph of her father that stood on her desk in a silver frame. With a nail she scratched a small 'R' on the back of the frame, to remind herself where little Tom's college education was when the time came for it.

She put a portable typewriter, a Rolleiflex camera, and the box for the vicar in the trunk compartment of the car, and next day she drove them to Golders Green. First, she mailed the fur coats. Then, carrying the typewriter, she got on a bus that was going someplace she'd never even heard of. When she got on, the conductor was upstairs taking fares, and very casually she put the typewriter in the parcels compartment. Five stops later, when he was on the upper deck again, she got off and left it behind.

The Rolleiflex almost stymied her. She didn't want to be so lacking in imagination as to try the bus thing again, and yet she didn't want to throw it away. She wanted somebody—anybody—to have it; any idiot could see it was worth a lot, and it was a pity to waste it.

She headed for Notting Hill Gate, parked the car, and walked slowly down a slummy street, looking for a likely candidate. There were plenty around, but they all had drawbacks. Some were too young. Some looked too honest. Some weren't alone. She had almost given up, and then she saw him. He came out of a betting shop and was slouching off down the street, shredding his losing ticket as he went.

He was alone and, better luck than she'd counted on, he was drunk. More important, he was old enough and shabby enough to know what to do with a £300 camera, and she could tell there wasn't an honest bone in his body. He wouldn't go to the police, not him. And he'd know how to unload it so the police didn't go to him, either.

She followed him a short way and then broke into a ladylike run. "I say." It was, as upper-class English accents go, a real three-dollar bill, but he wouldn't know that, even if he'd been sober. "I say, can you help me, please?" He turned around unsteadily and stood weaving on the sidewalk in front of her.

"Oh, thanks awfully for stopping, and it's absolutely

ridiculous, I know, but I was returning this"—his eyes followed the Rolleiflex as she swung it back and forth—"to Mrs. Banks, who lives just there at number fifteen, and the awful thing is she's not in. I'm in the most ghastly rush myself, and so I wondered if you'd be good enough to wait here for her to come back."

A little glint of avarice came into his eyes, but he stifled it and shook his head. "And here's this, to make it worth your while." She opened her bag, gave him a pound note, and put the camera in his other hand. "Now don't forget. Mrs. Banks. Number fifteen. And you'll wait right here, won't you? She really won't be long, but I've simply got to run."

The gold pocket watch with the heavy gold chain and "To H. G. Purdy, on his retirement—June 1927" engraved on the back she put in a paper bag with some tangerines and walked out to the very centre of Westminister Bridge. Unhurriedly she ate two of the tangerines, put the peels back in the bag, and, with the rest of the tangerines left in for ballast, dropped it over the side.

The silver, unidentifiably ordinary Victorian forks and spoons and a cigarette box of the kind that Asprey's sells by the hundred, was easier. She gave the forks and spoons to Mrs. Bush to make up a little for Tom's having robbed her, and the cigarette box she wrapped in white tissue paper and took to Mr. Wilkinson at the bank. She knew his birthday was in December because once, working around to talking about her overdraft by way of a little conversation about astrology, he'd told her he was Sagittarius. Now he told her he was quite, quite touched by her remembering. Such a magnificent gift! And so unexpected, too.

The Bessinghome silver salver and the Georgian coffeepot she kept. She put them out in full sight on the oak chest so it couldn't look as if she were worried about them, and if anyone ever asked where they'd come from, she was going to say Anthony had given them to her—and that he could have them back any time he wanted. That way—if it came to that—they could be filtered back to the Bessinghomes, and that would be that. But it wouldn't, she knew, come to that. As soon as she could get the coffeepot and salver to the house with the wdlnd frntge and the wbf, they'd be safe.

When Tom's cupboard was empty she slept much easier, and once she'd moved the skis and things back into it she no longer woke at four a.m. in a cold sweat, absolutely certain that Sergeant Dodds was on his way over that minute. That she'd relearned to masturbate might have had something to do with the sleeping easier too, but all she really could have sworn to was that it was a tremendous load off her mind that Tom's things were gone and the trail was stone-cold.

She wasn't actually lonely. Little Tom was too much fun, and she had too many things to do to get ready to go, for loneliness to be what she felt, but she did miss Franklin terribly. She ached for him, and though she'd heard of that happening to cowlike faithful wives whose husbands were off selling insurance in Indianapolis or something, she was very taken aback to find it could happen to her too. How had it? Why did she want this one man so much? Did it happen sooner or later to everybody? It must, if it could happen to her.

His letters were long, they came regularly, and they were the kind of letters that if you were in love with the man who wrote them seemed marvellous. Philadelphia was cold. He missed her. The Princeton football team was having a winning streak. How was the baby? Had she any idea what had become of his second-best tennis racket? He had been busy and had missed out on that house he'd told her about, but somebody had told him about another one only a little farther out and where there'd be room for a tennis court.

When was she thinking of coming? All systems were go, and he'd got a tremendous amount of help from the formidable lady at Johns Hopkins, who had turned out to be not formidable at all but young and, although a little earnest, very nice and a great cook. Jane would like her.

Would I? Like hell I would. And what does he mean, help? What kind of help?

The jealousy was so sharp and so sudden that it startled her, and immediately she reasoned it away. No. He wasn't like that, and she was an idiot. He was a grown-up man not some cocksure boy with a permanent hard-on and a permanent eye out for where to soften it up. He knew what he wanted, and what he wanted was her. He'd said so. Often, he'd said so. She could hear his voice saying it. She could feel his body saying it. It was true, and no earnest, helpful lady scientist from Johns Hopkins could make it not true. He didn't even *like* earnest women.

He did like a good cook, though. That was true, and she began to regret all the hamburgers she'd given him. . . .

When two weeks had gone by she phoned Sergeant Dodds, and he said yes, he'd heard from Glasgow and she could drop by any time. Could she, she asked, come that afternoon? Well, Friday would suit him better, actually. It was tit for tat.

She accepted the ritual mug of tea and held it in both hands to warm them.

"I'm afraid it's all pretty much of a muchness, what we've come up with, Miss Cornell. I hope you won't be too disappointed."

He pulled a new papers from a manila folder and handed them to her. The top sheet was some kind of official form and was headed GREGORY, T.

Date of birth:	*not known*
Place of birth:	*not known*
Mother's name:	*not known*
Father's name:	*not known*
Midwife assisting at birth:	*not known*

The next page was a photostat of another form. The heading was THE CONVENT OF THE MOST BLESSED HOLY VIRGIN MOTHER, and on it and five more sheets Tom's whole life was recorded.

He had been found just short of twenty-four years ago on the floor of the Church of the Holy Sepulchre, on Phillimore Street in Glasgow. "Eyes, blue. Hair, brown. Age, approx. 2 wks."

After two years with the nuns, he had been fostered out to a Mrs. Maclachlan—"present address not known"—and again, when he was five, to Mrs. R. Stowell—"now deceased." A year later he had been placed in the care of the Boys' Shelter. Two years after that he had been transferred to the Overton Street Orphanage run by The Merciful Christian Brotherhood of God.

Here, a picture of something more substantial than a shuttling, infinitely transferable object began to emerge. On a small sheet of paper headed "Interim Report" it said: "Intractable. Uncooperative. Defiant. (See Punishment Sheets attached hereto)."

The Punishment Sheets were divided into three columns. On the left, INCIDENTS. In the center column, ACTION TAKEN. To the right, AUTHORITY.

Late for Mass:	six strokes	Bro. Chas.
Bedwetting:	one week's forfeiture dinner	Matron
Stealing from larder:	six strokes	Bro. Benjamin
Blasphemous:	six strokes daily /3 days	Father John
Boots dirty:	scrub basement floor	Matron
Bedwetting:	sleep on floor/1 wk.	Matron
Disobedient:	orderly duty, infirmary/3 Sats	Bro. Kevin

There was more, but there was very little variation in either the crimes or the punishments.

The last entry of his stay at the Overton Street Orphanage was the longest page in Tom's biography:

"A not unintelligent boy but wilful and rebellious and a disturbing influence on the entire Home, notably among the younger boys. No possibility of fostering out due to previous history unsuccessful attempts and age (12). In view of the above and his behaviour, which is now believed to be incorrigible, steps being taken to effect transfer to Brocklehurst County Home, where, it is hoped, strict discipline and a routine of healthy outdoor work will effect an improvement."

From the arms of the Church, Tom had been lobbed into the arms of the state. And, shortly after that, into the arms of the law.

For raiding Woolworth's, a Mrs. Margaret Balfour, Magistrate, South Grangetown Juvenile Court, had sent him to Aylesworth Valley Approved School. At fifteen, he was released and started a very short-lived apprenticeship as a cooper in Lanarkshire.

"What's a cooper?" she asked Sergeant Dodds.

"A cooper? It's a chap that makes barrels."

"Oh."

From there—"apprehended in possession of a quantity of cigarettes, believed to have been stolen"—he was taken to court again, and the recommendation was that he be sent to Borstal. "For Borstal training," the phrase was. Waiting for a place at Borstal—those Etons of the delinquent classes are very crowded and sometimes as difficult to get into as the real Eton itself—Tom had spent six months in the Remand section of the Mickleforth County Jail.

After that, there was almost nothing. "Defected from working party at Claymore Grange," was where Tom's recorded life ended. The only page after that was the coroner's report. "Death by Misadventure."

Jane squared the sheets of paper up neatly and handed them back to Sergeant Dodds. "Thank you," she said.

There was a lot of hemming and hawing about it and more papers to be signed than there were in Tom's whole file, but in the end they let her arrange his funeral.

A few days later she sat alone in a chapel at the crematorium, and watched the wooden coffin with his body in it slide through a black velvet curtain. Two days later she walked out on Westminster Bridge to the same spot where she'd thrown the watch in, and licked her fingertip and held it up to test the wind.

Dodging the traffic, she crossed over to the other side of the bridge and very gently sprinkled Tom back into the river that had finished the job so well begun by the Church, the state, and the law. Instead of a prayer she silently repeated all she could remember of one of his favorite poems. It was the one by Shelly that went:

> I met Murder on the way—
> He had a mask like Castlereagh—
> Very smooth he looked, but grim,
> And seven bloodhounds followed him.
>
> All were fat, and well they might be,
> . . . .
> For one by one, and two by two,
> He tossed them human hearts to chew.
>
> Next came Fraud, and he had on,
> An ermined gown;
> His big tears, for he wept well,
> Turned to millstones as they fell.
>
> And the little children, who
> Round his feet played to and fro,
> Thinking every tear a gem,
> Had their brains knocked out by them.
>
> Clothed with the Bible, as with light,
> . . . .
> Next, Hypocrisy
> On a crocodile rode by.

> And many more Destructions played
> In this ghastly masquerade,
> All disguised, even to the eyes,
> Like Bishops, lawyers, peers, or spies.
>
> Last came . . .

Jane couldn't remember what it was. One more line was all she knew.

> Blood is on the grass like dew.

Her next move was to tell Prairie Jim and Mike Tyrone that she was quitting, and that if it was all the same to them she would like to be released from the six-months-notice clause in her contract so she could leave as soon as possible.

They were awfully nice about it. They were glad, they said, to see her so happy and to hear she was getting married. They wished her all the best, and she wasn't to worry about the six-months clause because that was not the kind of thing that mattered between friends.

On the other hand, finding a replacement would not be easy.

"It won't be, will it, Mike?"

"No, Jim, I doubt it will. What about David Perrin? He's not as good as Jane, of course, but he's—"

"Not on, Mike. He's just taken over from Ingrams on the *Telegram*."

"Oh. Pity."

"What about Peter Farley?"

"I doubt it. He's got his eye on the *Examiner*, and he's got a pretty good chance of getting it, too."

For several minutes they tossed names back and forth and got nowhere. When Mike Tyrone turned to her and asked if she'd consider staying on, as a personal favour to him, for three months, she wanted to scream, "No," and run.

But she had worked a long time for the *Orbit*. Mike

Tyrone had always been very kind to her. Even the Master-Mind of Medicine Hat didn't look so bad, now she knew she wouldn't have to look at him much longer. And, after all, three months wasn't very long. Not really.

"OK, Mike, just for you. Three months."

She wrote to Franklin and told him about the three months and why she'd agreed, and how the baby smiled real smiles now, not just gassy grimaces, and that it was sad he hadn't been able to come for Christmas.

She even managed to make an almost-joke out of the grim, lonely fiasco that had been Christmas, and told him how she'd sat alone in the kitchen, chewing on half-raw turkey, while Tun Maung had wrung his hands and said, "Very big bird. I think long enough oven. But not long enough."

The half-raw turkey had, she said, finally been made into turkey soup—a truly awful lot of turkey soup. Too much even for the rats. Although, brave, indestructible British rats that they were, they had eaten up every scrap of the plum pudding, leaving only the sprig of plastic holly that had been on top.

22

Now it would be a long time before she'd see Franklin again. And what she should have done, of course, was tell Mike Tyrone that she was sorry to have made a promise she couldn't keep and all that, but that she had to leave now. Now, this minute.

Less drastic, she could have taken little Tom and Tun Maung and gone to cover the minor but rather chic little film festival that was on in New York. It would have been easy to fix it with Mike—he didn't care what she covered, so long as he had a movie page that he could set on Friday and then forget about. She rather longed to see New York again, too. And Philadelphia would be only minutes away. She and Franklin would hunt around for houses with wbfs and be together.

But she didn't go. Tun Maung was in the midst of a series of special lectures that were important to him, and also it would be mad to take a new baby off to germy, smoggy New York in the dead of January. Not that the dead of January in germy, smoggy Covent Garden was exactly nature's remedy for anything, but she had an unshakable theory that it wasn't so much germs that were dangerous as new germs, germs you didn't know.

Even new germs that came in weren't so bad, because when germs crossed the threshold they became your germs, and benign. But going out was different; if it was you that crossed the threshold, not the germs, the ones you met outside stayed other people's germs and were hostile. Those were the ones you had to avoid.

That it had worked diametrically the opposite way with the Eskimos and the Polynesians, she knew. Nor was it a theory that she would have chosen to defend against a gathering of distinguished bacteriologists. It was just something that, like rubbing on castor oil makes your eyelashes grow, she believed.

The Hostile Germ Theory didn't keep her from taking little Tom out, though—to go out in London was all right, because London was where he lived. And so sometimes she'd push him in his big-wheeled shiny black pram up Drury Lane, past the theatrical shoemakers with dusty windows full of shoes that always reminded her of Busby Berkeley musicals, by the grubby little secondhand jewellery stores and the one-track-minded bookstores that stocked nothing but the *Thoughts of Chairman Mao* and, mysteriously, never seemed either to sell a copy or go out of business.

Then sometimes they'd go the other way. Past the Opera House and the iron and glass arcades of the flower market, by the shops where they sold florists' ribbon and moss, down the hill and across the Strand to the Thames. If it was a sunny day and there weren't too many new germs around, she'd hold little Tom up and show him the boats—not that he could see them, but he did like being held and talked to about them. What he liked, she decided, was the *idea* of boats.

He liked, in fact, the idea of pretty much anything, when you got right down to it, provided the conversation was animated enough, directed straight at him, and nonstop. Like anybody, baby or not, who is kissed and fed and wafted from treat to treat, talked to and made much of, he had very little to be disagreeable about and so wasn't. He hardly ever even cried.

She did, though. That postnatal depression the books had harped on was real. The short empty days and long black nights were real too, and nowadays anything could make her cry. A poached egg that broke before it got on the toast. Mozart's last winter in Vienna. All the little Michelangelos that had died before the age of five in back streets in Florence. Songs like "Over There" or "Joe Hill." Anything.

It got so bad she even went to the doctor—her regular doctor, who didn't know she'd had a baby, and whom she now couldn't think how to tell that she had. To make her jittery, tearful state plausible, she told him her grandmother had died.

For a man with a waiting room full of coughing children and parchment-faced men with skinny necks, he looked suitably if fleetingly sympathetic at the sad news and scribbled her a prescription. She couldn't read it but, as he was a healthy, gin-drinking, anti-drug puritan whose idea of a holiday was another try at the north face of the Eiger, she knew it wouldn't be much, and it wasn't. For the ten days that the green-and-black cheer-up capsules lasted, she was fine. She felt very confident and wandered vaguely through whole days as placidly euphoric as the Queen Mother touring a nuts-and-bolts factory.

On the eleventh day, though, she began to come down. By noon on the twelfth day, after a night when even she had begun to wonder about Covent Garden as a place to live, she looked and felt like the Absinthe Drinker again. And what could she do then? Go back and tell him her grandmother was still dead?

February wasn't too bad. Small hints of spring cheered her up. Little Tom was doing more and more miraculously clever things every day. Tun Maung had quit trying to boil corn long enough to get the cob soft in the center. Miss Fletcher and her "Mummy kissums baby night-night now" had long since gone. And there were letters from Franklin.

He was working hard. He missed her. He'd had to go to Harrisburg—but he didn't say why. He'd been in New York for a few days, too—"seeing people"—and New York was worse than ever, all dirty grey snow and the now-unemployed Santa Clauses back on skid row and blind drunk.

He hadn't had a chance to look at any more houses, and now he had to go to Georgia, where he'd promised to help a voters' registration group. He'd be away a couple of weeks, at least.

He had met a lot of new people, and had never really realized till now just how phony and sheltered and protected a life he had led. The scene in America terrified him. He wasn't sure at all any more, or even particularly hopeful, that any of the old ways to change things would work; the rot had gone too deep for that, and not just in politics; it was in everything. He felt—he didn't know how to explain it—uneasy. Unsettled. Everything he did seemed as futile as shoveling shit against the tide. . . .

She wrote to him that night, so it would get to him before he left for Georgia. But obviously it hadn't got there by then, because his next letter was from Georgia and it didn't say anything about the things she'd told him in hers or even whether he'd been able to get the Carter's sleeping suits for little Tom. About all it did say was that the weather was cold and that he'd write again.

Which he did. A postcard. "Slight hitch, shall have to stay another week at least. Raining here. Hope all well."

It was a hotel postcard, too. Not a bought one, just one of those lying photographs of themselves that hotels give away free and that are taken corner-on by someone who's had to crouch down in a manhole to get the one angle that makes a seven-story firetrap look good. "Hope all well." What kind of a way was that to talk?

She sent him back a postcard of the Old Curiosity Shop, also taken corner-on. "Raining here too."

Two days later, just so he wouldn't think she'd really been as petulant as that sounded, she sent another.

> A ditch-digging young man in a ditch
> Said if that silly old bitch
> Wants a letter, she'd better
> Cut it out or we'll never get rich.

It didn't scan, it wasn't very funny, and it was, she knew, labouring the point. But he probably never got it anyway, because when she next heard from him he was back in Philadelphia. It had been a nightmare of a trip. Now work had piled up and he had a couple of very difficult cases on his hands. Everything was happening fast, especially his idea about the psychiatric caseworkers, and he had to go see Sue Collins again at Johns Hopkins. She'd been a fantastic help, and now she even had a couple of people lined up that she thought might be just right for the job.

Even? What was so even about that? It was her job, wasn't it? What was so fantastic about finding a couple of psychiatric caseworkers in a country where psychiatric caseworkers were so deep on the sidewalks that if you dropped one they practically made you scoop it up and carry it away in a plastic bag?

It wasn't until mid-March that he was able to get away and come to London, and then it was all of a sudden that he came. She hadn't had a letter in days, but on Friday she got a cable saying he'd be there Monday.

She spent the whole weekend getting ready. She went through the complete hair ritual and shaved her legs and under her arms, plucked her eyebrows, dyed her lashes, and gave herself a viciously vigorous shampoo. She even bought some heat-up rollers that made her look like Shirley Temple in, and for, ten minutes.

She'd never been so happy. She even, and this was

an even, put bright red polish on her toenails and started taking the Pill.

She cleaned the apartment and got flowers from the market. Twice a day for three days she lay on the bathroom floor to do the exercises that were supposed to tighten up the stomach muscles and make stretch marks go away. Much oftener than twice a day she swooped little Tom up into the air and made him laugh so hard that he drooled long, stringy spits down on her. "Your dad's coming, he is. All the way from America he's coming." She had always called Franklin "dad" to Tom; it was a switchover she'd made very early on and easily.

The Monday-morning movie was too important a one to skip, but she sat way in the back and made enough notes on the first part to get by on, and sneaked out halfway through.

She ran down Wardour Street, caught a taxi at Shaftesbury Avenue, and—the driver was one of the old ones who yank the handbrake on at every red light and only let it off slowly five full seconds after the light turns green again—all the way home she sat on the edge of the back seat willing the decrepit old man to go faster.

She was paying the fare when she looked up at her front window on the outside chance that Franklin might be there watching for her, and some of the change the driver gave her fell under the cab.

The old man gave her an angry look and started to open his door. "No, honestly, don't bother," she said. "It's only money."

"*Only money?*"

Now she took in the arthritic, cigarette-stained fingers that poked out of grey knitted mitts, and the white-bread-and-marge look of hunger about him. She felt ashamed and braced herself for the speech about the General Strike of '26 and the years on the dole afterwards. But, like a symbolic nasty out of a Bergman film, he only tapped a crooked finger against his forehead. "Aye, and wot I say is there's them as has more money than wot they've got up here."

Disagreeable old bugger.

He was still muttering and shaking his head while he started up his wheezy engine and chugged off down the street. From the bottom of the stairs she yelled up, "Franklin? I'm home."

He hadn't heard. She put her keys away, ran up the stairs, and pounded on the door. "Hey, MacArthur. Open up."

He still hadn't heard. Anticlimactically she had to dig the keys out again and let herself in.

His almost white raincoat was on the oak chest, and she put it on over her own and, doing up the buttons and hitching the collar up in back, she walked down the hall to the open bedroom door. He had his back to her and was leaning on the windowsill, looking out over the flat roof.

"Spade. Sam Spade. They say a guy name of Rodgers lives here. He in?"

He turned round slowly. "Hi." It was a very tired, jet-lag voice.

She ran and kissed him and leaned back to look at the new mustache and sideburns and the Afro that was still embryonic but getting there.

"Man, you're like outasight. You read the part the way you look it, and we'll sign you, man, we'll sign you."

He undid her arms from around his neck. "Jane, I—"

"Aw, come on, don't be touchy." She smoothed the mustache. "It's lovely. And not only beautiful, but useful too. Think of all the things Hirsute Harry will never have to buy in sex shops now."

Still with both coats on, she kicked off her shoes and lay down on the bed. "Let me have a real look." She shut one eye and held up her thumb. "Yes. Very pretty, the hairy bit. The rest—" she ran a coolly measuring eye down over the black turtleneck sweater and jeans. "The rest I'm not so sure about, and god knows what Brooks Brothers feel about people who jump ship. But—well, welcome aboard battleship *Potemkin* anyway. And I kid you not-ski, we run a taut one."

"That all? You finished?"

She patted the bed beside her. "Come here. No more teasing. Cross my heart."

He sat down, and she held his hand against her cheek. "God, I've missed you. It's been hellish. I had a crying jag that lasted a whole month."

"I'm sorry. It's been pretty rough back there too." She felt ashamed again and jumped up.

"Darling, I'm an idiot! I always forget how awful that flight is. Here, you lie down. Me, I'll get us a drink. OK?"

"OK."

She took off the coats, hung them in Tom's cupboard, and stuck her head round the door into the kitchen. "Tun Maung?"

Smiling that wide happy Buddha smile, he stopped stirring something in a pot and wiped his hands on his apron. "Is ready. Is in ice bucket living room. You want now?"

"Yes, please, and could you bring it to the bedroom? Mr. Rodgers is very tired and lying down. Is Tom still asleep?"

"Yes, baba sleeping. You want I wake up?"

"No. Gosh, no. But bring him when he does wake up. He'll be very hungry."

Franklin wasn't lying down at all, he was back at the window again. She put her arms around his waist. "Hey, you were supposed to be resting. Remember?"

He undid her hands and turned around. It was too small a silence to be called pregnant, but it was a silence.

"Jane, I've—"

Tun Maung knocked, and she called, "Come in," and turned back to Franklin. "Sorry, darling. You were saying?"

Giving her shoulders a squeeze, he stepped around her. "Nothing. It'll keep. Tun Maung, is that champagne I see?"

"Yes, Mr. Lodgers. Is champagne. Miss Jane she save for you come. For silly brayshun."

It was out of nothing but pure happiness that Jane laughed, but it made Tun Maung look uncertain. "Is not now silly brayshun?"

"Oh, yes, is now," she said. "Is right now. And you have some too, Tun Maung. Everybody celebrate."

"No, please. I thank you very much and I very glad you here, Mr. Lodgers, but champagne like gin. Make head funny. You forgive?"

"Sure, Tun Maung, I forgive. But it's nice to see you again." Franklin gestured with his glass and took a sip. "How's the course going?"

"Course going fine. I light paper now and soon I light jesus."

"Hey, that's—that's really something."

When he'd gone, Franklin looked at Jane. "Where'd he get the address? I know a lot of people who'd pay good money for that."

She laughed a lot harder than the joke really deserved. "Thesis, you silly man. Belly tlicky language, English."

"Oh."

There was another silence that she broke with a bright, "Well, tell me what you've been—"

"I've—"

"Mm?"

"I've been—no, there's something we've got to talk about."

"Darling, there's lots we've got to talk about. Millions of things we've got to—"

"No, there's really only one thing. It's something that—well, that's happened to me."

The agony on his face was so raw and plain that she thought: My god, he's ill. Cancer. Like a subliminal flash the word jumped into her brain and pulsated there in hideous Day-Glo red.

"I've never lied to you, Jane. You know that, don't you?"

She was so frightened she could hardly move her mouth to say, "Yes."

"And you wouldn't want me to lie now, would you?"

Whatever it was, it wasn't cancer. She relaxed enough to take a sip of champagne. "Gosh, no. But what is it? What's happened?"

"I don't know."

"You don't know?" She laughed and sat down on the bed. "Well, it can't be much, then, can it? I mean, you're here and I'm here and we're still—"

He sat down beside her on the bed and picked up one of her hands and looked at it. "No. That's it, we're not."

"We're not?"

She knew she sounded half-witted, and when he didn't say anything she started edging her hand away from his. He let it go with no struggle at all, and she could hear Tun Maung's sandals coming slip-slop down the hall.

Little Tom wasn't crying but he was very hungry and had his fist in his mouth, sucking at it. Sitting on the bed, she clung to him tightly and rocked him back and forth. It seemed like a long time that she did that, and maybe it was, because now he was crying and so was she.

She laid him across her knees and quickly unbuttoned her silk shirt. As she lifted him up she leaned forward and wiped her eyes on a corner of his flannelette wrapper. "There. No more crying. OK, Tom?"

He made his piggish swallowing noises and Franklin, who'd gone back to the safety of the window, came and looked at him. "He's grown."

"Hasn't he?" Her voice was very tea-party. "He weighs—well, he weighs quite a lot now."

She reached for her glass and wiped the bottom of it on Tom's wrapper so it wouldn't drip on his head. "But you were telling me . . ."

His hands in his pockets, he walked to the window again. "I don't know if it's any use. I don't know if I can explain it so you'll understand. I can hardly explain it to myself."

"Try me." She meant it encouragingly, but it came out sounding curt and aggressive. He looked at her sharply, and she knew his male mind was trying to estimate just how much time stood between him and the moment when all hell was going to break loose. OK, she'd make it easy for him.

"Oh, come, Franklin, this is silly. I know I sounded a little stupid and all, but I've got it now, the message—I really have." She smiled at him over the top of the glass. "And so OK. Roger. Wilco. Over and out. There's no need to explain. These things happen. I know that."

"No. That's too easy. I can't duck it like that. Let me at least try to explain."

"Well—" She drew the word out long.

"Well, what?"

"Well, that all depends."

"Depends on what?"

"Depends on whether it's to make me feel better or you feel better. Remember the icepick?"

"I remember. It's not to make anybody feel better."

"Then why bother? Maybe you've read some good books lately. Or dropped some wild acid. Or squared the circle. I mean, there must be something we can talk about—we're two adults, aren't we? Two liberated, grown-up adults. I ask you, if people like that can't find something to—"

"Jane, stop it. Don't be so—"

"Don't be so what? Go on, say it."

"So . . . unreal."

"Unreal? Me, unreal? God. With one shove you tip my seventy-five thousand eggs out of my basket into the traffic at Hyde Park Corner at high noon. When I start dodging the cars to pick them up again, you say stop being unreal. Jesus. I tell you these trucks and buses are coming thick and fast, and that they are real, baby, real."

The momentum ran out, and she wiped her eyes

again. "Sorry," she whispered. "I didn't mean to get all fishwify."

Franklin put the box of Kleenex on the table near her. "I know."

She brushed her hair back out of her eyes and stood up. "I think I'll go finish feeding Tom in his room. It isn't fair to get him all fussed too."

After Tom had gone to sleep she sat for a long time in his room, trying to get used to it. Then she buttoned her shirt and walked down the hall to the living room, detouring by the bedroom to get the champagne bottle.

She waved it in his direction, but he shook his head, and so she poured herself some and sat down on the sofa with her feet on the slate-topped table. "Right. Ann Hysteric has regained her icy cool. So tell me. What happened? Where did I go wrong?"

"You didn't go wrong. I did."

"What's she like?"

"There's no she. It's not that."

"No? What is it, then? What is there can happen except a she?"

"Jane, I'm black."

"I thought you knew. *I* knew."

"No, listen. Please listen."

"OK. So I'm listening. But it had better improve."

"What had?"

"The script. They were throwing this one out when my father was a third assistant director."

"I doubt it. I very much doubt it."

"All right. So they were saving it in a bank vault until the world was ready for a story so human, so shocking, and so honest that it couldn't be told till now. You like that better?"

He sat on the table and looked down at his hands. "I don't think you understand what it means being black."

"It never seemed to bother you much before."

He looked for a split second as if he were going to

tell her something, but then he changed his mind. "No, it didn't much."

"And no wonder. I mean, face it, Franklin. You were brought up white—whiter than white. Miss Johnson. Boarding school. Yale. That pony. You haven't any better idea than I have what it's really like to be black because you're—"

"Because I'm not. That's what you were going to say, isn't it?"

"Well, I know it sounds funny, but you know what I mean."

"I do. Jesus, I do. And it's true what you say, except it—"

"Except it isn't."

"Right."

"And so?"

"So I can't do it any more, that's all. It's been one crazy, total, lousy, con fraud for ever since I can remember. For ever since I can remember, and that's a long time now, I've been a white nigger—even, like you say, whiter than white. But no more. I won't do it any more, not one more goddamned day. I know it's taken me a hell of a long time to find out, but I know what I am now. And I'm not white."

The champagne had run out; she dropped the heavy green bottle upside down into the wastebasket, and mixed them each a hefty vodka and tonic. "Here," she said and handed him his. "Got no gin. Gin's a nigger's drink and I wasn't expecting a nigger."

"I'm going back to Africa." He said it flatly and gloomily.

"What do you mean, back to Africa? You've never been to Africa."

"All right. I'm going to Africa. To Ghana."

"What in god's name for?"

"I don't know. But I've got to."

"Jesus."

"And I can't take you."

"No?"

"No."

"And you don't *mind?*" She shook her head as if she couldn't believe it.

"Jesus christ, of course I mind. I mind it like—no, more than—I mind a lot of things I've got used to having. I mind losing you. I mind hurting you. I mind having offered something I can't deliver. I mind having believed, and having believed so much, in something that can't be. I mind goddamned all of it. But my minding doesn't change it. There's nothing can change it."

He stood up and walked back and forth in front of her. "I've thought about it until I thought I'd go crazy thinking about it. I've thought of you and of all we've had and all the much, much more we could have, and I've tried to kid myself that it could still happen. I thought of how your face would look when I told you." He stopped for a moment and looked at her.

"And I thought of how I've loused up your life— well, part of your life, I never fooled myself I was irreplaceable or anything—and a couple of times when I thought of all that, it even began to seem the best thing to do would be to kick this ego trip, just never even mention it even, and bring you to Philadelphia so we could go on like before."

"But?"

"But I couldn't. I can't. It would be a lie, and nobody can live like that. Not forever."

"No, it's too crazy. *Africa?*" She smiled at him the way people smile when a child has said something preposterous. "Darling, it's mad. It's a mad little burst of jungly blackness. It's some fuzzy Jungian thing about the happy days of yore around the village tom-tom."

"No, it's not that."

"You sure?"

"I'm sure."

"Careful. You said that once before, you know."

"I know. God, please. Please don't make it worse than it is."

"But why can't I come? I mean, I don't *want* to go to Africa but I will." She smiled the indulgent smile

306

again. "Maybe, dazzled by the blinding whiteness of my Kelvinator, not to mention my face, black bwana has merely failed to notice what a great hewer of wood and drawer of water I could be."

"Jane, I can't. There's no halfway. There's two worlds, and I'm kicking the one we grew up in. There, I'm a kind of unplaceable schizo. A black man that was brought up white. I don't fit, I don't fit in black America and I don't fit in white America. I've tried. Ever since I went back I've tried, and it doesn't work. I can't—" His voice dwindled off.

"Darling, you can't what?"

"I can't work both sides of the street any longer."

It began to dawn on her that he meant it. But she still couldn't take it seriously; if she did that, it would make it real.

"Oy, oy, you are a nut, Franklin, you really are. What makes you think you're going to fit in Africa, of all places? Africa's foreign, darling. They talk funny languages. Who are you going to play tennis with? Who's going to produce Beckett plays for you?"

"Nobody. That's part of what I've got to leave behind. And of course it'll be foreign, foreign as hell. But don't you see? I've got to find some—I know you'll laugh and say I'm talking like a Harvard freshman, but I've got to find some identity. I've got to find some roots that are real."

"My god, you're not talking like a Harvard freshman, you're talking like a CCNY graduate student. Which is worse."

"OK. Right. But that's it."

"Oh, come on, darling. What will you do there? What will you live on? Franklin, it's crazy."

"I've sold everything I own and I've got about fifteen thousand dollars. That ought to last me awhile. And I can write. Pieces. Maybe even a book."

"Oh christ, Franklin. You, a remittance man? Living off pieces in *Holiday* magazine and General Motors stock? What's so noble and identity-making about that?"

"I never said it was noble."

"But darling, why don't you—we—just stay here, then? In England."

"No. I fit here least of all. And I can't marry you, Jane. If I do that, I'm back to both sides of the street again, no matter where I live. And I can't do it any more." His voice trembled, and she had never seen him so close to tears before. "I wish I could for your—for our sake. But I can't."

23

Playing for time, she got up and fixed two more drinks, and Tun Maung padded in, carrying a big tray. "Is last bottle. But I make *kaoshway*. For silly brayshun. I find light noodles Soho bazaar." Giggling, he set the tray down and wagged a finger at Jane. "Miss Jane, she say no light noodles in London and so no more *kaoshway*. But I find—I find."

"That *is* kind, Tun Maung. And we didn't have it that other time when I promised, did we? Poor Mr. Rodgers. We must give him a real big plateful."

"He like? You think he like?"

"I know he'll like. Prawn *balachong* too. Don't forget to give him some of that, Tun Maung."

"I bring bigger plates."

"What a good idea."

Tun Maung clucked about like a mother hen serving them, and when he'd closed the door and gone back to the kitchen, Franklin took a careful taste of the noodle mess.

"Jesus christ, it tastes like horseshit."

"That's right." Jane hadn't touched hers, and didn't.

"That's because it is. Like Catholicism, the Olympic Games, bound feet, Dior dresses, or any other crummy idea based on group exclusivity, it is undoubtedly horseshit."

"Right. You don't have to be subtle about it. But there is such a thing as identity; it isn't *just* something kids talk about."

"Certainly. Identity. There are people. And there are creeps. The creeps are the ones who think up the horseshit."

She locked the hall door, got a plastic bag from her desk, and scraped both plates of kaoshway into it. When she pointed to the window, he got up and opened it, and, leaning out, she lobbed the bag into the back of a truck parked below. "There. Birmingham or bust."

After she'd unlocked the door to the hall she sat down again. "And that's how to deal with horseshit."

"Sure. If you can fit it all in a bag, who wouldn't? But what if your whole life has been horseshit, what then? What if it's all around you? What if it's in everything you've been taught and in everything you believed? What if the horseshit values of the horseshit society you live in are something you can't take any more? Where's the handy window you can throw all that out of and then sit down and have another drink and feel better? You *show* me that window. You show me that window, and I'll show you a mirage that only looks like a window."

It had been a mistake; it hadn't jollied him out of it at all, it had only made things worse. Ignoring the champagne, she made them two more vodkas and stood in front of him with the tips of her fingers hooked together. "When evah I feel uf-raid, I strike a careless pose, and whistle a heppy choon, and no one evah knows I'm uf-raid . . ." She stopped singing. "Come on, identity-finder, who am I?"

He wasn't all that sober either. He leaned back in the leather chair and almost smiled. "Well, I tell you. You think you're Gertie Lawrence. And me—christ,

I'd swear you were Gertie Lawrence. But what would Gertie Lawrence say?" He took a long swallow of vodka. "No matter how you look at it, two of us have got to be wrong."

"Why?"

God. She was drunker than she'd thought.

"Because something is either true or not true."

"There's nothing in between?"

"Nothing. Nothing that isn't an error. Or a delusion."

"Or a lie."

"Or a lie."

"But a toy trumpet makes a real noise."

"And that Dutchman painted Vermeers. So what?"

"Ah, but they weren't real Vermeers, were they?"

"They got real Vermeer prices for them."

It was maudlin, drunken talk, and she ran her fingers through the wilting Shirley Temple curls, trying to remember what it was she'd started out to prove.

"Jane, this is getting us nowhere."

"So? That's where we were going anyway, isn't it? Unless you count Africa, and I definitely, absolutely don't count Africa."

"Won't you let me try and explain a little?"

"You have. You're black and I'm white and the chess game's off. All off your chess, the chess game is."

God. She was *much* drunker than she'd thought, and she wasn't going to retake Hill 237 this way.

Like Pluto skidding to a stop, she put the brakes on the drunkenness. She had to lay a plan. She had to lay a good plan. Or, better—the Great Idea of Western Woman formed itself slowly in her mind—lay him. In bed, and only in bed, could she show him again what was true and what was not true and how crazy this talk of Africa was.

While he talked and poured half her drink into his own glass, she fixed an intelligent listening-dog expression on her face.

How? He was off on ethnic awareness, and bed was very far from his mind. But she had to do it. It was her last chance, and she knew it. He'd forgotten, that's all it was. He'd forgotten that it didn't matter if she was white or striped or went for Groucho more than Karl. What did matter was he loved her. He did, too. She knew he did. And he'd know it too—once she got him there. But it had to look like chance. *Jesus, if he'd only stop talking . . .*

Pacing up and down, he had gone from ethnic awareness to the necessity for self-determination, and now to the too narrow, already corrupt, and hate-poisoned outlook of the American blacks.

"... don't you see, they hate too indiscriminately. They hate all whites, good, bad, or indifferent. And yet, what they hate they want to be. They want the same things the white man's got. The money. The power. The big shiny cars. The schools. The jobs. And you can't blame them; the white man's values have spewed out at them on white man's television all their lives. What else do they know? What else *is* there to know? What they don't know is that having those things, or even just wanting those things and hating other people for having more of them than they've got, is going to make them into the same brand of son of a bitch the white man is. It's like saying wolves are no good and must all be shot, and then going to Wolf School nights."

"Darling, of course I see. Or anyhow, I think I see. But—I don't know, maybe it's all a sort of *Zeitgeist* that can't be fought. I don't think it'll be much different in Af—"

He looked at his watch. "Jesus, it's two o'clock."

He was wrong. It was four minutes past two. At half past, Tun Maung would take little Tom out for his walk and not be back until four-thirty. She had two hours. Two and a quarter, with luck.

"*Is* it? Gosh, what shall we do about food? You must be starving."

"Go out somewhere?"

"Yuk."

"Why 'yuk'? We've got to eat."

312

"I know, but I'm not dressed or anything—I mean, look at me. No. You go. I'll—I'll just stay here."

"Don't be stupid. You've got to eat something."

As throwaway casually as Ray Milland stealing the handbag in The Lost Weekend, she took a pack of cards from the box on the table and started to shuffle them slowly. "I'll get something out of the icebox."

"You can't. He'd know then that we didn't eat the horseshit."

He sat down again, and she let the cards trickle from one hand to the other. "Not if I eat it in bed under the covers, he won't."

"No. I don't want you to be—"

"Be what?"

"Alone."

Still shuffling slowly, she kept the sad smile just this side of either bathos or cynicism; he was moving towards the trap nicely, but this was no time to overact.

She let a card fall on the floor, and he picked it up and said, "OK. I tell you what. I'll cut you for it. I win, we go out. You win, we stay here."

"What a crazy idea."

"No, come on. It's fair, isn't it?"

"OK. You go first." She handed him the cards. "Here, shuffle."

He shuffled them fast and expertly, and cut. "Jack of clubs."

"Hey, that's pretty big stuff to beat."

She turned the cards around on the table, evened them up and cut. "Well, what d'you know? The King of spades."

It had taken Tom a long time to teach her that trick, and she could remember the night when she'd finally learned.

He had been sitting just where Franklin was sitting now. When she goofed for the twentieth time and slammed the pack down on the table, he'd laughed and said, "Try it again. But remember, always let the mark shuffle. No sucker ever thinks he's been had, so

313

long as it was him that shuffled." Tom had picked up the scattered cards then, and she tried again.

When Tun Maung had gone out with little Tom, she brought cold chicken and a bottle of Pouilly Fuissé to the bedroom and "just in case he comes back" she locked the door.

It was as natural as it had always been. When she put her arms around his neck this time, he didn't undo her hands but held her head with his fingers twined in her hair and kissed her. It had worked.

In bed he was as overwhelmingly and terrifyingly, hungrily in need of her as he had been before. He held her and kissed her slowly, and they laughed about the ridiculous butter scene in *Last Tango*. "My god, who needs butter? Butter is for popcorn." And then he melted so deep and gradually into her that she could hardly tell where his body left off and hers began. More than ever it seemed impossible that there could ever come a time when he wouldn't be with her and part of her.

And she was right, it wasn't possible. He could never know or want another woman as thoroughly as he knew and wanted her. Even when she couldn't hold back any more and whispered, "Now. Please now," and really thought she meant it, he knew her too well and wanted her too much more to give in. "No, not now. Not yet." His teeth were hard and they hurt, but his hands and his tongue were gentle as he slowed her down.

He even said the things she'd hoped he'd say. He loved her. He was unhappy without her. He had never even come close to this with anyone else. Everything was so right, so good—so unbelievably good—"Not yet, baby. Not yet."

But even he had to give in sometime and then, the beautiful black shoulders still shiny with sweat, he lay on his back and covered his eyes with his arm. "Jesus christ. How can we ever quit? How can anyone walk away from this? How can I do it? I must be crazy."

She'd won.

314

She lifted her head from his chest and kissed his shoulder. It tasted salty and she licked his arm and his chest slowly. "Maybe not crazy. Maybe just forgetful. Temporarily a little forgetful."

The dark Coca-Cola eyes opened very slowly, and looked at her. "No. I never forgot—and I never will."

Even as he looked at her and said it, his eyes changed. She would have been hard put to say exactly how it was that they changed, but they changed. And she knew she hadn't won at all.

He touched her cheek with his finger, and his eyes changed again, but this time they went hazy and soft. "No, don't say it, baby. It's no go."

"Honestly, no?"

"Honestly, no."

He held her and stroked her hair while she cried, and before he got up to get the box of Kleenex he said, "I wish it weren't so. I wish to jesus it weren't so. I love you so much I—but what's the use? It is so. I can't change it. You can't change it. There's nobody on god's earth can change it."

He phoned for a cab and, the way cabs do when you don't want them to, it came so quickly that she would have been almost willing to bet it was the old Bergman nasty who'd brought her home and had been lurking just around the corner ever since.

She got his almost white raincoat out of Tom's cupboard and held it for him.

At the door he put his arms around her and buried his face in her hair. To keep the tears away she giggled. "God. It's awful, isn't it? Worse than I'd have guessed."

"Will you be all right?"

"Me? Sure. I'm always all right. It's the world that's all wrong." She laughed. "Ain't it the truth? By mere coincidence, of course, and it couldn't happen again in a million years, but ain't it the lousy truth?"

"It is, baby. It is the lousy truth."

She laughed again. A little too much she laughed again.

"What's so funny? Even the truth isn't that funny."

"I just happened to think of something Gary Cooper used to say, or that anyhow they say he used to say."

The laugh had turned the corner and become tears. He put his arms around her again. "What did Gary Cooper use to say?"

"He used to say, 'Fucking around is OK, but falling in love gets you in trouble.' I mean, I don't know if he really did say it, but they say he did. I only thought of it because it's the lousy truth too, isn't it?"

She kissed him on the cheek. "Darling, don't *look* like that. I'll be OK, honestly I will. After all, I'm free, white, and almost thirty-six, aren't I?"

He started down the stairs, but she still couldn't quite let him go. "Oh, I forgot—"

He turned around and looked up at her.

"Well, it's nothing really. Except that if I find your tennis racket, I'll send it on."

"It doesn't matter. My tennis days are over; it was only to give to a kid I know who wants one. I can always give him one of the other ones."

"Oh. Well, finders keepers, then."

Now he was all the way down and had his hand on the doorknob.

"Franklin?"

"Yes?"

"Is that formidable lady black?"

"What formidable lady?"

"The one at Johns Hopkins."

"Oh, her. Yes, she's black. Why?"

"You'll see."

Now it was he who laughed unconvincingly. "Baby you're off your head. I told you it wasn't that. Anyhow, she's married. She's a very serious, respectable married lady."

"And what's her husband?"

"A physicist."

"I don't mean that. Is he black or white?"

"White."

"Then maybe you'll see even quicker than I thought."

She couldn't hold him any longer. He shook his head once more, as if to say that women were too mad for any rational man ever to hope to fathom, and then he was gone.

She picked the plates of chicken off the bedroom floor and made the bed so Tun Maung wouldn't be shocked when he came back. And, because she was very particular about being fair and honest with restaurants, she phoned Rule's to say that Mr. Rodgers wouldn't be needing the table for two after all.

Then, because she had to do something and there wasn't much else to do, she lay on the bed and read the *New York Times* he'd left behind. The whole thing. Even the pieces on land reform in Brazil and how to make your own *sukiyaki*.

Nothing registered. But she read it all anyway. And after that, there really wasn't anything else to do, and so she just lay there, looking up at the skylight and waiting for little Tom to come back.

THE BIG BESTSELLERS
ARE AVON BOOKS!

The Eye of the Storm
Patrick White
21527 $1.95

Jane
Dee Wells
21519 $1.75

Theophilus North
Thornton Wilder
19059 $1.75

Daytime Affair
Joshua Lorne
20743 $1.50

The Secret Life of Plants
Peter Tompkins and Christopher Bird
19901 $1.95

The Wildest Heart
Rosemary Rogers
20529 $1.75

Come Nineveh, Come Tyre
Allen Drury
19026 $1.75

World Without End, Amen
Jimmy Breslin
19042 $1.75

The Amazing World of Kreskin
Kreskin
19034 $1.50

The Oath
Elie Wiesel
19083 $1.75

A Different Woman
Jane Howard
19075 $1.95

The Alchemist
Les Whitten
19919 $1.75

The Wolf and the Dove
Kathleen E. Woodiwiss
18457 $1.75

Sweet Savage Love
Rosemary Rogers
17988 $1.75

I'm OK—You're OK
Thomas A. Harris, M.D.
14662 $1.95

Jonathan Livingston Seagull
Richard Bach
14316 $1.50

Where better paperbacks are sold, or directly from the publisher. Include 25¢ per copy for mailing; allow three weeks for delivery. Avon Books, Mail Order Dept., 250 West 55th Street, New York, N.Y. 10019

BBI-75

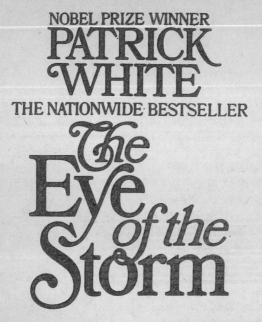

NOBEL PRIZE WINNER

PATRICK WHITE

THE NATIONWIDE BESTSELLER

The Eye of the Storm

"A BRILLIANT LITERARY ACHIEVE-
MENT." *Newsday*

"EXCITING...TOTALLY INVOLV-
ING." *Boston Globe*

"A BOOK OF ASTONISHING ENTER-
TAINMENT AND REWARDS."
Philadelphia Bulletin

"One seeks among debased superlatives
for words that would convey the gran-
deur of THE EYE OF THE STORM...
Every passage merits attention and gives
satisfaction." *The New York Times*

Now an Avon paperback on sale everywhere, or order direct from
the publisher. Address Avon Books, Mail Order Department, 250
West 55th St., New York, N.Y. 10019. Include 25¢ per copy for
mailing; allow three weeks for delivery.

26 WEEKS ON
THE NEW YORK TIMES BESTSELLER LIST

A LITERARY GUILD
FEATURED ALTERNATE

AMERICA'S MOST HONORED WRITER

ThorntonWilder

HIS LATEST,
WONDROUS BESTSELLING NOVEL

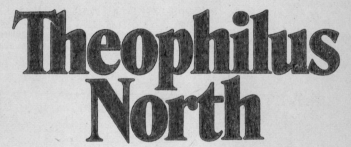

Theophilus North

America's celebrated writer explores, through Theophilus
North, the lives of the saints and the sinners, the rich and
the servants, in the Newport, Rhode Island of the '20s.

"EXTRAORDINARILY ENTERTAINING."
The New York Times

10059/$1.75